# PRAISE FOR THESE AUTHORS

## TESS GERRITSEN

"Tess Gerritsen is tops in her genre."
—*USA TODAY*

"Tess Gerritsen brings us action,
adventure and compelling romance."
—*Romantic Times*

"The reigning champion
of the medical thriller."
—*San Jose Mercury News*

## AMANDA STEVENS

"Prepare to be thrilled."
—*USA TODAY* bestselling author
Patricia Kay

## KAY DAVID

"Crisp, passionate, edgy and fast-paced—
a true winner!"
—*Romantic Times* on *The Target*

**Tess Gerritsen** is an accomplished woman with an interesting background. Once a practicing physician, she has chosen instead to write full-time. A woman of many talents, she even plays the fiddle in a band! Tess has cowritten *Adrift,* a CBS screenplay, and has several other screenplays optioned by HBO. Having lived in Hawaii, she now resides in Camden, Maine, with her physician husband and two sons.

**Amanda Stevens** knew at an early age that she wanted to be a writer, and began her first novel at the age of thirteen. While majoring in English at Houston Community College and the University of Houston, she was encouraged to write a romance novel by one of her instructors, who was himself writing a historical. Her first romance was sold to the Silhouette Intimate Moments line in 1985. Amanda lives in Houston, Texas, with her husband of seventeen years and their twins.

**Kay David** was born and reared in Texas, and has lived all over the world from the Middle East to South America. She frequently draws on these exotic locations for her books. Kay has undergraduate degrees in both English and management of information sciences, and has a master's degree in behavioral science. She has worked at NASA, designed and built homes, and has even owned her own jewelry company, but her true love is writing. Along with her husband of twenty-seven years, Pieter, and their globe-trotting cat, Leroy, Ms. David divides her time between the Texas Gulf coast and the Hill Country.

# TESS GERRITSEN

## IN THEIR FOOTSTEPS

**Plus two bonus short stories from
Amanda Stevens and Kay David**

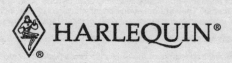

HARLEQUIN®

TORONTO • NEW YORK • LONDON
AMSTERDAM • PARIS • SYDNEY • HAMBURG
STOCKHOLM • ATHENS • TOKYO • MILAN • MADRID
PRAGUE • WARSAW • BUDAPEST • AUCKLAND

ISBN 0-373-83621-X

IN THEIR FOOTSTEPS

Copyright © 2004 by Harlequin Books S.A.

Amanda Stevens is acknowledged as the author of BEDROOM WINDOW.
Kay David is acknowledged as the author of 24 HOURS.

The publisher acknowledges the copyright holders of the individual works as follows:

IN THEIR FOOTSTEPS
Copyright © 1994 by Terry Gerritsen

BEDROOM WINDOW
Copyright © 2003 by Harlequin Books S.A.

24 HOURS
Copyright © 2001 by Harlequin Books S.A.

# CONTENTS

# IN THEIR FOOTSTEPS

## Tess Gerritsen

# *PROLOGUE*

*Paris, 1973*

HE WAS LATE. It was not like Madeline, not like her at all.

Bernard Tavistock ordered another café au lait and took his time sipping it, every so often glancing around the outdoor café for a glimpse of his wife. He saw only the usual Left Bank scene: tourists and Parisians, red-checked tablecloths, a riot of summertime colors. But no sign of his raven-haired wife. She was half an hour late now; this was more than a traffic delay. He found himself tapping his foot as the worries began to creep in. In all their years of marriage, Madeline had rarely been late for an appointment, and then only by a few minutes. Other men might moan and roll their eyes in masculine despair over their perennially tardy spouses, but Bernard had no such complaints—he'd been blessed with a punctual wife. A beautiful wife. A woman who, even after fifteen years of marriage, continued to surprise him, fascinate him, tempt him.

Now where the dickens *was* she?

He glanced up and down Boulevard Saint-Germain. His uneasiness grew from a vague toe-tapping anxiety to outright worry. Had there been a traffic accident? A last-minute alert from their French Intelligence contact, Claude Daumier? Events had been moving at a frantic pace these last two weeks. Those rumors of a NATO intelligence leak—of a mole in their midst—had them all glancing over their shoulders, wondering who among them could not be trusted.

For days now, Madeline had been awaiting instructions from MI6 London. Perhaps, at the last minute, word had come through.

Still, she should have let him know.

He rose to his feet and was about to head for the telephone when he spotted his waiter, Mario, waving at him. The young man quickly wove his way past the crowded tables.

"M. Tavistock, there is a telephone message for you. From *madame*."

Bernard gave a sigh of relief. "Where is she?"

"She says she cannot come for lunch. She wishes you to meet her."

"Where?"

"This address." The waiter handed him a scrap of paper, smudged with what looked like tomato soup. The address was scrawled in pencil: 66, Rue Myrha, #5.

Bernard frowned. "Isn't this in Pigalle? What on earth is she doing in that neighborhood?"

Mario shrugged, a peculiarly Gallic version with tipped head, raised eyebrow. "I do not know. She tells me the address, I write it down."

"Well, thank you." Bernard reached for his wallet and handed the fellow enough francs to pay for his two café au laits, as well as a generous tip.

*"Merci,"* said the waiter, beaming. "You will return for supper, M. Tavistock?"

"If I can track down my wife," muttered Bernard, striding away to his Mercedes.

He drove to Place Pigalle, grumbling all the way. What on earth had possessed her to go there? It was not the safest part of Paris for a woman—or a man, either, for that matter. He took comfort in the knowledge that his beloved Madeline could take care of herself quite well, thank you very much. She was a far better marksman than he was, and that automatic she carried in her purse was always kept fully loaded—a precaution he insisted upon ever since that near-disaster in Berlin. Distressing how one couldn't trust one's own people these days. Incompetents everywhere, in MI6, in NATO, in French Intelligence. And there had been Madeline, trapped in that building with the East Germans, and no one to back her up. *If I hadn't arrived in time...*

No, he wouldn't relive that horror again.

She'd learned her lesson. And a loaded pistol was now a permanent accessory to her wardrobe.

He turned onto Rue de Chapelle and shook his head in disgust at the deteriorating street scene, the tawdry night-clubs, the scantily clad women poised on street corners. They saw his Mercedes and beckoned to him eagerly. Desperately. "Pig Alley" was what the Yanks used to call this neighborhood. The place one came to for quick delights, for guilty pleasures. *Madeline,* he thought, *have you gone completely mad? What could possibly have brought you here?*

He turned onto Boulevard Bayes, then Rue Myrha, and parked in front of number 66. In disbelief, he stared up at the building and saw three stories of chipped plaster and sagging balconies. Did she really expect him to meet her in this firetrap? He locked the Mercedes, thinking, *I'll be lucky if the car's still here when I return.* Reluctantly he entered the building.

Inside there were signs of habitation: children's toys in the stairwell, a radio playing in one of the flats. He climbed the stairs. The smell of frying onions and cigarette smoke seemed to hang permanently in the air. Numbers three and four were on the second floor; he kept climbing, up a narrow staircase to the top floor. Number five was the attic flat; its low door was tucked between the eaves.

He knocked. No answer.

"Madeline?" he called. "Really now, this isn't some sort of practical joke, is it?"

Still there was no answer.

He tried the door; it was unlocked. He pushed inside, into

the garret flat. Venetian blinds hung over the windows, casting slats of shadow and light across the room. Against one wall was a large brass bed, its sheets still rumpled from some prior occupant. On a bedside table were two dirty glasses, an empty champagne bottle and various plastic items one might delicately refer to as "marital aids." The whole room smelled of liquor, of sweating passion and bodies in rut.

Bernard's puzzled gaze gradually shifted to the foot of the brass bed, to a woman's high-heeled shoe lying discarded on the floor. Frowning, he took a step toward it and saw that the shoe lay in a glistening puddle of crimson. As he rounded the foot of the bed, he froze in disbelief.

His wife lay on the floor, her ebony hair fanned out like a raven's wings. Her eyes were open. Three sunbursts of blood stained her white blouse.

He dropped to his knees beside her. "No," he said. *"No."* He touched her face, felt the warmth still lingering in her cheeks. He pressed his ear to her chest, her bloodied chest, and heard no heartbeat, no breath. A sob burst forth from his throat, a disbelieving cry of grief. *"Madeline!"*

As the echo of her name faded, there came another sound behind him—footsteps. Soft, approaching...

Bernard turned. In bewilderment, he stared at the pistol—Madeline's pistol—now pointed at him. He looked up at the face hovering above the barrel. It made no sense—no sense at all!

"Why?" asked Bernard.

The answer he heard was the dull thud of the silenced automatic. The bullet's impact sent him sprawling to the floor beside Madeline. For a few brief seconds, he was aware of her body close beside him, and of her hair, like silk against his fingers. He reached out and feebly cradled her head. *My love,* he thought. *My dearest love.*

And then his hand fell still.

# CHAPTER ONE

*Buckinghamshire, England*
*Twenty years later*

JORDAN TAVISTOCK lounged in Uncle Hugh's easy chair and amusedly regarded, as he had a thousand times before, the portrait of his long-dead ancestor, the hapless Earl of Lovat. Ah, the delicious irony of it all, he thought, that Lord Lovat should stare down from that place of honor above the mantelpiece. It was testimony to the Tavistock family's sense of whimsy that they'd chosen to so publicly display their one relative who'd, literally, lost his head on Tower Hill—the last man to be officially decapitated in England—unofficial decapitations did not count. Jordan raised his glass in a toast to the unfortunate earl and tossed back a gulp of sherry. He was tempted to pour a second glass, but it was already five-thirty, and the guests would soon be arriving for the Bastille Day reception. *I should keep at least a few gray cells in working order,* he thought. *I might need them to hold up my end of the chitchat.* Chitchat being one of Jordan's least favorite activities.

For the most part, he avoided these caviar and black-tie bashes his Uncle Hugh seemed so addicted to throwing. But tonight's event—in honor of their house guests, Sir Reggie and Lady Helena Vane—might prove more interesting than the usual gathering of the horsey set. This was the first big affair since Uncle Hugh's retirement from British Intelligence, and a number of Hugh's former colleagues from MI6 would make an appearance. Throw into the brew a few old chums from Paris—all of them in London for the recent economic summit—and it could prove to be a most intriguing night. Anytime one threw a group of ex-spies and diplomats together in a room, all sorts of surprising secrets tended to surface.

Jordan looked up as his uncle came grumbling into the study. Already dressed in his tuxedo, Hugh was trying, without success, to fix his bow tie; he'd managed, instead, to tie a stubborn square knot.

"Jordan, help me with this blasted thing, will you?" said Hugh.

Jordan rose from the easy chair and loosened the knot. "Where's Davis? He's much better at this sort of thing."

"I sent him to fetch that sister of yours."

"Beryl's gone out again?"

"Naturally. Mention the words 'cocktail party,' and she's flying out the door."

Jordan began to loop his uncle's tie into a bow. "Beryl's never been fond of parties. And just between you and me, I think she's had just a bit too much of the Vanes."

"Hmm? But they've been lovely guests. Fit right in—"

"It's the nasty little barbs flying between them."

"Oh, *that.* They've always been that way. I scarcely notice it anymore."

"And have you seen the way Reggie follows Beryl about, like a puppy dog?"

Hugh laughed. "Around a pretty woman, Reggie *is* a puppy dog."

"Well, it's no wonder Helena's always sniping at him." Jordan stepped back and regarded his uncle's bow tie with a frown.

"How's it look?"

"It'll have to do."

Hugh glanced at the clock. "Better check on the kitchen.

See that things are in order. And why aren't the Vanes down yet?"

As if on cue, they heard the sound of querulous voices on the stairway. Lady Helena, as always, was scolding her husband. "*Someone* has to point these things out to you," she said.

"Yes, and it's always you, isn't it?"

Sir Reggie fled into the study, pursued by his wife. It never failed to puzzle Jordan, the obvious mismatch of the pair. Sir Reggie, handsome and silver haired, towered over his drab little mouse of a wife. Perhaps Helena's substantial inheritance explained the pairing; money, after all, was the great equalizer.

As the hour edged toward six o'clock, Hugh poured out glasses of sherry and handed them around to the foursome. "Before the hordes arrive," he said, "a toast, to your safe return to Paris." They sipped. It was a solemn ceremony, this last evening together with old friends.

Now Reggie raised his glass. "And here's to English hospitality. Ever appreciated!"

From the front driveway came the sound of car tires on gravel. They all glanced out the window to see the first limousine roll into view. The chauffeur opened the door and out stepped a fiftyish woman, every ripe curve defined by a green gown ablaze with bugle beads. Then a young man in a shirt of purple silk emerged from the car and took the woman's arm.

"Good heavens, it's Nina Sutherland and her brat," Helena muttered. "What broom did *she* fly in on?"

Outside, the woman in the green gown suddenly spotted them standing in the window. "Hello, Reggie! Helena!" she called in a voice like a bassoon.

Hugh set down his sherry glass. "Time to greet the barbarians," he said, sighing. He and the Vanes headed out the front door to welcome the first arrivals.

Jordan paused a moment to finish his drink, giving himself time to paste on a smile and get the old handshake ready. Bastille Day—what an excuse for a party! He tugged at the coattails of his tuxedo, gave his ruffled shirt one last pat, and resignedly headed out to the front steps. Let the dog and pony show begin.

Now where in blazes was his sister?

AT THAT MOMENT, the subject of Jordan Tavistock's speculation was riding hell-bent for leather across a grassy field. *Poor old Froggie needs the workout,* thought Beryl. *And so do I.* She bent forward into the wind, felt the lash of Froggie's mane against her face, and inhaled that wonderful scent of horseflesh, sweet clover and warm July earth. Froggie was enjoying the sprint just as much as she was, if not more. Beryl could feel those powerful muscles straining for ever more speed. *She's a demon, like me,* thought Beryl, suddenly laughing aloud—the same wild laugh that always made poor Uncle Hughie cringe. But out here, in the open fields, she could laugh like a wanton woman and no one would hear. If only she could keep on riding, forever and ever! But fences and walls seemed to be everywhere in her life. Fences of the mind, of the heart. She urged her mount still faster, as though through speed she could outrun all the devils pursuing her.

Bastille Day. What a desperate excuse for a party.

Uncle Hugh loved a good bash, and the Vanes *were* old family friends; they deserved a decent send-off. But she'd seen the guest list, and it was the same tiresome lot. Shouldn't ex-spies and diplomats lead more interesting lives? She couldn't imagine James Bond, retired, pottering about in his garden.

Yet that's what Uncle Hugh seemed to do all day. The highlight of *his* week had been harvesting the season's first hybrid Nepal tomato—his earliest tomato ever! And as for her uncle's friends, well, she couldn't imagine *them* ever sneaking around the back alleys of Paris or Berlin. Philippe

St. Pierre, perhaps—yes, she could picture *him* in his younger days; at sixty-two, he was still charming, a Gallic lady-killer. And Reggie Vane might have cut a dashing figure years ago. But most of Uncle Hugh's old colleagues seemed so, well…used up.

*Not me. Never me.*

She galloped harder, letting Froggie have free rein.

They raced across the last stretch of field and through a copse of trees. Froggie, winded now, slowed to a trot, then a walk. Beryl pulled her to a halt by the church's stone wall. There she dismounted and let Froggie wander about untethered. The churchyard was deserted and the gravestones cast lengthening shadows across the lawn. Beryl clambered over the low wall and walked among the plots until she came to the spot she'd visited so many times before. A handsome obelisk towered over two graves, resting side by side. There were no curlicues, no fancy angels carved into that marble face. Only words.

Bernard Tavistock, 1930–1973
Madeline Tavistock, 1934–1973
On earth, as it is in heaven, we are together.

Beryl knelt on the grass and gazed for a long time at the resting place of her mother and father. *Twenty years ago tomorrow,* she thought. *How I wish I could remember you more clearly! Your faces, your smiles.* What she did remember were odd things, unimportant things. The smell of leather luggage, of Mum's perfume and Dad's pipe. The crackle of paper as she and Jordan would unwrap the gifts Mum and Dad brought home to them. Dolls from France. Music boxes from Italy. And there was laughter. Always lots of laughter…

Beryl sat with her eyes closed and heard that happy sound through the passage of twenty years. Through the evening buzz of insects, the clink of Froggie's bit and bridle, she heard the sounds of her childhood.

The church bell tolled—six chimes.

At once Beryl sat up straight. Oh, no, was it already that late? She glanced around and saw that the shadows had grown, that Froggie was standing by the wall regarding her with frank expectation. *Oh Lord,* she thought, *Uncle Hugh will be royally cross with me.*

She dashed out of the churchyard and climbed onto Froggie's back. At once they were flying across the field, horse and rider blended into a single sleek organism. *Time for the shortcut,* thought Beryl, guiding Froggie toward the trees. It meant a leap over the stone wall, and then a clip along the road, but it would cut a mile off their route. Froggie seemed to understand that time was of the essence. She picked up speed and approached the stone wall with all the eagerness of a seasoned steeplechaser. She took the jump cleanly, with inches to spare. Beryl felt the wind rush past, felt her mount soar, then touch down on the far side of the wall. The biggest hurdle was behind them. Now, just beyond that bend in the road—

She saw a flash of red, heard the squeal of tires across pavement. Froggie swerved sideways and reared up. The sudden lurch caught Beryl by surprise. She tumbled out of the saddle and landed with a stunning thud on the ground.

Her first reaction, after her head had stopped spinning, was astonishment that she had fallen at all—and for such a stupid reason.

Her next reaction was fear that Froggie might be injured.

Beryl scrambled to her feet and ran to snatch the reins. Froggie was still spooked, nervously trip-trapping about on the pavement. The sound of a car door slamming shut, of someone running toward them, only made the horse edgier.

"Don't come any closer!" hissed Beryl over her shoulder.

"Are you all right?" came the anxious inquiry. It was a man's voice, pleasantly baritone. American?

"I'm fine," snapped Beryl.

"What about your horse?"

Murmuring softly to Froggie, Beryl knelt down and ran her hands along Froggie's foreleg. The delicate bones all seemed to be intact.

"Is he all right?" said the man.

"It's a she," answered Beryl. "And yes, she seems to be just fine."

"I really *can* tell the difference," came the dry response. "When I have a view of the essential parts."

Suppressing a smile, Beryl straightened and turned to look at the man. Dark hair, dark eyes, she noted. And the definite glint of humor—nothing stiff-upper-lip about this one. Forty plus years of laughter had left attractive creases about his eyes. He was dressed in formal black tie, and his broad shoulders filled out the tuxedo jacket quite impressively.

"I'm sorry about the spill," he said. "I guess it *was* my fault."

"This is a country road, you know. Not exactly the place to be speeding. You never can tell what lies around the bend."

"So I've discovered."

Froggie gave her an impatient nudge. Beryl stroked the horse's neck, all the time intensely aware of the man's gaze.

"I do have something of an excuse," he said. "I got turned around in the village back there, and I'm running late. I'm trying to find some place called Chetwynd. Do you know it?"

She cocked her head in surprise. "You're going to Chetwynd? Then you're on the wrong road."

"Am I?"

"You turned off a half mile too soon. Head back to the

main road and keep going. You can't miss the turn. It's a private drive, flanked by elms—quite tall ones.''

"I'll watch for the elms, then.''

She remounted Froggie and gazed down at the man. Even viewed from the saddle, he cut an impressive figure, lean and elegant in his tuxedo. And strikingly confident, not a man to be intimidated by anyone—even a woman sitting astride nine hundred muscular pounds of horseflesh.

"Are you sure you're not hurt?" he asked. "It looked like a pretty bad fall to me.''

"Oh, I've fallen before.'' She smiled. "I have quite a hard head.''

The man smiled, too, his teeth straight and white in the twilight. "Then I shouldn't worry about you slipping into a stupor tonight?''

"*You're* the one who'll be slipping into a stupor tonight.''

He frowned. "Excuse me?''

"A stupor brought on by dry and endless palaver. It's a distinct possibility, considering where you're headed.'' Laughing, she turned the horse around. "Good evening,'' she called. Then, with a farewell wave, she urged Froggie into a trot through the woods.

As she left the road behind, it occurred to her that she would get to Chetwynd before he did. That made her laugh again. Perhaps Bastille Day would turn out more interesting than she'd expected. She gave the horse a nudge of her boot. At once Froggie broke into a gallop.

RICHARD WOLF STOOD BESIDE his rented M.G. and watched the woman ride away, her black hair tumbling like a horse's mane about her shoulders. In seconds she was gone, vanished from sight into the woods. He never even caught her name, he thought. He'd have to ask Lord Lovat about her. *Tell me, Hugh. Are you acquainted with a black-haired witch tearing about your neighborhood?* She was dressed like one of the village girls, in a frayed shirt and grass-stained jodhpurs, but her accent bespoke the finest of schools. A charming contradiction.

He climbed back into the car. It was almost six-thirty now; that drive from London had taken longer than he'd expected. Blast these backcountry lanes! He turned the car around and headed for the main road, taking care this time to slow down for curves. No telling what might be lurking around the bend. A cow or a goat.

Or another witch on horseback.

*I have quite a hard head.* He smiled. A hard head, indeed. She slips off the saddle—bump—and she's right back on her feet. And cheeky to boot. As if I couldn't tell a mare from a stallion. All I needed was the right view.

Which he certainly had had of her. There was no doubt whatsoever that it was the female of the species he'd been looking at. All that raven hair, those laughing green eyes. *She almost reminds me of...*

He suppressed the thought, shoved it into the quicksand of bad memories. Nightmares, really. Those terrible echoes of his first assignment, his first failure. It had colored his career, had kept him from ever again taking anything for granted. That was the way one *should* operate in this business. Check the facts, never trust your sources, and always, always watch your back.

It was starting to wear him down. *Maybe I should kick back and retire early. Live the quiet country life like Hugh Tavistock.* Of course Tavistock had a title and estate to keep him in comfort, though Richard had to laugh when he thought of the rotund and balding Hugh Tavistock as earl of anything. *Yeah, I should just settle down on those ten acres in Connecticut. Declare myself Earl of Whatever and grow cucumbers.*

But he'd miss the work. Those delicious whiffs of danger, the international chess game of wits. The world was changing so fast, and you didn't know from day to day who your enemies were....

He spotted, at last, the turnoff to Chetwynd. Flanked by majestic elms, it was as the black-haired woman had described it. That impressive driveway was more than matched by the manor house standing at the end of the road. This was no mere country cottage; this was a castle, complete with turrets and ivy-covered stone walls. Formal gardens stretched out for acres, and a brick path led to what looked like a medieval maze. So this was where old Hugh Tavistock had repaired to after those forty years of service to queen and country. Earldom must have its benefits—one certainly didn't acquire this much wealth in government service. And Hugh had struck him as such a down-to-earth fellow! Not at all the country nobleman type. He had no airs, no pretensions; he was more like some absentminded civil servant who'd wandered, quite by accident, into MI6's inner sanctum.

Amused by the grandeur of it all, Richard went up the steps, breezed through the security gauntlet, and walked into the ballroom.

Here he saw a number of familiar faces among the dozens of guests who'd already arrived. The London economic summit had drawn in diplomats and financiers from across the continent. He spotted at once the American ambassador, swaggering and schmoozing like the political appointee he was. Across the room he saw a trio of old acquaintances from Paris. There was Philippe St. Pierre, the French finance minister, deep in conversation with Reggie Vane, head of the Paris Division, Bank of London. Off to the side stood Reggie's wife, Helena, looking ignored and crabby as usual. Had Richard *ever* seen that woman look happy?

A woman's loud and brassy laugh drew Richard's attention to another familiar figure from his Paris days—Nina Sutherland, the ambassador's widow, shimmering from throat to ankle in green silk and bugle beads. Though her husband was long dead, the old gal was still working the crowd like a seasoned diplomat's wife. Beside her was her twenty-year-old son, Anthony, rumored to be an artist. In his purple shirt, he cut just as flashy a figure as his mother did. What a resplendent pair they were, like a couple of peacocks! Young Anthony had obviously inherited his ex-actress mother's gene for flamboyance.

Judiciously avoiding the Sutherland pair, Richard headed to the buffet table, which was graced with an elaborate ice sculpture of the Eiffel Tower. This Bastille Day theme had been carried to ridiculous extremes. *Everything* was French tonight: the music, the champagne, the tricolors hanging from the ceiling.

"Rather makes one want to burst out singing the 'Marseillaise,' doesn't it?" said a voice.

Richard turned and saw a tall blond man standing beside him. Slenderly built, with the stamp of aristocracy on his face, he seemed elegantly at ease in his starched shirt and tuxedo. Smiling, he handed a glass of champagne to Richard. The chandelier light glittered in the pale bubbles. "You're Richard Wolf," the man said.

Richard nodded, accepting the glass. "And you are...?"

"Jordan Tavistock. Uncle Hugh pointed you out as you walked into the room. Thought I'd come by and introduce myself."

The two men shook hands. Jordan's grip was solid and connected, not what Richard expected from such smoothly aristocratic hands.

"So tell me," said Jordan, casually picking up a second glass of champagne for himself, "which category do you fit into? Spy, diplomat or financier?"

Richard laughed. "I'm expected to answer that question?"

"No. But I thought I'd ask, anyway. It gets things off to a flying start." He took a sip and smiled. "It's a mental exercise of mine. Keeps these parties interesting. I try to pick up on the cues, deduce which ones are with Intelligence. And half of these people are. Or were." Jordan gazed around the room. ''Think of all the secrets contained in all these heads—all those little synapses snapping with classified data.''

''You seem to have more than a passing acquaintance with the business.''

''When one grows up in this household, one lives and breathes the game.'' Jordan regarded Richard for a moment. ''Let's see. You're American....''

''Correct.''

''And whereas the corporate executives arrived in groups by stretch limousine, you came on your own.''

''Right so far.''

''And you refer to intelligence work as *the business*.''

''You noticed.''

''So my guess is...CIA?''

Richard shook his head and smiled. ''I'm just a private security consultant. Sakaroff and Wolf, Inc.''

Jordan smiled back. ''Clever cover.''

''It's not a cover. I'm the real thing. All these corporate executives you see here want a safe summit. An IRA bomb could ruin their whole day.''

''So they hire you to keep the nasties away,'' finished Jordan.

''Exactly,'' said Richard. And he thought, *Yes, this is Madeline and Bernard's son, all right. He resembles Bernard, has got the same sharply observant brown eyes, the same finely wrought features. And he's quick. He notices things—an indispensable talent.*

At that moment, Jordan's attention suddenly shifted to a new arrival. Richard turned to see who had just entered the ballroom. At his first glimpse of the woman, he stiffened in surprise.

It was that black-haired witch, dressed not in old jodhpurs and boots this time, but in a long gown of midnight blue silk. Her hair had been swept up into an elegant mass of waves. Even from this distance, he could feel the magical spell of her attraction—as did every other man in the room.

"It's her," murmured Richard.

"You mean you two have met?" asked Jordan.

"Quite by accident. I spooked her horse on the road. She was none too pleased about the fall."

"You actually unhorsed her?" said Jordan in amazement. "I didn't think it was possible."

The woman glided into the room and swept up a glass of champagne from a tray, her progress cutting a noticeable swath through the crowd.

"She certainly knows how to fill a dress," Richard said under his breath, marveling.

"I'll tell her you said so," Jordan said dryly.

"You wouldn't."

Laughing, Jordan set down his glass. "Come on, Wolf. Let me properly introduce you."

As they approached her, the woman flashed Jordan a smile of greeting. Then her gaze shifted to Richard, and instantly her expression went from easy familiarity to a look of cautious speculation. *Not good,* thought Richard. *She's remembering how I knocked her off that horse. How I almost got her killed.*

"So," she said, civilly enough, "we meet again."

"I hope you've forgiven me."

"Never." Then she smiled. What a smile!

Jordan said, "Darling, this is Richard Wolf."

The woman held out her hand. Richard took it and was surprised by the firm, no-nonsense handshake she returned. As he looked into her eyes, a shock of recognition went through him. *Of course. I should have seen it the very first time we met. That black hair. Those green eyes. She has to be Madeline's daughter.*

"May I introduce Beryl Tavistock," said Jordan. "My sister."

"SO HOW DO YOU HAPPEN to know my Uncle Hugh?" Beryl asked as she and Richard strolled down the garden path. Dusk had fallen, that soft, late dusk of summer, and the flowers had faded into shadow. Their fragrance hung in the air, the scent of sage and roses, lavender and thyme. *He moves like a cat in the darkness,* Beryl thought. *So quiet, so unfathomable.*

"We met years ago in Paris," he said. "We lost touch for a long time. And then, a few years ago, when I set up my consulting firm, your uncle was kind enough to advise me."

"Jordan tells me your company's Sakaroff and Wolf."

"Yes. We're security consultants."

"And is that your real job?"

"Meaning what?"

"Have you a, shall we say, *unofficial* job?"

He threw back his head and laughed. "You and your brother have a knack for cutting straight to the chase."

"We've learned to be direct. It cuts down on the small talk."

"Small talk is society's lubricant."

"No, small talk is how society avoids telling the truth."

"And you want to hear the truth," he said.

"Don't we all?" She looked up at him, trying to see his eyes in the darkness, but they were only shadows in the silhouette of his face.

"The truth," he said, "is that I really am a security consultant. I run the firm with my partner, Niki Sakaroff—"

"Niki? That wouldn't be Nikolai Sakaroff?"

"You've heard the name?" he asked, in a tone that was just a trifle too innocent.

"Former KGB?"

There was a pause. "Yes, at one time," he said evenly. "Niki may have had connections."

"Connections? If I recall correctly, Nikolai Sakaroff was a full colonel. And now he's your business partner?" She laughed. "Capitalism does indeed make strange bedfellows."

They walked a few moments in silence. She asked quietly, "Do you still do business for the CIA?"

"Did I say I did?"

"It's not a difficult conclusion to come to. I'm very discreet, by the way. The truth is safe with me."

"Nevertheless I refuse to be interrogated."

She looked up at him with a smile. "Even under torture, I assume?"

Through the darkness she could see his teeth gleaming in a grin. "That depends on the type of torture. If a beautiful woman nibbles on my ear, well, I might admit to anything."

The brick path ended at the maze. For a while, they stood contemplating that leafy wall of shadow.

"Come on, let's go in," she said.

"Do you know the way out?"

"We'll see."

She led him through the opening and they were quickly swallowed up by hedge walls. In truth, she knew every turn, every blind end, and she moved through the maze with confidence. "I could do this blindfolded," she said.

"Did you grow up at Chetwynd?"

"In between boarding schools. I came to live with Uncle Hugh when I was eight. After Mum and Dad died."

They rustled through the last slot in the hedge and emerged into the center. In a small clearing there was a stone bench and enough moonlight to faintly see each other's face.

"They were in the business, too," she said, circling the grassy clearing slowly. "Or did you already know that?"

"Yes, I've…heard of your parents."

At once she sensed an undertone of caution in his voice and wondered why he'd gone evasive on her. She saw that he was standing by the stone bench, his hands in his pockets.

*All these family secrets. I'm sick of it. Why can't anyone ever tell the truth in this house?*

"What have you heard about them?" she asked.

"I know they died in Paris."

"In the line of duty. Uncle Hugh says it was a classified mission and refuses to talk about it, so we never do." She stopped circling and turned to face him. "I seem to be thinking about it a lot these days."

"Why?"

"Because it happened on the fifteenth of July. Twenty years ago tomorrow."

He moved toward her, his face still hidden in shadow. "Who reared you, then? Your uncle?"

She smiled. "'Reared' is a bit of an exaggeration. Uncle Hugh gave us a home, and then he pretty much turned us loose to grow up as we pleased. Jordan's done quite well for himself, I think. Gone to university and all. But then, Jordie's the smart one in the family."

Richard moved closer—so close she thought she could see his eyes glittering above her in the darkness. "And which one are you?"

"I suppose…I suppose I'm the wild one."

"The wild one," he murmured. "Yes, I think I can tell…."

He touched her face. With that one brief contact, he left her skin tingling. She was suddenly aware of her pounding heart, her quickening breath. *Why am I letting this happen?* she wondered. *I thought I'd sworn off romance. But now this man I scarcely know is dragging me back into the game—a game at which I've proved myself a miserable failure. It's stupid, it's impulsive. It's insanity itself.*

*And it's leaving me quite hungry for more….*

His lips grazed hers; it was the lightest of kisses, but it was heady with the taste of champagne. At once she craved another kiss, a longer kiss. For a moment, they stared at each other, both hovering on the edge of temptation.

Beryl surrendered first. She swayed toward him, against him. His arms went around her, trapping her in their embrace. Eagerly she met his lips, met his kiss with one just as fierce.

"The wild one," he whispered. "Yes, definitely the wild one."

"Demanding, too..."

"I don't doubt it."

"...and *very* difficult."

"I hadn't noticed...."

They kissed again, and by the ragged sound of his breathing, she knew that he, too, was a helpless victim of desire. Suddenly a devilish impulse seized her.

She pulled away. Coyly she asked, "Now will you tell me?"

"Tell you what?" he asked, plainly confused.

"Whom you really work for?"

He paused. "Sakaroff and Wolf, Inc.," he said. "Security consultants."

"Wrong answer," she said. Then, laughing wickedly, she turned and scampered out of the maze.

*Paris*

AT 8:45, AS WAS HER HABIT, Marie St. Pierre patted on her bee pollen face cream, ran a brush through her stiff gray hair, and then slipped under the covers of her bed. She flicked on the TV remote control and awaited her favorite program of the week—"Dynasty." Though the voices were obviously dubbed and the settings garishly American, the stories were close to her heart. Love and power. Pain and retribution. Yes, Marie knew all about love and pain. It was the retribution part she hadn't quite mastered. Every time the anger bubbled up inside her and those old fantasies of revenge began to play out in her mind, she had only to consider the consequences of such action, and all thoughts of vengeance died. No, she loved Philippe too much. And they had come so far together! From finance minister to prime minister would be such a short, short climb....

She suddenly focused on the TV as a brief news item flashed on the screen—the London economic summit. Would Philippe's face appear? No, just a pan of the conference table, a five-second view of two dozen men in suits and ties. No Philippe. She sat back in disappointment and wondered, for the hundredth time, if she should have accompanied her husband to London. She hated to fly, and he'd warned her the trip would be tiresome. Better to stay home, he'd told her; she would hate London.

Still, it might have been nice to go away with him for a few days. Just the two of them in a hotel room. A change of scenery, a new bed. It might have been the spark their marriage so terribly needed—

A thought suddenly crossed her mind. A thought so painful that it twisted her heart in knots. *Here I am. And there is Philippe, alone in London....*

Or was he alone?

She sat trembling for a moment, considering the possibilities. The images. At last she could resist the impulse no longer. She reached for the telephone and dialed Nina Sutherland's Paris apartment.

The phone rang and rang. She hung up and dialed again. Still it rang unanswered. She stared at the receiver. So Nina has gone to London, too, she thought. And there they would be together, in his hotel room. *While I wait at home in Paris.*

She rose from the bed. "Dynasty" had just come on the TV; she ignored it. Instead she got dressed. *Perhaps I am jumping to conclusions,* she thought. *Perhaps Nina is really home and refuses to answer her telephone.*

She would drive past Nina's apartment in Neuilly. Check the windows to see if her lights were on inside.

*And if they were not?*

No, she wouldn't think about that, not yet.

Fully dressed now, she hurried downstairs, picked up her purse and keys in the darkened living room, and opened the front door. Just as she felt the night air against her face, her ears were blasted by a deafening roar.

The explosion threw her off her feet, flinging her forward down the front steps. Only her outstretched arms beneath her prevented her head from slamming against the concrete. She was vaguely aware of glass raining down around her and then of the soft crackle of flames. Slowly she managed to roll over onto her back. There she lay, staring upward at the fingers of fire shooting through her bedroom window.

It was meant for her, she thought. The bomb was meant for her.

As fire sirens wailed closer, she lay on her back in the broken glass and thought, *Is this what it's come to, my love?*

And she watched her bedroom burn above her.

# CHAPTER TWO

*Buckinghamshire, England*

THE EIFFEL TOWER was melting. Jordan stood beside the buffet table and watched the water drip, drip from the ice sculpture into the silver platter of oysters below it. So much for Bastille Day, he thought wearily. Another night, another party. And this one's about run its course.

"You have had more than enough oysters for one night, Reggie," said a peevish voice. "Or have you forgotten your gout?"

"Haven't had an attack in months."

"Only because *I've* been watching your diet," said Helena.

"Then tonight, dear," said Reggie, plucking up another oyster, "would you mind looking the other way?" He lifted the shell to his mouth and tipped the oyster. Nirvana was written on his face as the slippery glob slid into his throat.

Helena shuddered. "It's disgusting, eating a live animal." She glanced at Jordan, noting his quietly bemused look. "Don't you agree?"

Jordan gave a diplomatic shrug. "A matter of upbringing, I suppose. In some cultures, they eat termites. Or quivering fish. I've even heard of monkeys, their heads shaved, immobilized—"

"Oh, please," groaned Helena.

Jordan quickly escaped before the marital spat could escalate. It was not a healthy place to be, caught between a feuding husband and wife. Lady Helena, he suspected, normally held the upper hand; money usually did.

He wandered over to join Finance Minister Philippe St. Pierre and found himself trapped in a lecture on world economics. The summit was a failure, Philippe declared. The Americans want trade concessions but refuse to learn fiscal responsibility. And on and on and on. It was almost a relief when bugle-beaded Nina Sutherland swept into the conversation, trailing her peacock son, Anthony.

"It's not as if Americans are the only ones who have to clean up their act," snorted Nina. "We're none of us doing very well these days, even the French. Or don't you agree, Philippe?"

Philippe flushed under her direct gaze. "We are all of us having difficulties, Nina—"

"Some of us more than others."

"It is a worldwide recession. One must be patient."

Nina's jaw shot up. "And what if one cannot afford to wait?" She drained her glass and set it down sharply. "What then, Philippe, darling?"

Conversation suddenly ceased. Jordan noticed that Helena was watching them amusedly, that Philippe was clutching his glass in a white-knuckled fist. What the blazes was going on here? he wondered. Some private feud? Bizarre tensions were weaving through the gathering tonight. Perhaps it's all that free-flowing champagne. Certainly Reggie had had too much. Their portly houseguest had wandered from the oyster tray to the champagne table. With an unsteady hand, he picked up yet another glass and raised it to his lips. No one was acting quite right tonight. Not even Beryl.

*Certainly* not Beryl.

He spied his sister as she reentered the ballroom. Her cheeks were flushed, her eyes glittering with some unearthly fire. Close on her heels was the American, looking just as flushed and more than a little bothered. Ah, thought Jordan with a smile. A bit of hanky-panky in the garden, was it?

Well, good for her. Poor Beryl could use some fresh romance in her life, anything to make her forget that chronically unfaithful surgeon.

Beryl whisked up a glass of champagne from a passing servant and headed Jordan's way. "Having fun?" she asked him.

"Not as much as you, I suspect." He glanced across at Richard Wolf, who'd just been waylaid by some American businessman. "So," he whispered, "did you wring a confession out of him?"

"Not a thing." She smiled over her champagne glass. "Extremely tight-lipped."

"Really?"

"But I'll have another go at him later. After I let him cool his heels for a while."

Lord, how beautiful his baby sister could be when she was happy, thought Jordan. Which, it seemed, wasn't very often lately. Too much passion in that heart of hers; it made her far more vulnerable than she'd ever admit. For a year now she'd been lying doggo, had dropped out entirely from the old mating game. She'd even given up her charity work at St. Luke's—a job she'd dearly loved. It was too painful, always running into her ex-lover on the hospital grounds.

But tonight the old sparkle was back in her eyes and he was glad to see it. He noticed how it flared even more brightly as Richard Wolf glanced her way. All those flirtatious looks passing back and forth! He could almost feel the crackle of electricity flying between them.

"...a well-deserved honor, of course, but a bit late, don't you think, Jordan?"

Jordan glanced in puzzlement at Reggie Vane's flushed face. The man had been drinking entirely too much. "Excuse me," he said, "I'm afraid I wasn't following."

"The Queen's medal for Leo Sinclair. You remember Leo, don't you? Wonderful chap. Killed a year and a half ago. Or was it two years?" He gave his head a little shake, as though to clear it. "Anyway, they're just getting 'round to giving the widow his medal. I think that's inexcusable."

"Not everyone who was killed in the Gulf got a medal," Nina Sutherland cut in.

"But Leo was Intelligence," said Reggie. "He deserved some sort of honor, considering how he...died."

"Perhaps it was just an oversight," said Jordan. "Papers getting mislaid, that sort of thing. MI6 does try to honor its dead, and Leo sort of fell through the cracks."

"The way Mum and Dad did," said Beryl. "They died in the line of duty. And they never got a medal."

"Line of duty?" said Reggie. "Not exactly." He lifted the champagne glass unsteadily to his lips. Suddenly he paused, aware that the others were staring at him. The silence stretched on, broken only by the clatter of an oyster shell on someone's plate.

"What do you mean by 'not exactly'?" asked Beryl.

Reggie cleared his throat. "Surely...Hugh must have told you...." He looked around and his face blanched. "Oh, no," he murmured, "I've put my foot in it this time."

"Told us what, Reggie?" Jordan persisted.

"But it was public knowledge," said Reggie. "It was in all the Paris newspapers...."

"Reggie," Jordan said slowly. Deliberately. "Our understanding was that my mother and father were shot in Paris. That it was murder. Is that not true?"

"Well, of course there was a murder involved—"

"A murder?" Jordan cut in. "As in singular?"

Reggie glanced around, befuddled. "I'm not the only one here who knows about it. You were all in Paris when it happened!"

For a few heartbeats, no one said a thing. Then Helena added, quietly, "It was a very long time ago, Jordan. Twenty years. It hardly makes a difference now."

"It makes a difference to *us*," Jordan insisted. "What happened in Paris?"

Helena sighed. "I told Hugh he should've been honest with you, instead of trying to bury it."

"Bury *what?*" asked Beryl.

Helena's mouth drew tight.

It was Nina who finally spoke the truth. Brazen Nina, who had never bothered with subtleties. She said flatly, "The police said it was a murder. Followed by a suicide."

Beryl stared at Nina. Saw the other woman's gaze meet hers without flinching. "No," she whispered.

Gently Helena touched her shoulder. "You were just a child, Beryl. Both of you were. And Hugh didn't think it was appropriate—"

Beryl said again, "No," and pulled away from Helena's outstretched hand. Suddenly she whirled and fled in a rustle of blue silk across the ballroom.

"Thank you. All of you," said Jordan coldly. "For your most refreshing candor." Then he, too, turned and headed across the room in pursuit of his sister.

He caught up with her on the staircase. "Beryl?"

"It's not true," she said. "I don't believe it!"

"Of course it's not true."

She halted on the stairs and looked down at him. "Then why are they all saying it?"

"Ugly rumors. What else can it be?"

"Where's Uncle Hugh?"

Jordan shook his head. "He's not in the ballroom."

Beryl looked up toward the second floor. "Come on, Jordie," she said, her voice tight with determination. "We're going to set this thing straight."

Together they climbed the stairs.

Uncle Hugh was in his study; through the closed door, they could hear him speaking in urgent tones. Without knocking, they pushed inside and confronted him.

"Uncle Hugh?" said Beryl.

Hugh cut her off with a sharp motion for silence. He

turned his back and said into the telephone, "It *is* definite, Claude? Not a gas leak or anything like that?"

"Uncle Hugh!"

Stubbornly he kept his back turned to her. "Yes, yes," he said into the phone, "I'll tell Philippe at once. God, this is horrid timing, but you're right, he has no choice. He'll have to fly back tonight." Looking stunned, Hugh hung up and stared at the telephone.

"Did you tell us the truth?" asked Beryl. "About Mum and Dad?"

Hugh turned and frowned at her in bewilderment. "What? What are you talking about?"

"You told us they were killed in the line of duty," said Beryl. "You never said anything about a suicide."

"Who told you that?" he snapped.

"Nina Sutherland. But Reggie and Helena knew about it, too. In fact, the whole world seems to know! Everyone except us."

"Blast that Sutherland woman!" roared Hugh. "She had no right."

Beryl and Jordan stared at him in shock. Softly Beryl said, "It *is* a lie. Isn't it?"

Abruptly Hugh started for the door. "We'll discuss it later," he said. "I have to take care of this business—"

"Uncle Hugh!" cried Beryl. "Is it a lie?"

Hugh stopped. Slowly he turned and looked at her. "I never believed it," he said. "Not for a second did I think Bernard would ever hurt her...."

"What are you saying?" asked Jordan. "That it was Dad who killed her?"

Their uncle's silence was the only answer they needed. For a moment, Hugh lingered in the doorway. Quietly he said, "Please, Jordan. We'll talk about it later. After everyone leaves. Now I really must see to this phone call." He turned and left the room.

Beryl and Jordan looked at each other. They each saw, in the other's eyes, the same shock of comprehension.

"Dear God, Jordie," said Beryl. "It must be true."

FROM ACROSS THE BALLROOM, Richard saw Beryl's hasty exit and then, seconds later, the equally rapid departure of a grim-faced Jordan. What the hell was going on? he wondered. He started to follow them out of the room, then spotted Helena, shaking her head as she moved toward him.

"It's a disaster," she muttered. "Too much bloody champagne flowing tonight."

"What happened?"

"They just heard the truth. About Bernard and Madeline."

"Who told them?"

"Nina. But it was Reggie's fault, really. He's so drunk he doesn't know what he's saying."

Richard looked at the doorway through which Jordan had just vanished. "I should talk to them, tell them the whole story."

"I think that's their uncle's responsibility. Don't you? He's the one who kept it from them all these years. Let him do the explaining."

After a pause, Richard nodded. "You're right. Of course you're right. Maybe I'll just go and strangle Nina Sutherland instead."

"Strangle my husband while you're at it. You have my permission."

Richard turned and spotted Hugh Tavistock reentering the ballroom. "Now what?" he muttered as the man hurried toward them.

"Where's Philippe?" snapped Hugh.

"I believe he was headed out to the garden," said Helena. "Is something wrong?"

"This whole evening's turned into a disaster," muttered

Hugh. "I just got a call from Paris. A bomb's gone off in Philippe's flat."

Richard and Helena stared at him in horror.

"Oh, my God," whispered Helena. "Is Marie—"

"She's all right. A few minor injuries, but nothing serious. She's in hospital now."

"Assassination attempt?" Richard queried.

Hugh nodded. "So it would seem."

IT WAS LONG PAST MIDNIGHT when Jordan and Uncle Hugh finally found Beryl. She was in her mother's old room, huddled beside Madeline's steamer trunk. The lid had been thrown open, and Madeline's belongings were spilled out across the bed and the floor: silky summer dresses, flowery hats, a beaded evening purse. And there were silly things, too: a branch of sea coral, a pebble, a china frog—items of significance known only to Madeline. Beryl had removed all of these things from the trunk, and now she sat surrounded by them, trying to absorb, through these inanimate objects, the warmth and spirit that had once been Madeline Tavistock.

Uncle Hugh came into the bedroom and sat down in a chair beside her. "Beryl," he said gently, "it's time...it's time I told you the truth."

"The time for the truth was years ago," she said, staring down at the china frog in her hand.

"But you were both so very young. You were only eight, and Jordan was ten. You wouldn't have understood—"

"We could've dealt with the facts! Instead you hid them from us!"

"The facts were painful. The French police concluded—"

"Dad would *never* have hurt her," said Beryl. She looked up at him with a ferocity that made Hugh draw back in surprise. "Don't you remember how they were together, Uncle Hugh? How much in love they were? *I* remember!"

"So do I," said Jordan.

Uncle Hugh took off his spectacles and wearily rubbed his eyes. "The truth," he said, "is even worse than that."

Beryl stared at him incredulously. "How could it be any worse than murder and suicide?"

"Perhaps...perhaps you should see the file." He rose to his feet. "It's upstairs. In my office."

They followed their uncle to the third floor, to a room they seldom visited, a room he always kept locked. He opened the cabinet and pulled a folder from the drawer. It was a classified MI6 file labeled Tavistock, Bernard and Madeline.

"I suppose I...I'd hoped to protect you from this," said Hugh. "The truth is, I myself don't believe it. Bernard didn't have a traitorous bone in his body. But the evidence was there. And I don't know any other way to explain it." He handed the file to Beryl.

In silence she opened the folder. Together she and Jordan paged through the contents. Inside were copies of the Paris police report, including witness statements and photographs of the murder scene. The conclusions were as Nina Sutherland had told them. Bernard had shot his wife three times at close range and had then put the gun to his own head and pulled the trigger. The crime photos were too horrible to dwell on; Beryl flipped quickly past those and found herself staring at another report, this one filed by French Intelligence. In disbelief, she read and reread the conclusions.

"This isn't possible," she said.

"It's what they found. A briefcase with classified NATO files. Allied weapons data. It was in the garret, where their bodies were discovered. Bernard had those files with him when he died—files that shouldn't have been out of the embassy building."

"How do you know *he* took them?"

"He had access, Beryl. He was our Intelligence liaison to NATO. For months, Allied documents were showing up in East German hands, delivered to them by someone they code-named Delphi. We knew we had a mole, but we couldn't identify him—until those papers were found with Bernard's body.''

''And you think Dad was Delphi,'' said Jordan.

''No, that's what French Intelligence concluded. I couldn't believe it, but I also couldn't dispute the facts.''

For a moment, Beryl and Jordan sat in silence, dismayed by the weight of the evidence.

''You don't really believe it, Uncle Hugh?'' said Beryl softly. ''That Dad was the one?''

''I couldn't argue with the findings. And it *would* explain their deaths. Perhaps they knew they were on the verge of being discovered. Disgraced. So Bernard took the gentleman's way out. He would, you know. Death before dishonor.''

Uncle Hugh sank back in the chair and wearily ran his fingers through his gray hair. ''I tried to keep the report as quiet as possible,'' he said. ''The search for Delphi was halted. I myself had a few sticky years in MI6. Brother of a traitor and all, can we trust him, that sort of thing. But then, it was forgotten. And I went on with my career. I think…I think it was because no one at MI6 could quite believe the report. That Bernard had gone to the other side.''

''I don't believe it, either,'' said Beryl.

Uncle Hugh looked at her. ''Nevertheless—''

''I *won't* believe it. It's a fabrication. Someone at MI6, covering up the truth—''

''Don't be ridiculous, Beryl.''

''Mum and Dad can't defend themselves! Who else will speak up for them?''

''Your loyalty's commendable, darling, but—''

''And where's *your* loyalty?'' she retorted. ''He was your brother!''

''I didn't want to believe it.''

"Then did you confirm that evidence? Did you discuss it with French Intelligence?"

"Yes, and I trusted Daumier's report. He's a thorough man."

"Daumier?" queried Jordan. "Claude Daumier? Isn't he chief of their Paris operations?"

"At the time, he was their liaison to MI6. I asked him to review the findings. He came to the same conclusions."

"Then this Daumier fellow is an idiot," said Beryl. She turned to the door. "And I'm going to tell him so myself."

"Where are you going?" asked Jordan.

"To pack my things," she said. "Are you coming, Jordan?"

"Pack?" said Hugh. "Where in blazes are you headed?"

Beryl threw a glance over her shoulder. "Where else," she answered, "but Paris?"

RICHARD WOLF GOT THE CALL at six that morning. "They are booked on a noon flight to Paris," said Claude Daumier. "It seems, my friend, that someone has pried open a rather nasty can of worms."

Still groggy with sleep, Richard sat up in bed and gave his head a shake. "What are you talking about, Claude? Who's flying to Paris?"

"Beryl and Jordan Tavistock. Hugh has just called me. I think this is not a good development."

Richard collapsed back on his pillow. "They're adults, Claude," he said, yawning. "If they want to jet off to Paris—"

"They are coming to find out about Bernard and Madeline."

Richard closed his eyes and groaned. "Oh, wonderful, just what we need."

"My sentiments precisely."

"Can't Hugh talk them out of it?"

"He tried. But this niece of his..." Daumier sighed. "You have met her. So you would understand."

Yes, Richard knew exactly how stubborn Miss Beryl Tavistock could be. Like mother, like daughter. He remembered that Madeline had been just as unswerving, just as unstoppable.

Just as enchanting.

He shook off those haunting memories of a long-dead woman and said, "How much do they know?"

"They have seen my report. They know about Delphi."

"So they'll be digging in all the right places."

"All the dangerous places," amended Daumier.

Richard sat up on the side of the bed and clawed his fingers through his hair as he considered the possibilities. The perils.

"Hugh is concerned for their safety," said Daumier. "So am I. If what we think is true—"

"Then they're walking into quicksand."

"And Paris is dangerous enough as it is," added Daumier, "what with the latest bombing."

"How is Marie St. Pierre, by the way?"

"A few scratches, bruises. She should be released from the hospital tomorrow."

"Ordnance report back?"

"Semtex. The upper apartment was completely demolished. Luckily Marie was downstairs when the bomb went off."

"Who's claiming responsibility?"

"There was a telephone call shortly after the blast. It was a man, said he belonged to some group called Cosmic Solidarity. They claim responsibility."

"Cosmic Solidarity? Never heard of that one."

"Neither have we," said Daumier. "But you know how it is these days."

Yes, Richard knew only too well. Any wacko with the right connections could buy a few ounces of Semtex, build a bomb, and join the revolution—any revolution. No wonder his business was booming. In this brave new world, terrorism was a fact of life. And clients everywhere were willing to pay top dollar for security.

"So you see, my friend," said Daumier, "it is not a good time for Bernard's children to be in Paris. And with all the questions they will ask—"

"Can't you keep an eye on them?"

"Why should they trust me? It was *my* report in that file. No, they need another friend here, Richard. Someone with sharp eyes and unerring instincts."

"You have someone in mind?"

"I hear through the grapevine that you and Miss Tavistock shared a degree of...simpatico?"

"She's way too rich for my blood. And I'm too poor for hers."

"I do not usually ask for favors," said Daumier quietly. "Neither does Hugh."

*And you're asking for one now,* thought Richard. He sighed. "How can I refuse?"

After he'd hung up, he sat for a moment contemplating the task ahead. This was a baby-sitting job, really—the sort of assignment he despised. But the thought of seeing Beryl Tavistock again, and the memory of that kiss they'd shared in the garden, was enough to make him grin with anticipation. *Way too rich for my blood,* he thought. *But a man can dream, can't he? And I do owe it to Bernard and Madeline.*

Even after all these years, their deaths still haunted him. Perhaps the time had come to close the mystery, to answer all those questions he and Daumier had raised twenty years ago. The same questions MI6 and Central Intelligence had firmly suppressed.

Now Beryl Tavistock was poking her aristocratic nose into the mess. And a most attractive nose it was, he thought. He hoped it didn't get her killed.

He rose from the bed and headed for the shower. So much

to do, so many preparations to make before he headed to the airport.

Baby-sitting jobs—how he hated them.

But at least this one would be in Paris.

ANTHONY SUTHERLAND STARED out his airplane window and longed fervently for the flight to be over and done with. Of all the rotten luck to be booked on the same Air France flight as the Vanes! And then to be seated straight across the first-class aisle from them—well, this really was intolerable. He considered Reggie Vane a screaming bore, especially when intoxicated, which at the moment Reggie was well on the way to becoming. Two whiskey sours and the man was starting to babble about how much he missed jolly old England, where food was boiled as it should be, not sautéed in all that ghastly butter, where people lined up in proper queues, where crowds didn't reek of garlic and onions. He'd lived too many years in Paris now—surely it was time to retire from the bank and go home? He'd put in many years at the Bank of London's Paris branch. Now that there were so many clever young V.P.s ready to step into his place, why not let them?

Lady Helena, who appeared to be just as fed up with her husband as Anthony was, simply said, "Shut up, Reggie," and ordered him a third whiskey sour.

Anthony didn't much care for Helena, either. She reminded him of some sort of nasty rodent. Such a contrast to his mother! The two women sat across the aisle from each other, Helena drab and proper in her houndstooth skirt and jacket, Nina so striking in her whitest-white silk pantsuit. Only a woman with true confidence could wear white silk, and his mother was one who could. Even at fifty-three, Nina was stunning, her dark, upswept hair showing scarcely a trace of gray, her figure the envy of any twenty-year-old. *But of course,* thought Anthony, *she's my mother.*

And, as usual, she was getting in her digs at Helena.

"If you and Reggie hate it so much in Paris," sniffed Nina, "why do you stay? If you ask me, people who don't adore the city don't deserve to live there."

"Of course, you *would* love Paris," said Helena.

"It's all in the attitude. If you'd kept an open mind…"

"Oh, no, we're much too stuffy," muttered Helena.

"I didn't say that. But there is a certain British attitude. God is an Englishman, that sort of thing."

"You mean He isn't?" Reggie interjected.

Helena didn't laugh. "I just think," she said, "that a certain amount of order and discipline is needed for the world to function properly."

Nina glanced at Reggie, who was noisily slurping his whiskey. "Yes, I can see you both believe in discipline. No wonder the evening was such a disaster."

"We weren't the ones who blurted out the truth," snapped Helena.

"At least *I* was sober enough to know what I was saying!" Nina declared. "They would have found out in any event. After Reggie there let the cat out of the bag, I just decided it was time to be straight with them about Bernard and Madeline."

"And look at the result," moaned Helena. "Hugh says Beryl and Jordan are flying to Paris this afternoon. Now they'll be mucking around in things."

Nina shrugged. "Well, it was a long time ago."

"I don't see why you're so nonchalant. If anyone could be hurt, it's you," muttered Helena.

Nina frowned at her. "What do you mean by that?"

"Oh, nothing."

"No, really! What do you mean by that?"

"Nothing," Helena snapped.

Their conversation came to an abrupt halt. But Anthony could tell his mother was fuming. She sat with her hands balled up in her lap. She even ordered a second martini. When she rose from her seat and headed down the aisle for a bit of exercise, he followed her. They met at the rear of the plane.

"Are you all right, Mother?" he asked.

Nina glanced in agitation toward first class. "It's all Reggie's bloody fault," she whispered. "And Helena's right, you know. I *am* the one who could be hurt."

"After all these years?"

"They'll be asking questions again. Digging. Lord, what if those Tavistock brats find something?"

Anthony said quietly, "They won't."

Nina's gaze met his. In that one look they saw, in each other's eyes, the bond of twenty years. "You and me against the world," she used to sing to him. And that's how it had felt—just the two of them in their Paris flat. There'd been her lovers, of course, insignificant men, scarcely worth noting. But mother and son—what love could be stronger?

He said, "You've nothing to worry about, darling. Really."

"But the Tavistocks—"

"They're harmless." He took her hand and gave it a reassuring squeeze. "I guarantee it."

# CHAPTER THREE

FROM THE WINDOW of her suite at the Paris Ritz, Beryl looked down at the opulence of Place Vendôme, with its Corinthian pilasters and stone arches, and saw the evening parade of well-heeled tourists. It had been eight years since she'd last visited Paris, and then it had been on a lark with her girlfriends—three wild chums from school, who'd preferred the Left Bank bistros and seedy nightlife of Montparnasse to this view of unrepentant luxury. They'd had a grand time of it, too, had drunk countless bottles of wine, danced in the streets, flirted with every Frenchman who'd glanced their way—and there'd been a lot of them.

It seemed a million years ago. A different life, a different age.

Now, standing at the hotel window, she mourned the loss of all those carefree days and knew they would never be back. *I've changed too much,* she thought. *It's more than just the revelations about Mum and Dad. It's me. I feel restless. I'm longing for…I don't know what. Purpose, perhaps? I've gone so long without purpose in my life.…*

She heard the door open, and Jordan came in through the connecting door from his suite. "Claude Daumier finally returned my call," he said. "He's tied up with the bomb investigation, but he's agreed to meet us for an early supper."

"When?"

"Half an hour."

Beryl turned from the window and looked at her brother.

They'd scarcely slept last night, and it showed in Jordan's face. Though freshly shaved and impeccably dressed, he had that ragged edge of fatigue, the lean and hungry look of a man operating on reserve strength. *Like me.*

"I'm ready to leave anytime," she said.

He frowned at her dress. "Isn't that…Mum's?"

"Yes. I packed a few of her things in my suitcase. I don't know why, really." She gazed down at the watered-silk skirt. "It's eerie, isn't it? How well it fits. As if it were made for me."

"Beryl, are you sure you're up to this?"

"Why do you ask?"

"It's just that—" Jordan shook his head "—you don't seem at all yourself."

"Neither of us is, Jordie. How could we be?" She looked out the window again, at the lengthening shadows in Place Vendôme. The same view her mother must have looked down upon on *her* visits to Paris. The same hotel, perhaps even the same suite. *I'm even wearing her dress.* "It's as if—as if we don't know who we are anymore," she said. "Where we spring from."

"Who you are, who I am, has never been in doubt, Beryl. Whatever we learn about them doesn't change us."

She looked at him. "So you think it might be true."

He paused. "I don't know," he said. "But I'm preparing myself for the worst. And so should you." He went to the closet and took out her wrap. "Come on. It's time to confront the facts, little sister. Whatever they may be."

At seven o'clock, they arrived at Le Petit Zinc, the café where Daumier had arranged to meet them. It was early for the usual Parisian supper hour, and except for a lone couple dining on soup and bread, the café was empty. They took a seat in a booth at the rear and ordered wine and bread and a *remoulade* of mustard and celeriac to stave off their hunger. The lone couple finished their meal and departed. The appointed time came and went. Had Daumier changed his mind about meeting them?

Then, at seven-twenty, the door opened and a trim little Frenchman in suit and tie walked into the dining room. With his graying temples and his briefcase, he could have passed for any distinguished banker or lawyer. But the instant his gaze locked on Beryl, she knew, by his nod of acknowledgment, that this must be Claude Daumier.

But he had not come alone. He glanced over his shoulder as the door opened again, and a second man entered the restaurant. Together they approached the booth where Beryl and Jordan were seated. Beryl stiffened as she found herself staring not at Daumier but at his companion.

"Hello, Richard," she said quietly. "I had no idea you were coming to Paris."

"Neither did I," he said. "Until this morning."

Introductions were made, hands shaken all around. Then the two men slid into the booth. Beryl faced Richard straight across the table. As his gaze met hers, she felt the earlier sparks kindle between them, the memory of their kiss flaring to mind. *Beryl, you idiot,* she thought in irritation, *you're letting him distract you. Confuse you. No man has a right to affect you this way—certainly not a man you've only kissed once in your life. Not to mention one you met only twenty-four hours ago.*

Still, she couldn't seem to shake the memory of those moments in the garden at Chetwynd. Nor could she forget the taste of his lips. She watched him pour himself a glass of wine, watched him raise the glass to sip. Again, their eyes met, this time over the gleam of ruby liquid. She licked her own lips and savored the aftertaste of Burgundy.

"So what brings you to Paris?" she asked, raising her glass.

"Claude, as a matter of fact." He tilted his head at Daumier.

At Beryl's questioning look, Daumier said, "When I

heard my old friend Richard was in London, I thought why not consult him? Since he is an authority on the subject.''

''The St. Pierre bombing,'' Richard explained. ''Some group no one's ever heard of is claiming responsibility. Claude thought perhaps I'd be able to shed some light on their identity. For years I've been tracking every reported terrorist organization there is.''

''And did you shed some light?'' asked Jordan.

''Afraid not,'' he admitted. ''Cosmic Solidarity doesn't show up on my computer.'' He took another sip of wine, and his gaze locked with hers. ''But the trip isn't entirely wasted,'' he added, ''since I discover you're in Paris, as well.''

''Strictly business,'' said Beryl. ''With no time for pleasure.''

''None at all?''

''None,'' she said flatly. She pointedly turned her attention to Daumier. ''My uncle did call you, didn't he? About why we're here?''

The Frenchman nodded. ''I understand you have both read the file.''

''Cover to cover,'' said Jordan.

''Then you know the evidence. I myself confirmed the witness statements, the coroner's findings—''

''The coroner could have misinterpreted the facts,'' Jordan asserted.

''I myself saw their bodies in the garret. It was not something I am likely to forget.'' Daumier paused as though shaken by the memory. ''Your mother died of three bullet wounds to the chest. Lying beside her was Bernard, a single bullet in his head. The gun had his fingerprints. There were no witnesses, no other suspects.'' Daumier shook his head. ''The evidence speaks for itself.''

''But where's the motive?'' said Beryl. ''Why would he kill someone he loved?''

"Perhaps that is the motive," said Daumier. "Love. Or loss of love. She may have found someone else—"

"That's impossible," Beryl objected vehemently. "She loved him."

Daumier looked down at his wineglass. He said quietly, "You have not yet read the police interview with the landlord, M. Rideau?"

Beryl and Jordan looked at him in puzzlement. "Rideau? I don't recall seeing that interview in the file," said Jordan.

"Only because I chose to exclude it when I sent the file to Hugh. It was a...matter of discretion."

Discretion, thought Beryl. Meaning he was trying to hide some embarrassing fact.

"The attic flat where their bodies were found," said Daumier, "was rented out to a Mlle Scarlatti. According to the landlord, Rideau, this Scarlatti woman used the flat once or twice a week. And only for the purpose of..." He paused delicately.

"Meeting a lover?" Jordan said bluntly.

Daumier nodded. "After the shooting, the landlord was asked to identify the bodies. Rideau told the police that the woman he called Mlle Scarlatti was the same one found dead in the garret. Your mother."

Beryl stared at him in shock. "You're saying my mother met a *lover* there?"

"It was the landlord's testimony."

"Then we'll have to talk face-to-face with this landlord."

"Not possible," said Daumier. "The building has been sold several times over. M. Rideau has left the country. I do not know where he is."

Beryl and Jordan sat in stunned silence. So that was Daumier's theory, thought Beryl. That her mother had a lover. Once or twice a week she would meet him in that attic flat on Rue Myrha. And then her father found out. So he killed her. And then he killed himself.

She looked up at Richard and saw the flicker of sympathy

in his eyes. He believes it, too, she thought. Suddenly she resented him simply for being here, for hearing the most shameful secret of her family.

They heard a soft beeping. Daumier reached under his jacket and frowned at his pocket pager. "I am afraid I will have to leave," he said.

"What about that classified file?" asked Jordan. "You haven't said anything about Delphi."

"We'll speak of it later. This bombing, you understand—it is a crisis situation." Daumier slid out of the booth and picked up his briefcase. "Perhaps tomorrow? In the meantime, try to enjoy your stay in Paris, all of you. Oh, and if you dine here, I would recommend the duckling. It is excellent." With a nod of farewell, he turned and swiftly walked out of the restaurant.

"We just got the royal runaround," muttered Jordan in frustration. "He drops a bomb in our laps, then he scurries for cover, never answering our questions."

"I think that was his plan from the start," said Beryl. "Tell us something so horrifying, we'll be afraid to pursue it. Then our questions will stop." She looked at Richard. "Am I right?"

He met her gaze without wavering. "Why are you asking me?"

"Because you two obviously know each other well. Is this the way Daumier usually operates?"

"Claude's not one to spill secrets. But he also believes in helping out old friends, and your uncle Hugh's a good friend of his. I'm sure Claude's keeping your best interests at heart."

Old friends, thought Beryl. Daumier and Uncle Hugh and Richard Wolf—all of them linked together by some shadowy past, a past they would not talk about. This was how it had been, growing up at Chetwynd. Mysterious men in limousines dropping in to visit Hugh. Sometimes Beryl would hear snatches of conversation, would pick up whis-

pered names whose significance she could only guess at.
Yurchenko. Andropov. Baghdad. Berlin. She had learned
long ago not to ask questions, never to expect answers.
"Not something to bother your pretty head about," Hugh
would tell her.

This time, she wouldn't be put off. This time she demanded answers.

The waiter came to the table with the menus. Beryl shook
her head. "We won't be staying," she said.

"You're not interested in supper?" asked Richard.
"Claude says it's an excellent restaurant."

"Did Claude ask you to show up?" she demanded.
"Keep us well fed and entertained so we won't trouble
him?"

"I'm delighted to keep you well fed. And, if you're willing, entertained." He smiled at her then, a smile with just
a spark of mischief. Looking into his eyes, she found herself
wavering on the edge of temptation. *Have supper with me*,
she read in his smile. *And afterward, who knows? Anything's possible.*

Slowly she sat back in the booth. "We'll have supper
with you, on one condition."

"What's that?"

"You play it straight with us. No dodging, no games."

"I'll try."

"Why are you in Paris?"

"Claude asked me to consult. As a personal favor. The
summit's over now, so my schedule's open. Plus, I was
curious."

"About the bombing?"

He nodded. "Cosmic Solidarity is a new one for me. I
try to keep up with new terrorist groups. It's my business."
He held a menu out to her and smiled. "And that, Miss
Tavistock, is the unadulterated truth."

She met his gaze and saw no flicker of avoidance in his

eyes. Still, her instincts told her there was something more behind that smile, something yet unsaid.

"You don't believe me," he said.

"How did you guess?"

"Does this mean you're not having supper with me?"

Up until that moment, Jordan had sat watching them, his gaze playing Ping-Pong. Now he cut in impatiently. "We are definitely having supper. Because I'm hungry, Beryl, and I'm not moving from this booth until I've eaten."

With a sigh of resignation, Beryl took the menu. "I guess that answers that. Jordie's stomach has spoken."

AMIEL FOCH'S TELEPHONE rang at precisely seven-fifteen.

"I have a new task for you," said the caller. "It's a matter of some urgency. Perhaps this time around, you'll prove successful."

The criticism stung, and Amiel Foch, with twenty-five years' experience in the business, barely managed to suppress a retort. The caller held the purse strings; he could afford to hurl insults. Foch had his retirement to consider. Requests for his services were few and far between these days. One's reflexes, after all, did not improve with age.

Foch said, with quiet control, "I planted the device as you instructed. It went off at the time specified."

"And all it did was make a lot of bloody noise. The target was scarcely hurt."

"She did the unexpected. One cannot control such things."

"Let's hope this time you keep things under better control."

"What is the name?"

"Two names. A brother and sister, Beryl and Jordan Tavistock. They're staying at the Ritz. I want to know where they go. Who they see."

"Nothing more?"

"For now, just surveillance. But things may change at

any time, depending on what they learn. With any luck, they'll simply turn around and run home to England.''

"If they do not?"

"Then we'll take further action.''

"What about Mme St. Pierre? Do you wish me to try again?''

The caller paused. "No,'' he said at last, "she can wait. For now, the Tavistocks take priority.''

OVER A MEAL OF poached salmon and duck with raspberry sauce, Beryl and Richard thrusted and parried questions and answers. Richard, an accomplished verbal duelist, revealed only the barest sketch of his personal life. He was born and reared in Connecticut. His father, a retired cop, was still living. After leaving Princeton University, Richard joined the U.S. State Department and served as political officer at embassies around the world. Then, five years ago, he left government service to start up business as a security consultant. Sakaroff and Wolf, based in Washington, D.C., was born.

"And that's what brought me to London last week," he said. "Several American firms wanted security for their executives during the summit. I was hired as consultant.''

"And that's all you were doing in London?'' she asked.

"That's all I was doing in London. Until I got Hugh's invitation to Chetwynd.'' His gaze met hers across the table.

His directness unsettled her. *Is he telling me the truth, fiction or something in between?* That matter-of-fact recitation of his career had struck her as rehearsed, but then, it would be. People in the intelligence business always had their life histories down pat, the details memorized, fact blending smoothly with fantasy. What did she really know about him? Only that he smiled easily, laughed easily. That his appetite was hearty and he drank his coffee black.

And that she was intensely, insanely, attracted to him.

After supper, he offered to drive them back to the Ritz. Jordan sat in the back seat, Beryl in the front—right next to Richard. She kept glancing sideways at him as they drove up Boulevard Saint-Germain toward the Seine. Even the traffic, outrageously rude and noisy, did not seem to ruffle him. At a stoplight, he turned and looked at her and that one glimpse of his face through the darkness of the car was enough to make her heart do a somersault.

Calmly he shifted his attention back to the road. "It's still early," he said. "Are you sure you want to go back to the hotel?"

"What's my choice?"

"A drive. A walk. Whatever you'd like. After all, you're in Paris. Why not make the most of it?" He reached down to shift gears, and his hand brushed past her knee. A shiver ran through her—a warm, delicious sizzle of anticipation.

*He's tempting me. Making me dizzy with all the possibilities. Or is it the wine? What harm can there be in a little stroll, a little fresh air?*

She called over her shoulder, "How about it, Jordie? Do you feel like taking a walk?" She was answered by a loud snore.

Beryl turned and saw to her astonishment that her brother was sprawled across the back seat. A sleepless night and two glasses of wine at supper had left him dead to the world. "I guess that's a negative," she said with a laugh.

"What about just you and me?"

That invitation, voiced so softly, sent another shiver of temptation up her spine. After all, she thought, she was in Paris....

"A short walk," she agreed. "But first, let's put Jordan to bed."

"Valet service coming up," Richard said, laughing. "First stop, the Ritz."

Jordan snored all the way back to the hotel.

THEY WALKED IN THE Tuileries, a stroll that took them along a gravel path through formal gardens, past statues glowing a ghostly white under the street lamps.

"And here we are again," said Richard, "walking through another garden. Now if only we could find a maze with a nice little stone bench at the center."

"Why?" she asked with a smile. "Are you hoping for a repeat scenario?"

"With a slightly different ending. You know, after you left me in there, it took me a good five minutes to find my way out."

"I know." She laughed. "I was waiting at the door, counting the minutes. Five minutes wasn't bad, really. But other men have done better."

"So that's how you screen your men. You're the cheese in the maze—"

"And you were the rat."

They both laughed then, and the sound of their voices floated through the night air.

"And my performance was only...adequate?" he said.

"Average."

He moved toward her, his smile gleaming in the shadows. "Better than adquate?"

"For you, I'll make allowances. After all, it was dark...."

"Yes, it was." He moved closer, so close she had to tilt her head up to look at him. So close she could almost feel the heat radiating from his body. "Very dark," he whispered.

"And perhaps you were disoriented?"

"Extremely."

"And it *was* a nasty trick I played...."

"For which you should be soundly punished."

He reached up and took her face in his hands. The taste of his lips on hers sent a shudder of pleasure through her body. *If this is my punishment,* she thought, *oh, let me commit the crime again....* His fingers slid through her hair, tangling in the strands as his kiss pressed ever deeper. She felt her legs wobble and melt away, but she had no need of them; he was there to support them both. She heard his murmur of need and knew that these kisses were dangerous, that he, too, was fast slipping toward the same cliff's edge. She didn't care—she was ready to make the leap.

And then, without warning, he froze.

One moment he was kissing her, and an instant later his hands went rigid against her face. He didn't pull away. Even as she felt his whole body grow tense against her, he kept her firmly in his embrace. His lips glided to her ear.

"Start walking," he whispered. "Toward the Concorde."

"What?"

"Just move. Don't show any alarm. I'll hold your hand."

She focused on his face, and through the shadows she saw his look of feral alertness. Swallowing back the questions, she allowed him to take her hand. They turned and began to walk casually toward the Place de la Concorde. He gave her no explanation, but she knew just by the way he gripped her hand that something was wrong, that this was not a game. Like any other pair of lovers, they strolled through the garden, past flower beds deep in shadow, past statues lined up in ghostly formation. Gradually she became more and more aware of sounds: the distant roar of traffic, the wind in the trees, their shoes crunching across the gravel...

And the footsteps, following somewhere behind them.

Nervously she clutched his hand. His answering squeeze of reassurance was enough to dull the razor edge of fear. *I've known this man only a day,* she thought, *and already I feel that I can count on him.*

Richard picked up his pace—so gradually she almost didn't notice it. The footsteps still pursued them. They veered right and crossed the park toward Rue de Rivoli. The sounds of traffic grew louder, obscuring the footsteps of their pursuer. Now was the greatest danger—as they left the darkness behind them and their pursuer saw his last chance to make a move. Bright lights beckoned from the street ahead. *We can make it if we run,* she thought. *A dash through the trees and we'll be safe, surrounded by other people.* She prepared for the sprint, waiting for Richard's cue.

But he made no sudden moves. Neither did their pursuer. Hand in hand, she and Richard strolled nonchalantly into the naked glare of Rue de Rivoli.

Only as they joined the stream of evening pedestrians did Beryl's pulse begin to slow again. There was no danger here, she thought. Surely no one would dare attack them on a busy street.

Then she glanced at Richard's face and saw that the tension was still there.

They crossed the street and walked another block.

"Stop for a minute," he murmured. "Take a long look in that window."

They paused in front of a chocolate shop. Through the glass they saw a tempting display of confections: raspberry creams and velvety truffles and Turkish delight, all nestled in webs of spun sugar. In the shop, a young woman stood over a vat of melted chocolate, dipping fresh strawberries.

"What are we waiting for?" whispered Beryl.

"To see what happens."

She stared in the window and saw the reflections of people passing behind them. A couple holding hands. A trio of students in backpacks. A family with four children.

"Let's start walking again," he said.

They headed west on Rue de Rivoli, their pace again leisurely, unhurried. She was caught by surprise when he suddenly pulled her to the right, onto an intersecting street.

"Move it!" he barked.

All at once they were sprinting. They made another sharp right onto Mont Thabor, and ducked under an arch. There, huddled in the shadow of a doorway, he pulled her against him so tightly that she felt his heart pounding against hers, his breath warming her brow. They waited.

Seconds later, running footsteps echoed along the street. The sound moved closer, slowed, stopped. Then there was no sound at all. Almost too terrified to look, Beryl slowly shifted in Richard's arms, just enough to see a shadow slide past their archway. The footsteps moved down the street and faded away.

Richard chanced a quick look up the street, then gave Beryl's hand a tug. "All clear," he whispered. "Let's get out of here."

They turned onto Castiglione Street and didn't stop running until they were back at the hotel. Only when they were safely in her suite and he'd bolted the door behind them, did she find her voice again.

"What happened out there?" she demanded.

He shook his head. "I'm not sure."

"Do you think he meant to rob us?" She moved to the phone. "I should call the police—"

"He wasn't after our money."

"What?" She turned and frowned at him.

"Think about it. Even on Rue de Rivoli, with all those witnesses, he didn't stop following us. Any other thief would've given up and gone back to the park. Found himself another victim. But he didn't. He stayed with us."

"I didn't even see him! How do you know there *was* any—"

"A middle-aged man. Short, stocky. The sort of face most people would forget."

She stared at him, her agitation mounting. "What are you saying, Richard? That he was following us in particular?"

"Yes."

"But why would anyone follow you?"

"I could ask the same question of you."

"I'm of no interest to anyone."

"Think about it. About why you came to Paris."

"It's just a family matter."

"Apparently not. Since you now seem to have strange men following you around town."

"How do I know he wasn't following you? You're the one who works for the CIA!"

"Correction. I work for myself."

"Oh, don't palm off that rubbish on me! I practically grew up in MI6! I can smell you people a mile away!"

"Can you?" His eyebrow shot up. "And the odor didn't scare you off?"

"Maybe it should have."

He was pacing the room now, moving about like a restless animal, locking windows, pulling curtains. "Since I can't seem to deceive your highly perceptive nose, I'll just confess it. My job description is a bit looser than I've admitted to."

"I'm astonished."

"But I'm still convinced the man was following *you.*"

"Why would anyone follow me?"

"Because you're digging in a mine field. You don't understand, Beryl. When your parents were killed, there was more involved than just another sex scandal."

"Wait a minute." She crossed toward him, her gaze hard on his face. "What do you know about it?"

"I knew you were coming to Paris."

"Who told you?"

"Claude Daumier. He called me in London. Said that Hugh was worried. That someone had to keep an eye on you and Jordan."

"So you're our nanny?"

He laughed. "In a manner of speaking."

"And how much do you know about my mother and father?"

She knew by his brief silence that he was debating his answer, weighing the consequences of his next words. She fully expected to hear a lie.

Instead he surprised her with the truth. "I knew them both," he said. "I was here in Paris when it happened."

The revelation left her stunned. She didn't doubt for an instant that it was the truth—why would he fabricate such a story?

"It was my very first posting," he said. "I thought it was incredible luck to draw Paris. Most first-timers get sent to some bug-infested jungle in the middle of nowhere. But I drew Paris. And that's where I met Madeline and Bernard." Wearily he sank into a chair. "It's amazing," he murmured, studying Beryl's face, "How very much you look like her. The same green eyes, the same black hair. She used to sweep hers back in this sort of loose chignon. But strands of it were always coming loose, falling about her neck...." He smiled fondly at the memory. "Bernard was crazy about her. So was every man who ever met her."

"Were you?"

"I was only twenty-two. She was the most enchanting woman I'd ever met." His gaze met hers. Softly he added, "But then, I hadn't met her daughter."

They stared at each other, and Beryl felt those silken threads of desire tugging her toward him. Toward a man whose kisses left her dizzy, whose touch could melt even stone. A man who had not been straight with her from the very start.

*I'm so tired of secrets, so tired of trying to tease apart the truths from the half truths. And I'll never know which is which with this man.*

Abruptly she went to the door. "If we can't be honest with each other," she said, "there's no point in being together at all. So why don't we say good-night. And good-bye."

"I don't think so."

She turned and frowned at him. "Excuse me?"

"I'm not ready to say goodbye. Not when I know you're being followed."

"You're concerned about my welfare, is that it?"

"Shouldn't I be?"

She shot him a breezy smile. "I'm very good at taking care of myself."

"You're in a foreign city. Things could happen—"

"I'm not exactly alone." She crossed the room to the connecting door leading to Jordan's suite. Yanking it open, she called, "Wake up, Jordie! I'm in need of some brotherly assistance."

There was no answer from the bed.

"Jordie?" she said.

"Your bodyguard stays right on his toes, doesn't he?" said Richard.

Annoyed, Beryl flicked on the wall switch. In the sudden flood of light, she found herself blinking in astonishment.

Jordan's bed was empty.

# CHAPTER FOUR

*THAT WOMAN is staring at me again.*

Jordan stirred a teaspoon of sugar into his cappuccino and casually glanced in the direction of the blonde sitting three tables away. At once she averted her gaze. She was attractive enough, he noted. Mid-twenties, with a lean, athletic build. Nothing overripe about that one. Her hair was cut like a boy's, with elfin wisps feathering her forehead. She wore a black sweater, black skirt, black stockings. Fashion or camouflage? He shifted his gaze ahead to the street and the evening parade of pedestrians. Out of the corner of his eye, he spied the woman again looking his way. Ordinarily it would have flattered him to know he was the object of such intense feminine scrutiny. But something about this particular woman made him uneasy. Couldn't a fellow wander the streets of Paris these days without being stalked by carnivorous females?

It had been such a pleasant outing up till now. Minutes after sending Beryl and Richard on their way, he'd slipped out of his hotel room in search of a decent watering hole. A stroll across Place Vendôme, a visit to the Olympia Music Hall, then a midnight snack at Café de la Paix—what better way to spend one's first evening in Paris?

But perhaps it was time to call it a night.

He finished his cappuccino, paid the tab, and began walking toward the Rue de la Paix. It took him only half a block to realize the woman in black was following him.

He had paused at a shop window and was gazing in at a

display of men's suits when he spotted a fleeting glimpse of a blond head reflected in the glass. He turned and saw her standing across the street, intently staring into a window. A lingerie shop, he noted. Judging by the rest of her outfit, she'd no doubt choose her knickers in black, as well.

Jordan continued walking in the direction of Place Vendôme.

Across the street, the woman was parralleling his route.

*This is getting tiresome,* he thought. *If she wants to flirt, why doesn't she just come over and bat her eyelashes?* The direct approach, he could appreciate. It was honest and straightforward, and he liked honest women. But this stalking business unnerved him.

He walked another half block. So did she.

He stopped and pretended to study another shop window. She did likewise. *This is ridiculous,* he thought. *I am not going to put up with this nonsense.*

He crossed the street and walked straight up to her. *"Mademoiselle?"* he said.

She turned and regarded him with a startled look. Plainly she had not expected a face-to-face confrontation.

*"Mademoiselle,"* he said, "may I ask why you're following me?"

She opened her mouth and shut it again, all the time staring at him with those big gray eyes. Rather pretty eyes, he observed.

"Perhaps you don't understand me? *Parlez-vous anglais?*"

"Yes," she murmured, "I speak English."

"Then perhaps you can explain why you're following me."

"But I am not following you."

"Yes, you are."

"No, I am not!" She glanced up and down the street. "I am taking a walk. As you are."

"You're dogging my every step. Stopping where I stop. Watching every move I make."

"That is preposterous." She pulled herself up, a spark of outrage lighting her eyes. Real or manufactured? He couldn't be sure. "I have no interest in you, *Monsieur!* You must be imagining things."

"Am I?"

In answer, she spun around and stalked away up the Rue de la Paix.

"I don't think I am imagining things!" he called after her.

"You English are all alike!" she flung over her shoulder.

Jordan watched her storm off and wondered if he had jumped to conclusions. If so, what a fool he'd made of himself! The woman rounded a corner and vanished, and he felt a moment's regret. After all, she had been rather attractive. Lovely gray eyes, unbeatable legs.

Ah, well.

He turned and continued on his way toward the Place Vendôme and the hotel. Only as he reached the lobby doors of the Ritz did that sixth sense of his begin to tingle again. He paused and glanced back. In a distant archway, he spied a flicker of movement, a glimpse of a blond head just before it ducked into the shadows.

She was still following him.

DAUMIER ANSWERED the phone on the fifth ring. *"Allo?"*

"Claude, it's me," said Richard. "Are you having us tailed?"

There was a pause, then Daumier said, "A precaution, my friend. Nothing more."

"Protection? Or surveillance?"

"Protection, naturally! A favor to Hugh—"

"Well, it scared the living daylights out of us. The least you could've done was warn me." Richard glanced toward Beryl, who was anxiously pacing the hotel room. She hadn't admitted it, but he knew she was shaken, and that for all her bravado, all her attempts to throw him out of her suite, she was relieved he'd stayed. "Another thing," he said to Daumier, "we seem to have misplaced Jordan."

"Misplaced?"

"He's not in his suite. We left him here hours ago. He's since vanished."

There was a silence on the line. "This is worrisome," said Daumier.

"Do your people have any idea where he is?"

"My agent has not yet reported in. I expect to hear from her in another—"

*"Her?"* Richard cut in.

"Not our most experienced operative, I admit. But quite capable."

"It was a man following us tonight."

Daumier laughed. "Richard, I am disappointed! I thought you, of all people, knew the difference."

"I can bloody well tell the difference!"

"With Colette, there is no question. Twenty-six, rather pretty. Blond hair."

"It was a man, Claude."

"You saw the face?"

"Not clearly. But he was short, stocky—"

"Colette is five foot five, very slender."

"It wasn't her."

Daumier said nothing for a moment. "This is disturbing," he concluded. "If it was not one of our people—"

Richard suddenly pivoted toward the door. Someone was knocking. Beryl stood frozen, staring at him with a look of fear.

"I'll call you back, Claude," Richard whispered into the phone. Quietly he hung up.

There was another knock, louder this time.

"Go ahead," he murmured, "ask who it is."

Shakily she called out, "Who is it?"

"Are you decent?" came the reply. "Or should I try again in the morning?"

"Jordan!" cried a relieved Beryl. She ran to open the door. "Where have you been?"

Her brother sauntered in, his blond hair tousled from the night wind. He saw Richard and halted. "Sorry. If I've interrupted anything—"

"Not a thing," snapped Beryl. She locked the door and turned to face her brother. "We've been worried sick about you."

"I just went for a walk."

"You could have left me a note!"

"Why? I was right in the neighborhood." Jordan flopped lazily into a chair. "Having quite a nice evening, too, until some woman started following me around."

Richard's chin snapped up in surprise. "Woman?"

"Rather nice-looking. But not my type, really. A bit vampirish for my taste."

"Was she blond?" asked Richard. "About five foot five? Mid-twenties?"

Jordan shook his head in amazement. "Next you'll tell me her name."

"Colette."

"Is this a new parlor trick, Richard?" Jordan said with a laugh. "ESP?"

"She's an agent working for French Intelligence," said Richard. "Protective surveillance, that's all."

Beryl gave a sigh of relief. "So that's why we were followed. And you had me scared out of my wits."

"You *should* be scared," said Richard. "The man following us wasn't working for Daumier."

"You just said—"

"Daumier had only one agent assigned to surveillance tonight. That woman, Colette. Apparently she stayed with Jordan."

"Then who was following us?" demanded Beryl.

"I don't know."

There was a silence. Then Jordan asked peevishly, "Have I missed something? Why are we all being followed? And when did Richard join the fun?"

"Richard," said Beryl tightly, "hasn't been completely honest with us."

"About what?"

"He neglected to mention that he was here in Paris in 1973. He knew Mum and Dad."

Jordan's gaze at once shot to Richard's face. "Is that why you're here now?" he asked quietly. "To prevent us from learning the truth?"

"No," said Richard. "I'm here to see that the truth doesn't get you both killed."

"Could the truth really be that dangerous?"

"It's got someone worried enough to have you both followed."

"Then you don't believe it *was* a simple murder and suicide," said Jordan.

"If it was that simple—if it was just a case of Bernard shooting Madeline and then taking his own life—no one would care about it after all these years. But someone obviously does care. And he—or she—is keeping a close watch on your movements."

Beryl, strangely silent, sat down on the bed. Her hair, which she'd gathered back with pins, was starting to loosen, and silky tendrils had drifted down her neck. All at once Richard was struck by her uncanny resemblance to Madeline. It was the hairstyle and the watered-silk dress. He recognized that dress now—it was her mother's. He shook himself to dispel the notion that he was looking at a ghost.

He decided it was time to tell the truth, and nothing but. "I never did believe it," he said. "Not for a second did I think Bernard pulled that trigger."

Slowly Beryl looked up at him. What he saw in her gaze—the wariness, the mistrust—made him want to reach

out to her, to make her believe in him. But trust wasn't
something she was about to give him, not now. Perhaps not
ever.

"If he didn't pull the trigger," she asked, "then who
did?"

Richard moved to the bed. Gently he touched her face.
"I don't know," he said. "But I'm going to help you find
out."

AFTER RICHARD LEFT, Beryl turned to her brother. "I don't
trust him," she said. "He's told us too many lies."

"He didn't lie to us exactly," Jordan observed. "He just
left out a few facts."

"Oh, right. He conveniently neglects to mention that he
knew Mum and Dad. That he was here in Paris when they
died. Jordie, for all we know, *he* could've pulled the trigger!"

"He seems quite chummy with Daumier."

"So?"

"Uncle Hugh trusts Daumier."

"Meaning we should trust Richard Wolf?" She shook her
head and laughed. "Oh, Jordie, you must be more exhausted
than you realize."

"And you must be more smitten than you realize," he
said. Yawning, he crossed the floor toward his own suite.

"What's that supposed to mean?" she demanded.

"Only that your feelings for the man obviously run hot
and heavy. Because you're fighting them every inch of the
way."

She pursued him to the connecting door. "Hot?" she said
incredulously. "Heavy?"

"There, you see?" He breathed a few loud pants and
grinned. "Sweet dreams, baby sister. I'm glad to see you're
back in circulation."

Then he closed the door on her astonished face.

WHEN RICHARD ARRIVED at Daumier's flat, he found the Frenchman still awake but already dressed in his bathrobe and slippers. The latest reports on the bombing of the St. Pierre residence were laid out across his kitchen table, along with a plate of sausage and a glass of milk. Forty years with French Intelligence hadn't altered his preference for working in close proximity to a refrigerator.

Waving at the reports, Daumier said, "It is all a puzzle to me. A Semtex explosive planted under the bed. A timing mechanism set for 9:10—precisely when the St. Pierres would be watching Marie's favorite television program. It has all the signs of an inside operation, except for one glaring mistake—Philippe was in England." He looked at Richard. "Does it not strike you as an inconceivable blunder?"

"Terrorists are usually brighter than that," admitted Richard. "Maybe they intended it only as a warning. A statement of purpose. 'We can reach you if we want to,' that sort of thing."

"I still have no information on this Cosmic Solidarity League." Wearily Daumier ran his hands through his hair. "The investigation, it goes nowhere."

"Then maybe you can turn your attention for a moment to my little problem."

"Problem? Ah, yes. The Tavistocks." Daumier sat back and smiled at him. "Hugh's niece is more than you can handle, Richard?"

"Someone else was definitely tailing us tonight," said Richard. "Not just your agent, Colette. Can you find out who it was?"

"Give me something to work with," said Daumier. "A middle-aged man, short and stocky—that tells me nothing. He could have been hired by anyone."

"It was someone who knew they were coming to Paris."

"I know Hugh told the Vanes. They, in turn, could have mentioned it to others. Who else was at Chetwynd?"

Richard thought back to the night of the reception and

the night of Reggie's indiscretion. Blast Reggie Vane and his weakness for booze. That was what had set this off. A few too many glasses of champagne, a wagging tongue. Still, he couldn't bring himself to dislike the man. Poor Reggie was a harmless soul; certainly he'd never meant to hurt Beryl. Rather, it was clear he adored her like a daughter.

Richard said, "There were numbers of people the Vanes might have spoken to. Philippe St. Pierre. Nina and Anthony. Perhaps others."

"So we are talking about any number of people," Daumier said, sighing.

"Not a very short list," Richard had to admit.

"Is this such a wise idea, Richard?" The question was posed quietly. "Once before, if you recall, we were prevented from learning the truth."

How could he not remember? He'd been stunned to read that directive from Washington: "Abort investigation." Claude had received similar orders from his superior at French Intelligence. And so the search for Delphi and the NATO security breach had come to an abrupt halt. There'd been no explanation, no reasons given, but Richard had formed his own suspicions. It was clear that Washington had been clued in to the truth and feared the repercussions of its airing.

A month later, when U.S. Ambassador Stephen Sutherland leaped off a Paris bridge, Richard thought his suspicions confirmed. Sutherland had been a political appointee; his unveiling as an enemy spy would have embarrassed the president himself.

The matter of the mole was never officially resolved.

Instead, Bernard Tavistock had been posthumously implicated as Delphi. Conveniently tried and found guilty, thought Richard. Why not pin the blame on Tavistock? A dead man can't deny the charges.

*And now, twenty years later, the ghost of Delphi is back to haunt me.*

With new determination, Richard rose from the chair. "This time, Claude," he said, "I'm tracking him down. And no order from Washington is going to stop me."

"Twenty years is a long time. Evidence has vanished. Politics have changed."

"One thing hasn't changed—the guilty party. What if we were wrong? What if Sutherland wasn't the mole? Then Delphi may still be alive. And operational."

To which Daumier added, "And very, very worried."

BERYL WAS AWAKENED the next morning by Richard knocking on her door. She blinked in astonishment as he handed her a paper sack, fragrant with the aroma of freshly baked croissants.

"Breakfast," he announced. "You can eat it in the car. Jordan's already waiting for us downstairs."

"Waiting? For what?"

"For you to get dressed. You'd better hurry. Our appointment's for eight o'clock."

Bewildered, she shoved back a handful of tangled hair. "I don't recall making any appointments for this morning."

"I made it for us. We're lucky to get one, considering the man doesn't see many people these days. His wife won't allow it."

"Whose wife?" she said in exasperation.

"Chief Inspector Broussard. The detective in charge of your parents' murder investigation." Richard paused. "You do want to speak to him, don't you?"

*He knows I do,* she thought, clutching together the edges of her silk robe. *He's got me at a disadvantage. I'm scarcely awake and he's standing there like Mr. Sunshine himself.* And since when had Jordan turned into an early riser? Her brother almost never rolled out of bed before eight.

"You don't have to come," he said, turning to leave. "Jordan and I can—"

"Give me ten minutes!" she snapped and closed the door on him.

She made it downstairs in nine minutes flat.

Richard drove with the self-assurance of a man long familiar with the streets of Paris. They crossed the Seine and headed south along crowded boulevards. The traffic was as insane as London's, thought Beryl, gazing out at the crush of buses and taxis. *Thank heavens he's behind the wheel.*

She finished her croissant and brushed the crumbs off the file folder lying in her lap. Contained in that folder was the twenty-year-old police report, signed by Inspector Broussard. She wondered how much the man would remember about the case. After all this time, surely the details had blended together with all the other homicide investigations of his career. But there was always the chance that some small unreported detail had stayed with him.

"Have you met Broussard?" she asked Richard.

"We met during the course of the investigation. When I was interviewed by the police."

"They questioned you? Why?"

"He spoke to all your parents' acquaintances."

"I never saw your name in the police file."

"A number of names didn't make it to that file."

"Such as?"

"Philippe St. Pierre. Ambassador Sutherland."

"Nina's husband?"

Richard nodded. "Those were politically sensitive names. St. Pierre was in the Finance Ministry, and he was a close friend of the prime minister's. Sutherland was the American ambassador. Neither were suspects, so their names were kept out of the official report."

"Meaning the good inspector protected the high and mighty?"

"Meaning he was discreet."

"Why did your name escape the report?"

"I was just a bit player asked to comment on your parents' marriage. Whether they ever argued, seemed unhappy, that's all. I was only on the periphery.''

She touched the file on her lap. "So tell me," she said, "why are you getting involved now?"

"Because you and Jordan are. Because Claude Daumier asked me to look after you." He glanced at her and added quietly, "And because I owe it to your father. He was…a good man." She thought he would say more, but then he turned and gazed straight ahead at the road.

"Wolf," asked Jordan, who was sitting in the back seat, "are you aware that we're being followed?"

"What?" Beryl turned and scanned the traffic behind them. "Which car?"

"The blue Peugeot. Two cars back."

"I see it," said Richard. "It's been tailing us all the way from the hotel."

"You knew the car was there all the time?" said Beryl. "And you didn't think of mentioning it?"

"I expected it. Take a good look at the driver, Jordan. Blond hair, sunglasses. Definitely a woman."

Jordan laughed. "Why, it's my little vampiress in black. Colette."

Richard nodded. "One of the friendlies."

"How can you be sure?" asked Beryl.

"Because she's Daumier's agent. Which makes her protection, not a threat." Richard turned off Boulevard Raspail. A moment later, he spotted a parking space and pulled up at the curb. "In fact, she can keep an eye on the car while we're inside."

Beryl glanced at the large brick building across the street. Over the entrance archway were displayed the words *Maison de Convalescence.* "What is this place?"

"A nursing home."

"This is where Inspector Broussard lives?"

"He's been here for years," said Richard, as he gazed up at the building with a look of pity. "Ever since his stroke."

JUDGING BY THE PHOTOGRAPH tacked to the wall of his room, ex-Chief Inspector Broussard had once been an impressive man. The picture showed a beefy Frenchman with a handlebar mustache and a lion's mane of hair, posing regally on the steps of a Paris police station.

It bore little resemblance to the shrunken creature now propped up, his body half-paralyzed, in bed.

Mme Broussard bustled about the room, all the time speaking with the precise grammar of a former teacher of English. She fluffed her husband's pillow, combed his hair, wiped the drool from his chin. "He remembers everything," she insisted. "Every case, every name. But he cannot speak, cannot hold a pen. And that is what frustrates him! It is why I do not let him have visitors. He wishes so much to talk, but he cannot form the words. Only a few, here and there. And how it upsets him! Sometimes, after a visit with friends, he will moan for days." She moved to the head of the bed and stood there like a guardian angel. "You ask him only a few questions, do you understand? And if he becomes upset, you must leave immediately."

"We understand," said Richard. He pulled up a chair next to the bedside. As Beryl and Jordan watched, he opened the police file and slowly laid the crime-scene photos on the coverlet for Broussard to see. "I know you can't speak," he said, "but I want you to look at these. Nod if you remember the case."

Mme Broussard translated for her husband. He stared down at the first photo—the gruesome death poses of Madeline and Bernard. They lay like lovers, entwined in a pool of blood. Clumsily Broussard touched the photo, his fingers lingering on Madeline's face. His lips formed a whispered word.

"What did he say?" asked Richard.

"*La belle.* Beautiful woman," said Mme Broussard. "You see? He does remember."

The old man was gazing at the other photos now, his left hand beginning to quiver in agitation. His lips moved helplessly; the effort to speak came out in grunts. Mme Broussard leaned forward, trying to make out what he was saying. She shook her head in bewilderment.

"We've read his report," said Beryl. "The one he filed twenty years ago. He concluded that it was a murder and suicide. Did he truly believe that?"

Again, Mme Broussard translated.

Broussard looked up at Beryl, his gaze focusing for the first time on her black hair. A look of wonder came over his face, almost a look of recognition.

His wife repeated the question. Did he believe it was a murder and suicide?

Slowly Broussard shook his head.

Jordan asked, "Does he understand the question?"

"Of course he does!" snapped Mme Broussard. "I told you, he understands everything."

The man was tapping at one of the photos now, as though trying to point something out. His wife asked a question in French. He only slapped harder at the photo.

"Is he trying to point at something?" asked Beryl.

"Just a corner of the picture," said Richard. "A view of empty floor."

Broussard's whole body seemed to be quivering with the effort to speak. His wife leaned forward again, straining to make out his words. She shook her head. "It makes no sense."

"What did he say?" asked Beryl.

"*Serviette.* It is a napkin or a towel. I do not understand." She snatched up a hand towel from the sink and held it up to her husband. "*Serviette de toilette?*"

He shook his head and angrily batted away the towel.

"I do not know what he means," Mme Broussard said with a sigh.

"Maybe I do," said Richard. He bent close to Broussard. *"Porte documents?"* he asked.

Broussard gave a sigh of relief and collapsed against his pillows. Wearily he nodded.

"That's what he was trying to say," said Richard. *"Serviette porte documents.* A briefcase."

"Briefcase?" echoed Beryl. "Do you think he means the one with the classified file?"

Richard frowned at Broussard. The man was exhausted, his face a sickly gray against the white linen.

Mme Broussard took one look at her husband and moved in to shield him from Richard. "No further questions, Mr. Wolf! Look at him! He is drained—he cannot tell you more. Please, you must leave."

She hurried them out of the room and into the hallway. A nun glided past, carrying a tray of medicines. At the end of the hall, a woman in a wheelchair was singing lullabies to herself in French.

"Mme Broussard," said Beryl, "we have more questions, but your husband can't answer them. There was another detective's name on that report—an Etienne Giguere. How can we get in touch with him?"

"Etienne?" Mme Broussard looked at her in surprise. "You mean you do not know?"

"Know what?"

"He was killed nineteen years ago. Hit by a car while crossing the street." Sadly she shook her head. "They did not find the driver."

Beryl caught Jordan's startled look; she saw in his eyes the same dismay she felt.

"One last question," said Jordan. "When did your husband have his stroke?"

"1974."

"Also nineteen years ago?"

Mme Broussard nodded. "Such a tragedy for the department! First, my husband's stroke. Then three months later, they lose Etienne." Sighing, she turned back to her husband's room. "But that is life, I suppose. And there is nothing we can do to change it...."

Back outside again, the three of them stood for a moment in the sunshine, trying to shake off the gloom of that depressing building.

"A hit and run?" said Jordan. "The driver never caught? I have a bad feeling about this."

Beryl glanced up at the archway. *"Maison de Convalescence,"* she murmured sarcastically. "Hardly a place to recover. More like a place to die." Shivering, she turned to the car. "Please, let's just get out of here."

They drove north, to the Seine. Once again, the blue Peugeot followed them, but none of them paid it much attention; the French agent had become a fact of life—almost a reassuring one.

Suddenly Jordan said, "Hold on, Wolf. Let me off on Boulevard Saint-Germain. In fact, right about here would be fine."

Richard pulled over to the curb. "Why here?"

"We just passed a café—"

"Oh, Jordan," groaned Beryl, "you're not hungry already, are you?"

"I'll meet you back at the hotel," said Jordan, climbing out of the car. "Unless you two care to join me?"

"So we can watch you eat? Thank you, but I'll pass."

Jordan gave his sister an affectionate squeeze of the shoulder and closed the car door. "I'll catch a taxi back. See you later." With a wave, he turned and strolled down the boulevard, his blond hair gleaming in the sunshine.

"Back to the hotel?" asked Richard softly.

She looked at him and thought, *It's always there shimmering between us—the attraction. The temptation. I look in his eyes, and suddenly I remember how safe it feels to be in his arms. How easy it would be to believe in him. And that's where the danger lies.*

"No," she said, looking straight ahead. "Not yet."

"Then where to?"

"Take me to Pigalle. Rue Myrha."

He paused. "Are you certain you want to go there?"

She nodded and stared down at the file in her lap. "I want to see the place where they died."

CAFÉ HUGO. YES, THIS WAS the place, thought Jordan, gazing around at the crowded outdoor tables, the checkered tablecloths, the army of waiters ferrying espresso and cappuccino. Twenty years ago, Bernard had visited this very café. Had sat drinking coffee. And then he had paid the bill and left, to meet his death in a building in Pigalle. All this Jordan had learned from the police interview with the waiter. But it happened a long time ago, thought Jordan. The man had probably moved on to other jobs. Still, it was worth a shot.

To his surprise, he discovered that Mario Cassini was still employed as a waiter. Well into his forties now, his hair a salt-and-pepper gray, his face creased with the lines of twenty years of smiles, Mario nodded and said, "Yes, yes. Of course I remember. The police, they come to talk to me three, four times. And each time I tell them the same thing. M. Tavistock, he comes for café au lait, every morning. Sometimes, *madame* is with him. Ah, beautiful!"

"But she wasn't with him on that particular day?"

Mario shook his head. "He comes alone. Sits at that table there." He pointed to an empty table near the sidewalk, red-checked cloth fluttering in the breeze. "He waits a long time for *madame*."

"And she didn't come?"

"No. Then she calls. Tells him to meet her at another place. In Pigalle. I take the message and give it to M. Tavistock."

"She spoke to you? On the telephone?"

"*Oui.* I write down address, give to him."

"That would be the address in Pigalle?"

Mario nodded.

"My father—M. Tavistock—did he seem at all upset that day? Angry?"

"Not angry. He seems—how do you say?—worried. He does not understand why *madame* goes to Pigalle. He pays for his coffee, then he leaves. Later I read in the newspaper that he is dead. Ah, *horrible!* The police, they are asking for information. So I call, tell them what I know." Mario shook his head at the tragedy of it all. At the loss of such a lovely woman as Mme Tavistock and such a generous man as her husband.

No new information here, thought Jordan. He turned to leave, then stopped and turned back.

"Are you certain it was Mme Tavistock who called to leave the message?" he asked.

"She says it is her," said Mario.

"And you recognized her voice?"

Mario paused. It lasted just the blink of an eye, but it was enough to tell Jordan that the man was not absolutely certain. "Yes," said Mario. "Who else would it be?"

Deep in thought, Jordan left the café and walked a few paces along Boulevard Saint-Germain, intending to return on foot to the hotel. But half a block away, he spotted the blue Peugeot. His little blond vampiress, he thought, still following him about. They were headed in the same direction; why not ask her for a ride?

He went to the Peugeot and pulled open the passenger door. "Mind dropping me off at the Ritz?" he asked brightly.

An outraged Colette stared at him from the driver's seat. "What do you think you are doing?" she demanded. "Get out of my car!"

"Oh, come, now. No need for hysterics—"

"Go away!" she cried, loudly enough to make a passerby stop and stare.

Calmly Jordan slid into the front seat. He noted that she was dressed in black again. What was it with these secret agent types? "It's a long walk to the Ritz. Surely it's not *verboten*, is it? To give me a lift back to my hotel?"

"I do not even know who you are," she insisted.

"I know who *you* are. Your name's Colette, you work for Claude Daumier, and you're supposed to be keeping an eye on me." Jordan smiled at her, the sort of smile that usually got him exactly what he wanted. He said, quite reasonably, "Rather than sneaking around after me all the way up the boulevard, why not be sensible about it? Save us both the inconvenience of this silly cat-and-mouse game."

A spark of laughter flickered in her eyes. She gripped the steering wheel and stared straight ahead, but he could see the smile tugging at her lips. "Shut the door," she snapped. "And use the seat belt. It is regulation."

As they drove up Boulevard Saint-Germain, he kept glancing at her, wondering if she was really as fierce as she appeared. That black leather skirt and the scowl on her face couldn't disguise the fact she was actually quite pretty.

"How long have you worked for Daumier?" he asked.

"Three years."

"And is this your usual sort of assignment? Following strange men about town?"

"I follow instructions. Whatever they are."

"Ah. The obedient type." Jordan sat back, grinning. "What did Daumier tell you about this particular assignment?"

"I am to see you and your sister are not harmed. Since today she is with M. Wolf, I decide to follow you." She paused and added under her breath, "Not as simple as I thought."

"I'm not all that difficult."

"But you do the unexpected. You catch me by surprise."

A car was honking at them. Annoyed, Colette glanced up at the rearview mirror. "This traffic, it gets worse every—"

At her sudden silence, Jordan glanced at her. "Is something wrong?"

"No," she said after a pause, "I am just imagining things."

Jordan turned and peered through the rear window. All he saw was a line of cars snaking down the boulevard. He looked back at Colette. "Tell me, what's a nice girl like you doing in French Intelligence?"

She smiled—the first real smile he'd seen. It was like watching the sun come out. "I am earning a living."

"Meeting interesting people?"

"Quite."

"Finding romance?"

"Regrettably, no."

"What a shame. Perhaps you should find a new line of work."

"Such as?"

"We could discuss it over supper."

She shook her head. "It is not allowed to fraternize with a subject."

"So that's all I am," he said with a sigh. "A subject."

She dropped him off on a side street, around the corner from the Ritz. He climbed out, then turned and said, "Why not come in for a drink?"

"I am on duty."

"It must get boring, sitting in that car all day. Waiting for me to make another unexpected move."

"Thank you, but no." She smiled—a charmingly impish grin. It carried just a hint of possibility.

Jordan left the car and walked into the hotel.

Upstairs, he paced for a while, pondering what he'd just learned at Café Hugo. That phone call from Madeline—it just didn't fit in. Why on earth would she arrange to meet Bernard in Pigalle? It clearly didn't go along with the theory of a murder-suicide. Could the waiter be lying? Or was he simply mistaken? With all the ambient noise of a busy café, how could he be certain it was really Madeline Tavistock making that phone call?

*I have to go back to the café. Ask Mario, specifically, if the voice was an Englishwoman's.*

Once again he left the hotel and stepped into the brightness of midday. A taxi sat idling near the front entrance, but the driver was nowhere to be seen. Perhaps Colette was still parked around the corner; he'd ask her to drive him back to Boulevard Saint-Germain. He turned up the side street and spotted the blue Peugeot still parked there. Colette was sitting inside; through the tinted windshield, he saw her silhouette behind the steering wheel.

He went to the car and tapped on the passenger window. "Colette?" he called. "Could you give me another lift?"

She didn't answer.

Jordan swung open the door and slid in beside her. "Colette?"

She sat perfectly still, her eyes staring rigidly ahead. For a moment, he didn't understand. Then he saw the bright trickle of blood that had traced its way down her hairline and vanished into the black fabric of her turtlenecked shirt. In panic, he reached out to her and gave her shoulder a shake. *"Colette?"*

She slid toward him and toppled into his lap.

He stared at her head, now resting in his arms. In her temple was a single, neat bullet hole.

He scarcely remembered scrambling out of the car. What he did remember were the screams of a woman passerby. Then, moments later, he focused on the shocked faces of people who'd been drawn onto this quiet side street by the screams. They were all pointing at the woman's arm hanging limply out of the car. And they were staring at him.

Numbly, Jordan looked down at his own hands.

They were smeared with blood.

## CHAPTER FIVE

FROM THE CROWD of onlookers standing on the corner, Amiel Foch watched the police handcuff the Englishman and lead him away. An unintended development, he thought. Not at all what he'd expected to happen.

Then again, he hadn't expected to see Colette LaFarge ever again. Or, even worse, to be seen by her. They'd worked together only once, and that was three years ago in Cyprus. He'd hoped, when he walked past her car, with his head down and his shoulders hunched, that she would not notice him. But as he'd headed away, he'd heard her call out his name in astonishment.

He'd had no alternative, he thought as he watched the attendants load her body into the ambulance. French Intelligence thought he was dead. Colette could have told them otherwise.

It hadn't been an easy thing to do. But as he'd turned to face her, his decision was already made. He had walked slowly back to her car. Through the windshield, he'd seen her look of wonder at a dead colleague come back to life. She'd sat frozen, staring at the apparition. She had not moved as he approached the driver's side. Nor did she move as he thrust his silenced automatic into her car window and fired.

*Such a waste of a pretty girl,* he thought as the ambulance drove away. But she should have known better.

The crowd was dispersing. It was time to leave.

He edged toward the curb. Quietly he dropped his pistol

in the gutter and kicked it down the storm drain. The weapon was stolen, untraceable; better to have it found near the scene of the crime. It would cement the case against Jordan Tavistock.

Several blocks away, he found a telephone. He dialed his client.

"Jordan Tavistock has been arrested for murder," said Foch.

"Whose murder?" came the sharp reply.

"One of Daumier's agents. A woman."

"Did Tavistock do it?"

"No. I did."

There was a sudden burst of laughter from his client. "This is priceless! Absolutely priceless! I ask you to follow Jordan, and you have him framed for murder. I can't wait to see what you do with his sister."

"What do you wish me to do?" asked Foch.

There was a pause. "I think it's time to resolve this mess," he said. "Finish it."

"The woman is no problem. But her brother will be difficult to reach, unless I can find a way into the prison."

"You could always get yourself arrested."

"And when they identify my fingerprints?" Foch shook his head. "I need someone else for that job."

"Then I'll find you someone," came the reply. "For now, let's work on one thing at a time. Beryl Tavistock."

A TURKISH MAN NOW OWNED the building on Rue Myrha. He'd tried to improve it. He'd painted the exterior walls, shored up the crumbling balconies, replaced the missing roof slates, but the building, and the street on which it stood, seemed beyond rehabilitation. It was the fault of the tenants, explained Mr. Zamir, as he led them up two flights of stairs to the attic flat. What could one do with tenants who let their children run wild? By all appearances, Mr. Zamir was a successful businessman, a man whose tailored suit and excellent English bespoke prosperous roots. There were four families in the building, he said, all of them reliable enough with the rent. But no one lived in the attic flat—he'd always had difficulty renting that one out. People had come to inspect the place, of course, but when they heard of the murder, they quickly backed out. These silly superstitions! Oh, people claim they do not believe in ghosts, but when they visit a room where two people have died...

"How long has the flat been empty?" asked Beryl.

"A year now. Ever since I have owned the building. And before that—" he shrugged "—I do not know. It may have been empty for many years." He unlocked the door. "You may look around if you wish."

A puff of stale air greeted them as they pushed open the door—the smell of a room too long shut away from the world. It was not an unpleasant room. Sunshine washed in through a large, dirt-streaked window. The view looked down over Rue Myrha, and Beryl could see children kicking a soccer ball in the street. The flat was completely empty of furniture; there were only bare walls and floor. Through an open door, she glimpsed the bathroom with its chipped sink and tarnished fixtures.

In silence Beryl circled the flat, her gaze moving across the wood floor. Beside the window, she came to a halt. The stain was barely visible, just a faint brown blot in the oak planks. *Whose blood?* she wondered. *Mum's? Dad's? Or is it both of theirs, eternally mingled?*

"I have tried to sand the stain away," said Mr. Zamir. "But it goes very deep into the wood. Even when I think I have erased it, in a few weeks the stain seems to reappear." He sighed. "It frightens them away, you know. The tenants, they do not like to see such reminders on their floor."

Beryl swallowed hard and turned to look out the window. *Why on this street?* she wondered. *In this room? Of all the places in Paris, why did they die here?*

She asked quietly, "Who owned this building, Mr. Zamir? Before you did?"

"There were many owners. Before me, it was a M. Rosenthal. And before him, a M. Dudoit."

"At the time of the murder," said Richard, "the landlord was a man named Jacques Rideau. Did you know him?"

"I am sorry, I do not. That would have been many years ago."

"Twenty."

"Then I would not have met him." Mr. Zamir turned to the door. "I will leave you alone. If you have questions, I will be down in number three for a while."

Beryl heard the man's footsteps creak down the stairs. She looked at Richard and saw that he was standing off in a corner, frowning at the floor. "What are you thinking?" she asked.

"About Inspector Broussard. How he kept trying to point at that photo. The spot he was pointing to would be somewhere around here. Just to the left of the door."

"There's nothing to look at. And there was nothing in the photo, either."

"That's what bothers me. He seemed so troubled by it. And there was something about a briefcase...."

"The NATO file," she said softly.

He looked at her. "How much have you been told about Delphi?"

"I know it wasn't Mum or Dad. They would never have gone to the other side."

"People go over for different reasons."

"But not them. They certainly didn't need the money."

"Communist sympathies?"

"Not the Tavistocks!"

He moved toward her. With every step he took, her pulse seemed to leap faster. He came close enough to make her feel threatened. And tempted. Quietly he said, "There's always blackmail."

"Meaning they had secrets to hide?"

"Everyone does."

"Not everyone turns traitor."

"It depends on the secret, doesn't it? And how much one stands to lose because of it."

In silence they gazed at each other, and she found herself wondering how much he really did know about her parents. How much he wasn't admitting to. She sensed he knew a lot more than he was letting on, and that suspicion loomed like a barrier between them. Those secrets again. Those unspoken truths. She had grown up in a household where certain conversational doors were always kept locked. *I refuse to live my life that way. Ever again.*

She turned away. "They had no reason to be vulnerable to blackmail."

"You were just a child, eight years old. Away at boarding school in England. What did you really know about them? About their marriage, their secrets? What if it was your mother who rented this flat? Met her lover here?"

"I don't believe it. I won't."

"Is it so difficult to accept? That she was human, that she might have had a lover?" He took her by the shoulders, willing her to meet his gaze. "She was a beautiful woman, Beryl. If she'd wanted to, she could have had any number of lovers."

"You're making her out to be a tramp!"

"I'm considering all the possibilities."

"That she sold out Queen and country? To keep some vile little secret from surfacing?" Angrily she wrenched away from him. "Sorry, Richard, but my faith runs a little deeper than that. And if you'd known them, really known them, you'd never consider such a thing." She pivoted away and walked to the door.

"I did know them," he said. "I knew them rather well."

She stopped, turned to face him. "What do you mean by 'rather well'?"

"We...moved in the same circles. Not the same team, exactly. But we worked at similar purposes."

"You never told me."

"I didn't know how much I *should* tell you. How much you should know." He began to slowly circle the room, carefully considering each word before he spoke. "It was my first assignment. I'd just completed my training at Langley—"

"CIA?"

He nodded. "I was recruited straight out of the university. Not exactly my first career choice. But somehow they'd gotten hold of my master's thesis, an analysis of Libyan arms capabilities. It turned out to be amazingly close to the mark. They knew I was fluent in a few languages. And that I had taken out quite a large sum in student loans. That was the carrot, you see—the loan payoff. The foreign travel. And, I have to admit, the idea intrigued me, the chance to work as an Intelligence analyst..."

"Is that how you met my parents?"

He nodded. "NATO knew it had a security leak, originating in Paris. Somehow weapons data were slipping through to the East Germans. I'd just arrived in Paris, so there was no question that I was clean. They assigned me to work with Claude Daumier at French Intelligence. I was asked to compose a dummy weapons report, something close to, but not quite, the truth. It was encoded and transmitted to a few select embassy officials in Paris. The idea was to pinpoint the possible source of the leak."

"How were my parents involved?"

"They were attached to the British embassy. Bernard in Communications, Madeline in Protocol. Both were really working for MI6. Bernard was one of a few who had access to classified files."

"So he was a suspect?"

Richard nodded. "Everyone was. British, American, French. Right up to ambassadorial level." Again he began to pace, carefully measuring his words. "So the dummy file went out to the embassies. And we waited to see if it would turn up, like the others, in East German hands. It didn't. It ended up here, in a briefcase. In this very room." He stopped and looked at her. "With your parents."

"And that closed the file on Delphi," she said. Bitterly she added, "How neat and easy. You had your culprit. Lucky for you he was dead and unable to defend himself."

"I didn't believe it."

"Yet you dropped the matter."

"We had no choice."

"You didn't care enough to learn the truth!"

"No, Beryl. We didn't have the choice. We were instructed to call off the investigation."

She stared at him in astonishment. "By whom?"

"My orders came straight from Washington. Claude's from the French prime minister. The matter was dropped."

"And my parents went on record as traitors," she said. "What a convenient way to close the file." In disgust she turned and left the room.

He followed her down the stairs. "Beryl! I never really believed Bernard was the one!"

"Yet you let him take the blame!"

"I told you, I was ordered to—"

"And of course you always follow orders."

"I was sent back to Washington soon afterward. I couldn't pursue it."

They walked out of the building into the bedlam of Rue Myrha. A soccer ball flew past, pursued by a gaggle of tattered-looking children. Beryl paused on the sidewalk, her eyes temporarily dazzled by the sunshine. The street sounds, the shouts of the children, were disorienting. She turned and looked up at the building, at the attic window. The view suddenly blurred through her tears.

"What a place to die," she whispered. "God, what a horrible place to die...."

She climbed into Richard's car and pulled the door closed. It was a blessed relief to shut out the noise and chaos of Rue Myrha.

Richard slid in behind the driver's seat. For a moment, they sat in silence, staring ahead at the ragamuffins playing street soccer.

"I'll take you back to the hotel," he said.

"I want to see Claude Daumier."

"Why?"

"I want to hear his version of what happened. I want to confirm that you're telling me the truth."

"I am, Beryl."

She turned to him. His gaze was steady, unflinching. *An honest look if ever I've seen one,* she thought. *Which only proves how gullible I am.* She wanted to believe him, and there was the danger. It was that blasted attraction between them—the feverish tug of hormones, the memory of his kisses—that clouded her judgment. *What is it about this man? I take one look at his face, inhale a whiff of his scent, and I'm aching to tear off his clothes. And mine, as well.*

She looked straight ahead, trying to ignore all those heated signals passing between them. "I want to talk to Daumier."

After a pause, he said, "All right. If that's what it'll take for you to believe me."

A phone call revealed that Daumier was not in his office; he'd just left to conduct another interview with Marie St. Pierre. So they drove to Cochin Hospital, where Marie was still a patient.

Even from the far end of the hospital corridor, they could tell which room was Marie's; half a dozen policemen were stationed outside her door. Daumier had not yet arrived. Madame St. Pierre, informed that Lord Lovat's niece had arrived, at once had Beryl and Richard escorted into her room.

They discovered they weren't the only visitors Marie was

entertaining that afternoon. Seated in chairs near the patient's bed were Nina Sutherland and Helena Vane. A little tea party was in progress, complete with trays of biscuits and finger sandwiches set on a rolling cart by the window. The patient, however, was not partaking of the refreshments; she sat propped up in bed, a sad and weary-looking French matron dressed in a gray robe to match her gray hair. Her only visible injuries appeared to be a bruised cheek and some scratches on her arms. It was clear from the woman's look of unhappiness that the bomb's most serious damage had been emotional. Any other patient would have been discharged by now; only her status as St. Pierre's wife allowed her such pampering.

Nina poured two cups of tea and handed them to Beryl and Richard. "When did you arrive in Paris?" she said.

"Jordan and I flew in yesterday," said Beryl. "And you?"

"We flew home with Helena and Reggie." Nina sat back down and crossed her silk-stockinged legs. "First thing this morning, I thought to myself, I really should drop in to see how Marie's doing. Poor thing, she does need cheering up."

Judging by the patient's glum face, Nina's visit had not yet achieved the desired result.

"What's the world coming to, I ask you?" said Nina, balancing her cup of tea. "Madness and anarchy! No one's immune, not even the upper class."

"Especially the upper class," said Helena.

"Has there been any progress on the case?" asked Beryl.

Marie St. Pierre sighed. "They insist it is a terrorist attack."

"Well, of course," said Nina. "Who else plants bombs in politicians' houses?"

Marie's gaze quickly dropped to her lap. She looked at her hands, the bony fingers woven together. "I have told Philippe we should leave Paris for a while. Tonight, perhaps, when I am released. We could visit Switzerland...."

"An excellent idea," murmured Helena gently. She reached out to squeeze Marie's hand. "You need to get away, just the two of you."

"But that's turning tail," said Nina. "Letting the criminals know they've won."

"Easy for you to say," muttered Helena. "It wasn't your house that was bombed."

"And if it was my house, I'd stay right in Paris," Nina retorted. "I wouldn't give an inch—"

"You've never had to."

"What?"

Helena looked away. "Nothing."

"What are you muttering about, Helena?"

"I only think," said Helena, "that Marie should do exactly what she wants. Leaving Paris for a while makes perfect sense. Any friend would back her up."

"I *am* her friend."

"Yes," murmured Helena, "of course you are."

"Are you saying I'm not?"

"I didn't say anything of the kind."

"You're muttering again, Helena. Really, it drives me up a wall. Is it so difficult to come right out and say things?"

"Oh, please," moaned Marie.

A knock on the door cut short the argument. Nina's son, Anthony, entered, dressed with his usual offbeat flair in a shirt of electric blue, a leather jacket. "Ready to leave, Mum?" he asked Nina.

At once Nina rose huffily to her feet. "More than ready," she sniffed and followed him to the door. There she stopped and gave Marie one last glance. "I'm only speaking as a friend," she said. "And I, for one, think you should stay in Paris." She took Anthony's arm and walked out of the room.

"Good heavens, Marie," muttered Helena, after a pause. "Why do you put up with the woman?"

Marie, looking small as she huddled in her bed, gave a

small shrug. *They are so very much alike,* thought Beryl, comparing Marie St. Pierre and Helena. Neither one blessed with beauty, both on the fading side of middle age, and trapped in marriages to men who no longer adored them.

"I've always thought you were a saint just to let that bitch in your door," said Helena. "If it were up to me…"

"One must keep the peace" was all Marie said.

They tried to carry on a conversation, the four of them, but so many silences intervened. And overshadowing their talk of bomb blasts and ruined furniture, of lost artwork and damaged heirlooms, was the sense that something was being left unsaid. That even beyond the horror of these losses was a deeper loss. One had only to look in Marie St. Pierre's eyes to know that she was reeling from the devastation of her life.

Even when her husband, Philippe, walked into the room, Marie did not perk up. If anything, she seemed to recoil from Philippe's kiss. She averted her face and looked instead at the door, which had just swung open again.

Claude Daumier entered, saw Beryl, and halted in surprise. "You are *here?*"

"We were waiting to see you," said Beryl.

Daumier glanced at Richard, then back at Beryl. "I have been trying to find you both."

"What's wrong?" asked Richard.

"The matter is…delicate." Daumier motioned for them to follow. "It would be best," he said, "to discuss this in private."

They followed him into the hallway, past the nurses' station. In a quiet corner, Daumier stopped and turned to Richard.

"I have just received a call from the police. Colette was found shot to death in her car. Near Place Vendôme."

"Colette?" said Beryl. "The agent who was watching Jordan?"

Grimly Daumier nodded.

"Oh, my God," murmured Beryl. "Jordie—"

"He is safe," Daumier said quickly. "I assure you, he's not in danger."

"But if they killed her, they could—"

"He has been placed under arrest," said Daumier. His gaze, quietly sympathetic, focused on Beryl's shocked face. "For murder."

LONG AFTER EVERYONE ELSE had left the hospital room, Helena remained by Marie's bedside. For a while they said very little; good friends, after all, are comfortable with silence. But then Helena could not hold it in any longer. "It's intolerable," she said. "You simply can't stand for this, Marie."

Marie sighed. "What else am I to do? She has so many friends, so many people she could turn against me. Against Philippe...."

"But you must do something. Anything. For one, refuse to speak to her!"

"I have no proof. Never do I have proof."

"You don't need proof. Use your eyes! Look at the way they act together. The way she's always around him, smiling at him. He may have told you it was over, but you can see it isn't. And where is he, anyway? You're in the hospital and he scarcely visits you. When he does, it's just a peck on the cheek and he's off again."

"He is preoccupied. The economic summit—"

"Oh, yes," Helena snorted. "Men's business is always so bloody important!"

Marie started to cry, not sobs, but noiseless, pitiful tears. Suffering in silence—that was her way. Never a complaint or a protest, just a heart quietly breaking. *The pain we endure,* thought Helena bitterly, *all for the love of men.*

Marie said in a whisper, "It is even worse than you know."

"How can it possibly be any worse?"

Marie didn't reply. She just looked down at the abrasions on her arms. They were only minor scrapes, the aftermath of flying glass, but she stared at them with what looked like quiet despair.

*So that's it,* thought Helena, horrified. *She thinks they're trying to kill her. Why doesn't she strike back? Why doesn't she fight?*

But Marie hadn't the will. One could see that, just by the slump of her shoulders.

*My poor, dear friend,* thought Helena, gazing at Marie with pity, *how very much alike we are. And yet, how very different.*

A MAN SAT ON THE BENCH across from him, silently eyeing Jordan's clothes, his shoes, his watch. A well-pickled fellow by the smell of him, thought Jordan with distaste. Or did that delightful odor, that unmistakable perfume of cheap wine and ripe underarms, emanate from the other occupant of the jail cell? Jordan glanced at the man snoring blissfully in the far corner. Yes, there was the likely source.

The man on the bench was still staring at him. Jordan tried to ignore him, but the man's gaze was so intrusive that Jordan finally snapped, "What are you looking at?"

*"C'est en or?"* the man asked.

"Pardon?"

*"La montre. C'est en or?"* The man pointed at Jordan's watch.

"Yes, of course it's gold!" said Jordan.

The man grinned, revealing a mouthful of rotted teeth. He rose and shuffled across the cell to sit beside Jordan. Right beside him. His gaze dropped speculatively to Jordan's shoes. *"C'est italienne?"*

Jordan sighed. "Yes, they're Italian."

The man reached over and fingered Jordan's linen jacket sleeve.

"All right, that's it," said Jordan. "Hands to yourself, chap! *Laissez-moi tranquille!*"

The man simply grinned wider and pointed to his own shoes, a pair of cardboard and plastic creations. "You like?"

"Very nice," groaned Jordan.

The sound of footsteps and clinking keys approached. The man sleeping in the corner suddenly woke up and began to yell, *"Je suis innocent! Je suis innocent!"*

"M. Tavistock?" called the guard.

Jordan jumped at once to his feet. "Yes?"

"You are to come with me."

"Where are we going?"

"You have visitors."

The guard led him down a hall, past holding cells jammed full with prisoners. Good grief, thought Jordan, and he'd thought his cell was bad. He followed the guard through a locked door into the booking area. At once his ears were assaulted with the sounds of bedlam. Everywhere phones seemed to be ringing, voices arguing. A ragtag line of prisoners waited to be processed, and one woman kept yelling that it was a mistake, all a mistake. Through the babble of French, Jordan heard his name called.

"Beryl?" he said in relief.

She ran to him, practically knocking him over with the force of her embrace. "Jordie! Oh, my poor Jordie, are you all right?"

"I'm fine, darling."

"You're really all right?"

"Never better, now that you're here." Glancing over her shoulder, he saw Richard and Daumier standing behind her. The cavalry had arrived. Now this terrible business could be cleared up.

Beryl pulled away and frowned at his face. "You look ghastly."

"I probably smell even worse." Turning to Daumier, he said, "Have they found out anything about Colette?"

Daumier shook his head. "A single bullet, nine millimeters, in the temple. Plainly an execution, with no witnesses."

"What about the gun?" asked Jordan. "How can they accuse me without having a murder weapon?"

"They do have one," said Daumier. "It was found in the storm drain, very near the car."

"And no witnesses?" said Beryl. "In broad daylight?"

"It is a side street. Not many passersby."

"But someone must have seen something."

Daumier gave an unhappy nod. "A woman did report seeing a man force his way into Colette's car. But it was on Boulevard Saint-Germain."

Jordan groaned. "Oh, great. That would've been me."

Beryl frowned. "You?"

"I talked her into giving me a ride back to the hotel. My fingerprints will be all over the inside of that car."

"What happened after you got into the car?" Richard asked.

"She let me off at the Ritz. I went up to the room for a few minutes, then came back down to talk to her. That's when I found…" Groaning, he clutched his head. "Lord, this can't be happening."

"Did you see anything?" Richard pressed him.

"Not a thing. But…" Jordan's head slowly lifted. "Colette may have."

"You're not sure?"

"While we were driving to the hotel, she kept frowning at the mirror. Said something about imagining things. I looked, but all I saw was traffic." Miserable, he turned to Daumier. "I blame myself, really. I keep thinking, if only I'd paid more attention, if I hadn't been so wrapped up—"

"She knew how to protect herself," interrupted Daumier. "She should have been prepared."

''That's what I don't understand,'' said Jordan. ''That she was caught so off guard.'' He glanced at his watch. ''There's still plenty of daylight. We could go back to Boulevard Saint-Germain. Retrace my steps. Something might come back to me.''

His suggestion was met with dead silence.

''Jordie,'' said Beryl, softly, ''you can't.''

''What do you mean, I can't?''

''They won't release you.''

''But they have to release me! I didn't do it!'' He looked at Daumier. To his dismay, the Frenchman regretfully shook his head.

Richard said, ''We'll do whatever it takes, Jordan. Somehow we'll get you out of here.''

''Has anyone called Uncle Hugh?''

''He's not at Chetwynd,'' said Beryl. ''No one knows where he is. It seems he left last night without telling anyone. So we're going to see Reggie and Helena. They've friends in the embassy. Maybe they can pull some strings.''

Dismayed by the news, Jordan could only stand there, surrounded by the chaos of milling prisoners and policemen. *I'm in prison and Uncle Hugh's vanished,* he thought. *This nightmare is getting worse by the second.*

''The police think I'm guilty?'' he ventured.

''I am afraid so,'' said Daumier.

''And you, Claude? What do you think?''

''Of course he knows you're innocent!'' declared Beryl. ''We all do. Just give me time to clear things up.''

Jordan turned to his sister, his beautiful, stubborn sister. The one person he cared most about in the world. He took off his watch and firmly pressed it into her hand.

She frowned. ''Why are you giving me this?''

''Safekeeping. I may be in here a rather long time. Now, I want you to go home, Beryl. The next plane to London. Do you understand?''

''But I'm not going anywhere.''

"Yes, you are. And Richard is damn well going to see to it."

"How?" she retorted. "By dragging me off by the hair?"

"If that's what it takes."

"You need me here!"

"Beryl." He took her by the shoulders and spoke quietly. Sensibly. "A woman's been killed. And she was trained to defend herself."

"It doesn't mean I'm next."

"It means they're frightened. Ready to strike back. You have to go home."

"And leave you in this place?"

"Claude will be here. And Reggie—"

"So I fly home and leave you to rot in prison?" She shook her head in disagreement. "Do you really think I'd do that?"

"If you love me, you will."

Her chin came up. "If I love you," she said, "I'll do no such thing." She threw her arms around him in a fierce, uncompromising embrace. Then, brushing away tears, she turned to Richard. "Let's go. The sooner we talk to Reggie, the sooner we'll clear up this mess."

Jordan watched his sister walk away. It was just like her, he thought, to steer her own straight and stubborn course through that unruly crowd of pickpockets and prostitutes. "Beryl!" he yelled. "Go home! Don't be a bloody idiot!"

She stopped and looked back at him. "But I can't help it, Jordie. It runs in the family." Then she turned and walked out the door.

# CHAPTER SIX

"YOUR BROTHER'S RIGHT," said Richard. "You should go home."

"Don't *you* start now," she snapped over her shoulder.

"I'll drive you to the hotel to pack. Then I'm taking you to the airport."

"You and what regiment?"

"For once will you take some advice?" he yelled.

She spun around on the crowded sidewalk and turned to confront him. "Advice, yes. Orders, no."

"Okay, then just listen for a minute. Your coming to Paris was a crazy move to begin with. Sure, I understand why you did it. I understand that you'd want to know the truth about your parents. But things have changed, Beryl. A woman's been killed. It's a whole new ball game now."

"What am I supposed to do about Jordan? Just leave him there?"

"I'll take care of it. I'll talk to Reggie. We'll get him the best lawyer there is—"

"And I run home? Wash my hands of the whole mess?" She looked down at the watch she was holding. Jordan's watch. Quietly she said, "He's my family. Did you see how wretched he looked? It would kill him to stay in that place. If I left him there, I'd never forgive myself."

"And if something happened to you, Jordan would never forgive himself. And neither would I."

"I'm not your responsibility."

"But you are."

"And who decided that?"

He reached for her then, trapping her face in his hands. "I did," he whispered, and pressed his lips to hers. She was so stunned by the ferocity of his kiss that at first she couldn't react; too many glorious sensations were assaulting her at once. She heard his murmurings of need, felt the hot surge of his tongue into her mouth. Her own body responded, every nerve singing with desire. She was oblivious to the traffic, the passersby on the sidewalk. There were only the two of them and the way their bodies and mouths melted together. All day they'd been fighting this, she thought. And all day she knew it was hopeless. She knew it would come to this—one kiss on a Paris street, and she was lost.

Gently he pulled away and gazed down at her. "*That's* why you have to leave Paris," he murmured.

"Because you command it?"

"No. Because it makes sense."

She stepped back, desperate to put space between them, to regain some control—any control—over her emotions. "Sense to you, perhaps," she said softly. "But not to me." Then she turned and climbed into his car.

He slid in beside her and shut the door. Though they sat in silence, she could feel his frustration radiating throughout the car.

"What can I say that would make you change your mind?" he asked.

"*My* mind?" She looked at him and managed a tight, uncompromising smile. "Absolutely nothing."

"IT'S RATHER a sticky situation," said Reggie Vane. "If the charges weren't so serious—theft, perhaps, or even assault—then the embassy might be able to do something. But murder? I'm afraid that's beyond diplomatic intervention."

They were talking in Reggie's private study, a masculine, dark-paneled room very much like her Uncle Hugh's at Chetwynd. The bookshelves were lined with English classics, the walls hung with hunting scenes of foxes and hounds and gentlemen on horseback. The stone fireplace was an exact copy, Reggie had told them, of the hearth in his childhood home in Cornwall. Even the smell of Reggie's pipe tobacco reminded Beryl of home. How comforting to discover that here, on the outskirts of Paris, was a familiar world transplanted straight from England.

"Surely the ambassador can do something?" said Beryl. "This is Jordan we're talking about, not some soccer-club hooligan. Besides, he's innocent."

"Of course he's innocent," said Reggie. "Believe me, if there was anything I could do about it, our Jordan wouldn't stay in that cell a moment longer." He sat down on the couch beside her and clasped her hands, the whole time focusing his mild blue eyes on her face. "Beryl, darling, you have to understand. Even the ambassador himself can't work miracles. I've spoken to him, and he's not optimistic."

"Then there's nothing you or he can do?" Beryl asked miserably.

"I'll arrange for a lawyer—one our embassy recommends. He's an excellent fellow, someone they call in for just this sort of thing. Specializes in English clients."

"And that's all we can hope for? A good attorney?"

Reggie's answer was a regretful nod.

In her disappointment, Beryl didn't hear Richard move to stand close behind her, but she did feel his hands coming to rest protectively on her shoulders. *How I've come to rely on him,* she thought. *A man I shouldn't trust. And yet I do.*

Reggie looked at Richard. "What about the Intelligence angle?" he asked. "Any evidence forthcoming?"

"French Intelligence is working with the police. They'll be running ballistic tests on the gun. No fingerprints were found on it. The fact that he's Lord Lovat's nephew will get him some special consideration. But in the end, it's still a murder charge. And the victim's a Frenchwoman. Once the local papers get hold of the story, it will sound like some spoiled English brat trying to slither out of criminal charges.''

''And there's enough ill will toward us British as it is,'' said Reggie. ''After thirty years in this country, I should know. I tell you, as soon as my year's up at the bank, I'm going home.'' His gaze wandered longingly to the painting over the mantelpiece. It was of a country home, its walls festooned with blue wisteria blossoms. ''Helena hated it in Cornwall—thought the house was far too primitive. But it suited my parents. And it suits me.'' He looked at Beryl. ''It's a frightening thing, getting into trouble so far from home. One is always aware that one is vulnerable. And neither class nor money can make things right.''

''I've told Beryl she should fly home,'' said Richard.

Reggie nodded. ''My feelings exactly.''

''I can't,'' said Beryl. ''I'd feel like a rat jumping ship.''

''At least you'd be a live rat,'' said Richard.

Angrily she shrugged off his touch. ''But a rat all the same.''

Reggie reached for her hand. ''Beryl,'' he said quietly, ''listen to me. I was your mother's oldest friend—we grew up together. So I feel a special responsibility. And you have no idea how painful it is for me to see one of Madeline's children in such a fix. It's awful enough that Jordan's in trouble, but to worry about you, as well...'' He gave her hand a squeeze. ''Listen to your Mr. Wolf here. He's a sensible fellow. Someone you can trust.''

*Someone I can trust.* Beryl felt Richard's gaze on her back, felt it as acutely as a touch, and her spine stiffened. She focused firmly on Reggie. Dear Reggie, whose shared past with Madeline made him part of her family.

She said, ''I know you mean only the best, Reggie, but I can't leave Paris.''

The two men looked at each other, exchanging shared expressions of frustration, but not surprise. After all, they had both known Madeline; they could expect nothing less than stubbornness from her daughter.

There was a knock on the study door. Helena poked her head in. "All right for me to come in?"

"Of course," said Beryl.

Helena entered, carrying a tray of tea and biscuits, which she set down on the end table. "I'm always careful to ask first," she said with a smile as she poured out four cups, "before I trespass in Reggie's private abode." She handed Beryl a cup. "Have we made any headway, then?"

From the silence that greeted her question, Helena knew the answer. She looked at once apologetic. "Oh, Beryl. I'm so sorry. Isn't there *something* you can do, Reggie?"

"I'm already doing it," said Reggie, with more than a hint of impatience. Turning his back to her, he took a pipe down from the mantelpiece and lit it. For a moment, there was only the sound of the teacups clinking on saucers and the soft put-put-put of Reggie's lips on the pipe stem.

"Reggie?" ventured Helena again. "It seems to me that calling an attorney is merely being reactive. Isn't there something, well, *active* that could be done?"

"Such as?" asked Richard.

"For instance, the crime itself. We all know Jordan couldn't have done it. So who did?"

Reggie grunted. "You're hardly qualified as a detective."

"Still, it's a question that will have to be answered. That young woman was killed while watching over Jordan. So this may all stem from the reason Jordan's in Paris to begin with. Though I can't quite see how a twenty-year-old case of murder could be so dangerous to someone."

"It was more than murder," Beryl observed. "Espionage was involved."

"That business with the NATO mole," Reggie said to Helena. "You remember. Hugh told us about it."

"Oh, yes. Delphi." Helena glanced at Richard. "MI6 never actually identified him, did they?"

"They had their suspicions," said Richard.

"I myself always wondered," said Helena, reaching for a biscuit, "about Ambassador Sutherland. And why he committed suicide so soon after Madeline and Bernard died."

Richard nodded. "You and I think along the same lines, Lady Helena."

"Though I can't say he didn't have other reasons to jump off that bridge. If I were a man married to Nina, I'd have killed myself long ago." Helena bit sharply into the biscuit; it was a reminder that even mousy women have teeth.

Reggie tapped his pipe and said, "It's not right for us to speculate."

"Still, one can't help it, can one?"

By the time Reggie walked his guests to the front door, darkness had fallen and the night had taken on a damp, unseasonable chill. Even the high walls surrounding the Vanes' private courtyard couldn't seem to shut out the sense of danger that hung in the air that night.

"I promise you," said Reggie, "I'll do everything I can."

"I don't know how to thank you," Beryl murmured.

"Just give me a smile, dear. Yes, that's it." Reggie took her by the shoulders and planted a kiss on her forehead. "You look more and more like your mother every day. And from me, there is no higher compliment." He turned to Richard. "You'll look out for the girl?"

"I promise," said Richard.

"Good. Because she's all we have left." Sadly he touched Beryl's cheek. "All we have left of Madeline."

"WERE THEY ALWAYS that way together?" asked Beryl. "Reggie and Helena?"

Richard kept his eyes on the road as he drove. "What do you mean?"

"The sniping at each other. The put-downs."

He chuckled. "I'm so used to hearing it, I hardly notice it anymore. Yes, I guess it was that way when I met them twenty years ago. I'm sure part of it's due to his resentment of Helena's money. No man likes to feel, well, kept.''

"No," she said quietly, looking straight ahead. "I suppose no man would." *Is that how it would be between us?* she wondered. *Would he hold my money against me? Would his resentment build up over the years, until we ended up like Reggie and Helena, sharing a lifetime of hell together?*

"Part of it, too," said Richard, "is the fact that Reggie never really liked being in Paris, and he never liked being a banker. Helena talked him into taking the post."

"She doesn't seem to like it here much, either."

"No. And so there they are, always sniping at each other. I'd see them at parties with your parents, and I was always struck by the contrast. Bernard and Madeline seemed so much in love. Then again, every man who met your mother couldn't help but fall in love, just a little."

"What was it about her?" asked Beryl. "You said once that she was...enchanting."

"When I met her, she was about forty. Oh, she had a gray hair here and there. A few laugh lines. But she was more fascinating than any twenty-year-old woman I'd ever met. I was surprised to hear that she wasn't born to nobility."

"She was from Cornwall. Old Spanish blood. Dad met her one summer while on holiday." Beryl smiled. "He said she beat him in a footrace. In her bare feet. And that's when he knew she was the one for him."

"They were well matched, in every way. I suppose that's what fascinated me—their happiness. My parents were divorced. It was a pretty nasty split, and it soured me on the whole idea of marriage. But your parents made it look so easy." He shook his head. "I was more shocked than anyone about their deaths. I couldn't believe that Bernard would—"

"He didn't do it. I know he didn't."

After a pause, Richard said, "So do I."

They drove for a moment without speaking, the lights of passing traffic flashing at them through the windshield.

"Is that why you never married?" she asked. "Because of your parents' divorce?"

"It was one reason. The other is that I've never found the right woman." He glanced at her. "Why didn't you marry?"

She shrugged. "Never the right man."

"There must have been someone in your life."

"There was. For a while." She hugged herself and stared out at the darkness rushing past.

"Didn't work out?"

She managed a laugh. "I'm lucky it didn't."

"Do I detect a trace of bitterness?"

"Disillusionment, really. When we first met, I thought he was quite extraordinary. He was a surgeon about to leave on a mercy mission to Nigeria. It's so rare to find a man who really cares about humanity. I visited him, twice, in Africa. He was in his element out there."

"And what happened?"

"We were lovers for a while. And then I came to realize how he saw himself. The great white savior. He'd swoop into a primitive hospital, save a few lives, then fly home to England for a bracing dose of adulation. Which, it turned out, he could never get enough of. One adoring woman wasn't sufficient. He had to have a dozen." Softly she added, "And I wanted to be the only one." She leaned back against the car seat and stared out at the glow of Paris. The City of Light, she thought. Still, there were those shadows, those dark alleys and even darker secrets.

Back at the Place Vendôme, they sat for a moment in the parked car, not speaking, just sitting side by side in the gloom. *We're both exhausted,* she thought. *And the night isn't over yet. I'll have to pack Jordan's things. A tooth-brush, a change of clothes. Bring them back to the prison....*

"Then I can't talk you into leaving," he said.

She looked out at the plaza, at the silhouette of two lovers strolling arm in arm through the darkness. "No. Not until he's free. Not until we see this through to the end."

"I was afraid you'd say that. But I'm not surprised. Just the other day you told me you had a hard head."

She looked at his face, saw the gleam of his smile in the shadows. "This isn't hardheadedness, Richard. This is loyalty. To Jordan. To my parents. We're Tavistocks, you see, and we stand by each other."

"Standing by Jordan, I can see. But your parents are dead."

"It's a matter of honor."

He shook his head. "Bernard and Madeline aren't around to care about honor. It's a medieval concept, to march into battle for something as abstract as the family name."

She climbed out of the car. "Obviously the Wolf family name means nothing to you," she said coldly.

He was out of the car and moving right beside her as she walked through the hotel lobby and stepped into the elevator. "Maybe it's my peculiarly American point of view, but my name is what *I* make of it. I don't wear the family crest tattooed on my forehead."

"You couldn't possibly understand."

"Of course not," he retorted as they stepped out of the elevator. "I'm just a dumb Yank."

"I never called you any such thing!"

He followed her into the suite and shut the door with a thud. "Still, it's clear I'm not up to her Ladyship's standards."

She whirled around and faced him in anger. "You're holding it against me, aren't you? My name. My wealth."

"What's bothering me has nothing to do with your being a Tavistock."

"What *is* bothering you, then?"

"The fact that you won't listen to reason."

"Ah. My hard head."

"Yes, your hard head. And your dumb sense of honor. And your...your..."

She moved right up to him. Tilting up her chin, she stared him straight in the eye. "My what?"

He took her face in his hands and planted a kiss on her mouth, a kiss so long and hard that she had difficulty catching her breath. When at last he pulled back, her legs were wobbly and her pulse was roaring in her ears.

"*That's* what's bothering me," he said. "I can't think straight when you're around. Can't concentrate long enough to tie my own shoelaces. You brush past me, or just look at me, and my mind goes off on certain tangents I'd rather not specify. It's the kind of situation that leads to mistakes. And I don't like to make mistakes."

"You're the one who can't concentrate. And I'm the one who has to fly home?" She turned and started across the room toward the connecting door to Jordan's suite. "Sorry, Richard," she said, moving past the window, "but you'll just have to keep those lusty male hormones under—"

Her words were cut off by the crack of the shattering window.

Reflexes made her pivot away from the sting of flying glass. In the next instant, Richard lunged at her and sent her sprawling to the shard-littered floor.

Another bullet zinged through the window and thudded into the far wall.

"The light!" shouted Richard. "Got to kill the light!" He began to crawl toward the bedside lamp and had almost reached it when the second window shattered. Broken glass rained on top of him.

"Richard!" screamed Beryl.

"Stay down!" He took a deep breath, then rolled across the floor. He grabbed the lamp cord and yanked the plug from the outlet. Instantly the room was plunged into darkness. The only light came through the windows, shining dimly in from the Place Vendôme. An eerie silence fell over the room, broken only by the hammering of Beryl's heart-beat in her ears.

She started to rise to her knees.

"Don't move!" warned Richard.

"He can't see us."

"He might have an infrared scope. Stay down."

Beryl dropped back to the floor and felt the bite of broken glass through her sleeves. "Where's it coming from?"

"Has to be one of the buildings across the plaza. Long-range rifle."

"What do we do now?"

"We call for reinforcements." She heard him crawling in the darkness, then heard the clang of the telephone hitting the floor. An instant later, he muttered an oath. "Line's dead! Someone's cut the wire."

New panic shot through Beryl. "You mean they've been in the room?"

"Which means—" Suddenly he fell silent.

"Richard?"

"Shh. Listen."

Over her pounding heartbeat, she heard the faint whine of the hotel elevator as it came to a stop at their floor.

"I think we're in trouble," said Richard.

# CHAPTER SEVEN

"HE CAN'T GET IN," said Beryl. "The door's locked."

"They'll have a passkey. If they managed to get in here earlier..."

"What do we do?"

"Jordan's room. Move!"

At once she was on her knees and crawling toward the connecting door. Only when she'd reached it did she realize Richard wasn't following her.

"Come on!" she whispered.

"You go. I'll hold them off."

She glanced back in disbelief. "What?"

"They'll check this room first to see if we've been hit. I'll slow them down. You get out through Jordan's suite. Head for the stairwell and don't stop running."

Beryl crouched frozen in the connecting doorway. *This is suicide. He has no gun, no weapon at all.* Already he was slipping through the shadows. She could just make out his figure, poised by the door. Waiting for the attack.

The knock on the door made her jerk in panic. "Mlle Tavistock?" called a man's voice. Beryl didn't answer; she didn't dare to. *"Mademoiselle?"* the voice called again.

Richard was gesturing frantically at her through the darkness. *Get out! Now.*

*I can't leave him,* she thought. *I can't let him fight this alone.*

A key grated in the lock.

There was no time to consider the risks. Beryl grabbed

the bedside lamp, scrambled toward Richard, and planted herself right beside him.

"What the hell are you doing?" he whispered.

"Shut up," she hissed back.

They both flattened against the wall as the door swung open in front of them. There was a pause, the span of just a few heartbeats, and then they heard footsteps cross the threshold into the room. The door slowly swung closed, revealing the silhouettes of the intruders—two men, standing in the darkness. Beryl could feel Richard coil up beside her, could almost hear his silent one-two-three countdown. Suddenly he was flying at the nearest man; the force of the impact sent both men slamming to the floor.

Beryl raised the lamp and brought it crashing down on the head of the second intruder. He collapsed at her feet, facedown and groaning. She dropped beside him and began patting his clothes for a gun. Through his jacket, she felt a hard lump under his arm. A holster? She rolled him over onto his back. Only then, as a crack of light through the partially closed door spilled across his face, did she realize their mistake.

"Oh, my God," she said. She glanced at Richard, who'd just grabbed his opponent by the collar and was about to shove him against the wall. "Richard, don't!" she yelled. "Don't hurt him!"

He paused, still clutching the other man's collar in his fists. "Why the hell not?" he muttered.

"Because these are the wrong men, that's why!" She went to the wall switch and flicked on the overhead light.

Richard blinked in the sudden brightness. He stared at the hotel manager, cowering in his grip. Then he turned and looked at the man who lay groaning by the door. It was Claude Daumier.

At once Richard released the manager, who promptly shrank away in terror. "Sorry," said Richard. "My mistake."

"IF I'D KNOWN IT WAS YOU," said Beryl, pressing a bag of ice to Daumier's head, "I wouldn't have whacked you so hard."

"If you had known it was me," muttered Daumier, "I would hope you wouldn't have whacked me at all." He sat up on the couch and caught the bag of ice before it could slide off. "*Zut alors,* what did you use, *chérie?* A brick?"

"A lamp. And not a very big one, either." She glanced at Richard and the hotel manager. Both men were looking slightly the worse for wear—especially the manager. That black eye of his was colorful testimony to the damaging potential of Richard's fist. Now that the crisis was over, and they were safely barricaded in the manager's office, the situation struck Beryl as more than a little hilarious. A senior French Intelligence agent, beaned by a lamp? Richard, still nursing his bruised knuckles. And the poor hotel manager, assiduously maintaining a safe distance from those same knuckles. She could have laughed—if the whole affair hadn't been so frightening.

There was a knock on the door. Instantly Beryl tensed, only to relax again when she saw that it was a policeman. *I'm still high on adrenaline,* she thought as she watched Daumier and the cop converse in French. *Still expecting the worst.*

The policeman withdrew, closing the door behind him.

"What did he say?" Beryl asked.

"The shots were fired from across the plaza," said Daumier. "They have found bullet casings on the rooftop."

"And the gunman?" asked Richard.

Regretfully Daumier shook his head. "Vanished."

"Then he's still on the loose," said Richard. "And we don't know when he'll strike again." He looked at the manager. "What about that telephone wire? Who could've cut it?"

The man shrank back a step, as though expecting another

blow. "I do not know, *monsieur!* One of the maids, she says her passkey was misplaced for a few hours today."

"So anyone could have gotten in."

"No one from our staff! They are thoroughly checked. You see, we have many important guests."

"I want your employees revetted. Every last one of them."

The manager nodded meekly. Then, still wincing in pain from the black eye, he left the office.

Richard began to pace, carelessly yanking his tie loose as he moved. "We have an intruder who cuts the phone line. A marksman stationed across the plaza. A high-powered rifle positioned for a shot straight into Beryl's room. Claude, this is sounding worse by the minute."

"Why would they try to kill me?" asked Beryl. "What have I done?"

"You've asked too many questions, that's what." Richard turned to Daumier. "You had it right, Claude. The matter's not dead, not by a long shot."

"We were both in that room, Richard," said Beryl. "How do you know he was aiming at me?"

"I wasn't the one walking past that window."

"You're the one who's CIA."

"The qualifying prefix is *ex,* as in, no longer with the Company. I'm not a threat to anyone."

"And I am?"

"Yes. By virtue of your name—not to mention your curiosity." He glanced at Daumier. "We need a safe house, Claude. Can you arrange it?"

"We keep a flat in Passy for protection of witnesses. It will serve your purpose."

"Who else knows about it?"

"My people. A few ministry officials."

"That's too many."

"It is the best I can offer. It has an alarm system. And I will assign guards."

Richard paused, thinking, weighing the risks. At last he nodded. "It will have to do for tonight. Tomorrow, we'll come up with something else. Maybe a plane ticket." He looked at Beryl.

This time she didn't protest. Already she could feel the adrenaline fading away. A moment ago, every nerve felt wired for action; now a plane home was beginning to sound sensible. All it took was a short flight across the Channel, and she'd be safe in the refuge of Chetwynd. It was all so easy, so tempting.

And she was so very, very tired.

With a numb sense of detachment, Beryl listened as Daumier made the necessary phone calls. He hung up and said, "I will have a car and escort brought around. Beryl's clothes will be delivered to the flat later. Oh, and Richard, you will no doubt want this." He reached under his suit jacket and withdrew a semiautomatic pistol from his shoulder holster. He handed it to Richard. "A loan. Just between us, of course."

"Are you sure you want to part with it?"

"I have another." Daumier slid off his holster, which he also gave to Richard. "You remember how to use one?"

Richard checked the ammunition clip and nodded grimly. "I think it'll come back."

A policeman knocked on the door. The car was waiting.

Richard took Beryl's arm and helped her to her feet. "Time to drop out of sight for a while. Are you ready?"

She looked at the gun he was holding, noted how easily he handled it, how comfortably he slid it into the holster. A professional, she thought. The transformation was almost frightening. *How well do I really know you, Richard Wolf?*

For now, the question was irrelevant. He was the one man she could count on, the one man she had to trust.

She folowed him out the door.

"WE SHOULD BE SAFE HERE. For tonight, at least." Richard double-bolted the apartment door and turned to look at her.

She was standing in the center of the living room, her arms wrapped around her shoulders, a dazed look in her eyes. This was not the brash and stubborn Beryl he knew, he thought. This was a woman who'd faced sheer terror and knew the worst wasn't over yet. He wanted to go to her, to take her in his arms and promise her that nothing would ever hurt her while he was around, but they both knew it was a promise he might not be able to keep. In silence, he circled the flat, checking to see that the windows were secure, the drapes closed. A glance outside told him there were two guards watching the building, one at the front entrance, one at the rear. A safety net, he thought. For when I let my attention slip. And it *would* slip. Sooner or later, he would have to sleep.

Satisfied that all was locked up tight, he went back to the living room. He found Beryl sitting on the couch, very quiet, very still. Almost...defeated.

"Are you all right?" he asked.

She gave a shrug, as though the question was irrelevant— as though they had far more important things to consider.

He took off his jacket and tossed it over a chair. "You haven't eaten. There's some food in the kitchen."

Her gaze focused on his shoulder holster. "Why did you quit the business?" she asked.

"You mean the Company?"

She nodded. "When I saw you holding that gun, it...it suddenly struck me. What you used to be."

He sat down beside her. "I've never killed anyone. If that makes a difference."

"But you're trained to do it."

"Only in self-defense. That's not the same thing as murder."

She nodded, as though trying very hard to agree with him.

He took the Glock from the holster and held it out to her. She regarded it with undisguised abhorrence.

"Yes, I understand how you feel," he said. "This gun's a semiautomatic. Nine millimeter bullets, sixteen cartridges to the magazine. Some people consider it a work of art. I think of it as a tool of last resort. Something I hope to God I never have to use." He set it on the coffee table, where it lay like an evil reminder of violence. "Pick it up if you want to. It's not very heavy."

"I'd rather not." She shuddered and looked away. "I'm not afraid of guns. I mean, I've handled rifles before. I used to go shooting with Uncle Hugh. But those were only clay pigeons."

"Not quite the same thing."

"No. Not quite."

"You asked why I quit the Company." He pointed to the Glock. "That was one of the reasons. I've never killed anyone, and I'm not itching to. For me, the intelligence business was a game. A challenge. The enemy was well-defined— the Russians, the East Germans. But now…" He picked up the gun and held it thoughtfully in his palm. "The world's turned into a crazy place. I can't tell who the enemy is anymore. And I knew that sooner or later, I'd lose my edge. I could already feel it happening."

"Your edge?"

"It's my age, you know. You hit forty and you don't react the way you did as a twenty-year-old. I like to think I've grown smarter, instead, but what I really am is more cautious. And a lot less willing to take risks." He looked at her. "With anyone's life."

She met his gaze. Looking into her eyes, he suddenly found himself wanting to babble all sorts of crazy things. To tell her that the one life he didn't want to risk was hers. When had this stopped being a mere baby-sitting job? he wondered. When had it become something much more? A mission. An obsession.

"You frighten me, Richard," she said.

"It's the gun."

"No, it's you. All the things I don't know about you. All the secrets you're keeping from me."

"From now on, I promise I'll be absolutely honest with you."

"But it started out as half truths. Not telling me you knew my parents. Or how they died. Don't you see, it's my childhood all over again! Uncle Hugh with his head full of classified secrets." She let out a breath of frustration and looked away. "Then I see you with that...thing."

He touched her face and gently turned it toward him. "It's just a temporary evil," he murmured. "Until this is over." She kept looking at him, her eyes bright and moist, her hair tumbling about her shoulders. *She wants to trust me*, he thought. *But she's afraid.*

He couldn't help himself. He kissed her. Once. Twice. The second time, he felt her lips yield under his, felt her whole body seem to turn liquid at his touch. He kissed her a third time and found his hands sliding through her hair, his fingers hopelessly becoming tangled in all that raven silk. She sighed, a delicious sound of surrender, invitation, and she sagged backward onto the couch.

Suddenly he, too, was falling, tumbling on top of her. Their lips met in a touch that instantly turned electric. She reached around his neck and pulled him down hard against her—

And flinched. That blasted gun again. The holster had pushed into her breast, had served as an ugly reminder of all the things that had happened today. All the things that could still happen.

He looked at her face, at her hair flung across the cushions, at the mingling of fear and desire he saw in her eyes. *Not now,* he thought. *Not this way.*

Slowly he pulled away and they both sat up. For a moment, they remained side by side on the couch, not touching, not speaking.

She said, "I'm not ready for this. I'll put my life in your hands, Richard. But my heart, that's a different matter."

"I understand."

"Then you'll also understand that I'm not a fan of James Bond, or anyone remotely like him. I'm not impressed by guns, or by the men who use them." She rose to her feet and moved pointedly away from the couch. Away from him.

"So what does impress you?" he asked. "If not a man's gun?"

She turned to him and he saw a flicker of humor cross her face. *The old Beryl,* he thought. *Thank God she's still there, somewhere.*

"Straight talk," she said. "That's what impresses me."

"Then that's what you'll get. I promise."

She turned and walked to the bedroom. "We'll see."

JORDAN WAS NOT IMPRESSED by this lawyer, no, he was not impressed at all.

The man had greasy hair and a greasy little mustache, and he spoke English with the exaggerated accent of a second-rate actor playing a stereotypical Frenchman. All those "eets" and "zees" and *"Mon Dieus."* Still, Jordan reasoned, since Beryl had hired the man, he must be one of the best attorneys in Paris.

*You could have fooled me,* thought Jordan, gazing across the prison interview table at the smarmy M. Jarre.

"Not to worry," said the man. "Everything will be taken care of. I am reviewing the papers now, and I believe we will soon reach an agreement to have you released."

"What about the investigation?" asked Jordan. "Any progress?"

"Very slow. You know how it is, M. Tavistock. In a city as large as Paris, the police, they are overworked. You cannot be impatient."

"And my uncle? Have you been able to reach him?"

"He is in complete agreement with my planned course of action."

"Is he coming to Paris?"

"He is detained. Business keeps him at home, I am afraid."

"At home? But I thought…" Jordan paused. Didn't Beryl say Uncle Hugh had left Chetwynd?

M. Jarre rose from the table. "Rest assured that all that can be done, will be done. I have instructed the police to transfer you to a more comfortable cell."

"Thank you," said Jordan, still puzzling over the reference to Uncle Hugh. As the attorney was leaving the room, Jordan called out, "M. Jarre? Did my uncle happen to mention how his…negotiations went in London?"

The attorney glanced back. "They are still in progress, I understand. But I am sure he will tell you himself." He gave a nod of farewell. "Good evening, M. Tavistock. I hope you find your new cell more agreeable." He walked out.

*What the dickens is going on?* thought Jordan. He wondered about this all the way to his cell—his new cell. One look at the pair of shady characters seated inside and his suspicions about M. Jarre deepened. *This* was more agreeable quarters?

Reluctantly Jordan stepped inside and flinched at the clang of the door shutting behind him. The jailer walked away, his footsteps echoing down the hall.

The two prisoners were staring at his fine Italian shoes, which contrasted dreadfully with the regulation prison garb he was wearing.

"Hello," said Jordan, for want of anything else to say.

*"Anglais?"* asked one of the men.

Jordan swallowed. *"Oui. Anglais."*

The man grunted and pointed to an empty bunk. "Yours."

Jordan went to the bunk, set his bundle of street clothes

on the foot of the bed, and stretched out on the mattress.
As the two prisoners babbled away in French, Jordan kept
wondering about that greasy attorney and why he had lied
about Uncle Hugh. If only he could get in touch with Beryl,
ask her what was going on...

He sat up at the sound of footsteps approaching the cell.
It was the guard, escorting yet another prisoner—this one a
balding, round-cheeked man with a definite waddle and a
pleasant enough face. The sort of fellow you'd expect to see
standing behind a bakery counter. *Not your typical criminal,*
thought Jordan. *But then, neither am I.*

The man entered the cell and was directed to the fourth
and last bunk. He sat down, looking stunned by the circumstances in which he found himself. François was his name,
and from what Jordan could gather using his elementary
command of French, the man's crime had something to do
with the fair sex. Solicitation, perhaps? François was not
eager to talk about it. He simply sat on his bed and stared
at the floor. *We're both new to this,* thought Jordan.

The other two cellmates were still watching him. Sullen
young men, obviously sociopathic. He'd have to keep his
eye on them.

Supper came—an atrocious goulash accompanied by
French bread. Jordan stared at the muddy brown gravy and
thought wistfully of his supper the night before—poached
salmon and roast duckling. Ah, well. One had to eat re-
gardless of one's circumstances. What a shame there wasn't
a bottle of wine to wash down the meal. A nice Beaujolais,
perhaps, or just a common Burgundy. He took a bite of
goulash and decided that even a bad bottle of wine would
be welcome—anything to dull the taste of this gravy. He
forced himself to eat it and made a silent vow that when he
got out of here—*if* he got out of here—the first place he'd
head for was a decent restaurant.

At midnight, the lights were turned off. Jordan stretched
out on the blanket and made every effort to sleep, but found

he couldn't. For one thing, his cellmates were snoring to wake the dead. For another, the day's events kept playing and replaying in his mind. That drive with Colette from Boulevard Saint-Germain. The way she had glanced at the rearview mirror. If only he had paid more attention to who might be following them back to the hotel. And then, against his will, he remembered the horror of finding her body in the car, remembered the stickiness of her blood on his hands.

Rage bubbled up inside him—an impotent sense of fury about her death. *It's my fault,* he thought. If she hadn't been watching over him, protecting him.

But that's not why she died, Jordan thought suddenly. He was nowhere nearby when it happened. So why did they kill her? Did she know something, see something...

... or someone?

His thoughts veered in a new direction. Colette must have spotted a face in her rearview mirror, a face in the car that was following them. After she'd dropped Jordan off at the Ritz, maybe she'd seen that someone again. Or he'd seen her and knew she could identify him.

Which made the killer someone Colette knew. Someone she recognized.

He was so intent on piecing together the puzzle, he didn't pay much attention to the creak of the bunk springs somewhere in the cell. Only when he heard the soft rustle of movement did he realize that one of his cellmates was approaching his bed.

It was dark; he could make out only faintly a shadowy figure moving toward him. One of those young hoods, he thought, come to rifle his jacket.

Jordan lay perfectly still and willed his breathing to remain deep and even. *Let the coward think I'm still asleep. When he moves close enough, I'll surprise him.*

The shadow slipped quietly through the darkness. Six feet away, now five. Jordan's heart was pounding, his muscles already tensed for action. *Just a little closer. A little closer. He'll be reaching for the jacket hanging at the foot of the bed....*

But the man moved instead to Jordan's head. There was a faint arc of shadow—an arm being raised to deliver a blow. Jordan's hand shot out just as his assailant attacked.

He caught the other man's wrist and heard a grunt of surprise. His attacker came at him with his free hand. Jordan deflected the blow and scrambled off the bunk. Still gripping his attacker's wrist, he gave it a vicious twist, eliciting a yelp of pain. The man was thrashing to get free now, but Jordan held on. He was not going to get away. Not without learning a lesson. He shoved the man backward and heard the satisfying thud of his opponent's body hitting the cinder-block wall. The man groaned and tried to pull free. Again, Jordan shoved. This time they both toppled over onto a cot, landing on its sleeping occupant. The man in Jordan's grasp began to writhe, to jerk. At once Jordan realized this was no longer a man fighting to free himself. This was a man in the throes of a convulsion.

He heard the sound of footsteps and then the cell lights flashed on. A guard yelled at him in French.

Jordan released his assailant and backed away in surprise. It was the moon-faced François. The man lay sprawled on the bed, his limbs twitching, his eyes rolled back. The young hood on whom François had landed frantically rolled away from beneath the body and stared in horror at the bizarre display.

François gave a last grunt of agony and fell still.

For a few seconds, everyone watched him, expecting him to move again. He didn't.

The guard gave a shout for assistance. Another guard came running. Yelling at the prisoners to stand back, they rushed into the cell and examined the motionless François. Slowly they straightened and looked at Jordan.

*"Est mort,"* one of them murmured.

"That-that's impossible!" said Jordan. "How can he be dead? I didn't hit him that hard!"

The guards merely stared at him. The other two prisoners regarded Jordan with new respect and backed away to the far side of the cell.

"Let me look at him!" demanded Jordan. He pushed past the guards and knelt by François. One glance at the body and he knew they were right. François was dead.

Jordan shook his head. "I don't understand...."

"*Monsieur,* you come with us," said one of the guards.

"I couldn't have killed him!"

"But you see for yourself he is dead."

Jordan suddenly focused on a fine line of blood trickling down François's cheek. He bent closer. Only then did he spot the needle-thin dart impaled in the dead man's scalp. It was almost invisible among the salt-and-pepper hairs of his temple.

"What in blazes...?" muttered Jordan. Swiftly he glanced around the floor for a syringe, a dart gun—whatever might have injected that needle point. He saw nothing on the floor or on the bed. Then he looked down at the dead man's hand and saw something clutched in his left fist. He pried open the frozen fingers and the object slid out and landed on the bedcovers.

A ballpoint pen.

At once he was hauled back and shoved toward the cell door. "Go," said the guard. "Walk!"

"Where?"

"Where you can hurt no one." The guard directed Jordan into the corridor and locked the cell door. Jordan caught a fleeting glimpse of his cellmates, watching him in awe, and then he was hustled down the hallway and into a private cell, this one obviously reserved for the most dangerous prisoners. Double-barred, no windows, no furniture, only a concrete slab on which to lie. And a light blazing down relentlessly from the ceiling.

Jordan sank onto the slab and waited. For what? he wondered. Another attack? Another crisis? How could this nightmare possibly get any worse?

An hour passed. He couldn't sleep, not with that light shining overhead. Footsteps and the clank of keys alerted him to a visitor. He looked up to see a guard and a well-dressed gentleman with a briefcase.

"M. Tavistock?" said the gentleman.

"Since there's no one else here," muttered Jordan, rising to his feet, "I'm afraid that must be me."

The door was unlocked, and the man with the briefcase entered. He glanced around in dismay at the Spartan cell. "These conditions... Outrageous," he said.

"Yes. And I owe it all to my wonderful attorney," said Jordan.

"But *I* am your attorney." The man held out his hand in greeting. "Henri Laurent. I would have come sooner, but I was attending the opera. I received M. Vane's message only an hour ago. He said it was an emergency."

Jordan shook his head in confusion. "Vane? Reggie Vane sent you?"

"Yes. Your sister requested my immediate services. And M. Vane—"

"Beryl hired you? Then who the hell was..." Jordan paused as the bizarre events suddenly made sense. Horrifying sense. "M. Laurent," said Jordan, "a few hours ago, there was a lawyer here to see me. A M. Jarre."

Laurent frowned. "But I was not told of another attorney."

"He claimed my sister hired him."

"But I spoke to M. Vane. He told me Mlle Tavistock requested *my* services. What did you say was the other attorney's name?"

"Jarre."

Laurent shook his head. "I am not familiar with any such criminal attorney."

Jordan sat for a moment in stunned silence. Slowly he raised his head and looked at Laurent. "I think you'd better contact Reggie Vane. At once."

"But why?"

"They've already tried to kill me once tonight." Jordan shook his head. "If this keeps up, M. Laurent, by morning I may be quite dead."

# CHAPTER EIGHT

THEY WERE FOLLOWING her again. Black hounds, trotting across the dead leaves of the forest. She heard them rustle through the underbrush and knew they were moving closer.

She gripped Froggie's bridle, struggled to calm her, but the mare panicked. Suddenly Froggie yanked free of Beryl's grasp and reared up.

The hounds attacked.

Instantly they were at the horse's throat, ripping, tearing with their razor teeth. Froggie screamed, a human scream, shrill with terror. *Have to save her,* thought Beryl. *Have to beat them away.* But her feet seemed rooted to the ground. She could only stand and watch in horror as Froggie dropped to her knees and collapsed to the forest floor.

The hounds, mouths bloodied, turned and looked at Beryl.

She awakened, gasping for breath, her hands clawing at the darkness. Only as her panic faded did she hear Richard calling her name.

She turned and saw him standing in the doorway. A lamp was shining in the room behind him, and the light gleamed faintly on his bare shoulders.

"Beryl?" he said again.

She took a deep breath, still trying to shake off the last threads of the nightmare. "I'm awake," she said.

"I think you'd better get up."

"What time is it?"

"Four a.m. Claude just phoned."

"Why?"

"He wants us to meet him at the police station. As soon as possible."

"The police station?" She sat up sharply as a terrible thought came to mind. "Is it Jordan? Has something happened to him?"

Through the shadows, she saw Richard nod. "Someone tried to kill him."

"AN INGENIOUS DEVICE," said Claude Daumier, gingerly laying the ballpoint pen on the table. "A hypodermic needle, a pressurized syringe. One stab, and the drug would be injected into the victim."

"Which drug?" asked Beryl.

"It is still being analyzed. The autopsy will be performed in the morning. But it seems clear that this drug, whatever it was, was the cause of death. There is not enough trauma on the body to explain otherwise."

"Then Jordan won't be blamed for this?" said Beryl in relief.

"Hardly. He will be placed in isolation, no other prisoners, a double guard. There should be no further incidents."

The conference room door opened. Jordan appeared, escorted by two guards. *Dear Lord, he looks terrible,* thought Beryl as she rose from her chair and went to hug him. Never had she seen her brother so disheveled. The beginnings of a thick blond beard had sprouted on his jaw, and his prison clothes were mapped with wrinkles. But as they pulled apart, she gazed in his eyes and saw that the old Jordan was still there, good-humored and ironic as ever.

"You're not hurt?" she asked.

"Not a scratch," he answered. "Well, perhaps a few," he amended, frowning down at his bruised fist. "It's murder on the old manicure."

"Jordan, I swear I never hired any lawyer named Jarre. The man was a fraud."

"I suspected as much."

"The man I did hire, M. Laurent, Reggie swears he's the best there is."

"I'm afraid even the best won't get me out of this fix," Jordan observed disconsolately. "I seem destined to be a long-term resident of this fine establishment. Unless the food kills me first."

"Will you be serious for once?"

"Oh, but you haven't tasted the goulash."

Beryl turned in exasperation to Daumier. "What about the dead man? Who was he?"

"According to the arrest record," said Daumier, "his name was François Parmentier, a janitor. He was charged with disorderly conduct."

"How did he end up in Jordan's cell?" asked Richard.

"It seems that his attorney, Jarre, made a special request for both his clients to be housed in the same cell."

"Not just a request," amended Richard. "It must've been a bribe. Jarre and the dead man were a team."

"Working on whose behalf?" asked Jordan.

"The same party who tried to kill Beryl," said Richard. *"What?"*

"A few hours ago. It was a high-powered rifle, fired at her hotel window."

"And she's still in Paris?" Jordan turned to his sister. "That's it. You're going home, Beryl. And you're leaving at once."

"I've been trying to tell her the same thing," said Richard. "She won't listen."

"Of course she won't. My darling little sister never does!" Jordan scowled at Beryl. "This time, though, you don't have a choice."

"You're right, Jordie," said Beryl. "I don't have a choice. That's why I'm staying."

"You could get yourself killed."

"So could you."

They stood facing each other, neither one willing to give ground. *Deadlock,* thought Beryl. *He's worried about me, and I'm worried about him. And we're both Tavistocks, which means neither of us will ever concede defeat.*

*But I have the upper hand on this one. He's in jail. I'm not.*

In disgust, Jordan turned and flopped into a chair. "For Pete's sake, work on her, Wolf!" he muttered.

"I'm trying to," said Richard. "Meanwhile, we still haven't answered a basic question—who wants you both dead?"

They fell silent for a moment. Through a cloud of fatigue, Beryl looked at her brother, thinking that he was supposed to be the clever one in the family. If he couldn't figure it out, who could?

"The key to all this," said Jordan, "is François, the dead man." He looked at Daumier. "What else do you know about him? Friends, family?"

"Only a sister," said Daumier. "Living in Paris."

"Have your people spoken to her yet?"

"There is no point to it."

"Why not?"

"She is, how do you say...?" Daumier tapped his forehead. "*Retardataire.* She lives at the Sacred Heart Nursing Home. The nuns say she cannot speak, and she is in very poor health."

"What about his job?" said Richard. "You said he worked as a janitor."

"At Galerie Annika. An art gallery, in Auteuil. It is a reputable establishment. Known for its collection of works by contemporary artists."

"What does the gallery say about him?"

"I spoke only briefly to Annika. She says he was a quiet man, very reliable. She will be in later this morning to answer questions." He glanced at his watch. "In the meantime, I suggest we all try to catch some sleep. For a few hours, at least.''

"What about Jordan?'' asked Beryl. "How do I know he'll be safe here?''

"As I said, he will be kept in a private cell. Strict isolation—''

"That might be a mistake,'' said Richard. "There'd be no witnesses.''

*If anything happens to him...* Beryl shivered.

Jordan nodded. "Wolf's right. I'd feel a whole lot safer sharing a cell with someone.''

"But they could lock you up with another hired killer,'' said Beryl.

"I know just the fellows to share my cell,'' said Jordan. "A pair of harmless enough chaps. I hope.''

Daumier nodded. "I will arrange it.''

It was wrenching to see Jordan marched away. In the doorway, he paused and gave her a farewell wave. That's when Beryl realized she was taking this far harder than he was. But that's old Jordie for you, she mused. Never one to lose his good humor.

Outside, the first streaks of daylight had appeared in the sky, and the sound of traffic had already begun its morning crescendo. Beryl, Richard and Daumier stood on the sidewalk, all of them tottering on the edge of collapse.

"Jordan will be safe,'' said Daumier. "I will see to it.''

"I want him to be more than safe,'' said Beryl. "I want him out of there.''

"For that, we must prove him innocent.''

"Then that's exactly what we'll do,'' she said.

Daumier looked at her with bloodshot eyes. He seemed far older tonight, this kindly Frenchman in whose face the years had etched deep furrows. He said, "What you must do, *chérie,* is stay alert. And out of sight.'' He turned toward his car. "Tonight, we talk again.''

By the time Beryl and Richard had returned to the flat in

Passy, Beryl could feel herself nodding off. The latest jolt of tension had worn off, and her energy was on a fast down-hill slide. Thank God Richard still seemed to be operating on all cylinders, she thought as they climbed out of the car. If she collapsed, he could drag her up those steps.

He practically did. He put his arm around her and walked her through the door, up the hall and into the bedroom. There, he sat her down on the bed.

"Sleep," he said, "as long as you need to."

"A week should about do it," she murmured.

He smiled. And though sleep was blurring her vision, she saw his face clearly enough to register, once again, that flicker of attraction between them. It was always there, ready to leap into full flame. Even now, exhausted as she was, images of desire were weaving into shape in her mind. She remembered how he'd stood, shirtless, in the bedroom doorway, the lamplight gleaming on his shoulders. She thought how easy it would be to invite him into her bed, to ask for a hug, a kiss. And then, much, much more. *Too much bloody chemistry between us,* she pondered. *It addles my brain, keeps me from concentrating on the important issues. I take one look at him, I inhale one whiff of his scent, and all I can think about is pulling him down on top of me.*

Gently he kissed her forehead. "I'll be right next door," he said, and left the room.

Too tired to undress, she lay down fully clothed on the bed. Daylight brightened outside the window, and the sounds of traffic drifted up from the street. If this nightmare was ever over, she thought, she'd have to stay away from him for a while. Just to get her bearings again. Yes, that's what she'd do. She'd hide out at Chetwynd. Wait for that crazy attraction between them to fade.

But as she closed her eyes, the images returned, more vivid and tempting than ever. They pursued her, right into her dreams.

RICHARD SLEPT FIVE HOURS and rose just before noon. A shower, a quick meal of eggs and toast, and he felt the old engines fire up again. There were too few hours in the day, too many matters to attend to; sleep would have to assume a lower priority.

He peeked in on Beryl and saw that she was still asleep. Good. By the time she woke up, he should be back from making his rounds. Just in case he wasn't, though, he left a note on the nightstand. "Gone out. Back around three. R." Then, as an afterthought, he laid the gun beside the note. If she needed it, he figured, it'd be there for her.

After confirming that the two guards were still on duty, he left the flat, locking the door behind him.

His first stop was 66 Rue Myrha, the building where Madeline and Bernard died.

He had gone over the Paris police report again, had read and reread the landlord's statement. M. Rideau claimed he'd discovered the bodies on the afternoon of July 15, 1973, and had at once notified the police. Upon being questioned, he'd told them that the attic was rented to a Mlle Scarlatti, who used the place only infrequently and paid her rent in cash. On occasion, he had heard moans, whimpers, and a man's voice emanating from the flat. But the only person he ever saw face-to-face was Mlle Scarlatti, whose head scarves and sunglasses made it difficult for him to be specific about her appearance. Nevertheless, M. Rideau was certain that the dead woman in the flat was indeed the lusty Scarlatti woman. And the dead man? The landlord had never seen him before.

Three months after this testimony, M. Rideau had sold the building, packed up his family, and left the country.

That last detail had garnered only a footnote in the police report: "Landlord no longer available for statements. Has left France."

Richard had a hunch that the landlord's departure from the country just might be the most important clue they had.

If he could locate Rideau's current whereabouts and question him about those events of twenty years before...

He knocked at each flat in the building, but came up with no leads. Twenty years was a long time; people moved in, moved out. No one remembered any M. Rideau.

Richard went outside and stood for a moment on the sidewalk. A ball hurtled past, pursued by a pack of scruffy kids. The endless soccer match, he mused, watching the tangle of dirty arms and legs.

Over the children's heads, he spotted an elderly woman sitting on her stoop. At least seventy years old, he guessed. Perhaps she'd lived here long enough to know the former residents of this street.

He went over to the woman and spoke to her in French. "Good afternoon."

She smiled a sweet, toothless grin.

"I am trying to find someone who remembers M. Jacques Rideau. The man who used to own that building over there." He pointed to number 66.

Also in French, she answered: "He moved away."

"You knew him, then?"

"His son was all the time visiting in my house."

"I understand the whole family left France."

She nodded. "They went to Greece. And how do you suppose he managed that, eh? Him, with that old car! And the clothes their children wore! But off they go to their villa." She sighed. "And I am here, where I'll always be."

Richard frowned. "Villa?"

"I hear they have a villa, near the sea. Of course, it may not be true—the boy was always making up stories. Why should he start telling the truth? But he claimed it was a villa, with flowers growing up the posts." She laughed. "They must all be dead by now."

"The family?"

"The flowers. They could not even remember to water their pots of geraniums."

"Do you know where in Greece they moved to?"

The woman shrugged. "Somewhere near the sea. But then, isn't all of Greece near the sea?"

"The name of the village?"

"Why should I remember these things? He was not *my* boyfriend."

Frustrated, Richard was about to turn away when he suddenly registered what the woman had just said. "You mean, the landlord's son—he was your daughter's boyfriend?"

"My granddaughter."

"Did he call her? Write her any letters?"

"A few. Then he stopped." She shook her head. "That is how it is with young people. No devotion."

"Did she keep any of those letters?"

The woman laughed. "All of them. To remind her husband what a fine catch he made."

It took a bit of persuasion for Richard to be invited inside the old woman's apartment. It was a dark, cramped flat. Two small children sat at the kitchen table, gnawing fistfuls of bread. Another woman—most likely in her mid-thirties, but with much older eyes—sat spooning cereal into an infant's mouth.

"He wants to see your letters from Gerard," said the grandmother.

The younger woman eyed Richard with suspicion.

"It's important I speak with his father," explained Richard.

"His father doesn't want to be found," she said, and resumed feeding the baby.

"Why not?"

"How should I know? Gerard didn't tell me."

"Does it have to do with the murders? The two English people?"

She paused, the spoon halfway to the baby's mouth. "You are English?"

"No, American." He sat down across from her. "Do you remember the murders?"

"It was a long time ago." She wiped the baby's face. "I was only fifteen."

"Gerard wrote you letters, then stopped. Why?"

The woman gave a bitter laugh. "He lost interest. Men always do."

"Or something could have happened to him. Maybe he couldn't write to you. And he wanted to, very much."

Again, she paused.

"If I go to Greece, I can inquire on your behalf. I only need to know the name of the village."

She sat for a moment, thinking. Wiping up the baby's mess. She looked at her two children, both of them runny nosed and whining. *She's longing to escape,* he imagined. *Wishing her life had turned out some other way. Any other way. And she's thinking about this long-lost boyfriend, and how things might have been, for the two of them, in a villa by the sea....*

She stood up and went into another room. A moment later, she returned and laid a thin bundle of letters down on the table.

There were only four—not exactly a record of devotion. All were still tucked in their envelopes. Richard skimmed their contents, noting an outpouring of adolescent yearnings. "I will come back for you. I will love you always. Do not forget me...." By the fourth letter, the passion was clearly cooling.

There was no return address, either on the letters or on the envelopes. The family's whereabouts were obviously meant to be kept secret. But on one of the envelopes, a postmark was clearly printed: Paros, Greece.

Richard handed the letters back to the woman. She cradled them for a moment, as though savoring the memories. *So many years ago, a lifetime ago, and see what has become of me....*

"If you find Gerard...if he is still alive," she said, "ask him..."

"Yes?" Richard said gently.

She sighed. "Ask him if he remembers me."

"I will."

She held the letters a moment longer. And then, with a sigh, she laid them aside and picked up the spoon. In silence, she began to feed the baby.

HE MADE ONE MORE STOP before returning to the flat, this time at the Sacred Heart Nursing Home.

It was a far grimmer institution than the one Richard had visited the day before. No private rooms here, no sweet-faced nuns gliding down the halls. This was one step above a prison, and a crowded one at that, with three or four patients to a room, many of them restrained in their beds. Julee Parmentier, François's retarded sister, occupied one of the grimmest rooms of all. Barely clothed, she lay on top of a plastic-lined mattress. Protective mitts covered her hands; around her waist was a wide belt, its ends secured to the bed with just enough slack for her to shift from side to side, but not sit up. She barely seemed to register Richard's presence; instead she moaned and stared relentlessly at the ceiling.

"She has been like this for many years," said the nurse. "An accident, when she was twelve. She fell from a tree and hit her head on some stones."

"She can't speak at all? Can't communicate?"

"When her brother François would visit, he said she would smile. He insisted he saw it. But..." The nurse shrugged. "I saw nothing."

"Did he visit often?"

"Every day. The same time, nine o'clock in the morning. He would stay until lunch, then he would go to his work at the gallery."

"He did this every day?"

"Yes. And on Sunday he would stay later—until four o'clock."

Richard gazed at the woman in the bed and tried to imagine what it must have been like for François to sit for hours in this room with its noise and its smells. To devote every free hour of his life to a sister who could not even recognize his face.

"It is a tragedy," said the nurse. "He was a good man, François."

They left the room and walked away from the sight of that pitiful creature lying on her plastic sheet.

"What will happen to her now?" asked Richard. "Will someone see that she's cared for?"

"It hardly matters now."

"Why do you say that?"

"Her kidneys are failing." The nurse glanced up the hall, toward Julee Parmentier's room, and shook her head sadly. "Another month, two months, and she will be dead."

"BUT YOU MUST KNOW where he went," insisted Beryl.

The French agent merely shrugged. "He did not say, *Mademoiselle*. He only instructed me to watch over the flat. And see that you came to no harm."

"And that's all he said? And then he drove off?"

The man nodded.

In frustration, Beryl turned and went back into the flat, where she reread Richard's note: "Gone out. Back around three." No explanations, no apologies. She crumpled it up and threw it at the rubbish can. And what was she supposed to do now? Wait around all day for him to return? What about Jordan? What about the investigation?

What about lunch?

Her hunger pangs could no longer be ignored. She went to the kitchen and opened the refrigerator. She stared in dismay at the contents: a carton of eggs, a loaf of bread and a shriveled sausage. No fruit, no vegetables, not even a puny carrot. Stocked, no doubt, by a man.

*I'm not going to eat that,* she determined, closing the refrigerator door. *But I'm not going to starve, either. I'm going to have a proper meal—with or without him.*

Daumier's men had delivered her belongings to the flat the night before. From the closet, she chose her most nondescript black dress, pinned up her hair under a wide-brimmed hat, and slid on a pair of dark glasses. *Not too hideous,* she decided, glancing at herself in the mirror.

She walked out of the flat into the sunshine.

The guard stationed at the front door confronted her at once. "*Mademoiselle,* you are not allowed to leave."

"But you let *him* leave," she countered.

"Mr. Wolf specifically instructed—"

"I'm hungry," she said. "I get quite cranky when I'm hungry. And I'm not about to live on eggs and toast. So if you can just direct me to the nearest Métro station…"

"You are going *alone?*" he asked in horror.

"Unless you'd care to escort me."

The man glanced uneasily up and down the street. "I have no instructions in this matter."

"Then I'll go alone," she said, and breezily started to walk away.

"Come back!"

She kept walking.

"*Mademoiselle!*" he called. "I will get the car!"

She turned and flashed him her most brilliant smile. "My treat."

Both guards accompanied her to a restaurant in the nearby neighborhood of Auteuil. She suspected they chose the place not for the quality of its food, but for the intimate dining room and the easily surveyed front entrance. The meal itself was just a shade above mediocre: bland vichyssoise and a cut of lamb that could have doubled for leather. But Beryl was hungry enough to savor every morsel and still have an appetite for the *tarte aux pommes.*

By the time the meal was over, her two companions were in a much more jovial mood. Perhaps this bodyguard business was not such a bad thing, if the lady was willing to spring for a meal every day. They even relented when Beryl asked them to make a stop on the drive back to the flat. It would only take a minute, she said, to look over the latest art exhibit. After all, she might find something to strike her fancy.

And so the men accompanied her to Galerie Annika.

The exhibit area was one vast, soaring gallery—three stories, connected by open walkways and spiral staircases. Sunlight shone down through a skylit dome, illuminating a collection of bronze sculptures displayed on the first floor.

A young woman, her spiky hair a startling shade of red, came forward to greet them. Was there something in particular *Mademoiselle* wished to see?

"May I just look around a bit?" asked Beryl. "Or perhaps you could direct me to some paintings. Nothing too modern—I prefer classical artists."

"But of course," said the woman, and guided Beryl and her escorts up the spiral stairs.

Most of what she saw hanging on the walls was hideous. Landscapes populated by deformed animals. Birds with dog heads. City scenes with starkly cubist buildings. The young woman stopped at one painting and said, "Perhaps this is to your liking?"

Beryl took one look at the nude huntress holding aloft a dead rabbit and said, "I don't think so." She moved on, taking in the eccentric collection of paintings, fabric hangings and clay masks. "Who chooses the work to be displayed here?" she asked.

"Annika does. The gallery owner."

Beryl stopped at a particularly grotesque mask—a man with a forked tongue. "She has a...unique eye for art."

"Quite daring, don't you think? She prefers artists who take risks."

"Is she here today? I'd very much like to meet her."

"Not at the moment." The woman shook her head sadly. "One of our employees died last night, you see. Annika had to speak to the police."

"I'm sorry to hear that."

"Our janitor." The woman sighed. "It was quite unexpected."

They returned to the first-floor gallery. Only then did Beryl spot a work she'd consider purchasing. It was one of the bronze sculptures, a variation on the Madonna-and-child theme. But as she moved closer to inspect it, she realized it wasn't a human infant nursing at the woman's breast. It was a jackal.

"Quite intriguing, don't you think?"

Beryl shuddered and looked at her spiky-haired guide. "What brilliant mind dreamed *this* one up?"

"A new artist. A young man, just building his reputation here in Paris. We are hosting a reception in his honor tonight. Perhaps you will attend?"

"If I can."

The woman reached into a basket and plucked out an elegantly embossed invitation. This she handed to Beryl. "If you are free tonight, please drop in."

Beryl was about to slip the card carelessly into her purse when she suddenly focused on the artist's name. A name she recognized.

*Galerie Annika presente:*
*Les sculptures de* Anthony Sutherland
*17 juillet 7–9 du soir.*

# CHAPTER NINE

"THIS IS CRAZY," said Richard. "An unacceptable risk."

To his annoyance, Beryl simply waltzed over to the closet and stood surveying her wardrobe. "What do you think would be appropriate tonight? Formal or semi?"

"You'll be out in the open," said Richard. "An art reception! I can't think of a more public place."

Beryl took out a black silk sheath, turned to the mirror, and calmly held the dress to her body. "A public place is the safest place to be," she observed.

"You were supposed to stay here! Instead you go running around town—"

"So did you."

"I had business...."

She turned and walked into the bedroom. "I did, too," she called back cheerfully.

He started to follow her, but halted in the doorway when he saw that she was undressing. At once he turned around and stood with his back pressed against the doorjamb. "A craving for a three-star meal doesn't constitute necessity!" he snapped over his shoulder.

"It wasn't a three-star meal. It wasn't even a half star. But it was better than eggs and moldy bread."

"You're like some finicky kitten, you know that? You'd rather starve than deign to eat canned food like every other cat."

"You're quite right. I'm a spoiled Persian and I want my cream and chicken livers."

"I would've brought you back a meal. Catnip included."

"You weren't here."

And that was his mistake, he realized. He couldn't leave this woman alone for a second. She was too damn unpredictable.

No, actually she *was* predictable. She'd do whatever he *didn't* want her to do.

And what he didn't want her to do was leave the flat tonight.

But he could already hear her stepping into the black dress, could hear the whisper of silk sliding over stockings, the hiss of the zipper closing over her back. He fought to suppress the images those sounds brought to mind—the long legs, the curve of her hips... He found himself clenching his jaw in frustration, at her, at himself, at the way events and passions were spinning out of his control.

"Do me up, will you?" she asked.

He turned and saw that she'd moved right beside him. Her back was turned and the nape of her neck was practically within kissing distance.

"The hook," she said, tossing her hair over one shoulder. He inhaled the flowery scent of shampoo. "I can't seem to fasten it."

He attached the hook and eye and found his gaze lingering on her bare shoulders. "Where did you get that dress?" he asked.

"I brought it from Chetwynd." She breezed over to the dresser and began to slip on earrings. The silk sheath seemed to mold itself to every luscious curve of her body. "Why do you ask?"

"It's Madeline's dress. Isn't it?"

She turned to look at him. "Yes, it is," she said quietly. "Does that bother you?"

"It's just—" he let out a breath "—it's a perfect fit. Curve for curve."

"And you think you're seeing a ghost."

"I remember that dress. I saw her wear it at an embassy reception." He paused. "God, it's really eerie, how that dress seems made for you."

Slowly she moved toward him, her gaze never wavering from his face. "I'm not her, Richard."

"I know."

"No matter how much you may want her back—"

"Her?" He took her wrists and pulled her close to him. "When I look at you, I see only Beryl. Of course, I notice the resemblance. The hair, the eyes. But *you're* the one I'm looking at. The one I want." He bent toward her and gently grazed her lips with a kiss. "That's why I want you to stay here tonight."

"Your prisoner?" she murmured.

"If need be." He kissed her again and heard an answering purr of contentment from her throat. She tilted her head back, and his lips slid to her neck, so smooth, so deliciously perfumed.

"Then you'll have to tie me up..." she whispered.

"Whatever you want."

"...because there's no other way you're going to keep me here tonight." With a maddening laugh, she wriggled free and walked into the bathroom.

Richard suppressed a groan of frustration. From the doorway, he watched as she pinned up her hair. "Exactly what do you expect to get out of this event, anyway?" he demanded.

"One never knows. That's the joy of intelligence gathering, isn't it? Keep your ears and eyes open and see what turns up. I think we've learned quite a lot already about François. We know he has a sister who's ill. Which means François needed money. Working as a janitor in an art gallery couldn't possibly pay for all the care she needed. Perhaps he was desperate, willing to do anything for money. Even work as a hired assassin."

"Your logic is unassailable."

"Thank you."

"But your plan of action is insane. You don't need to take this risk—"

"But I do." She turned to him, her hair now regally swept into a chignon. "Someone wants me and Jordan dead. And there I'll be tonight. A perfectly convenient target."

*What a magnificent creature she is,* he thought. *It's that unbeatable bloodline, those Bernard and Madeline genes. She thinks she's invincible.*

"That's the plan, is it?" he said. "Tempt the killer into making a move?"

"If that's what it takes to save Jordan."

"And what's to stop the killer from carrying it out?"

"My two bodyguards. And you."

"I'm not infallible, Beryl."

"You're close enough."

"I could make a mistake. Let my attention slip."

"I trust you."

"But I don't trust myself!" Agitated, he began to pace the bedroom floor. "I've been out of the business for years. I'm out of practice, out of condition. I'm forty-two, Beryl, and my reflexes aren't what they used to be."

"Last night they seemed quick enough to me."

"Walk out that door, Beryl, and I can't guarantee your safety."

She came toward him, looking him coolly in the eye. "The fact is, Richard, you can't guarantee my safety anywhere. In here, out on the streets, at an artist's reception. Wherever I am, there's a chance things could go wrong. If I stay in this flat, if I stare at these walls any longer, thinking of all the things that could happen, I'll go insane. It's better to be out *there.* Doing something. Jordan isn't able to, so I have to be the one."

"The one to set yourself up as bait?"

"Our only lead is a dead man—François. Someone hired

him, Richard. Someone who may have connections to Galerie Annika.''

For a moment Richard stood gazing at her, thinking, *She's right, of course. It's the same conclusion I came to. She's clever enough to know exactly what needs to be done. And reckless enough to do it.*

He went to the nightstand and picked up the Glock. A pound and a half of steel and plastic, that's all he had to protect her with. It felt flimsy, insubstantial, against all the dangers lurking beyond the front door.

''You're coming with me?'' she said.

He turned and looked at her. ''You think I'd let you go alone?''

She smiled, so full of confidence it frightened him. It was Madeline's old smile. Madeline, who'd been every bit as confident.

He slid the Glock into his shoulder holster. ''I'll be right beside you, Beryl,'' he said. ''Every step of the way.''

ANTHONY SUTHERLAND STOOD posing like a little emperor beside his bronze cast of the Madonna with jackal. He was wearing a pirate shirt of purple silk, black leather pants and snakeskin boots, and he seemed not in the least bit fazed by all the photographers' flashbulbs that kept popping around him. The art critics were in vapors over the show. ''Frightening.'' ''Disturbing.'' ''Images that twist convention.'' These were some of the comments Beryl overheard being murmured as she wandered through the gallery.

She and Richard stopped to look at another of Anthony's bronzes. At first glance, it had looked like two nude figures entwined in a loving embrace. Closer inspection, however, revealed it to be a man and woman in the process of devouring each other alive.

''Do you suppose that's an allegory for marriage?'' said a familiar voice. It was Reggie Vane, balancing a glass of champagne in one hand and two dainty plates of canapés in the other.

He bent forward and gave Beryl an affectionate kiss on the cheek. "You're absolutely stunning tonight, dear. Your mother would be proud of you."

"Reggie, I had no idea you were interested in modern art," said Beryl.

"I'm not. Helena dragged me here." In disgust, he glanced around at the crowd. "Lord, I hate these things. But the St. Pierres were coming, and of course Marie always insists Helena show up as well, just to keep her company." He set his empty champagne glass on top of the bronze couple and laughed at the whimsical effect. "An improvement, wouldn't you say? As long as these two are going to eat each other, they might as well have some bubbly to wash each other down."

An elegantly attired woman swooped in and snatched away the glass. "Please, be more respectful of the work, Mr. Vane," she scolded.

"Oh, I wasn't being disrespectful, Annika," said Reggie. "I just thought it needed a touch of humor."

"It is absolutely perfect as it is." Annika gave the bronze heads a swipe of her napkin and stood back to admire the interwoven figures. "Whimsy would ruin its message."

"What message is that?" asked Richard.

The woman turned to look at him, and her head of boyishly cropped hair suddenly tilted up with interest. "The message," she said, gazing intently at Richard, "is that monogamy is a destructive institution."

"That's marriage, all right," grunted Reggie.

"But free love," the woman continued, "love that has no constraints and is open to all pleasures—that is a positive force."

"Is that Anthony's interpretation of this piece?" asked Beryl.

"It's how *I* interpret it." Annika shifted her gaze to Beryl. "You are a friend of Anthony's?"

"An acquaintance. I know his mother, Nina."

"Where is Nina, by the way?" asked Reggie. "You'd think she'd be front-and-center stage for *darling* Anthony's night of *glory*."

Beryl had to laugh at Reggie's imitation of Nina. Yes, when Queen Nina wanted an audience, all she had to do was throw one of these stylish bashes, and an audience would invariably turn up. Even poor Marie St. Pierre, just out of the hospital, had put in an appearance. Marie stood off in a corner with Helena Vane, the two women huddled together like sparrows in a gathering of peacocks. It was easy to see why they'd be such close friends; both of them were painfully plain, neither one was happily married. That their marriages were not happy was only too clear tonight. The Vanes were avoiding each other, Helena off in her corner darting irritated looks, Reggie standing as far away as possible. And as for Marie St. Pierre—her husband wasn't even in the room at the moment.

"So this is in praise of free love, is it?" said Reggie, eyeing the bronze with new appreciation.

"That is how I see it," said Annika. "How a man and a woman should love."

"I quite agree," said Reggie with a sudden burst of enthusiasm. "Banish marriage entirely."

The woman looked provocatively at Richard. "What do you think, Mr....?"

"Wolf," said Richard. "I'm afraid I don't agree." He took Beryl's arm. "Excuse us, will you? We still have to see the rest of the collection."

As he led Beryl away toward the spiral staircase, she whispered, "There's nothing to see upstairs."

"I want to check out the upper floors."

"Anthony's work is all on the first floor."

"I saw Nina slink up the stairs a few minutes ago. I want to see what she's up to."

They climbed the stairs to the second-floor gallery. From the open walkway, they paused to look over the railing at the crowd on the first floor. It was a flashy gathering, a sea of well-coiffed heads and multicolored silks. Annika had moved into the limelight with Anthony, and as a new round of flashbulbs went off, they embraced and kissed to the sound of applause.

"Ah, free love," sighed Beryl. "She obviously has samples to pass around."

"So I can see."

Beryl gave him a sly smile. "Poor Richard. On duty tonight and can't indulge."

"*Afraid* to indulge. She'd eat me up alive. Like that bronze statue."

"Aren't you tempted? Just a little?"

He looked at her with amusement. "You're baiting me, Beryl."

"Am I?"

"Yes, you are. I know exactly what you're up to. Putting me to the test. Making me prove I'm not like your friend the surgeon. Who, as you implied, also believed in free love."

Beryl's smile faded. "Is that what I'm doing?" she asked softly.

"You have a right to." He gave her hand a squeeze and glanced down again at the crowd. *He's always alert, always watching out for me,* she thought. *I'd trust him with my life. But my heart? I still don't know....*

In the downstairs gallery, a pair of musicians began to play. As the sweet sounds of flute and guitar floated through the building, Beryl suddenly sensed a pair of eyes watching her. She looked down at the cluster of bronze statues and spotted Anthony Sutherland, standing by his Madonna with jackal. He was gazing right at her. And the expression in his eyes was one of cold calculation.

Instinctively she shrank away from the railing.

"What is it?" asked Richard.

"Anthony. It's the way he looks at me."

But by then Anthony had already turned away and was shaking Reggie Vane's hand. An odd young man, thought Beryl. What sort of mind dreams up these nightmarish visions? Women nursing jackals. Couples devouring each other. Had it been so difficult, growing up as Nina Sutherland's son?

She and Richard wandered through the second-floor gallery, but found no sign of Nina.

"Why are you so interested in finding her?" asked Beryl.

"It's not her so much as the way she went up those stairs. Obviously trying not to be noticed."

"And you noticed her."

"It was the dress. Those trademark bugle beads of hers."

They finished their circuit of the second floor and headed up the staircase to the third. Again, no sign of Nina. But as they moved along the walkway, the musicians in the first-floor gallery suddenly ceased playing. In the abrupt silence that followed, Beryl heard Nina's voice—a few loud syllables—just before it dropped to a whisper. Another voice answered—a man's, speaking softly in reply.

The voices came from an alcove, just ahead.

"It's not as if I haven't been patient," said Nina. "Not as if I haven't *tried* to be understanding."

"I know. I know—"

"Do you know what it's been *like* for me? For Anthony? Have you any *idea?* All those years, waiting for you to make up your mind."

"I never let you want for anything."

"Oh, how *fortunate* for us! My goodness, how generous of you!"

"The boy has had the best—everything he's ever wanted. Now he's twenty-one. My responsibility ends."

"Your responsibility," said Nina, "has only just *begun*."

Richard yanked Beryl around the corner just as Nina emerged from the alcove. She stormed right past them, too angry to notice her audience. They could hear her high heels tapping down the staircase to the lower galleries.

A moment later, a second figure emerged from the alcove, moving like an old man.

It was Philippe St. Pierre.

He went over to the railing and stared down at the crowd in the gallery below. He seemed to be considering the temptation of that two-story drop. Then, sighing deeply, he walked away and followed Nina down the stairs.

Down in the first-floor gallery, the crowd was starting to thin out. Anthony had already left; so had the Vanes. But Marie St. Pierre was still standing in her corner, the abandoned wife waiting to be reclaimed. A full room's length away stood her husband Philippe, nursing a glass of champagne. And standing between them was that macabre sculpture, the bronze man and woman devouring each other alive.

Beryl thought that perhaps Anthony had hit upon the truth with his art. That if people weren't careful, love would consume them, destroy them. As it had destroyed Marie.

The image of Marie St. Pierre, standing alone and forlorn in the corner, stayed with Beryl all the way back to the flat. She thought how hard it must be to play the politician's wife—forever poised and pleasant, always supportive, never the shrew. And all the time knowing that your husband was in love with another woman.

"She must have known about it. For years," said Beryl softly.

Richard kept his gaze on the road as he navigated the streets back to Passy. "Who?" he asked.

"Marie St. Pierre. She must have known about her husband and Nina. Every time she looks at young Anthony, she'd see the resemblance. And how it must hurt her. Yet all these years, she's put up with him.''

"And with Nina," said Richard.

Beryl sat back, puzzled. *Yes, she does put up with Nina. And that's the part I don't understand. How she can be so civil, so gracious, to her husband's mistress. To her husband's bastard son....*

"You think Philippe is Anthony's father?"

"That's what Nina meant, of course. All that talk about Philippe's responsibilities. She meant Anthony." She paused. "Art school must be very expensive."

"And Philippe must've paid a pretty bundle over the years, supporting the boy. Not to mention Nina, whose tastes are extravagant, to say the least. Her widow's pension couldn't have been enough to—"

"What is it?" asked Beryl.

"I just had a flash of insight about her husband, Stephen Sutherland. He committed suicide a month after your parents died—jumped off a bridge."

"Yes, you told me that."

"All these years, I've thought his death was related to the Delphi case. I suspected he was the mole, that he killed himself when he thought he was about to be discovered. But what if his reasons for jumping off that bridge were entirely personal?"

"His marriage."

"And young Anthony. The boy he discovered wasn't his son at all."

"But if Stephen Sutherland wasn't Delphi..."

"Then we're back to a person or persons unknown."

*Persons unknown.* Meaning someone who could still be alive. And afraid of discovery.

Instinctively she glanced over her shoulder, checking to see if they were being followed. Just behind them was the Peugeot with the two French agents; beyond that she saw only a stream of anonymous headlights. Richard was right, she thought. She should have stayed in the flat. She should have kept her head low, her face out of sight. Anyone could have spotted her this afternoon. Or they could be following her right this moment, could be watching her from somewhere in that sea of headlights.

Suddenly she longed to be back in the flat, safely surrounded by four walls. It began to seem endless, this drive to Passy, a journey through a darkness full of perils.

When at last they pulled up in front of the building, she was so anxious to get inside that she quickly started to climb out of the car. Richard pulled her back in.

"Don't get out yet," he said. "Let the men check it first."

"You don't really think—"

"It's a precaution. Standard operating procedure."

Beryl watched the two French agents climb the steps and unlock the front door. While one man stood watch on the steps, the other vanished inside.

"But how could anyone find out about the flat?" she asked.

"Payoffs. Leaks."

"You don't think Claude Daumier—"

"I'm not trying to scare you, Beryl. I just believe in being careful."

She watched as the lights came on inside the flat. First the living room, then the bedroom. At last, the man on the steps gave them the all-clear signal.

"Okay, it must be clean," said Richard, climbing out of the car. "Let's go."

Beryl stepped out onto the curb. She turned toward the building and took one step up the sidewalk—

—and was slammed backward against the car as an explosion rocked the earth. Shattered glass flew from the building and rained onto the street. Seconds later, the sky lit up with the hellish glow of flames shooting through the broken windows. Beryl sank to the ground, her ears still ringing from the blast. She stared numbly as tongues of flame slashed the darkness.

She couldn't hear Richard's shouts, didn't realize he was crouched right beside her until she felt his hands on her face. "Are you all right?" he cried. "Beryl, look at me!"

Weakly she nodded. Then her gaze traveled to the front walkway, to the body of the French agent lying sprawled near the steps.

"Stay put!" yelled Richard as he pivoted away from her. He dashed over to the fallen man and knelt beside him just long enough to feel for a pulse. At once he was back at Beryl's side. "Get in the car," he said.

"But what about the men?"

"That one's dead. The other one didn't stand a chance."

"You don't know that!"

"Just get in the car!" ordered Richard. He opened the door and practically shoved her inside. Then he scrambled around to the driver's side and slid behind the wheel.

"We can't just leave them there!" cried Beryl.

"We'll have to." He started the engine and sent the car screeching away from the curb.

Beryl watched as a succession of streets blurred past. Richard drove like a madman, but she was too stunned to feel afraid, too bewildered to focus on anything but the river of red taillights stretching ahead of them.

"Jordan," she whispered. "What about Jordan?"

"Right now I have to think about you."

"They found the flat. They can get to him!"

"I'll take care of it later. First we get you to a safe place."

"Where?"

He swerved across two lanes and shot onto an off ramp. "I'll come up with one. Somewhere."

*Somewhere.* She stared out at the night glow of Paris. A sprawling city, an ocean of light. A million different places to hide.

To die.

She shivered and shrank deep into the seat. "And then what?" she whispered. "What happens next?"

He looked at her. "We get out of Paris. Out of the country."

"You mean—go home?"

"No. It won't be safe in England, either." He turned his gaze back to the road. The car seemed to leap through the darkness. "We're going to Greece."

DAUMIER ANSWERED the phone on the second ring. *"Allo?"*

A familiar voice growled at him from the receiver. *"What the hell is going on?"*

"Richard?" said Daumier. "Where are you?"

"A safe place. You'll understand if I don't reveal it to you."

"And Beryl?"

"She's unhurt. Though I can't say the same for your two men. Who knew about the flat, Claude?"

"Only my people."

"Who else?"

"I told no one else. It should have been a safe enough place."

"Apparently you were wrong. Someone found out."

"You were both out of the flat earlier today. One of you could have been followed."

"It wasn't me."

"Beryl, then. You should not have allowed her out of the building. She could've been spotted at Galerie Annika this afternoon and followed back to the flat."

"My mistake. You're right, I shouldn't have left her alone. I can't afford to make any more mistakes."

Daumier sighed. "You and I, Richard, we have known each other too long. This is not the time to stop trusting each other."

There was a brief silence on the other end. Then Richard

said, "I'm sorry, but I have no choice, Claude. We're going under."

"Then I will not be able to help you."

"We'll go it alone. Without your help."

"Wait, Richard—"

But the line had already gone dead. Daumier stared at the receiver, then slowly laid it back in the cradle. There was no point in trying to trace the call; Richard would have used a pay phone—and it would be in a different neighborhood from where he'd be staying. The man was once a professional; he knew the tricks of the trade.

Maybe—just maybe—it would keep them both alive.

"Good luck, my friend," murmured Daumier. "I am afraid you will need it."

RICHARD RISKED one more call from the pay phone, this one to Washington, D.C.

His business partner answered with his usual charmless growl. "Sakaroff here."

"Niki, it's me."

"Richard? How is beautiful Paris? Having a good time?"

"A lousy time. Look, I can't talk long. I'm in trouble."

Niki sighed. "Why am I not surprised?"

"It's the old Delphi case. You remember? Paris, '73. The NATO mole."

"Ah, yes."

"Delphi's come back to life. I need your help to identify him."

"I was KGB, Richard. Not Stasi."

"But you had connections to the East Germans."

"Not directly. I had little contact with Stasi agents. The East Germans, you know...they preferred to operate independently."

"Then who would know about Delphi? There must be some old contact you can pump for information."

There was a pause. "Perhaps..."

"Yes?"

"Heinrich Leitner," said Sakaroff. "He is the one who could tell you. He oversaw Stasi's Paris operations. Not a field man—he never left East Berlin. But he would be familiar with Delphi's work."

"Okay, he's the man I'll talk to. So how do I get to him?"

"That is the difficult part. He is in Berlin—"

"No problem. We'll go there."

"—in a high-security prison."

Richard groaned. "That *is* a problem." In frustration, he turned and stared through the phone-booth door at the subway platform. "I've got to get in to see him, Niki."

"You'll need approval. That will take days. Papers, signatures..."

"Then that's what I'll have to get. If you could make a few calls, speed things up."

"No guarantees."

"Understood. Oh, and one more thing," said Richard. "We've been trying to get ahold of Hugh Tavistock. It seems he's vanished. Have you heard anything about it?"

"No. But I will check my sources. Anything else?"

"I'll let you know."

Sakaroff grunted. "I was afraid you would say that."

Richard hung up. Stepping away from the pay phone, he glanced around at the subway platform. He saw nothing suspicious, only the usual stream of nighttime commuters—couples holding hands, students with backpacks.

The train for Creteil-Préfecture rolled into the station. Richard stepped onto it, rode it for three stops, then got off. He lingered on the next platform for a few minutes, surveying the faces. No one looked familiar. Satisfied that he hadn't been followed, he boarded the Bobigny-Picasso train and rode it to Gare de l'Est. There he stepped off, walked out of the station, and headed briskly back to the *pension*.

He found Beryl still awake and sitting in an armchair by

# An Important Message from the Editors

Dear Reader,

Because you've chosen to read one of our fine romance novels, we'd like to say "thank you!" And, as a **special** way to thank you, we've selected <u>two more</u> of the books you love so well **plus** an exciting Mystery Gift to send you — absolutely <u>FREE!</u>

Please enjoy them with our compliments...

*Pam Powers*

Lift here

# *How to validate your Editor's*
## "Thank You"
# FREE GIFT

1. Peel off gift seal from front cover. Place it in space provided at right. This automatically entitles you to receive 2 FREE BOOKS and a fabulous mystery gift.

2. Send back this card and you'll get 2 brand-new *Romance* novels. These books have a cover price of $5.99 or more each in the U.S. and $6.99 or more each in Canada, but they are yours to keep absolutely free.

3. There's no catch. You're under no obligation to buy anything. We charge nothing—ZERO—for your first shipment. And you don't have to make any minimum number of purchases— not even one!

4. The fact is, thousands of readers enjoy receiving their books by mail from The Reader Service. They enjoy the convenience of home delivery...they like getting the best new novels at discount prices BEFORE they're available in stores... and they love their Heart to Heart subscriber newsletter featuring author news, horoscopes, recipes, book reviews and much more!

5. We hope that after receiving your free books you'll want to remain a subscriber. But the choice is yours— to continue or cancel, any time at all! So why not take us up on our invitation, with no risk of any kind. You'll be glad you did!

GET A *Free* MYSTERY GIFT...

SURPRISE MYSTERY GIFT COULD BE YOURS **FREE** AS A SPECIAL "THANK YOU" FROM THE EDITORS

*The Editor's "Thank You" Free Gifts Include:*

- ● *Two BRAND-NEW Romance novels!*
- ● *An exciting mystery gift!*

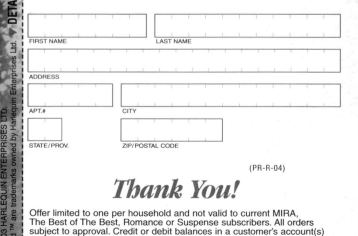

**DETACH AND MAIL CARD TODAY!** ▼

# Yes! I have placed my
Editor's "Thank You" seal in the
space provided above. Please
send me 2 free books and a
fabulous mystery gift. I
understand I am under no
obligation to purchase any
books, as explained on the
back and on the opposite page.

PLACE
FREE GIFT
SEAL
HERE

### 393 MDL DVFG          193 MDL DVFF

| | |
|---|---|
| FIRST NAME | LAST NAME |

ADDRESS

| | |
|---|---|
| APT.# | CITY |

| | |
|---|---|
| STATE/PROV. | ZIP/POSTAL CODE |

(PR-R-04)

## Thank You!

## The Reader Service — Here's How It Works:

Accepting your 2 free books and gift places you under no obligation to buy anything. You may keep the books and gift and return the shipping statement marked "cancel." If you do not cancel, about a month later we'll send you 3 additional books and bill you just $4.74 each in the U.S., or $5.24 each in Canada, plus 25¢ shipping & handling per book and applicable taxes if any.* That's the complete price and — compared to cover prices starting from $5.99 each in the U.S. and $6.99 each in Canada — it's quite a bargain! You may cancel at any time, but if you choose to continue, every month we'll send you 3 more books, which you may either purchase at the discount price or return to us and cancel your subscription.

*Terms and prices subject to change without notice. Sales tax applicable in N.Y. Canadian residents will be charged applicable provincial taxes and GST.

the window. She'd turned off all the lights, and in the darkness she was little more than a silhouette against the glow of the night sky. He shut and bolted the door. "Beryl?" he said. "Everything all right?"

He thought he saw her nod. Or was it just the quivering of her chin as she took a breath and let out a soft, slow sigh?

"We'll be safe here," he said. "For tonight, at least."

"And tomorrow?" came the murmured question.

"We'll worry about that when the time comes."

She leaned back against the chair cushions and stared straight ahead. "Is this how it was for you, Richard? Working for Intelligence? Living day to day, not daring to think about tomorrows?"

He moved slowly to her chair. "Sometimes it was like this. Sometimes I wasn't sure there'd be a tomorrow for me."

"Do you miss that life?" She looked at him. He couldn't see her face, but he felt her watching him.

"I left that life behind."

"But do you miss it? The excitement? That lovely promise of violence?"

"Beryl. Beryl, please." He reached for her hand; it was like a lump of ice in his grasp.

"Didn't you enjoy it, just a little?"

"No." He paused. Then softly he said, "Yes. For a short time. When I was very young. Before it turned all too real."

"The way it did tonight. Tonight, it was real for me. When I saw that man lying there…" She swallowed. "This afternoon, you see, we had lunch together, the three of us. They had the veal. And a bottle of wine, and ice cream. And I got them to laugh…." She looked away.

"It seems like a game, at first," said Richard. "A make-believe war. But then you realize that the bullets are real. So are the people." He held her hand in his and wished he could warm it, warm her. "That's what happened to me. All of a sudden, it got too real. And there was a woman...."

She sat very still, waiting, listening. "Someone you loved?" she asked softly.

"No, not someone I loved. But someone I liked, very much. It was in Berlin, before the Wall came down. We were trying to bring over a defector to the West. And my partner, she got trapped on the wrong side. The guard spotted her. Fired." He lifted Beryl's hand to his lips and kissed it, held it.

"She...didn't make it?"

He shook his head. "And it wasn't a game of make-believe any longer. I could see her body lying in the no-man's-zone. And I couldn't reach her. So I had to leave her there, for the other side...." He released her hand. He moved to the window and looked out at the lights twinkling over Paris. "That's when I left the business. I didn't want another death on my conscience. I didn't want to feel...responsible." He turned to her. In the faint glow from the city, her face looked pale, almost luminous. "That's what makes this so hard for me, Beryl. Knowing what could happen if I make a mistake. Knowing that your life depends on what I do next."

For a long time, Beryl sat very still, watching him. Feeling his gaze through the darkness. That spark of attraction crackled like fire between them as it always did. But tonight there was something more, something that went beyond desire.

She rose from the chair. Though he didn't move, she could feel the fever of his gaze as she glided toward him, could hear the sharp intake of his breath as she reached up and touched his beard-roughened face. "Richard," she whispered, "I want you."

At once she was swept into his arms. No other embrace, no other kiss, had ever stolen her breath the way this one did. *We are like that couple in bronze,* she thought. *Starved for each other. Devouring each other.*

But this was a feast of love, not destruction.

She whimpered and her head fell back as his mouth slid to her throat. She could feel every stroke of his hands through the silky fabric of her dress. Oh Lord, if he could do this to her with her clothes on, what lovely torment would he unleash on her naked flesh? Already her breasts were tingling under his touch, her nipples turned to tight buds.

He unzipped her dress and slowly eased it off her shoulders.

It hissed past her hips and slid into a silken ripple on the floor. He, too, traced the length of her torso, his lips moving slowly down her throat, her breasts, her belly. Shuddering with pleasure, she gripped his hair and moaned, "No fair..."

"All's fair," he murmured, easing her stockings down her thighs. "In love and war...."

By the time he had her fully undressed, by the time he'd shed his own clothes, she was beyond words, beyond protest. She'd lost all sense of time and space; there was only the darkness, and the warmth of his touch, and the hunger shuddering deep inside her. She scarcely realized how they found their way to the bed. Eagerly she sank backward onto the mattress, and heard the squeak of the springs, the quickening duet of their breathing. Then she pulled him down against her, drew him onto and into her.

*Starved for each other,* she thought as he captured her mouth under his, invaded it, explored it. *Devouring each other.*

And like two who were famished, they feasted.

He reached for her hands, and their fingers entwined in a tighter and tighter knot as their bodies joined, thrusted, exulted. Even as her last shudders of desire faded away, he was still gripping her hands.

Slowly he released them and cradled her face instead. He pressed gentle kisses to her lips, her eyelids. "Next time," he whispered, "we'll take it slower. I won't be in such a hurry, I promise."

She smiled at him. "I have no complaints."

"None?"

"None at all. But next time…"

"Yes?"

She twisted her body beneath him, and they tumbled across the sheets until her body was lying atop his. "Next time," she murmured, lowering her lips to his chest, "it's my turn to do the tormenting."

He groaned as her mouth slid hotly down to his belly. "We're taking turns?"

"You're the one who said it. All's fair…"

"…in love and war." He laughed. And he buried his hands in her hair.

THEY MET IN THE usual place, the warehouse behind Galerie Annika. Against the walls were stacked dozens of crates containing the paintings and sculptures of would-be artists, most of them no doubt talentless amateurs hoping for a spot on a gallery wall. *But who can really say which is art and which is rubbish?* thought Amiel Foch, gazing around at the room full of crated dreams. *To me, it is all the same. Pigment and canvas.*

Foch turned as the warehouse door swung open. "The bomb went off as planned," he said. "The job is done."

"The job is *not* done," came the reply. Anthony Sutherland emerged from the night and stepped into the warehouse. The thud of the door shutting behind him echoed across the bare concrete floor. "I wanted the woman neutralized. She is still alive. So is Richard Wolf."

Foch stared at Anthony. "It was a delayed fuse, set off two minutes after entry! It could not have ignited on its own."

"Nevertheless, they are still alive. Thus far, your record of success is abysmal. You could not finish off even that stupid creature, Marie St. Pierre."

"I will see to Mme St. Pierre—"

"Forget her! It's the Tavistocks I want dead! Lord, they're like cats! Nine bloody lives."

"Jordan Tavistock is still in custody. I can arrange—"

"Jordan will keep for a while. He's harmless where he is. But Beryl has to be taken care of soon. My guess is that she and Wolf are leaving Paris. Find them."

"How?"

"You're the professional."

"So is Richard Wolf," said Foch. "He will be difficult to trace. I cannot perform miracles."

There was a long silence. Foch watched the other man pace among the crates, and he thought, *This boy is nothing like his mother. This one has the ruthlessness to see things through. And the nerve not to flinch at the consequences.*

"I cannot search blindly," said Foch. "I must have a lead. Will they go to England, perhaps?"

"No, not England." Anthony suddenly stopped pacing. "Greece. The island of Paros."

"You mean...the Rideau family?"

"Wolf will try to contact him. I'm sure of it." Anthony let out a snort of disgust. "My mother should have taken care of Rideau years ago. Well, there's still time to do it."

Foch nodded. "I leave for Paros."

AFTER FOCH HAD LEFT, Anthony Sutherland stood alone in the warehouse, gazing about at the crates. *So many hopes and dreams locked away in here,* he reflected. *But not mine. Mine are on display for all to see and admire. The work of these poor slobs may molder into eternity. But I am the toast of Paris.*

It took more than talent, more than luck. It took the help

of Philippe St. Pierre's cold hard cash. Cash that would instantly dry up if his mother was ever exposed.

*My father Philippe,* thought Anthony with a laugh. *Still unsuspecting after all these years. I have to hand it to my lovely mother—she knows how to keep them under her spell.*

But feminine wiles could take one only so far.

If only Nina had cleaned up this matter years ago. Instead, she'd left a live witness, had even paid the man to leave the country. And as long as that witness lived, he was like a time bomb, ticking away on some lonely Greek island.

Anthony left the warehouse, walked down the alley, and climbed into his car. It was time to go home. Mustn't keep his mother awake; Nina did worry about him so. He tried never to distress her. She was, after all, the only person in this world who really loved him. Understood him.

*Like peas in a pod, Mother and I,* he thought with a smile. He started his car and roared off into the night.


THEY CAME TO ESCORT HIM from his cell at 9:00 a.m. No explanations, just the clink of keys in the door, and a gruff command in French.

Now what? wondered Jordan as he followed the guard up the corridor to the visitation room. He stepped inside, blinking at the glare of overhead fluorescent lights.

Reggie Vane was waiting in the room. At once he waved Jordan to a chair. "Sit down. You look bloody awful, my boy."

"I feel bloody awful," said Jordan, and sank into the chair.

Reggie sat down, too. Leaning forward, he whispered conspiratorially, "I brought what you asked for. There's a nice little *charcuterie* around the corner. Lovely duckling terrine. And a few *baguettes*." He shoved a paper bag under the table. *"Bon appétit."*

Jordan glanced in the bag and gave a sigh of pleasure. "Reggie, old man, you're a saint."

"Had some nice leek tarts to go with it, but the cop at the front desk insisted on helping himself."

"What about wine? Did you manage a decent bottle or two?"

Reggie shoved a second bag under the table, eliciting a musical clink from the contents. "But of course. A Beaujolais and a rather nice Pinot noir. Screw-top caps, I'm afraid—they wouldn't allow a corkscrew. And you'll have to hand over the bottles as soon as they're empty. Glass, you know."

Jordan regarded the Beaujolais with a look of sheer contentment. "How on earth did you manage it, Reggie?"

"Just scratched a few itchy palms. Oh, and those books you wanted—Helena will bring them by this afternoon."

"Capital!" Jordan folded the bag over the bottles. "If one must be in prison, one might as well make it a civilized experience." He looked up at Reggie. "Now, what's the latest news? I've had no word from Beryl since yesterday."

Reggie sighed. "I was dreading that question."

"What's happened?"

"I think she and Wolf have left Paris. After the explosion last night—"

"What?"

"I heard it from Daumier this morning. The flat where Beryl was staying was bombed last night. Two French agents killed. Wolf and your sister are fine, but they're dropping out for a while, leaving the country."

Jordan gave a sigh of relief. Thank God Beryl was out of the picture. It was one less problem to worry about. "What about the explosion?" he asked. "What does Daumier say about it?"

"His people feel there are similarities."

"To what?"

"The bombing of the St. Pierre residence."

Jordan stared at him. "But that was a terrorist attack. Cosmic Solidarity or some crazy group—"

"Apparently bombs are sort of like fingerprints. The way they're put together identifies their maker. And both bombs had identical wiring patterns. Something like that."

Jordan shook his head. "Why would terrorists attack Beryl? Or me? We're civilians."

"Perhaps they think otherwise."

"Or perhaps it wasn't terrorists in the first place," said Jordan, suddenly pushing out of his chair. He paced the room, pumping fresh blood to his legs, his brain. Too many hours in that cell had turned his body to mush; he needed a stiff walk, a slap of fresh air. "What if," he suggested, "that bombing of the St. Pierre place wasn't a terrorist attack at all? What if that Cosmic Solidarity nonsense was just a cover story to hide the real motive?"

"You mean it wasn't a political attack?"

"No."

"But who would want to kill Philippe St. Pierre?"

Jordan suddenly stopped dead as the realization hit him. "Not Philippe," he said softly. "His wife. Marie."

"*Marie* planted the bomb?"

"No! Marie was the *target!* She was the only one home when the bomb went off. Everyone assumes it was a mistake, an error in timing. But the bomber knew exactly what he was doing. He was trying to kill Marie, not her husband." Jordan looked at Reggie with new urgency. "You have to reach Wolf. Tell him what I just said."

"I don't know where he is."

"Ask Daumier."

"He doesn't know, either."

"Then find out where my uncle's gone off to. If ever I needed a family connection, it's right now."

After Reggie had left, the guard escorted Jordan back to his cell. The instant he stepped inside, the familiar smells assaulted him—the odor of sour wine and ripe bodies. Back with old friends, he thought, looking at the two Frenchmen snoring in their cots, the same two men whose cell he'd shared when he was first arrested. A drunk, a thief and him. What a happy little trio they made. He went to his cot and set down the two paper bags with the food and wine. At least he wouldn't have to gag on any more goulash.

Lying down, he stared at the cobwebs in the corner. So many leads to follow, to run down. *A killer's on the loose and here I am, locked up and useless. Unable to test my theories. If I could just get the help of someone I trust, someone I know beyond a doubt is on my side...*

*Where the hell is Beryl?*

THE GREEK TAVERN KEEPER slid two glasses of retsina onto their table. "Summertime, we have many tourists," he said with a shrug. "I cannot keep track of foreigners."

"But this man, Rideau, isn't a tourist," said Richard. "He's been living on this island twenty years. A Frenchman."

The tavern keeper laughed. "Frenchmen, Dutchmen, they are all the same to me," he grunted and went back into the kitchen.

"Another dead end," muttered Beryl. She took a sip of retsina and grimaced. "People actually *drink* this brew?"

"And some of them even enjoy it," said Richard. "It's an acquired taste."

"Then perhaps I'll acquire it another time." She pushed the glass away and looked around the gloomy taverna. It was midday, and passengers from the latest cruise ship had started trickling in from the heat, their shopping bags filled with the usual tourist purchases: Grecian urns, fishermen's caps, peasant dresses. Immersed in the babble of half a dozen languages, it was easy for Beryl to understand why the locals might not bother to distinguish a Frenchman from any other outsider. Foreigners came, they spent money, they left. What more did one need to know about them?

The tavern keeper reemerged from the kitchen carrying a sizzling platter of calamari. He set it on a table occupied by a German family and was about to head back to the kitchen when Richard asked, "Who might know about this Frenchman?"

"You waste your time," said the tavern keeper. "I tell you, there is no one on this island named Rideau."

"He brought his family with him," said Richard. "A wife and a son. The boy would be in his thirties now. His name is Gerard."

A dish suddenly clattered to the floor behind the counter of the bar. The dark-eyed young woman standing at the tap was frowning at Richard. "Gerard?" she said.

"Gerard Rideau," said Richard. "Do you know him?"

"She doesn't know anything," the tavern keeper insisted, and waved the young woman toward the kitchen.

"But I can see she does," said Richard.

The woman stood staring at him, as though not certain what to do, what to say.

"We've come from Paris," said Beryl. "It's very important we speak to Gerard's father."

"You are not French," said the woman.

"No, I'm English." Beryl nodded toward Richard. "He's American."

"He said...he said it was a Frenchman I should be careful of."

"Who did?"

"Gerard."

"He's right to be careful," said Richard. "But he should know things have gotten even more dangerous. There may be others coming to Paros, looking for his family. He has to talk to us, *now*." He pointed to the tavern keeper. "He'll be your witness. If anything goes wrong."

The woman hesitated, then went into the kitchen. A moment later, she reemerged. "He does not answer the telephone," she said. "I will have to drive you there."

It was a bumpy ride down a lonely stretch of road to Logaras beach. Clouds of dust flew in the open window and coated the jet black hair of their driver. Sofia was her name, and she had been born on the island. Her father managed the hotel near the harbor; now her three brothers ran the business. She could do a better job of it, she thought, but of course no one valued a woman's opinion, so she worked instead at Theo's tavern, frying calamari, rolling dolmas. She spoke four languages; one must, she explained, if one wished to live off the tourist trade.

"How do you know Gerard?" asked Beryl.

"We are friends" was the answer.

Lovers, guessed Beryl, seeing the other woman's cheeks redden.

"His family is French," said Sofia. "His mother died five years ago, but his father is still alive. But their name is not Rideau. Perhaps—" she looked at them hopefully "—it is a different family you are looking for?"

"They might have changed their name," said Beryl.

They parked near the beach and strode out across the rocks and sand. "There," said Sofia, pointing to a distant sailboard skimming the water. "That is Gerard." She waved and called to him in Greek.

At once the board spun around, the multicolored sail snapping about in a neat jibe. With the wind at his back, Gerard surfed to the beach like a bronzed Adonis and dragged the board onto the sand.

"Gerard," said Sofia, "these people are looking for a man named Rideau. Is that your father?"

Instantly Gerard dropped his sailboard. "Our name is not Rideau," he said curtly. Then he turned and walked away.

"Gerard?" called Sofia.

"Let me talk to him," said Richard, and he followed the other man up the beach.

Beryl stood by Sofia and watched the two men confront each other. Gerard was shaking his head, denying any knowledge of any Rideau family. Through the whistle of the wind, Beryl heard Richard's voice and the words "bomb" and "murder." She saw Gerard glance around nervously and knew that he was afraid.

"I hope I have done the right thing," murmured Sofia. "He is worried."

"He should be worried."

"What has his father done?"

"It's not what he's done. It's what he knows."

At the other end of the beach, Gerard was looking more and more agitated. Abruptly he turned and walked back to Sofia. Richard was right behind him.

"What is it?" asked Sofia.

"We go," snapped Gerard. "My father's house."

This time the drive took them along the coast, past groves of struggling olive trees on their left, and the gray-green Aegean on their right. The smell of Gerard's suntan lotion permeated the car. Such a dry and barren land, Beryl observed, looking out across the scrub grass. But to a man from a French slum, this would have seemed like a paradise.

"My father," said Gerard as he drove, "speaks no English. I will have to explain to him what you are asking. He may not remember."

"I'm sure he does remember," said Richard. "It's the reason you left Paris."

"That was twenty years ago. A long time…"

"Do you remember anything?" asked Beryl from the back seat. "You were…what? Fifteen, sixteen?"

"Fifteen," said Gerard.

"Then you must remember 66 Rue Myrha. The building where you lived."

Gerard gripped the steering wheel tightly as they bounced onto a dirt road. "I remember the police coming to see the attic. Asking my father questions. Every day, for a week."

"What about the woman who rented the attic?" asked Richard. "Her name was Scarlatti. Do you remember her?"

"Yes. She had a man," said Gerard. "I used to listen to them through the door. Every Wednesday. All the sounds they made!'' Gerard shook his head in amusement. ''Very exciting for a boy my age.''

''So this Mlle Scarlatti, she used the attic only as a love nest?'' asked Beryl.

''She was never there except to make love.''

''What did they look like, these two lovers?''

''The man was tall—that's all I remember. The woman, she had dark hair. Always wore a scarf and sunglasses. I do not remember her face very well, but I remember she was quite beautiful.''

Like her mother, thought Beryl. Could she be wrong? Had it really been her, meeting her lover in that run-down flat in Pigalle?

She asked softly, ''Was the woman English?''

Gerard paused. ''She could have been.''

''Meaning you're not certain.''

''I was young. I thought she was foreign, but I did not know from where. Then, after the murders, I heard she was English.''

''Did you see their bodies?''

Gerard shook his head. ''My father, he would not allow it.''

''So your father was the first to see them?'' asked Richard.

''No. It was the man.''

Richard glanced at Gerard in surprise. ''Which man?''

''Mlle Scarlatti's lover. We saw him climb the steps to the attic. Then he came running back down, quite frantic. That's when we knew something was wrong and called the police.''

''What happened to that man?''

''He drove away. I never saw him again. I assumed he was afraid of being accused. And that was why he sent us the money.''

''The payoff,'' said Richard. ''I guessed as much.''

''For silence?'' asked Beryl.

"Or false testimony." He asked Gerard, "How was the money delivered?"

"A man came with a briefcase only hours after the bodies were found. I'd never seen him before—a short, rather stocky Frenchman. He came to our flat, took my father into a back room. I did not hear what they said. Then the short man left."

"Your father never spoke to you about it?"

"No. And he told us we were not to speak of it to the police."

"You're certain that the briefcase contained money?"

"It must have."

"How do you know?"

"Because suddenly we had things. New clothes, a television. And then, soon afterward, we came to Greece. And we bought the house. There, you see?" He pointed. In the distance was a sprawling villa with a red-tiled roof. As they drove closer, Beryl saw bougainvillea trailing up the whitewashed walls and spilling over a covered veranda. Just below the house, waves lapped at a lonely beach.

They parked next to a dusty Citroën and climbed out. The wind whistled in from the sea, stinging their faces with sand. There was no other house in sight, only this solitary building, tucked into the crags of a barren hill.

"Papa?" called Gerard, climbing the stone steps. He swung open the wrought-iron gate. "Papa?"

No one answered.

Gerard pushed through the front door and stepped across the threshold, Beryl and Richard right behind him. Their footsteps echoed through silent rooms.

"I called here from the tavern," said Sofia. "There was no answer."

"His car is outside," said Gerard. "He must be here." He crossed the living room and started toward the dining room. "Papa?" he said, and halted in the doorway. An anguished cry was suddenly wrenched from his throat. He took a step forward and seemed to stumble to his knees. Over his shoulder, Beryl caught a view into the formal dining room beyond.

A wood table stretched the length of the room. At the far end of the table, a gray-haired man had slumped onto his dinner plate, scattering chick-peas and rice across the table's surface.

Richard pushed past Gerard and went to the fallen man. Gently he grasped the head and lifted the face from its pillow of mashed rice.

In the man's forehead was punched a single bullet-hole.

# CHAPTER TEN

AMIEL FOCH sat at an outdoor café table, sipping espresso and watching the tourists stroll past. Not the usual dentures-and-bifocals crowd, he observed as a shapely redhead wandered by. This must be the week for honeymooners. It was five o'clock, and the last public ferry to Piraeus would be sailing in half an hour. If the Tavistock woman planned to leave the island tonight, she'd have to board that ferry. He'd keep an eye on the gangplank.

He polished off his snack of stuffed grape leaves and started in on dessert, a walnut pastry steeped in syrup. Curious, how the completion of a job always left him ravenous. For other men, the spilling of blood resulted in a surge of libido, a sudden craving for hot, fast sex. Amiel Foch craved food instead; no wonder his weight was such a problem.

Dispatching the old Frenchman Rideau had been easy; killing Wolf and the woman would not be so simple. Earlier today he had considered an ambush, but Rideau's house stood on an empty stretch of shoreline, the only access a five-mile-long dirt road, and there was nowhere to conceal his car. Nowhere to lie in wait without being detected. Foch had a rule he never broke: always leave an escape route. The Rideau house, set in the midst of barren scrub, was too exposed for any such retreat. Richard Wolf was armed and would be watching for danger signs.

Amiel Foch was not a coward. But he was not a fool, either.

Far wiser to wait for another opportunity—perhaps in Piraeus, with its crowded streets and chaotic traffic. Pedestrians were killed all the time. An accident, two dead tourists—it would raise hardly a stir of interest.

Foch's gaze sharpened as the afternoon ferry pulled into port. There was only a brief unloading of passengers; the island of Paros was not, after all, on the usual Mykonos-Rhodes-Crete circuit made by tourists. At the bottom of the gangplank, a few dozen people had already gathered to board. Quickly Foch surveyed the crowd. To his consternation, he saw neither the woman nor Wolf. He knew they'd been on the island today; his contact had spotted the pair in a tavern this morning. Had they slipped away by some other route?

Then he noticed the man in the tattered Windbreaker and black fisherman's cap. Though his shoulders were hunched, there was no disguising the man's height—six feet tall, at least, with a tautly athletic build. The man turned sideways, and Foch caught a glimpse of his face, partly obscured by a few days' worth of stubble. It was, indeed, Richard Wolf. But he appeared to be traveling alone. Where was the woman?

Foch paid his café bill and wandered over to the landing. He mingled with the waiting passengers and studied their faces. There were a number of women, tanned tourists, Greek housewives clad modestly in black, a few hippies in blue jeans. Beryl Tavistock was not among them.

He felt a brief spurt of panic. Had the woman and Wolf separated? If so, he might never find her. He was tempted to stay on the island, to search her out....

The passengers were moving up the gangplank.

He weighed his choices and decided to follow Wolf. Better to stick with a flesh-and-blood quarry. Sooner or later, Wolf would reunite with the woman. Until then, Foch would have to bide his time, make no moves.

The man in the fisherman's cap walked up the gangplank and into the cabin. After a moment, Foch followed him inside and took a seat two rows behind him, next to an old man with a box of salted fish. It wasn't long before the engines growled to life and the ferry slid away from the dock.

Foch settled back for the ride, his gaze focused on the back of Wolf's head. The smell of fuel and dried fish soon became nauseating. The ferry pitched and heaved on the water, and his lunch of dolmas and espresso was threatening to come back up. Foch rose from his seat and scrambled outside. Standing at the rail, he gulped in a few breaths of fresh air and waited for the nausea to pass. At last it eased, and he reluctantly turned to go back into the cabin. He headed up the aisle, past Wolf—

Or the man he'd *thought* was Wolf.

He was wearing the same ratty Windbreaker, the same black fisherman's cap. But this man was clean shaven, younger. Definitely not the same man!

Foch glanced around the cabin. No Wolf. He hurried outside to the deck. No Wolf. He climbed the stairs to the upper level. Again, no Wolf.

He turned and saw the island of Paros receding behind them, and he let out a strangled curse. It was all a feint! They were still on the island—they had to be.

*And I'm trapped on this boat to Piraeus.*

Foch slapped the railing and cursed himself for his own stupidity. Wolf had outsmarted him—again. The old professional using his bag of tricks. There was no point interrogating the man in the cabin; he was probably just some local dupe hired to switch places with Wolf for the ferry ride.

He looked at his watch and calculated how many hours it would take him to get back to the island via a hired boat. With any luck, he could be stalking them tonight. If they were still there. He'd find them, he vowed. Wolf might be a professional. But then, so was he.

FROM INSIDE A NEARBY CAFÉ, Richard watched the ferry glide out of the harbor and heaved a sigh of relief. The old bait and switch had worked; no one had followed him off the boat. He'd been suspicious of one man in particular—a balding fellow in nondescript tourist clothes. Richard had noticed how the man had scanned the boarding passengers, how his gaze had paused momentarily on Richard's face.

Yes, he was the one. The bait was laid out for him.

The switch was a snap.

Once inside the ferry cabin, Richard had tossed his cap and jacket on a seat, walked up the aisle, and exited out the other door. By prior arrangement, Sofia's brother—six foot one and with black hair—had slid into that same seat, donned the cap and jacket, and promptly cradled his face in his arms, as though to sleep.

Richard had waited behind some crates on deck just long enough for all the passengers to board. Then he'd simply walked off the boat.

No one had followed him.

He left the café and climbed into Sofia's car.

It was a six-mile drive to the cove. Sofia and her brothers had *Melina,* the family fishing boat, ready to go, her engine running, her anchor line set to hoist. Richard scrambled out of the rowboat and up the rope ladder to *Melina*'s deck.

Beryl was waiting for him. He took her in his arms, hugged her, kissed her. "It's all right," he murmured. "I lost him."

"I was afraid I'd lose *you.*"

"Not a chance." He pulled back and smiled at her. With her black hair whipping in the wind, and her eyes the same crystalline green as the Aegean, she reminded him of some Greek goddess. Circe, Aphrodite. A woman who could hold a man forever bewitched.

The anchor thudded on deck. Sofia's brothers guided *Melina*'s bow around to face the open sea.

It started out a rough passage, the summer winds fierce

and constant, the sea a rolling carpet of swells. But at sunset, as the sky deepened to a glorious shade of red, the wind suddenly died and the water turned glassy. Beryl and Richard stood on deck and gazed at the darkening silhouettes of the islands.

Sofia said, "We arrive late tonight."

"Piraeus?" asked Richard.

"No. Too busy. We pull in at Monemvassia where no one will see us."

"And then?"

"You go your way. We go ours. It is safer, for all of us." Sofia glanced toward the stern at her two brothers, who were laughing and clapping each other on the back. "Look at them! They think this is a nice little adventure! If they had seen Gerard's father..."

"Will you be all right?" asked Beryl.

Sofia looked at her. "I worry more about Gerard. They may be looking for him."

"I don't think so," said Richard. "He was only a boy when he left Paris. His testimony can't hurt them."

"He remembered enough to tell *you*," countered Sofia.

Richard shook his head. "But I'm not sure what any of it meant."

"Perhaps the killer knows. And he will be looking for Gerard next." Sofia glanced back across the stern, toward the island. Toward Gerard, who had refused to flee. "His stubbornness. It will get him killed," she muttered, and wandered away into the cabin.

"What do you think it meant?" asked Beryl. "That business about the short man with the briefcase? Was it just a payoff to Rideau, to keep him silent?"

"Partly."

"You think there was something else in that briefcase," she said. "Something besides money."

He turned and saw the glow of the sunset on her face, the intensity of her gaze. *She's quick,* he thought. *She knows exactly what I'm thinking*. He said, "I'm sure there was. I think the lover of our mysterious Mlle Scarlatti found himself in a very sticky situation. Two dead bodies in his garret, the police certain to be notified. He sees a way to extricate himself from two crises at once. He sends his man to pay off Rideau, asks him not to identify him to police."

"And the second crisis?"

"His status as a mole."

"Delphi?"

"Maybe he knew Intelligence was about to close in. So he places the NATO documents in a briefcase…"

"And has his hired man plant the briefcase in the garret," finished Beryl. "Near my father's body."

Richard nodded. "*That's* what Inspector Broussard was trying to tell us—something about a briefcase. Remember that police photo of the murder scene? He kept pointing to an empty spot near the door. What if the briefcase was planted *after* that initial crime photo was taken? The inspector would have realized it was done postmortem."

"But he couldn't pursue the matter, because French Intelligence confiscated the briefcase."

"Exactly."

"They assumed my father was the one who brought the documents into the garret." She looked at him, her eyes glittering with determination. "How do we prove it? Any of it?"

"We identify Mlle Scarlatti's lover."

"But our only witness was Rideau. And Gerard was just a boy. He scarcely remembers what the man looked like."

"So we go to another source. A man who would know Delphi's true identity—his East German spymaster. Heinrich Leitner."

She stared at him in surprise. "Do you know how to reach him?"

"He's in a high-security prison in Berlin. Trouble is,

German Intelligence won't exactly allow us free access to their prisoners.''

"As a diplomatic favor?"

His laugh was plainly skeptical. "An ex-CIA agent isn't exactly on their most-favored list. Besides, Leitner might not want to see me. Still, it's a chance we'll take.'' He turned to gaze over the bow at the darkening sea.

He felt her move close beside him, felt her nearness as acutely as the warmth of the setting sun. It was enough to drive him crazy, having her so close and being unable to make love to her. He found himself counting the hours until they would be alone again, until he could undress her, make love to her. *And I once considered her too rich for my blood. Maybe she is. Maybe this is just a fever that'll burn itself out, leaving us both sadder and wiser. But for now she's all I think about, all I crave.*

"So that's where we're headed next," she whispered. "Berlin."

"There'll be risks." Their gazes met through the velvet dusk. "Things could go wrong...."

"Not while you're around," she said softly.

*I hope you're right,* he thought as he pulled her into his arms. *I hope to God you're right.*


THE DICE CLATTERED against the cell wall and came to rest with a five and a six showing.

"Ah-hah!" crowed Jordan, raising a fist in triumph. "What does that make it? Ten thousand francs? *Dix mille?*"

His cellmates, Leroi and Fofo, nodded resignedly.

Jordan held out his hand. "Pay up, gentlemen." Two grubby slips of paper were slapped into his palm. On each was written the number ten thousand. Jordan grinned. "Another round?"

Fofo shook the dice, threw them against the wall, and groaned. A three and a five. Leroi threw a pair of twos.

Jordan threw another five and six. His cellmates handed

over two more grubby slips of paper. *Why, I'll be a millionaire by tomorrow,* Jordan rejoiced, looking down at the growing pile of IOUs. On paper, anyway. He picked up the dice and was about to make another toss when he heard footsteps approach.

Reggie Vane was standing outside the cell, holding a basket of smoked salmon and crackers. "Helena sent these over," he said as he slid the basket through the small opening at the bottom of the cell door. "Oh, and there's fresh linen, napkins and such. One can't dine properly on paper, can one?"

"Certainly not," agreed Jordan, gratefully accepting the basket of goodies. "You are a true friend, indeed, Reggie."

"Yes, well…" Reggie grinned and cleared his throat. "Anything for a child of Madeline's."

"Any word from Uncle Hugh?"

"Still unreachable, according to your people at Chetwynd."

Jordan set the basket down in frustration. "This is most bizarre! I'm in prison. Beryl's vanished. And Uncle Hugh's probably off on some classified mission for MI6." He began to pace the cell, oblivious to the fact that Fofo and Leroi were hungrily raiding the contents of the basket. "What about that bomb investigation? Anything new?"

"The two bombings are definitely linked. The devices were manufactured by the same hand. It appears someone's targeted both Beryl and the St. Pierres."

"I think the target was Marie St. Pierre, in particular." Jordan stopped and looked at Reggie. "Let's say Marie *was* the target. What's the motive?"

Reggie shrugged. "She's not the sort of woman to pick up enemies."

"You should be able to come up with an answer. She and your wife are best chums, after all. Helena must know who'd want to kill Marie."

Reggie gave him a troubled look. "It's not as if there's any, well...proof."

Jordan moved toward him. "What are you thinking?"

"Just rumors. Things Helena might have mentioned."

"Was it about Philippe?"

Reggie looked down. "I feel a bit...well, ungentlemanly, bringing it up. You see, it happened years ago."

"What did?"

"The affair. Between Philippe and Nina."

Jordan stared at him through the bars. *There it is,* he thought. *There's the motive.* "How long have you known about this?" he asked.

"I heard about it fifteen, twenty years ago. You see, I couldn't understand why Helena disliked Nina so much. It was almost a...a hatred. You know how it is sometimes with females, all those catty looks. I assumed it was jealousy. My Helena's never been comfortable with more...well, attractive women. As a matter of fact, if I so much as glance at a pretty face, she gets downright nasty about it."

"How did she learn about Philippe and Nina?"

"Marie told her."

"Who else knew about it?"

"I doubt there were many. Poor Marie's not one to advertise her humiliation. To have one's husband dallying with a...a piece of baggage like Nina!"

"Yet she stayed married to Philippe all these years."

"Yes, she's loyal that way. And what good would it do to make a public stink of it? Ruin his career? Now he's finance minister. Chances are, he'll go to the top. And Marie will be with him. So in the long run, it was worth it."

"If she lives to see it."

"You're not saying Philippe would kill his own wife? And why now, at this late date?"

"Perhaps she issued an ultimatum. Think about it, Reggie! Here he is, inches away from being prime minister. And Marie says, 'It's your mistress or me. Choose.'"

Reggie looked thoughtful. "If he chooses Nina, he'd have to get rid of his wife."

"Ah, but what if he chooses Marie? And Nina's the one left out in the cold?"

They frowned at each other through the bars.

"Call Daumier," said Jordan. "Tell him what you just told me, about the affair. And ask him to put a tail on Nina."

"You don't really think—"

"I think," said Jordan, "that we've been looking at this from the wrong angle entirely. The bombing wasn't a political act. All that Cosmic Solidarity rubbish was merely a smoke screen, to cover up the real reason for the attack."

"You mean it was personal?"

Jordan nodded. "Murder usually is."

THE FLIGHT TO BERLIN was half-empty, so the only logical reason that disheveled pair of passengers in row two should be sitting in first class was that they must have actually paid the fare, a fact the flight attendant found difficult to believe, considering their appearance. Both wore dark sunglasses, wrinkled clothes and unmistakable expressions of exhaustion. The man had a week's worth of dark stubble on his jaw. The woman was deeply sunburned and her black hair was tangled and powdered with dust. Their only carryon was the woman's purse, a battered straw affair coated with sand. The attendant glanced at the couple's ticket stubs. Athens—Rome—Berlin. With a forced smile, she asked them if they wished to order cocktails.

"Bloody Mary," said the woman in the Queen's perfect English.

"A Rob Roy," said the man. "Hold the bitters."

The woman went to fetch their drinks. When she returned, the man and woman were holding hands and looking at each other with the weary smiles of fellow survivors. They took their drinks from the tray.

"To our health?" the man asked.

"Definitely," the woman answered.

And, grinning, they both tipped back their glasses in a toast.

The meal cart was wheeled out and on it were lobster patties, crown roast of lamb, wild rice and mushroom caps. The couple ate double servings of everything and topped their dinner off with a split of wine. Then, like a pair of exhausted puppies, they curled up against each other and fell asleep.

They slept all the way to Berlin. Only when the plane rolled to a stop at the terminal did they jerk awake, both of them instantly alert and on guard. As the passengers filed out, the flight attendant kept her gaze on that rumpled pair from Athens. There was no telling who they were or what they might be up to. First-class passengers did not usually travel the world dressed like bums.

The couple was the last to disembark.

The attendant followed the pair onto the passenger ramp and stood watching as they walked toward a small crowd of greeters. They made it as far as the waiting area.

Two men stepped into their path. At once the couple halted and pivoted as though to flee back toward the plane. Three more men magically appeared, blocking off their escape. The couple was trapped.

The attendant caught a glimpse of the woman's panicked face, the man's grim expression of defeat. She had been sure there was something wrong about them. They were terrorists, perhaps, or international thieves. And there were the police to make the arrest. She watched as the pair was led away through the murmuring crowd. Definitely not first class, she thought with a sniff of satisfaction. Oh, yes, one could always tell.

RICHARD AND BERYL were shoved forward into a window-less room. "Stay here!" came the barked command, then the door was slammed shut behind them.

"They were waiting for us," said Beryl. "How did they know?"

Richard went to the door and tested the knob. "Dead bolt," he muttered. "We're locked in tight." In frustration, he began to circle the room, searching for another way out. "Somehow they knew we were coming to Berlin...."

"We paid for the tickets in cash. There was no way they could have known. And those were airport guards, Richard. If they want us dead, why bother to arrest us?"

"To keep you from getting your heads shot off," said a familiar voice. "That's why."

Beryl wheeled around in astonishment at the portly man who'd just opened the door. "Uncle *Hugh?*"

Lord Lovat scowled at his niece's wrinkled clothes and tangled hair. "You're a fine mess. Since when did you adopt the gypsy look?"

"Since we hitchhiked halfway across Greece. Credit cards, by the way, are *not* the preferred method of payment in small Greek towns."

"Well, you made it to Berlin." He glanced at Richard. "Good work, Wolf."

"I could've used some assistance," growled Richard.

"And we would've happily provided it. But we had no idea where to find you, until I spoke with your man, Sakaroff. He said you'd be headed for Berlin. We only just found out you'd gone via Athens."

"What are *you* doing in Berlin, Uncle Hugh?" demanded Beryl. "I thought you were off on another one of your secret missions."

"I'm fishing."

"Not for fish, obviously."

"For answers. Which I'm hoping Heinrich Leitner will provide." He took another look at Beryl's clothes and sighed. "Let's get to the hotel and clean you both up. Then we'll pay a visit to Herr Leitner's prison cell."

"You have clearance to speak to him?" said Richard in surprise.

"What do you think I've been doing here these last few days? Wining and dining the necessary officials." He waved them out of the room. "The car's waiting."

In Uncle Hugh's hotel suite, they showered off three days' worth of Greek dust and sand. A fresh set of clothes was delivered to the room, courtesy of the concierge—sober business attire, outfits appropriate for a visit to a high-security prison.

"How do we know Leitner will tell us the truth?" asked Richard as they rode in the limousine to the prison.

"We don't," said Hugh. "We don't even know how much he *can* tell us. He oversaw Paris operations from East Berlin, so he'd be acquainted with code names, but not faces."

"Then we may come away with nothing."

"As I said, Wolf, it's a fishing expedition. Sometimes you reel in an old tire. Sometimes a salmon."

"Or, in this case, a mole."

"If he's cooperative."

"Are you prepared to hear the truth?" asked Richard. The question was directed at Hugh, but his gaze was on Beryl. Delphi could still be Bernard or Madeline, his eyes said.

"Right now, I'd say ignorance is far more dangerous," Hugh observed. "And there's Jordan to consider. I have people watching out for him. But there's always the chance things could go wrong."

Things have already gone wrong, thought Beryl, looking out the car window at the drab and dreary buildings of East Berlin.

The prison was even more forbidding—a massive concrete fortress surrounded by electrified fences. The very best of security, she noted, as they moved through the gauntlet of checkpoints and metal detectors. Uncle Hugh had obviously been expected, and he was greeted with the chilling disdain of an old Cold War enemy. Only when they'd arrived at the commandant's office was any courtesy extended to them. Glasses of hot tea were passed around, cigars offered to the men. Hugh accepted; Richard declined.

"Up until recently, Leitner was most uncooperative," said the commandant, lighting a cigar. "At first, he denied his role entirely. But our files on him are proof positive. He *was* in charge of Paris operations."

"Has Leitner provided any names?" asked Richard.

The commandant peered at Richard through the drifting cloud of cigar smoke. "You were CIA, were you not, Mr. Wolf?"

Richard gave only the briefest nod of acknowledgment. "It was years ago. I've left the business."

"But you understand how it is, to be dogged by one's past associations."

"Yes, I understand."

The commandant rose and went to look out his window at the barbed-wire fence enclosing his prison kingdom. "Berlin is filled with people running from their shadows. Their old lives. Whether it was for money or for ideology, they served a master. And now the master is dead and they hide from the past."

"Leitner's already in prison. He has nothing to lose by talking to us."

"But the people who worked for him—the ones not yet exposed—they have everything to lose. Now the East German files are open. And every day, some curious citizen opens one of those files and discovers the truth. Realizes that a friend or husband or lover was working for the enemy." The commandant turned, his pale blue eyes focused on Richard. "That's why Leitner has been reluctant to give names—to protect his old agents."

"But you say he's more cooperative these days?"

"In recent weeks, yes."

"Why?"

The commandant paused. "A bad heart, the doctors say. It fails, little by little. In two months, three…" He shrugged. "Leitner sees the end coming. And in exchange for a few last comforts, he's sometimes willing to talk."

"Then he may give us answers."

"If he is in the mood." The commandant turned to the door. "So, let us see what sort of mood Herr Leitner is in today."

They followed him down secured corridors, past mounted cameras and grim-faced guards, into the very core of the complex. Here there were no windows; the air itself seemed hermetically sealed from the outside world. *From here there is no escape*, thought Beryl. *Except through death*.

They stopped at cell number five. Two guards, each with his own key, opened separate locks. The door swung open.

Inside, on a wooden chair, sat an old man. Oxygen tubing snaked from his nostrils. His regulation prison garb—tan shirt and pants, no belt—hung loosely on his shrunken frame. The fluorescent lights gave his face a yellowish cast. Beside the man's chair stood an oxygen tank; except for the hiss of the gas flowing through his nasal prongs, the room was silent.

The commandant said, "*Guten Tag,* Heinrich."

Leitner said nothing. Only by a brief flicker of his eyes did he acknowledge the greeting.

"I have brought with me today, Lord Lovat, from England. You are familiar with the name?"

Again, a flicker in the old man's blue eyes. And a whisper, barely audible, "MI6."

"That's right," said Hugh. "Since retired."

"So am I," was the reply, not without a trace of humor. Leitner's gaze shifted to Beryl and Richard.

"My niece," said Hugh. "And a former associate. Richard Wolf."

"CIA?" said Leitner.

Richard nodded. "Also retired."

Leitner managed a faint smile. "How differently we enjoy our retirements." He looked once again at Hugh. "A social call on an old enemy? How thoughtful."

"Not a social call, exactly," said Hugh.

Leitner began to cough, and the effort seemed almost too much for him; when at last he settled back into his chair, his face had a distinctly blue tinge. "What is it you wish to know?"

"The identity of your double agent in Paris. Code name Delphi."

Leitner didn't speak.

"Surely the name is familiar, Herr Leitner. Over the years, Delphi must have passed on invaluable documents. He was your link to NATO operations. Don't you remember?"

"That was twenty years ago," murmured Leitner. "The world has changed."

"We want only his name. That's all."

"So you may put Delphi in a cage like this? Shut away from the sun and air?"

"So we can stop the killing," said Richard.

Leitner frowned. "What killing?"

"It's going on right now. A French agent, murdered in Paris. A man, shot to death in Greece. It's all linked to Delphi."

"That cannot be possible," said Leitner.

"Why?"

"Delphi has been put to sleep."

Hugh frowned at him. "Are you saying he's dead?"

"But that makes no sense," said Richard. "If Delphi's dead, why is the killing still going on?"

"Perhaps," said Leitner, "it has nothing at all to do with Delphi."

"Perhaps you are lying," said Richard.

Leitner smiled. "Always a possibility." Suddenly he began to cough again; it had the gurgling sound of a man drowning in his own secretions. When at last he could speak, it was only between gasps for oxygen. "Delphi was a paid recruit," he said. "Not a true believer. We preferred the believers, you see. They did not cost as much."

"So he did it for money?" asked Richard.

"A rather generous sum, over the years."

"When did it stop?"

"When it became a risk to all involved. So Delphi ended the association. Covered all tracks before your counterintelligence could close in."

"Is that why my parents were killed?" asked Beryl. "Because Delphi had to cover his tracks?"

Leitner frowned. "Your parents?"

"Bernard and Madeline Tavistock. They were shot to death in a garret in Pigalle."

"But that was a murder and suicide. I saw the report."

"Or were they both murdered? By Delphi?"

Leitner looked at Hugh. "I gave no such order. And that is the truth."

"Meaning some of what you told us is *not* the truth?" Richard probed.

Leitner took a deep breath of oxygen and painfully wheezed it out. "Truth, lies," he whispered. "What does it matter now?" He sank back in his chair and looked at the commandant. "I wish to rest. Take these people away."

"Herr Leitner," said Richard, "I'll ask this one last time. Is Delphi really dead?"

Leitner met his gaze with one so steady, so unflinching, it seemed that surely he was about to tell the truth. But the answer he gave was puzzling at best.

"Dormant," he said. "That is the word I would use."

"So he's not dead."

"For your purposes," Leitner said with a smile, "he is."

# CHAPTER ELEVEN

"A SLEEPER. That's what Delphi must be," said Richard. They had not dared discuss the matter in the limousine—no telling whom their driver really worked for. But here, in a noisy restaurant, with waiters whisking back and forth, Richard could finally spell out his theories. "I'm sure that's what he meant."

"A sleeper?" asked Beryl.

"Someone they recruit years in advance," said her uncle. "As a young adult. The person may be kept inactive for years. They live a normal life, try to gain influence in some trusted position. And then the signal's sent. And the sleeper's activated."

"So that's what he meant by dormant," said Beryl. "Not dead. But not active, either."

"Precisely."

"For this sleeper to be of any use to them, he'd have to be in a position of influence. Or close to it," said Beryl thoughtfully.

"Which describes Stephen Sutherland to a T," said Richard. "American ambassador. Access to all security data."

"It also describes Philippe St. Pierre," said Hugh. "Minister of Finance. In line for French prime minister—"

"And extremely vulnerable to blackmail," added Beryl, thinking of Nina and Philippe. And of Anthony, the son born of their illicit affair.

"I'll contact Daumier," said Hugh. "Have St. Pierre vetted again."

"While he's at it," said Richard, "ask him to vet Nina."

"Nina?"

"Talk about positions of influence! An ambassador's wife. Mistress to St. Pierre. She could've heard secrets from both sides of the bed."

Hugh shook his head. "Considering her double digit IQ, Nina Sutherland's the last person I'd expect to work for Intelligence."

"And the one person who'd get away with it."

Hugh glanced around impatiently for the waiter. "We have to leave for Paris at once," he said, and slapped enough marks on the table to pay for their coffees. "There's no telling what's happening to Jordan."

"If it is Nina, do you think she could get at Jordan?" asked Beryl.

"All these years, I've overlooked Nina Sutherland," said Hugh. "I'm not about to make the same mistake now."

DAUMIER MET THEM at Orly Airport. "I have reexamined the security files on Philippe and Nina," he said as they rode together in his limousine. "St. Pierre is clean. His record is unblemished. If he is the sleeper, we have no evidence of it."

"And Nina?"

Daumier gave a deep sigh. "Our dear Nina presents a problem. There was an item that was not addressed in her earlier vetting. She was eighteen when she first appeared on the London stage. A small part, quite insignificant, but it launched her acting career. At that time, she had an affair with one of her fellow actors—an East German by the name of Berte Klausner. He claimed he was a defector. But three years later, he vanished from England and was never heard from again."

"A recruiter?" asked Richard.

"Possibly."

"How on earth did this little affair make it past Nina's vetting?" asked Beryl.

Daumier shrugged. "It was noted when Nina and Sutherland were married. By then she'd retired from the theater to become a diplomat's wife. She didn't serve in any official capacity. As a rule, security checks on wives—especially if they are American—are not as demanding. So Nina slipped through."

"Then you have evidence of possible recruitment," said Beryl. "And she could have had access to NATO secrets by way of her husband. But you can't prove she's Delphi. Nor can you prove she's a murderer."

"True," admitted Daumier.

"I doubt you'll get her to confess, either," said Richard. "Nina was once an actress. She could probably brazen her way through anything."

"That is why I suggest the following action," said Daumier. "A trap. Tempt her into making a move."

"With what bait?" asked Richard.

"Jordan."

"That's out of the question!" said Beryl.

"He has already agreed to it. This afternoon, he will be released from prison. We move him to a hotel where he will attempt to be conspicuous."

Hugh laughed. "Not much of a stretch for our Jordan."

"My men will be stationed at strategic points in the hotel. If—and when—an attack occurs, we will be prepared."

"Things could go wrong," said Beryl. "He could be hurt—"

"He could be hurt in prison, as well," said Daumier. "At least this may provide us with answers."

"And possibly a dead body."

"Have you a better suggestion?"

Beryl glanced at Richard, then at her uncle. They were both silent. *I can't believe they're agreeing to this,* she thought.

She looked at Daumier. "What do you want *me* to do?"

"You'd complicate things, Beryl," said Hugh. "It's better for you to stay out of the picture."

"The Vanes' house has excellent security," said Daumier. "Reggie and Helena have already agreed that you should stay with them."

"But I haven't agreed," said Beryl.

"Beryl." It was Richard. He spoke quietly. Unbendingly. "Jordan will be protected from all angles. They'll be ready for the attack. This time, nothing will go wrong."

"Can you guarantee it? Can any of you?"

There was silence.

"Nothing can be guaranteed, Beryl," said Daumier quietly. "We have to take this chance. It may be the only way to catch Delphi."

In frustration, she looked out the window, thinking of the options. Realizing there were none—not if any of this was to be resolved—she said softly, "I'll agree to it on one condition."

"What's that?"

She looked at Richard. "I want you to be with him. I trust you, Richard. If you're watching Jordan, I know he'll be all right."

Richard nodded. "I'll be right by his side."

"Who else knows about this plan?" asked Hugh.

"Just a few of my people," said Daumier. "I was careful not to let any of this leak out to Philippe St. Pierre."

"What do Reggie and Helena know?" asked Beryl.

"Only that you need a safe place to stay. They are doing this as a favor to old friends."

As an old friend was exactly the way Beryl was greeted upon arrival at the Vanes' residence. As soon as the gates closed behind the limousine, and they were inside the high walls of the compound, she was swept into the comfort of their home. It all seemed so safe, so familiar: the English wallpaper, the tray of tea and biscuits on the end table, the vases of flowers perfuming the rooms. Surely nothing could hurt her here....

There was scarcely time to say goodbye to Richard. While Daumier and Hugh waited outside in the car, Richard pulled Beryl into his arms. They shared a last embrace, a last kiss.

"You'll be perfectly safe here," he whispered. "Don't leave the compound for any reason."

"*You're* the one I worry about. You and Jordan."

"I won't let anything happen to him." He tipped up her chin and pressed his lips to hers. "And that," he murmured, "is a promise." He touched her face and grinned, a confident grin that made her believe anything was possible.

Then he walked away.

She stood on the doorstep and watched the car drive out of the compound, saw the iron gates close shut behind it. *I'm with you,* she thought. *Whatever happens, Richard, I'm right there beside you.*

"Come, Beryl," said Reggie, affectionately draping his arm around her shoulders. "I have an instinct about these things. And I'm positive everything will turn out just fine."

She looked up at Reggie's smiling face. *Thank God for old friends,* she thought. And she let him lead her back into the house.

JORDAN WAS DOWN on all fours in his jail cell, rattling a pair of dice in his hand. His cellmates, the two shaggy, ripe-smelling ruffians—or could that odor be Jordan's?—hovered behind him, stamping their feet and yelling. Jordan threw the dice; they tumbled across the floor and clattered against the wall. Two fives.

"*Zut alors!*" groaned the cellmates.

Jordan raised his fist in triumph. "*Oh, là là!*" Only then did he see his visitors staring at him through the bars. "Uncle Hugh!" he said, jumping to his feet. "Am I glad to see you!"

Hugh's disbelieving gaze scanned the interior of the cell. Over the cot was draped a red-checked tablecloth, laid out with platters of sliced beef, poached salmon, a bowl of grapes. A bottle of wine sat chilling in a plastic bucket. And on a chair beside the bed was neatly stacked a half dozen leather-bound books and a vase of roses. "This is a prison?" quipped Hugh.

"Oh, I've spruced it up a bit," said Jordan. "The food was wretched, so I had some delivered. Brought in the reading material, as well. But," he said with a sigh, "I'm afraid it's still very much a prison." He tapped the bars. "As you can see." He looked at Daumier. "So, are we ready?"

"If you are still willing."

"Haven't much of a choice, have I? Considering the alternative."

The guard unlocked the door and Jordan stepped out, carrying his bundle of street clothes. But he couldn't walk away without a proper goodbye to his cellmates. He turned and found Fofo and Leroi staring at him mournfully. "Afraid this is it, fellows," he said. "It's been—" he thought a moment, struggling to come up with the right adjective "—a uniquely fragrant experience." On impulse, he tossed his tailored linen jacket to the disbelieving Fofo. "I think that might fit you," he said. "Wear it in good health." Then, with a farewell wave, he followed his companions out of the building and into Daumier's limousine.

They drove him to the Ritz—same floor, different room. A fashionably appropriate place for an assassination, he thought wryly as he came out of the shower and dressed in a fresh suit.

"Bulletproof windows," said Daumier. "Microphones in the front room. And there'll be two men, stationed across the hall. Also, you should have this." Daumier reached into his briefcase and pulled out an automatic pistol. He handed it to Jordan, who regarded the weapon with a raised eyebrow.

"Worst-case scenario? I'll actually have to defend myself?"

"A precaution. You know how to use one?"

"I suppose I can muddle through," said Jordan, expertly sliding in the ammunition clip. He looked at Richard. "Now what happens?"

"Have a meal in the restaurant downstairs," said Richard. "Take your time, make sure you're seen by as many employees as possible. Leave a big tip, be conspicuous. And return to your room."

"And then?"

"We wait and see who comes knocking."

"What if no one does?"

"They will," said Daumier grimly. "I guarantee it."

AMIEL FOCH RECEIVED the call a mere thirty minutes later. It was the hotel maid—the same woman who'd been so useful a week before, when he'd needed access to the Tavistocks' suites.

"He is back," she said. "The Englishman."

"Jordan Tavistock? But he's in prison—"

"I have just seen him in the hotel. Room 315. He seems to be alone."

Foch grimaced in amazement. Perhaps those Tavistock family connections had come through. Now he was a free man—and a vulnerable target. "I need to get into his room," said Foch. "Tonight."

"I cannot do it."

"You did it before. I'll pay double."

The maid gave a snort of disgust. "It's still not enough. I could lose my job."

"I'll pay more than enough. Just get me the passkey again."

There was a silence. Then the woman said, "First, you leave the envelope. Then, I get you the key."

"Agreed," said Foch, and hung up.

He immediately made a call to Anthony Sutherland. "Jordan Tavistock is out of prison," he said. "He's taken a room at the Ritz. Do you still wish me to proceed?"

"This time, I want it done right. Even if I have to supervise it myself. When do we move?"

"I do not think it is wise—"

*"When do we move?"*

Foch swallowed his angry response. It was a mistake letting Sutherland take part. The boy was just a voyeur, eager to experience the ultimate power—the taking of a life. Foch had sensed it years ago, from the day they'd first met. He'd known just by looking at him that he'd be addicted to thrills, to intensity, be it sexual or otherwise.

Now the young man wished to experience something novel. Murder. This was a mistake, surely, a mistake....

"Remember who's paying your fees, M. Foch," said Sutherland. "And outrageous fees, too. I'm the one who makes the decisions, not you."

*Even if they are stupid, dangerous decisions?* wondered Foch. At last he said, "It will be tonight. We wait for him to sleep."

"Tonight," agreed Sutherland. "I'll be there."


AT ELEVEN-THIRTY, JORDAN turned off the lights in his hotel room, stuffed three pillows under the bedspread, and fluffed it all up so that it vaguely resembled a human shape. Then he took his position by the door, next to Richard. In the darkness they sat and waited for something to happen. Anything to happen. So far, the evening had been a screaming bore. Daumier had made him a prisoner of his own hotel room. He'd watched two hours of telly, glanced through *Paris Match,* and completed five crossword puzzles. *What must I do to attract this assassin?* he wondered. *Send him an engraved invitation?*

Sighing, he leaned back against the wall. "Is this the sort of thing you used to do, Wolf?" he murmured.

"A lot of waiting around. A lot of boredom," said Richard. "And every so often, a moment of abject terror."

"What made you leave the business? The boredom or the terror?"

Richard paused. "The rootlessness."

"Ah. The man longs for home and hearth." Jordan smiled. "So tell me, does my sister figure into the equation?"

"Beryl is...one of a kind."

"You didn't answer the question."

"The answer is, I don't know," Richard admitted. He squared his shoulders to ease the tension in his muscles. "Sometimes, it seems like the world's worst possible match. Sure, I can put on a tuxedo, stand around swirling a snifter of brandy. But I don't fool anyone, least of all myself. And certainly not Beryl."

"You really think that's what she needs? A fop in black tie?"

"I don't know what she needs. Or what she wants. I know she probably thinks she's in love. But how the devil can anyone know for certain, when things are so crazy?"

"You wait till things *aren't* so crazy. Then you decide."

"And live with the consequences."

"You're already lovers, aren't you?"

Richard looked at him in surprise. "Are you always so inquisitive about your sister's love life?"

"I'm her closest male relative. And therefore responsible for defending her honor." Jordan laughed softly. "Someday, Wolf, I may have to shoot you. That is, if I survive the night."

They both laughed. And they settled back to wait.

At 1:00 a.m., they heard the faint click of a door closing in the hallway. Had someone just stepped out of the stairwell? Instantly Jordan snapped fully alert, his adrenaline kicking into overdrive. He whispered, "Did you hear—"

Richard was already rising to a crouch. Through the darkness, Jordan could sense the other man tensing for action. Where were Daumier's agents? he wondered frantically. Were the two of them on their own?

A key grated slowly in the lock. Jordan froze, heart thundering, the sweat breaking out on his palms. The gun felt slippery in his grasp.

The door swung open; two figures slowly edged into the room. The first took aim at the bed. A single bullet was all the gunman managed to squeeze off before Richard flew at him sideways. The force of his assault sent both men thudding to the floor.

Jordan shoved his gun into the ribs of the second intruder and barked, "Freeze!"

To Jordan's astonishment, the man didn't freeze, but turned and fled from the room.

Jordan dashed after him into the hall, just in time to see the two French agents tackle the fugitive to the floor. They yanked him, kicking and squirming, back to his feet. In amazement, Jordan stared at the man. *"Anthony?"*

"I'm bleeding!" spat Anthony Sutherland. "They broke my nose! I think they broke my nose!"

"Keep squealing, and they'll break a lot more," growled Richard.

Jordan turned and saw Richard haul the gunman out of the room. He yanked his head back, so Jordan could see his face. "Take a good look. Recognize him?"

"Why, it's my bogus attorney," said Jordan. "M. Jarre."

Richard nodded and forced the balding Frenchman to the floor. "Now let's find out his real name."

"IT'S EXTRAORDINARY," mused Reggie, "how very much you look like your mother."

The butler had long since cleared away the coffee cups, and Helena had vanished upstairs to see to the guest room. Beryl and Reggie sat alone together, enjoying a nip of brandy in his wood-paneled library. A fire crackled in the hearth—not for warmth on this July night, but for reassurance, the ancestral comfort of flames against the night, against the world's evils.

Beryl cradled the brandy snifter in her hands and watched the reflection of firelight in the golden liquid. She said, "When I remember her, it's from a child's point of view. So I remember only the things a child finds important. Her smile. The softness of her hands."

"Yes, yes. That was Madeline."

"I've been told she was quite enchanting."

"She was," said Reggie softly. "She was the loveliest, most extraordinary woman I've ever known...."

Beryl looked up and saw that he was staring at the fire as though seeing, in its flames, the faces of old ghosts. She gave him a fond look. "Mother told me once that you were her oldest and dearest friend."

"Did she?" Reggie smiled. "Yes, I suppose that's true. Did you know we played together, as children. In Cornwall..." He blinked and she thought she saw the faint gleam of tears on his lashes. "I was the first, you know," he murmured. "Before Bernard. Before..." Sighing, he sank back in his chair. "But that was a long time ago."

"You still think of her a great deal."

"It's difficult not to." He drained his brandy glass. Unsteadily he poured another—his third. "Every time I look at you, I think, 'There's Madeline, come back to life.' And I remember how much, how very much I miss her—" Suddenly he stiffened and glanced at the doorway. Helena was standing there, wearily shaking her head. "You've had more than enough for tonight, Reggie."

"It's only my third."

"And how many more will come after that one?"

"Bloody few, if you have your way."

Helena came into the room and took his arm. "Come, darling. You've kept Beryl up long enough. It's time for bed."

"It's only one o'clock."

"Beryl's tired. And you should be considerate."

Reggie looked at their guest. "Oh. Oh, yes, perhaps you're right." He rose to his feet and moved on unsteady legs toward Beryl. She turned her face as he bent over to plant a kiss on her cheek. It was a wet, sloppy kiss, heavy with the smell of brandy, and she had to suppress the urge to pull away. He straightened, and once again she saw the sheen of tears in his eyes. "Good night, dear," he murmured. "You'll be perfectly safe with us."

With a sense of pity, Beryl watched the old man shuffle out of the library.

"He's simply not able to tolerate spirits the way he used to," said Helena, sighing. "The years pass, you know, and he forgets that things change. Including his capacity for liquor." She gave Beryl a rueful smile. "I do hope he didn't bore you too much."

"Not at all. We talked about Mother. He said I remind him of her."

Helena nodded. "Yes, you do resemble her. Of course, I didn't know her nearly as well as Reggie did." She sat down on the armrest of a chair. "I remember the first time I met her. It was at my wedding. Madeline and Bernard were there, practically newlyweds themselves. You could see it, just by the way they looked at each other. Quite a lovely couple…" Helena picked up Reggie's brandy snifter, tidied the table. "When we met again in Paris, it was fifteen years later, and she hadn't aged a bit. It was eerie how unchanged she was. When all the rest of us felt so acutely the passage of time."

There was a long pause. Then Beryl asked, "Did she have a lover?" The question was asked softly, so softly it was almost swallowed in the gloom of that library.

The silence that followed stretched on so long, she thought perhaps her words had gone unnoticed. But then Helena said, "It shouldn't surprise you, should it? Madeline had that magic about her. That certain something the rest of us seem to lack. It's a matter of luck, you know. It's not something one achieves through effort or study. It's in one's genes. An inheritance, like a silver spoon in one's mouth.''

''My mother wasn't born with a silver spoon.''

''She didn't need one. She had that magic, instead.'' Abruptly Helena turned to leave. But in the doorway she caught herself and looked back at Beryl with a smile. ''I'll see you in the morning. Good night.''

Beryl nodded. ''Good night, Helena.''

For a long time, Beryl frowned at the empty doorway and listened to Helena ascend the stairs. She went to the hearth and stared at the dying embers. She thought of her mother, wondered if Madeline had ever stood here, in this library, in this house. Yes, of course she would have. Reggie was her oldest friend. They would have visited back and forth, the two couples, as they had in England years before....

Before Helena had insisted Reggie accept the Paris post.

The question suddenly came to her: *Why?* Was there some unspoken reason the Vanes had suddenly left England? Helena had grown up in Buckinghamshire; her ancestral home was a mere two miles from Chetwynd. Surely it must have been difficult to pack up her household, to leave behind all that was familiar, and move to a city where she couldn't even speak the language. One didn't blithely make such a move.

Unless one was fleeing *from* something.

Beryl's head lifted. She found herself staring at a ridiculous statuette on the mantelpiece—a fat little man holding a rifle. It had the inscription: ''Reggie Vane—most likely to shoot his own foot. Tremont Gun Club.'' Lined up beside it were various knickknacks from Reggie's past—a soccer medal, an old photo of a cricket team, a petrified frog. Judging by the items on display, this must be Reggie's private abode, the room to which he retreated from the world. The room that would hold his secrets.

She scanned the photos, and nowhere did she see a picture of Helena. Nor was there one on the desk or on the bookshelves—a fact she thought odd, for she remembered her father's library and all the snapshots of Madeline he kept so conspicuously in view. She moved to Reggie's cherry desk and quietly began to open the drawers. The first revealed the expected clutter of pens and paper clips. She opened the second and saw only a sheaf of cream-colored stationery and an address book. She closed the drawers and began to circle the room, thinking, *This is where you keep your most private treasures. The memories you hide, even from your wife....*

Her gaze came to rest on the leather footstool. It appeared to be a matched set with the easy chair, but it had been moved out of position, and instead sat at the side of the chair where it served no purpose...except to stand on.

She glanced directly up at the mahogany breakfront that stood against the wall. The shelves were filled with antique books, protected behind glass doors. The cabinet was at least eight feet tall, and on top was a matched pair of china bowls.

Beryl pushed the footstool over to the breakfront, climbed onto the stool, and reached up to retrieve the first bowl. It was empty and coated in dust. So was the second bowl. But as she slid the bowl back onto the cabinet, she met resistance. She reached back as far as she could, and her fingers met something flat and leathery. She grasped the edge and pulled it off the cabinet.

It was a photo album.

She took it over to the hearth and sat down by the dying fire. There she opened the cover to the first picture in the album. It was of a laughing, black-haired girl. The girl was twelve years old perhaps, and sitting on a swing, her skirt bunched up hoydenishly around her thighs, her bare legs dangling. On the next page was another photo—the same girl, a bit older now, dressed in May Day finery, flowers woven into her tangled hair. More photos, all of the black-haired girl: clad in waders and fishing in a stream, waving from a car, hanging upside down from a tree branch. And last—a wedding photo. It had been torn jaggedly in two, so that the groom was missing, and only the bride remained.

For an eternity, Beryl stared at the face she knew from her childhood—the face so very much like her own. She touched the smiling lips, traced the upswept tendrils of black hair. She thought about how it must be for a man to so desperately love a woman. To lose her to another man. To flee from those memories of her to a foreign city, only to have her reappear in that same city. And to find that, even fifteen years later, the feelings remain, and there is nothing you can do to ease your anguish, nothing at all...so long as she is alive.

Beryl shut the album and went to the telephone. She didn't know how to reach Richard, so she dialed Daumier's number instead and was greeted by a recorded message, intoned in businesslike French.

After the beep, she said, "Claude, it's Beryl. I have to speak to you at once. I think I've found some new evidence. Please, come get me! As soon as you—" She stopped, her hand suddenly frozen on the receiver. What was that click on the line?

She listened for other sounds, but heard only the pounding of her own heart—and silence. She hung up. The extension, she thought. Someone had been listening on the extension.

Quickly she rose to her feet. *I can't stay here, not in this house. Not under this roof. Not when I know he could have been the one.*

Clutching the album firmly in her arms, she left Reggie's library and hurried across the foyer. After disarming the security system, she stepped out the front door.

Outside, it was a cool night, the sky clear, the stars faintly twinkling against the distant haze of city light. She looked across the stone courtyard and saw that the iron gates were closed—no doubt locked, as well. As a bank executive in Paris, Reggie was a prime target for terrorists; he would install the very best security for his home.

*I have to get out of here,* she determined. *Without anyone knowing.*

And then what? Thumb a ride to the nearest police station? Daumier's flat? *Anywhere but here.*

She traced the perimeter of the courtyard, searching the high wall for a doorway, an exit. She spotted another gate, but it, too, was locked. No way around it, she thought. She'd have to climb over. Quickly she scanned the trees and spotted an apple tree with a branch overhanging the wall. Clutching the photo album in one hand, she scrambled up onto the lowest branch. It was an easy climb to the next branch, and the next, but every movement made the tree sway and sent apples thudding noisily to the ground. At the top of the wall, she tossed the album down on the other side and dropped to the ground beside it. At once she scooped up the album and turned toward the road.

The blinding beam of a flashlight made her freeze.

"So it's not a burglar after all," said a voice. "What on earth are you doing, Beryl?"

Squinting against the light, Beryl could barely make out Helena's silhouette standing before her. "I...I wanted to take a walk. But the gate was locked."

"I would have opened it for you."

"I didn't want to wake you." She turned her gaze from the flashlight. "Please, could you drop the torch? It hurts my eyes."

The beam slowly fell, and stopped at the photo album in Beryl's arms. Beryl had clasped the album to her chest, hoping Helena hadn't recognized it, but it was too late. She had already seen it.

"Where was it?" asked Helena softly. "Where did you find it?"

"The library," said Beryl. No point in lying now; the evidence was there, plainly in her grasp.

"All these years," murmured Helena. "He kept it all these years. And he swore to me—"

"What, Helena? What did he swear to?"

There was silence. "That he no longer loved her," came the whispered answer. Then a laugh, full of self-mockery. "I've lost out to a ghost. It was hopeless enough when she was alive. But now she's dead, and I can't fight back. The dead, you see, don't grow old. They stay young and beautiful. And perfect."

Beryl took a step forward, her arms extended in sympathy. "They weren't lovers, Helena. I know they weren't."

"I was never perfect enough."

"But he married you. There must have been love involved—"

Helena stepped away, angrily brushing off Beryl's offer of comfort. "Not love! It was spite. Some stupid, masculine gesture to show her he couldn't be hurt. We were married a month after she was. I was his consolation prize, you see. I gave him all the right connections. And the money. He happily accepted those. But he never really wanted my love."

Again, Beryl tried to reach out to her; again, Helena rebuffed the gesture. Beryl said softly, "It's time to move on, Helena. Make your own life, without him. While you're still young…"

"He *is* my life."

"But all these years, you must have known! You must have suspected that Reggie was the one who—"

"Not Reggie."

"Helena, please think about it!"

"*Not Reggie.*"

"He was obsessed, unable to let her go! To let another man have her—"

"It was me."

Those three words, uttered so quietly, chilled Beryl's blood to ice. She stared at the silhouette standing before her, her thoughts instantly shifting to ones of escape. She could flee down the road, pound at the nearest door.... She shifted onto the balls of her feet and was about to make a dash past Helena, when she heard the click of the pistol hammer.

"You look so very much like her," whispered Helena. "When I first saw you, years ago at Chetwynd, it was almost as if she'd come back. And now, I have to kill her all over again."

"But I'm not Madeline—"

"It makes no difference now who you are. Because you know." Helena raised her arm and Beryl saw, through the shadows, the faint gleam of the gun in her hand. "The garage, Beryl," she said. "We're going for a drive."

# CHAPTER TWELVE

"AMIEL FOCH," said Daumier, flipping through a file folder. "Age forty-six, formerly with French Intelligence. Presumed dead three years ago, after a helicopter crash off Cyprus—"

"He faked his own death?" asked Richard.

Daumier nodded. "It is not an easy matter to resign from Intelligence and simply start work as a mercenary. One would be subject to constraints."

"But if one is declared dead—"

"Precisely." Daumier skimmed the next page and stopped. "Here it is," he said. "The link we have been searching for. In 1972, M. Foch served as our liaison to the American mission. It seems there was a telephone threat against Ambassador Sutherland's family. For several years, Amiel Foch remained in contact with the Sutherland household. He was later reassigned to other duties, until his... death."

"When he became available for private clients. To perform any service," said Hugh.

"Including assassination." Daumier closed the folder and said to his assistant, "Bring in Mrs. Sutherland."

The woman who walked through the door was the same brash and confident Nina Sutherland that Richard had always known. She swept into the room, glanced around with disdain at her audience, then gracefully settled into a chair. "A bit late in the day for a command performance, don't you think?" she asked.

And a performance was just what they were going to get, thought Richard. Unless they shook her up. He pulled up a chair and sat down, facing her. "You know that Anthony's been taken into custody?"

A flicker of fear—just a flicker—rippled through her eyes. "It's a mistake, of course. He's never done anything wrong in his life."

"Murder through hire? Contracts with assassins?" Richard raised an eyebrow. "Ironclad charges, multiple witnesses. I'd say this is serious enough to warrant a very long stay behind bars."

"But he's only a boy and not—"

"He's of age. And fully responsible for his crimes." Richard glanced at Daumier. "Claude and I were just discussing what a shame it was. To be locked up so young. He'll be, how old when he's released, Claude? Fifty, do you think?"

"I would guess closer to sixty," said Daumier.

"Sixty." Richard shook his head and sighed. "His whole life behind him. No wife. No children." Richard looked Nina sympathetically in the eyes. "No grandchildren..."

Nina's face had turned ashen. She said in a whisper, "What do you want from me?"

"Cooperation."

"And what's my payback?"

"We can be lenient," said Daumier. "After all, he *is* just a boy."

Swallowing hard, Nina looked away. "It's not his fault. He doesn't deserve to be—"

"He's responsible for the deaths of two French agents. And the attempted murders of Marie St. Pierre and Jordan."

"He didn't do anything!"

"But he hired Amiel Foch to do his dirty work. What kind of a monster did you raise, Nina?"

"He was only trying to protect *me!*"

"From what?"

Nina's head drooped. "The past," she whispered. "It never goes away. Everything else changes, but the past..."

*The past,* thought Richard, remembering Heinrich Leitner's words. *We're always in its shadow.* "You were Delphi," he said. "Weren't you?"

Nina said nothing.

He leaned forward, and his voice dropped to a quiet, almost intimate murmur. "Perhaps it started out as a bit of a lark," he suggested. "An amusing game of spies and counterspies. Perhaps you liked the excitement. Or was it the money that tempted you? Whatever the reason, you passed a secret or two to the other side. Then it was classified documents. And suddenly you were in their pocket."

"It was only for a short time!"

"But by then it was too late. NATO intelligence got wind of it. And they were closing in. So you worked out a way to shift the blame. Somehow you lured Bernard and Madeline to your little love nest in Rue Myrha. There you shot them both."

"No."

"You planted the documents near Bernard's body."

*"No."*

Richard grabbed Nina by the shoulders and forced her to look at him. "And then you walked away and went on with your merry life. Isn't that how it went?"

Nina gave a pitiful sob. "I didn't kill them!"

*"Isn't it?"*

"I swear I didn't kill them! They were already dead!"

Richard released her. Nina sank back into the chair, her whole body shuddering with sobs.

"Who killed them?" demanded Richard. "Amiel Foch?"

"No, I never asked him to."

"Philippe?"

She looked up sharply. "No! He was the one who *found* them. He was frantic when he called me. Afraid he'd be accused of it. That's when I called in Foch. Asked him to make arrangements with Rideau, the landlord. A cash payment to change his testimony.''

"And the documents? Who planted them?''

"Foch did. By then, the police had already been called. Foch had to slip the briefcase into the garret.''

Jordan cut in, ''She's just admitted she's Delphi. Now we're supposed to believe some other mysterious culprit did the killing?''

"It's the truth!'' insisted Nina.

"Oh, right!'' sneered Jordan. "And the killer just happened to choose the very flat where you and Philippe met every week?''

Nina shook her head in bewilderment. "I don't know why he chose our flat.''

"It had to be you. Or Philippe,'' said Jordan.

"I would never...he would never...''

"Who else knew about the garret?'' asked Richard.

"No one.''

"Marie St. Pierre?''

"No.'' She paused, then whispered, "Yes, perhaps...''

"So Philippe's wife knew.''

Nina nodded miserably. "But no one else.''

"Wait,'' Jordan suddenly interjected. "Someone else *did* know about it.''

Everyone looked at him.

"What?'' said Richard.

"I heard it from Reggie. Helena knew about the affair—Marie told her. And if Marie knew about the garret on Rue Myrha, then—''

"So did Helena.'' Richard stared at Jordan. With that one look, they both knew what the other was thinking.

*Beryl.*

Instantly they both turned to leave. "Get us some backup!'' Richard snapped to Daumier. "Have them meet us there!''

"The Vanes' residence?''

Richard didn't answer; he was already running out the door.

"GET IN THE CAR," said Helena.

Beryl halted, her hand frozen on the door handle of the Mercedes. "There'll be questions, Helena."

"And I'll have the answers. I was asleep, you see. I slept all night. And when I woke up, you were gone. Left the compound on your own, never to be seen again."

"Reggie will remember—"

"Reggie won't remember a thing. He's stone drunk. As far as he knows, I never left the bed."

"They'll suspect you—"

"It's been twenty years, Beryl. And they still don't suspect." She raised the gun. "Get in. The driver's seat. Or do I have to change my story? Tell them I thought I was shooting a burglar?"

Beryl stared at the gun barrel pointed squarely at her chest. She had no choice. Helena really would shoot her. She climbed into the car.

Helena slid in beside her and tossed the keys into Beryl's lap. "Start the engine."

Beryl turned the key; the Mercedes purred to life like a contented cat. "My mother never meant to hurt you," said Beryl softly. "She was never interested in Reggie. She never wanted him."

"But he wanted *her*. Oh, I saw how he used to look at her! Do you know, he used to say her name in his sleep. There I'd be, lying next to him, and he'd be thinking of her. I never knew, I never really knew, if they were..." She swallowed. "Drive."

"Where?"

"Just go out the gate. Go!"

Beryl eased the Mercedes out of the garage and across the cobblestoned courtyard. Helena pressed a remote control and the iron gate automatically swung open. It closed again behind them as they drove through. Ahead stretched the tree-lined road. No other cars, no other witnesses.

The steering wheel felt slick with her sweat. Beryl gripped it tightly, just to keep her hands from shaking. "My father never hurt you," she whispered. "Why did you have to kill him?"

"Someone had to be blamed. Why not make it a dead man? And the fact it was Nina's secret flat—that made it all the more convenient." She laughed. "You should have seen how Nina and Philippe scrambled to cover things up."

"And Delphi?"

Helena shook her head in bewilderment. "What about Delphi?"

*So she knows nothing about it,* thought Beryl. *All this time, we've been chasing the wrong clues. Richard will never know—will never suspect—what really happened.*

The road began to curve and wind through the trees. They were headed into the depths of the Bois de Boulogne. *Is this where they'll find me?* she wondered, dismayed. *In some lonely copse of trees? At the muddy bottom of a pond?*

She peered ahead to the road beyond their headlights. They were approaching another curve.

*It may be my only chance. I can let her shoot me. Or I can go down fighting.* She pointed the car on a straight course. Then she hit the accelerator pedal. The engine roared and tires screamed. Beryl was thrust back against the seat as the Mercedes lurched forward.

Helena cried out, "No!" and clawed for control of the wheel. A split-second before they hit the trees, Helena managed to swerve them sideways. Suddenly they were tumbling like helpless riders in an out-of-control carnival ride. The Mercedes toppled over and over, windows shattered, and the two passengers were flung against the dashboard.

The car came to rest on its roof.

It was the blare of the horn that dragged Beryl back to consciousness. And the pain. Excruciating pain, tearing at her leg. She tried to move and realized that her chest was wedged against the steering wheel, and that her head was somehow cradled in the small space between the windshield and the upside-down dashboard. She pushed away from the steering wheel. The effort made her cry out in pain, but she managed to slide her body a few precious inches across the crumpled roof. For a moment, she rested, gasping for breath, waiting for the pain in her leg to ease. Then, gritting her teeth, she pushed again and managed to slide through into a larger pocket of space. The front seat? Everything seemed so mangled, so confusing in the darkness. The tumble had left her disoriented.

But she was not so dazed that she didn't smell the odor of gasoline growing stronger every second. *I have to get to a window—have to squeeze through before it explodes.* Blindly she reached out to feel her surroundings, and her hand shoved up against something warm. Something wet. She twisted her head around and came face-to-face with Helena's corpse.

Beryl screamed. Suddenly frantic to get out, to escape those sightless eyes, she squirmed away, clawing for the window. New pain, even more excruciating, ripped through her shattered leg and flooded her eyes with tears. She touched window frame, bits of glass and then…a branch! *I'm almost there. Almost there.*

Half crawling, half dragging herself, she managed to squeeze through the opening. Just as her body rolled onto the ground, the dirt beneath her seemed to give way and she began to slide down a leafy embankment. She landed in a ditch near some trees.

A burst of light suddenly shot into the sky. Through eyes blurred with agony, she looked up and saw the first flicker of the inferno. Seconds later, she heard the popping of glass, then a terrifying whoosh as a fountain of flames engulfed the vehicle.

*Why, Helena? Why?* The flames blurred, faded into a gathering darkness. She closed her eyes and shivered among the fallen leaves.

THREE MILES FROM the Vanes' residence, they spotted the fire. It was a car, upended, stretched diagonally across the road. A Mercedes.

"It's Helena's," shouted Richard. "My God, it's Helena's!" He leaped out and ran toward the burning car. He almost tripped over a shoe lying in the road. To his horror he saw it was a woman's pump. *"Beryl!"* he screamed. He was about to make a desperate lunge for the car door when the flames suddenly shot higher. A window burst out, scattering glass across the pavement. The searing heat sent him stumbling backward, his nostrils stinging with the stench of his own singed hair. He recovered his balance and was about to make another lunge through the flames when Jordan grabbed his arm.

"Wait!" cried Jordan.

Richard wrenched away. "Have to get her out!"

"No, *listen!*"

That's when he heard it—a moan, almost inaudible. It came not from the car, but from somewhere in the trees.

At once he and Jordan were scrambling along the roadside, yelling Beryl's name. Again, Richard heard the moan, closer now, coming from the shadows just below the road. He clambered down the dirt bank and stumbled into a drainage ditch.

That's where he found her, sprawled among the leaves. Barely conscious.

He gathered her up and was terrified by how limp, how cold her body felt in his arms. *She's in shock,* he realized. *We have precious little time....*

"Have to get her to a hospital!" he yelled.

Jordan ran ahead and yanked open the car door. Richard, clutching Beryl in his arms, slid into the back seat.

"Go!" he barked.

"Hang on," muttered Jordan, scrambling into the driver's seat. "It's going to be a wild ride."

With a screech of tires, their car shot off down the road. *Stay with me, Beryl,* Richard begged silently as he cradled her body in his arms. *Please, darling. Stay with me....*

But as the car sped through the darkness, she seemed to grow ever colder to his touch.

THROUGH THE HAZE of anesthesia, she heard him call her name, but the sound of his voice seemed so very far away, seemed to come from a distant place she could not possibly reach. Then she felt his hand close tightly over hers, and she knew he was right beside her. She could not see his face; she could not muster enough strength to open her eyes. Yet she knew he was there, that he would still be there when she awoke the next morning.

But it was Jordan whom she saw sitting by her bed. The late-morning sunlight streamed over his fair hair and a leather-bound book of poetry lay in his lap. He was reading Milton. *Dear Jordan,* she thought. *Ever reliable, ever serene. If only I had inherited such peace of mind.*

Jordan glanced up from the page and saw that she was awake. "Welcome back to the world, little sister," he said with a smile.

She groaned. "I'm not so sure I want to be back."

"The leg?"

"Killing me."

He reached for the call button. "Time to indulge in the miracle of morphine."

But even miracles take time. After the nurse delivered the injection, Beryl closed her eyes and waited for the pain to ease, for the blessed numbness to descend.

"Better?" asked Jordan.

"Not yet." She took a deep breath. "God, I hate being an invalid. Talk to me. Please."

"About what?"

*Richard,* she thought. *Please tell me about Richard. Why he isn't here. Why he's not the one sitting in that chair....*

Jordan said, quietly, "You know, he was here. Earlier this morning. But then Daumier called."

She lay still, not speaking. Waiting to hear more.

"He cares about you, Beryl. I'm sure he does." Jordan closed his book and set it on the bedside table. "Really, he seems an agreeable fellow. Quite capable."

"Capable," she murmured. "Yes, he is that."

"He didn't turn tail and run. He did look after you."

"As a favor," she amended. "To Uncle Hugh."

He didn't answer. And she thought that Jordie, too, had his doubts about their odds for happiness. And so did she. From the very beginning.

The morphine began to take effect. Little by little, she felt herself drift toward sleep. Only vaguely did she hear Richard enter the room and speak softly to Jordan. They murmured something about Helena and her body being burned beyond recognition. As the drug swept her brain toward unconsciousness, a memory suddenly flashed with horrifying vividness into her mind—the flames engulfing the car, engulfing Helena.

For loving too deeply, too fiercely, this was Helena's punishment.

She felt Richard take her hand and press it to his lips.

And what punishment, she wondered, would be hers?

# *EPILOGUE*

*Buckinghamshire, England*
*Six weeks later*

FROGGIE WAS RESTLESS, stamping about in her stall, whinnying for escape.

"Look at her, the poor thing," Beryl said and sighed. "She hasn't been run nearly enough, and I think she's going quite insane. You'll have to exercise her for me."

"Me? On the back of that…that maniac?" Jordan snorted. "I'm much too fond of my own neck."

Beryl hobbled over to the stall on her crutches. At once Froggie poked her head over the door and gave Beryl an insistent want-to-go-running nudge. "Oh, but she's such a pussycat."

"A pussycat with a foul temper."

"And she so badly needs a good, hard gallop."

Jordan looked at his sister, who was wobbling unsteadily on leg cast and crutches. She seemed so pale and thin these days. As if those long weeks in the hospital had drained something vital from her spirit. A bit of pallor was to be expected, of course, considering all the blood she'd lost, all the days of pain she'd suffered after the operation to pin her shattered femur. Now the leg was healing well, and the pain was only a memory, but she still seemed only a ghost of herself.

It was Richard Wolf's fault.

At least the fellow had been decent enough to hang

around during Beryl's hospitalization. In fact, he'd practically haunted her room, spending every daylight hour by her bed. And all the flowers! Every morning, a fresh bouquet.

Then, one day, he was gone. Jordan hadn't heard the explanation. He'd walked into his sister's hospital room that morning and found her staring out the window, all packed and ready to go home to Chetwynd.

Three weeks ago, they'd flown back. And she's been brooding ever since, he thought, looking at her wan face.

"Go on, Jordie," she said. "Give her a bit of a run. It'll be another month before I can ride her again."

Resignedly, Jordan swung open the stall door and led Froggie out to be saddled. "You'd better behave, young lady," he muttered to the beast. "No rearing. No bucking. And definitely no trampling your poor, defenseless rider."

Froggie gave him a look that could only be interpreted as the equine equivalent of *we'll see about that.*

Jordan mounted and gave Beryl a wave.

"Take care of her!" Beryl called out. "See she doesn't hurt herself!"

"Your concern is most touching!" he managed to blurt out just before Froggie took off at a mad gallop for the fields. Jordan managed a last backward glance at Beryl standing forlornly by the stable. How small she looked, how fragile. Not at all the Beryl he knew. Would she ever be herself again?

Froggie was bearing him toward the woods. He concentrated on hanging on for dear life as the beast made a beeline for the stone wall. "You just have to take that bloody hurdle, don't you?" he muttered as Froggie's mane whipped his face. "Which means *I* have to take the bloody hurdle—"

Together they flew over the wall, clearing it neatly. *Still in the saddle,* thought Jordan with a grin of triumph. *Not so easy to get rid of me, is it?*

It was the last thought in his head before Froggie tossed him off her back.

Jordan landed, fortunately enough, on a large clump of moss. As he sprawled beneath the wildly spinning treetops, he was vaguely aware of the sound of tires grinding across the dirt road, and then he heard someone call his name. Groggily he sat up.

Froggie was standing over him, looking not in the least bit apologetic. And behind her, climbing out of a red M.G., was Richard Wolf.

"Are you all right?" Richard called out, running toward him.

"Tell me, Wolf," Jordan groaned. "Are you out to kill all the Tavistocks? Or are you after one of us in particular?"

Laughing, Richard helped him to his feet. "I'd lay the blame where it belongs. On the horse."

Both men looked at Froggie. She answered with what sounded suspiciously like a laugh.

Richard asked quietly, "How's Beryl doing these days?"

Jordan began to clap the dirt from his trousers. "Her leg's healing fine."

"Besides the leg?"

"Not so fine." Jordan straightened and looked the other man in the eye. "Why did you walk out?"

Sighing, Richard looked off in the direction of Chetwynd. "She asked me to."

"What?" Jordan stared at him in bewilderment. "She never told me—"

"She's a Tavistock, like you. Doesn't believe in whining or complaining. Or losing face. It's that pride of hers."

"Ah, so it was like that, was it?" Jordan said. "An argument?"

"Not even that. It just seemed, with all those differences between us…" He shook his head and laughed. "Face it, Jordan. She's tea and crumpets, I'm coffee and doughnuts.

She'd hate it in Washington. And I'm not sure I could adjust to…this." He gestured to the rolling fields of Chetwynd.

*But you will adjust,* foresaw Jordan. *And so will she. Because it's plain for any idiot to see that you two belong together.*

"Anyway," said Richard, "when Niki called and reminded me we had a job in New Delhi, Beryl told me to go. She thought it would be a good test for us to be apart for a while. Said the Royal Family does it that way. To see if absence makes the heart—and hormones—forget."

"And does it?"

Richard grinned. "Not a chance," he said, and climbed back into his car. "I may be signing up with your wild and crazy family, after all. Any objections?"

"None," said Jordan. "But I *will* offer a bit of advice. That is, if you two expect to share a long and healthy life together."

"What's the advice?"

"Shoot the horse."

Laughing, Richard let out the brake and sped away toward Chetwynd.

Toward Beryl.

As Jordan watched the M.G. vanish around the bend, he thought, *Good luck to you, little sister. I'm glad one of us has finally found someone to love. Now if only I could be so fortunate…*

He turned to Froggie. "And as for you," he said aloud, "I am about to teach you exactly who's boss around here."

Froggie gave a snort. Then, with a triumphant toss of her mane, she turned and galloped away, riderless, toward Chetwynd.

"It's quite unlike you to be brooding this way," said Uncle Hugh as he picked another tomato and set it in his basket. He looked faintly ridiculous in his floppy gardening hat. More like the groundskeeper than the lord of the manor.

Crouching on his knees, he uncovered another bright red globe and carefully plucked the treasure. "Don't know why you're so gloomy these days. After all, the leg's almost healed."

"It's not the leg," said Beryl.

"One would think you were permanently crippled."

"It's not the leg."

"Well, what is it, then?" asked Hugh, moving on to the row of pole beans. Suddenly he stopped and glanced back at her. "Oh, it's him, isn't it?"

Sighing, Beryl reached for her crutches and rose from the garden bench. "I don't wish to discuss it."

"You never do."

"I still don't," she said, and stubbornly headed down the brick path toward the maze. She brushed past the edging of lavender, stirring the scents of the late summer garden. Once they'd walked this path together, she thought. And now she was walking it alone.

She entered the maze and, using her crutches, maneuvered around all the secret twists and turns. At last she emerged at the center and sat down on the stone bench. *Yes, I'm brooding again,* she realized. *Uncle Hugh's right. Have to stop this and get on with my life.*

But first, she would have to stop thinking of him. Had he stopped thinking of her? All the doubts, the fears, came back to assail her. She'd put him to the test, she thought. And he'd failed it.

From a distance, she heard someone call her name. It was so faint at first, she thought she might have imagined it. But there it was again—moving closer now!

She lurched to her feet, wobbling on the crutches. *"Richard?"*

"Beryl?" came the answering shout. "Where are you?"

"In the maze!"

His footsteps moved closer along the path. "Where?"

"The center!"

Through the high hedge walls, she heard his sheepish laughter. "And now I'm expected to find my way to the cheese?"

"Just think of it," she challenged him, "as a test of true love."

"Or true insanity," he muttered, rustling into the maze.

"I'm quite annoyed with you, you know," she called.

"I think I've noticed."

"You didn't write. You didn't call, not once!"

"I was too busy trying to catch planes back to London. And besides, I wanted you to miss me. Did you?"

"No, I didn't."

"You didn't?"

"Not at all." She bit her lip. "Oh, perhaps a bit..."

"Ah, so you *did* miss me—"

"But not much."

"I missed *you.*"

She paused. "Did you?" she asked softly.

"So much, in fact, that if I don't find the bloody center of this bloody maze pretty damn quick, I'm going to—"

"Going to what?" she asked breathlessly.

A rustle of branches made her turn. Suddenly he was there beside her, pulling her into his arms, covering her mouth with a kiss so deep, so insistent, she felt herself swaying dizzily. The crutches slipped away and fell to the ground. She didn't need them—not when he was there to hold her.

He drew away and smiled at her. "Hello again, Miss Tavistock," he whispered.

"You came back," she murmured. "You really came back."

"Did you think I wouldn't?"

"Does that mean you've thought about it? About us?"

He laughed. "I could scarcely concentrate on anything else. On the job, the client. Finally I had to call in Niki to pinch-hit for me, while I straighten out this mess with you."

She asked softly, "You think it *can* be straightened out?"

Gently he framed her face with his hands. "I don't know. Some folks would probably call us a long shot."

"And they'd be right. There are so many things that could pull us apart...."

"And just as many things that will keep us together." He lowered his face to hers, gently brushed her lips with his. "I confess, I'll never make a proper gentleman. Cricket's not my bag. And you'll have to put a gun to my head to get me up on a horse. But if you're willing to overlook those terrible flaws..."

She threw her arms around his neck. "What flaws?" she whispered, and their lips met again.

From the distance came the peal of the ancient church bells. Six o'clock. The coming of twilight and shadows, sweetly scented. *And love,* thought Beryl as he pulled her, laughing, into his arms.

Quite definitely, love.

# BEDROOM WINDOW

## Amanda Stevens

KAITLIN O'ROARKE reclined against a stack of pillows and watched her cousin's reaction with amusement. "Well? What do you think?"

"Quite the decadent little boudoir, isn't it?" Fiona Gallagher did a slow three-sixty, her expression ranging from shock and dismay to outright wonder. "Did you know about your friend's—shall we say—unusual tastes when you agreed to apartment-sit for her?"

Kaitlin grinned. "No, but I like what she's done with the place."

Fiona shot her a look. "You do not."

"I do, too. And furthermore, if I decide to get my own apartment, I'm calling her decorator."

"Where do you expect to find him? In the Yellow Pages under Fetishes R Us?" Fiona ran her hand along the telescope that was mounted on a tripod in front of a wall of windows framing the Chicago skyline. "Dollars to doughnuts she doesn't use this for stargazing."

"Maybe she likes to watch the boats on the lake."

"You can barely even see the lake from here. And stop trying to convince me you actually like this Kama Sutra nightmare. I know you too well. Down deep, you're still the same little Katie Gallagher who eloped with the first guy she ever slept with."

"All right, I won't try to convince you." But in the week since Kaitlin had first moved into the apartment, she really had come to appreciate the lavish colors and sumptuous textures, the erotic beauty of the artwork displayed on walls and in niches.

The décor was so far removed from the house she'd fled in the suburbs that Kaitlin had welcomed the change—any change—with open arms. What she hadn't been able to adjust to quite so easily, however, was the mirrored ceiling. She'd broken her foot that morning, and keeping it elevated meant that she had to spend a lot of time on her back. The woman who stared down at her from that mirror looked a little too lost and forlorn. A little too haunted by memories.

Fiona bent to the eyepiece on the telescope. "Your friend is obviously into some naughty stuff here, Kaitlin. Voyeurism is the word that comes to mind."

"Just because she collects erotic artwork and has a telescope in her bedroom doesn't mean she's...you know... kinky."

"Doesn't mean she's not, either.... *Hello*. What have we here?" Fiona adjusted the focus ring. "Seriously hot naked guy at twelve o'clock."

"Seriously?"

"No, wait. He's wearing pants. Damn." She didn't seem to appreciate the irony of her disappointment as she left the telescope and came to stand by the bed. "And speaking of hot guys, I was a little surprised to find your hubby here."

"Knowing how you feel about him, *I'm* a little surprised you'd admit that he's hot," Kaitlin said dryly.

Fiona shrugged. "Other than the horns and the cloven hooves, he's not so bad."

She was joking, but Kaitlin hadn't found anything remotely amusing about her family's feud with her husband's for a long time. The Gallaghers and the O'Roarkes had been enemies for generations, ever since William Gallagher and James O'Roarke had had a bitter falling out over a woman—Fiona and Kaitlin's grandmother, Colleen. William's sons and grandsons had followed him into the police department while James had gone on to found what would become one of the most notorious crime families in Chi-

# TEMPE MISSION PALMS

60 East Fifth Street • Tempe, Arizona 85281
480.894.1400 • Fax 480.968.7677 • 800.547.8705
www.missionpalms.com

cago. The O'Roarkes had long since mended their ways, but there was still no love lost between the two families. And now with Fiona a prosecutor and Dylan a defense attorney, they'd carried the feud over into the courtroom. Which left Kaitlin, as usual, caught in the middle.

"So what is he doing here?" Fiona persisted.

Kaitlin tried not to sound defensive. "He found out about the accident and came to check on me."

"And?"

"And nothing."

"Kaitlin, the man has set up a temporary office on the dining room table. He doesn't appear to be going anywhere anytime soon. That kind of defeats the purpose of a separation, doesn't it?"

"He's just staying for a little while in case I need anything. And stop looking at me like that," Kaitlin grumbled. "It doesn't mean...what you think it means."

"Are you sure?"

"Of course I'm sure. Look, we were married for seven years. We still care about each other. We just don't love each other anymore."

"So that's why you walked out on me," Dylan said from the doorway. "Thanks for the explanation, Kaitlin, because I never was too clear on your reason."

Even after everything they'd been through, the sight of Dylan in the doorway, tall, lean and incredibly handsome, still had the power to jump-start Kaitlin's heart. No matter what else they'd lost, the attraction was still there, sometimes stronger than ever. Kaitlin suspected that was because her husband had once again become a stranger to her. A man she hardly knew. A forbidden lover for whom she'd once been willing to sacrifice her mind, body and soul.

But no more. Kaitlin had awakened one morning to the realization that she could no longer go on the way they had been. The ugliness between the O'Roarkes and the Gallaghers had put a terrible strain on her and Dylan's relationship. Where once the hostility between their families had served to bring the two of them closer, now it was merely another broken stitch in a marriage that was fast coming apart at the seams.

Sensing the sudden tension, Fiona gathered up her coat and purse. "I need to be shoving off, but I'll see you soon, okay? Oh, I almost forgot. A little something for the invalid." She handed Kaitlin a plastic shopping bag from a movie rental store.

Kaitlin peeked inside. "Hitchcock! All my favorites, too. I can't believe you remembered."

"What are cousins for?" She shrugged into her coat, and then blew a kiss from the doorway.

DYLAN WAITED for the sound of Fiona's exit before he came slowly into the bedroom. He tried to keep his cool, but he felt as if he'd just been sucker-punched in the gut. "So we don't love each other anymore. When did you come to that conclusion?"

Kaitlin lay back against the pillows. "I don't want to talk about this right now. I'm tired."

Her cool dismissal made him so angry he had to wait a moment before he could speak. "And it's all about what you want, isn't it? You need some space. You need to find yourself. You need your independence. So you walk out on me and seven years of marriage without even once bothering to ask what I want."

She glared up at him. "Don't play the martyr, Dylan. If Aunt Maggie hadn't called you about the accident, you probably wouldn't even have noticed I was gone."

"Oh, I don't know. Coming home to find you packing your suitcases was a pretty big clue," he said with an edge of sarcasm.

Kaitlin shoved back her hair. "Okay, so I exaggerated. But you know what I mean. You put all your time and energy, your every waking hour into your career. And on the rare occasions when you are home, you're either on the phone or sequestered in your office going over briefs or depositions. And that's fine if it makes you happy, but what am I supposed to do? Sit around waiting for the walls to close in on me?''

''I didn't expect you to walk out.''

She sighed. ''It can't have been that much of a surprise. Things haven't been right between us for a long time. We were nothing more than polite roommates leading two separate lives before I left. We didn't even share the same bedroom anymore.''

Because you made me feel as if I was no longer welcome in your bed, he thought defensively. ''I started sleeping in the guest room because I didn't want to wake you up when I came in late.''

''Did it ever occur to you that I might want you to wake me up?''

''Did it ever occur to you that by the time I got home, I might be too exhausted to cater to your every *whim?*'' he shot back.

''Cater to my—'' Her eyes glittered with angry tears. ''You think wanting to have a conversation with my husband is a whim? Wanting to share my day with him, wanting to share my life with him, is a whim?''

''And do you think I enjoy spending fifteen and sixteen hours a day at the office? Damn it, Kaitlin, I do it because that's what it takes to become a senior partner at the firm. I'm trying to build something for us. Trying to provide for our future. I thought you understood that.''

''I do understand,'' Kaitlin said in a wounded tone. ''But what good is providing for the future if we're miserable in the here and now?''

*Miserable?* She'd been miserable? Dylan drew a long breath. ''So what's the next step here, Kaitlin? Divorce?''

*Divorce?* The word was like an arrow straight through Kaitlin's heart. ''I never said anything about a divorce.''

''Come on, Kaitlin. We both know where this is headed. A couple has to live separate and apart for a minimum of six months before a divorce can be granted on the grounds of irreconcilable differences. And that's only if neither spouse contests the petition. Don't tell me you didn't familiarize yourself with Illinois divorce laws before you moved in here.''

''I didn't.''

''Then what were you hoping to accomplish?'' he asked with a frown. ''Did you want me to come running after you? Beg you to come back to me? Promise to give up my career if it would make you happy? What is it you want from me, Kaitlin? Because I sure as hell don't know anymore.''

*I want you to be my husband again,* she silently cried. I want things to be the way they once were when you could look at me and make me melt. I want you to look at me that way again. I want you to hold me, kiss me, touch me the way you used to….

But instead, she said sadly, ''I don't want anything from you, Dylan. You're not responsible for my happiness. I realize that now. I didn't move into this apartment to establish a separate residence from you. I moved in here because I need to prove to myself that I can stand on my own two feet. That I can be alone without falling to pieces. And that maybe, just maybe, I can be happy again someday.''

''Without me, you mean?''

She closed her eyes briefly. ''I don't know. I just know I can't go back to the way things were.''

He shoved his hands into his pockets as he turned to stare out the window. ''You know what your problem is, Kaitlin? You still think our lives should be this great Romeo and Juliet love affair that defies all odds. But real life is more than just star-crossed lovers and fairy tales. It's mortgages and car payments and planning for a secure future.''

She sighed. ''I know that. And you're a wonderful provider, Dylan. You always have been.''

He glanced over his shoulder. ''Just a lousy husband, right?''

''I didn't say that.''

''Actions speak louder than words, Kaitlin.''

The bitterness in his tone brought fresh tears to her eyes. She'd never meant to hurt him. But after seven years of marriage, this is what they'd come to.

"Look, you really don't have to stay," she said. "I'm fine. You must have things you'd rather do."

He came back over to the bed. "What'll you do about dinner?"

"I'll fix a sandwich or order a pizza. I'm not completely helpless, you know. I'm perfectly capable of taking care of myself, and it's time we both realized that."

"That's the difference between us, Kaitlin. I've always known it."

Their gazes met in the falling darkness, and Kaitlin's heart constricted. "Don't," she whispered.

"Don't what?"

"Be nice to me."

"It's too little too late anyway, isn't it?" He turned back to the window.

Kaitlin cleared her throat. "If you insist on staying, maybe we should talk about something besides us."

He shrugged. "I'm open to suggestions."

She searched for something innocuous. "Tell me about work. You have a big case coming up, don't you?"

"I don't much feel like talking about work."

Kaitlin stared at him in shock. He lived and breathed work. "Okay, then. Tell me what you think of Jane's apartment."

He took a moment to study some of the erotic artwork on the walls, and when he glanced at Kaitlin, she saw something dark and knowing in his eyes. Something that made her shiver. Something that made her remember a time in the not-too-distant past when they had shared the same bedroom. And so much more.

"It's interesting. I'll say that for it." He leaned over to gaze through the telescope. "Do you ever use this thing?"

"No, not much." She paused. "Dylan, why do you think

Jane has a telescope in her bedroom? Do you think she's a voyeur?''

He looked slightly taken aback by the question, as if surprised Kaitlin would even think such a thing. "I don't know. But if she had a habit of watching someone, I'd say the chances are pretty good that someone was watching her back."

Kaitlin cast an uneasy glance toward the windows. "Do you think someone could be watching us right now?"

Dylan shrugged. "It's possible. I doubt your friend is the only one who uses these high-rises as her own personal peep show. And no blinds, I notice."

"That bothered me, too, at first. But you could do a striptease in front of those windows and it wouldn't matter how many people saw you because none of them know you. You'll never see them in real life."

Dylan looked simultaneously annoyed and intrigued by the notion. "Are you speaking from experience?"

"No, but I've thought about it," she admitted. "Ever since we were married, I've felt as if I were being pulled in a thousand different directions. It's hard to be the perfect wife and the perfect daughter when your husband and your father hate each other. No matter what I do, I always end up hurting someone I love. But it's different here. No pressures. No expectations. No one even knows me. Anonymity can be a very liberating experience."

"I never realized you felt so imprisoned by our marriage," Dylan said bitterly.

"I'm sorry. I don't mean to hurt you, but I'm trying to explain how I feel. Why I'm here. If there's any hope for us, we have to be honest with each other, don't we?"

"Maybe. But right now, I think I've had all the honesty I can stomach for one night." He strode across the room to the door.

"Dylan—" When he turned, Kaitlin bit her lip, not knowing what to say to him. "Where are you going?"

"To get you some dinner."

"You don't have to do that. I can—"

"Take care of yourself. Yeah, I got that, Kaitlin, so relax. I'm not trying to put a ball and chain around your ankle, okay? I'm just ordering you a pizza."

He slammed the door shut behind him, and Kaitlin lay in stunned silence. She'd never seen him so angry. Or hurt. Her first instinct was to go to him, but she knew that would be a mistake. He might get the wrong idea, and then she might lose her resolve. And they'd both end up back where they started.

Reaching for her crutches, she got up and limped into the bathroom, taking great care to avoid the mirror over the sink as she washed up. She'd become adept at brushing her teeth, fixing her hair, even putting on makeup without ever really looking at her reflection. Without ever really seeing the unhappy woman who stared back at her. That was why she had such a problem with that mirrored ceiling. It made it hard to avoid the truth.

Maneuvering back into the bedroom, she turned off the lamp, then stood at the bedroom window and studied the skyline. The view was breathtaking, the city lights so beautiful she could watch them forever. There was something at once isolating and intimate about all those windows.

Gazing through the telescope, she shifted the tube until she found the apartment she wanted. The lens had been fixed on the window directly across from hers when she'd moved in, but Kaitlin had come to think that it must have been by accident. In the week since she'd been there, the apartment across the way had remained dark. The unit was either empty or the owner away on business or vacation.

But to her surprise, a light was on tonight, and she could see a man inside. He was dressed all in black, and the way he paced back and forth reminded her of a caged animal. He had a phone to his ear, and suddenly he whirled and threw it against the wall with such force that Kaitlin could almost hear the crash. A shiver of unease crept up her backbone, but she couldn't turn away. She watched, mesmerized, as he stalked over to the window, and for a moment, he appeared to be staring at her.

Even though it was dark in the bedroom, Kaitlin shrank back. He couldn't see her and he didn't know who she was, but gooseflesh prickled along her skin just the same. She bent to the eyepiece again and saw that he'd rescued the phone. He lifted it to his ear and, evidently hearing a dial tone, punched in a number.

And then the phone in her bedroom started to ring.

The phone rang only twice before the answering machine kicked in. A dark, sensuous voice said on the tape, "Jane, if you're there, pick up. I have to talk to someone before I go crazy...."

The anxiety in his voice sent another chill up Kaitlin's spine. She bent to the eyepiece, and sure enough, the man in the apartment directly across from hers was still on the phone. Still pacing back and forth.

Kaitlin had no way of knowing if the voice on the answering machine belonged to him or not, but somehow she thought that it must. They seemed to fit. The timbre of the voice was deep and velvety. The man in the apartment was tall and sleek, with glossy black hair that brushed his shoulders and dark, smoldering eyes. He was the antithesis of Dylan. Her husband had light brown hair clipped very short and eyes that were as blue as an Irish sky. And Dylan would never lose control the way this man had. He would never sound so...desperate.

Kaitlin could never imagine Dylan dressing all in black, either, let alone in a silky shirt opened at the neck and pants so tight they fit the man like a second skin. Fit him so well that she could see the definition of his sinewy muscles and his...

"Jane, please pick up...."

Dylan wore custom-made suits, starchy white shirts and silk ties knotted so perfectly they sometimes set Kaitlin's teeth on edge. It made her feel as if she needed to go back and start all over with her own appearance.

"I need you...."

Kaitlin watched him through the telescope. He was facing her now, and she could see his features as clearly as if he were standing in the same room with her.

*Tall, dark, and handsome...*

The cliché could have been written for him. And yet he wasn't perfect. Kaitlin sensed that he was flawed somehow, and that made him even more attractive. She wondered if he was an artist or a writer. There was something eccentric about the way he dressed, something exotic about his looks. Something blatantly sexual about the way he prowled the apartment.

"If I don't talk to someone, I swear I'll go out of my mind."

He lifted a hand to gracefully drag it through his dark hair, and Kaitlin's stomach quivered in awareness.

"When I think about her with him, it kills me inside."

There was so much emotion in his voice...so much *passion.* What would it be like to have a man love you so desperately? Kaitlin wondered. A man who wanted you so badly? Dylan was upset and hurt at the moment, but deep down, Kaitlin suspected her leaving was more of an inconvenience to him than anything else. After he had time to get used to the idea, he might even be relieved.

"Jane..." The voice on the answering machine lowered. "You have to stop me. I'm afraid of what I might do—" The machine beeped.

In the apartment across from her, the man lifted his gaze to the window.

For the longest moment, they stared at one another, although he couldn't know for sure she was there. But somehow Kaitlin thought that he did. Somehow she could hear his silent appeal through the glass and distance that separated them. And for the space of a heartbeat it was as if they were the only two people in the world. Two needy souls reaching out in the darkness. And then Dylan said from the doorway behind her, "Kaitlin? What the hell do you think you're doing?"

As Kaitlin spun to face Dylan, she lost her balance and her weight came down hard on her injured foot. Yelping in pain, she tried to compensate by shifting to the other leg, but it was too late. Her knees buckled and she tumbled to the floor, banging her head on the velvet chaise near the telescope.

Dylan's heart leaped to his throat when he saw her collapse because he knew he couldn't get to her in time. It was like the slow disintegration of their marriage, he thought in a flash. He could see it coming, but he was powerless to stop it. He dropped to his knees beside her. "God, Kaitlin, are you okay?"

"I think so." She winced as she struggled to sit up.

He put his hand behind her back. "Here let me help you."

"I can do it myself!"

He sat back, wounded by her harshness. "Sorry."

"No, I'm sorry," she said contritely. "I didn't mean to snap at you. I just need to know that I can do this by myself. What if you hadn't been here?"

"But I am here."

"I know, but you won't always be."

A knife twisted in his heart. "Can I ask you something?"

"What is it?" She gritted her teeth as she reached for her crutches.

"Do you consider me weak?"

"Of course not, Dylan. We both know you're a rock. You can handle anything."

He ignored the edge of resentment in her tone. "If I found myself in your position," he said slowly. "I'd want your help. Would that make me weak? Would that make me too reliant?"

She slanted him a glance. "Look, I know what you're getting at, but I think the point here is, you would never find yourself in my position. You wouldn't have your head in the clouds and miss an icy patch on the sidewalk and embarrass yourself in front of half a dozen pedestrians.''

''Don't be too sure. Everyone slips now and then.''

''Not you, Dylan.''

He stared at her in surprise. ''You don't remember the time I fell off a ladder at home? We thought my leg was broken. I couldn't put any weight on it. You practically had to drag me to the car and then you drove me to the emergency room. I couldn't have made it without you. Did that make me weak?''

She sighed. ''No.''

''Then why is it such a big deal to let me help you now?''

''Because...''

''Look, Kaitlin.'' He raked a hand through his hair in frustration. ''I don't pretend to understand everything that's going on with you, but all I want to do is help you back to bed. No hidden agenda.''

She bit her lip, and then nodded. ''Okay. I could use a hand.''

Dylan lifted her into his arms and carried her to the bed. He half expected her to protest, to insist that he put her down, but instead she buried her face in his chest. And when he placed her gently on the bed, she clung to him, their lips only inches apart.

And as she gazed up at him, something stirred inside Dylan. She looked so small and vulnerable on the bed. So beautiful and sexy and desirable. And so lost, somehow.

He knew better than anyone what their marriage had cost her. In a very real sense, she'd lost her family because of him, and Dylan had made himself a promise on the day they'd eloped. He would spend the rest of his life making it up to her. He would take care of her, give her the kind of life she deserved, the kind of life he wanted her to have. But instead, he'd made her father's prophesy come true. He'd made her regret the day she'd ever met an O'Roarke.

As if reading his mind, she put a hand to his face. ''It

breaks my heart when you look that way,'' she said tenderly.

He cleared his throat. ''What way?''

''Like you have the weight of the world on your shoulders.''

He wanted to kiss her. At that moment, he wanted to kiss her more than he'd wanted anything in his life. And he could have sworn he saw the same hunger in her eyes. Their gazes held for the longest time, and then, as he lowered his head, the phone on the nightstand pealed loudly, a harsh intrusion that caused them both to jump.

Kaitlin lurched for the phone, although she didn't know why she was so frantic to answer, why she didn't want Dylan to hear the stranger's voice on the machine.

''Hello?'' Nothing but silence.

''Hello?'' More silence.

And then a deep, seductive voice said in her ear, ''You're not Jane, are you? The line went dead so abruptly Kaitlin started. And then it occurred to her that the stranger might not know who she was, but he knew who she wasn't. And he knew where she lived.

''Wrong number?'' Dylan asked, as he moved to the end of the bed.

''Some guy calling for Jane.'' Kaitlin couldn't quite meet her husband's gaze. Why did she feel so guilty when she hadn't done anything wrong?

''Whoever he was, I'm sure you gave him a thrill before he hung up,'' Dylan said unexpectedly.

Her gaze shot to his. *''What?''*

''Your voice is a real turn-on, Kaitlin. In fact, whoever that guy was, he's probably fantasizing right now about having phone sex with you.''

She gaped at him, speechless.

''I used to fantasize about it myself,'' he said calmly.

''You fantasized about…having phone sex…with me.'' Kaitlin found that revelation shocking on two levels. That Dylan had fantasies, and that she was in them.

His gaze on her intensified, so much so that it drew a shiver up Kaitlin's spine. "Sometimes when I'd be in a meeting with the senior partners, discussing my future with the firm or an upcoming case, my mind would wander and I'd find myself daydreaming about taking a phone call from you. I would imagine myself acting perfectly natural in front of the partners as I listened to you describe in graphic detail what you were wearing, what you wanted to do to me, and what you would make me do to you in return."

"Make you—" This man wasn't Dylan. This was some pod Dylan who'd done away with the real one. This Dylan was making Kaitlin's heartbeat way too fast.

"Are you telling me you not only fantasized about having phone sex with me, but having me…" How could she put this delicately? "Assume the dominant role?"

"Why is that so surprising?"

"Because you're always so in control, so strong. So…masterful in the bedroom. You're always the one—"

"On top?"

She cringed at that. "In a manner of speaking, yes."

"Maybe that's because I'm the one who always had to initiate sex between us."

"That's not true."

"Yes, it is. Think about it, Kaitlin. When did you ever make the first move? When did you ever let me know that you wanted me? I was the one who always had to put myself out there for rejection. It's understandable, I guess. You were a virgin when we started dating so I thought I had to be the one in control. The one who had to take care of you. But now it seems like I'm being penalized for playing a role that we both cast me in. And I'm not just talking about our sex life."

She couldn't believe he was speaking so candidly. Dylan had never been one to talk about his feelings. "Why are you telling me all this now?"

He looked suddenly angry. "Because I think you're right. I think it's time for a little honesty between us. You no longer want to play the damsel in distress? Well, maybe I'm a little tired of playing the stoic hero.''

He turned then and left the room, and Kaitlin could do nothing but stare at the closed door in astonishment. Why had they not had this discussion weeks ago, months ago, years ago? Why now, when it just might be too late? Now, when they'd drifted so far apart, Kaitlin wasn't sure they could ever find their way back to each other?

She wanted to go to him and try to make things right, but she knew that would be a mistake. She couldn't afford to rush into anything. She didn't want to act on an impulse that she might end up regretting tomorrow. Words were easy. Living by them was harder.

When the phone rang a third time, she turned to stare at it, but she didn't answer. Somehow, she knew that if she lifted that phone to her ear, if she let the dark-haired stranger into her life, even from a distance, it could be the final blow that severed her relationship with Dylan.

But Kaitlin couldn't seem to stop herself. She reached out and slowly lifted the receiver to her ear. There was nothing but silence at first. Then, after a moment, that velvety voice said in a near whisper, ''You must be Kaitlin.''

She gasped. ''How did—''

''I'm sorry,'' he said. ''I didn't mean to freak you out, but Jane told me you were coming to stay in her apartment while she's in Europe.''

A shiver ran up Kaitlin's spine. He not only knew where she lived, but he knew who she was. So much for anonymity.

Hang up! a little voice commanded.

Instead she gripped the phone tighter. ''You have me at a disadvantage,'' she said a bit breathlessly. ''You know who I am, but I don't know who you are.''

''Yes, you do.''

Her gaze flew to the telescope. Did he know she'd been watching him?

''We've met before,'' he said.

"That's impossible. If we'd met before, I'm sure I would have remembered you."

"How do you know?"

"Because I—" Kaitlin's gaze was still on the telescope, and she closed her eyes, realizing she'd almost given herself away. "You have a very distinctive voice. I don't think I would have forgotten it."

And suddenly something Dylan had said earlier came back to her. *"In fact, whoever that guy was, he's probably fantasizing right now about having phone sex with you."*

Now she understood perfectly what he'd meant by that. The stranger's voice was doing odd things to her insides.

She felt herself blush in the darkness. "I should go—"

"No, wait. Don't hang up." The teasing quality left his voice as desperation crept in. "I know this may sound a little strange, but do you think…would it be possible for us to…just keep on talking for a little while? I'm finding myself a bit on edge tonight."

Kaitlin imagined him in his apartment, pacing back and forth, dragging a hand through his dark, glossy hair….

"You have to stop me. I'm afraid of what I might do—"

And then she thought about all those long nights she'd waited on dinner for Dylan, only to find herself eating alone in front of the television set. She thought about all the anniversary and birthday plans they'd had to cancel because of an important case, all the vacations that had been put on hold because of a trial date. All the family celebrations she'd missed because she'd married an O'Roarke. Kaitlin knew about being on edge, that breathless, panicky feeling of having the walls close in on you. She knew about desperation and loneliness and needing to reach out to someone for a little understanding even if that someone was a stranger.

"Are you still there?" he asked softly.

"Yes."

"Shall I tell you why I'm on edge tonight?"

"Only if you tell me first where we've met before."

"I don't think I can do that, Kaitlin."

"Why not?"

He gave a low, masculine laugh. "Because I need to keep you guessing for a while. It'll make things so much more interesting later on."

A cold chill coursed through Kaitlin as she suddenly realized she might be playing with fire. "I'm really not in the mood for games," she said. "So if you're not going to tell me who you are or where we've met, I'm hanging up."

"I saw you with Jane a few weeks ago," he said, "At a restaurant on Michigan Avenue. I was meeting her there for dinner, and when I came in, I saw you two talking in the bar. But you left before I made it through the crowd, so I confess, we haven't really met. But Jane told me so much about you that I feel as if I know you."

Kaitlin knew the night he meant. She'd run into Jane, an old college friend, by accident at the restaurant, and the two of them had gotten to talking while they waited for their dinner partners. Jane had mentioned that she was going to Europe for several weeks and was looking for someone to apartment-sit for her. And before Kaitlin had quite known what she was doing, she'd volunteered. The separation had been building for months, but Dylan standing her up yet again that night had been the catalyst for her leaving.

She remembered what Dylan had said to her earlier. *"Then what were you hoping to accomplish? Did you want me to come running after you? Beg you to come back to me? Promise to give up my career if it would make you happy?"*

In all honesty, a part of her might have been hoping for all of those things. A part of her might have been hoping to shake him up enough that he would reevaluate his priorities. But another part of her had realized that she'd simply reached the end of her rope.

"So how do you like the apartment?" the stranger asked her.

Was that amusement in his voice? Kaitlin wondered. Had

he been in Jane's apartment before? In her bedroom? Just exactly what was their relationship? "It's very comfortable," Kaitlin said.

"What do you think of the view?"

Her gaze went back to the telescope. "It's different from what I'm used to," she murmured. Then realizing the implication, she added quickly, "The city takes a little getting used to."

"Not as quiet as the suburbs, is it?"

How did he know she lived in the suburbs?

*"...Jane told me so much about you that I feel as if I know you."*

Kaitlin couldn't believe she'd let the conversation go on for as long as it had. "I really need to be going," she said. "I have...someone here."

"Your husband?"

Gooseflesh prickled along the back her neck. How had he known that?

Okay, enough. Kaitlin put her finger on the off button, but before she could disconnect, that silken voice said in her ear, "Do you know what it's like to feel as if the walls are closing in on you, Kaitlin? To feel as if there is no one in the world who can understand what you're going through? To have people look at you and think, what a fortunate person she is. She has everything anyone could possibly want. A beautiful home. A loving husband. No good reason for her to be so unhappy. And yet...they can't see inside you, can they? They can't know what's going on in your mind and in your heart and in your soul. Do you know that feeling, Kaitlin?"

Her hand tightened on the phone. Yes, she knew that feeling. But how had *he* known?

"We're like kindred spirits, Kaitlin. Soul mates. That's why I understand you so well."

The chill inside her deepened. "You don't even know me," she whispered.

"I know you like to watch."

Kaitlin shivered at the stranger's tone, at his words. At his insight. And then she looked up to find Dylan watching her from the doorway. She had no idea how long he'd been there or how much he'd overheard. But all he said was, "The pizza's here. Shall I bring you in a tray?"

*"We're like kindred spirits, Kaitlin. Soul mates. That's why I understand you so well.... I know you like to watch."*

She shoved back her hair with a trembling hand. "Could you just put it in the oven? I'm really not hungry right now."

Dylan came slowly into the room, his gaze never leaving hers. "Is anything wrong?"

"No. Why?"

"I don't know. I get the impression whoever was on the phone just now upset you."

"It was just someone calling for Jane," she lied.

"Same guy as before?"

"I think so."

"Kaitlin, if he's harassing you, you need to tell me about it."

"Why?" she lashed out. "What could you do about it except turn off the phone? I'm perfectly capable of doing that on my own. And besides, I thought you were tired of playing the stoic hero."

"Then someone is harassing you."

"*No!* Look, I'm just tired, okay? There's nothing wrong. No one's harassing me. I'm fine."

"You're sure?"

"Yes! Dylan, you have to stop doing this."

"Stop what?" he asked angrily. "Stop caring about you?"

"Stop fussing over me. Stop worrying about me. Stop—"

"Being your husband?"

"Stop putting words in my mouth, okay?"

"Has it really come to this, Kaitlin? Can we not even

have a civil conversation without you getting all defensive?''

''*Me?* I'm not the one who—'' Kaitlin stopped herself short.

Dylan's gaze narrowed. ''What were you about to say, Kaitlin?''

She closed her eyes briefly. ''Nothing.''

''Something is obviously on your mind. Why won't you tell me what it is?''

''When have we ever been able to communicate?'' she asked bitterly.

''Are you blaming me for that, too?''

She drew a long breath. ''We're both to blame. We've let something precious slip away from us, Dylan. We've let too many things come between us. Your work. My family. Sometimes it just seems like nothing we can do will ever make it right again.''

He frowned down at her. ''You've never been a defeatist before.''

''I don't think I've ever felt this tired before.''

A shadow flickered in his eyes, an emotion Kaitlin couldn't quite define. ''They've finally gotten to you, haven't they?''

''I don't know what you mean.''

''Your family. They've worn you down. They've finally accomplished what they've been after for the past seven years.''

''What are you talking about, Dylan?''

His features hardened. ''They've turned you against me. They've made me a villain in your eyes.''

''That's not true.''

One brow lifted. ''No? Not even when those two thugs broke into our house last year? Not even when your father did his best to convince the investigating officer that the perpetrators were somehow connected to my family? Not when he stood in my own living room and tried his damnedest to persuade you that you would never be safe as long as you were married to me? Are you telling me none of that had an effect on you, Kaitlin? None of that had anything to do with your decision to move out?''

"Of course it didn't.''

"Are you sure? Because you were jumpy for weeks after the break-in. And I would see a certain look on your face at times when you didn't know I was watching you. I saw the doubt in your eyes.''

"That was your imagination,'' she said softly.

"Was it? I don't think so. But you know what hurt me the most, Kaitlin? It wasn't just having your father imply that I was responsible for putting your life in danger. It was his accusation that I couldn't protect you. And he was right.'' His hands balled into fists at his side. "But if I'd caught those creeps that night, I swear I would have killed them with my bare hands.''

Kaitlin had never heard him talk that way before. She had the oddest feeling that she was no longer listening to her husband but to a stranger. A man capable of violence. And as he turned to face her, she caught her breath. In the dim light from the window, he no longer even looked like her husband.

Dylan frowned. "Why are you looking at me like that?''

"Because of what you just said…'' Kaitlin put a hand to her throat. "It didn't sound like you at all.''

"What do you mean?''

"You still seem so angry. The break-in was months ago.''

His scowl deepened. "I'm not allowed to still be upset that a couple of street punks broke into our home and scared you half to death?''

She shook her head, her gaze still on him. "It was the way you said it. Like you meant it. Like you really could have killed them. I don't think I've ever heard you talk that way before, Dylan. You're always so in control. It's like… you're a different person suddenly.''

"That's ridiculous. I'm the same man I've always been.'' But in the dim light, he didn't look the same at all. He'd removed his jacket and tie, and his shirt was open at the neck, his cuffs rolled back. Even his hair was slightly mussed, as if he'd been running his fingers through it in agitation.

This was a Dylan she'd never seen before. A complex, driven man with deep emotions and dark secrets. A man who might very well fantasize about having phone sex with her. Who might even be willing to kill in order to protect her...

"Sometimes I wonder if I ever really knew you at all," she murmured.

"What's that supposed to mean?"

"You try so hard not to be an O'Roarke. Sometimes I wonder if *you* even know who you are."

He sighed. "I have no idea what you're talking about. But I guess that's part of the problem, isn't it?"

He turned back to the windows, staring into the night with a brooding frown.

"Can I ask you something, Dylan?"

He shrugged. "Go ahead."

She bit her lip. "What first attracted you to me?"

He gazed over his shoulder in disbelief. "Are you kidding? You see yourself in the mirror every day."

She felt a tingle of pleasure at his words. "I'm not talking about physical attraction. I mean, what made you fall in love with me? What made you want to marry me so quickly? We eloped after we'd known each other for only a few weeks. What made you decide I was the one?"

He gave her a long scrutiny. "What is it you're really asking, Kaitlin?"

"Was the fact that I'm a Gallagher part of the attraction?"

"Meaning?"

"Come on, Dylan. My family has been out to get yours for years. My father was one of the cops who helped send your cousin Daniel to prison for a murder he didn't commit. He and my uncle even suppressed evidence in that case."

Dylán's features tightened. "The evidence they suppressed wouldn't have cleared Daniel."

"No. But it could have made my own brother a suspect," Kaitlin said. "When the truth came out, my father got little more than a reprimand for what he'd done, while your cousin sat on death row for years. Can you honestly say that a part of you, maybe a very small part, but a part of you, nonetheless, didn't marry me out of revenge? You had to know what it would do to my father."

He walked slowly toward the bed, his eyes glittering angrily in the darkness. "If you believe that of me, then you're right. You never knew me at all."

Anger still gleamed in Dylan's eyes, but there was something else there, too. A terrible hurt that he'd buried so deep Kaitlin hadn't been able to see it until now.

And suddenly she realized what their marriage had cost *him*. All those years of knowing that no matter what he did, what he accomplished, he would never measure up. He would never be trusted, and for one simple reason. Because of his name.

After the break-in at their home, her father had made some terrible accusations. Kaitlin knew that a lot of it had been a result of his fear and frustration. He was a cop, but he hadn't been able to protect his own daughter. He'd had to lash out at someone, and the animosity between the Gallaghers and the O'Roarkes had made Dylan an easy target.

It had been a difficult, emotional time for all of them. Things had been said that could never be taken back, hurtful allegations that had only widened the gulf between Kaitlin and her father. And between her and Dylan because neither of them had been able to talk about their feelings. To express to each other their own fears and frustrations.

She gazed up at him now with tears in her eyes. "I'm sorry," she whispered. "I'm so sorry for everything my father said to you that night. For the way he's treated you all these years."

Dylan sat down on the edge of the bed and took her hands

in his. "I can handle your father, Kaitlin, as long as you know that I would never intentionally put you in danger."

"I do know that."

He squeezed her hands. "I've done some things I'm not proud of. And God knows my family hasn't been innocent of every crime they've been accused of. But I'd sooner take my own life than cause you pain."

A tear spilled over as she nodded. "I know that, too."

"And as for why I was attracted to you...why I'm still attracted to you..." He lifted a hand and gently wiped away her tears. "You're the most beautiful woman I've ever known. And I'm not just talking about physically, although you do take my breath away. You're beautiful inside, too, Kaitlin, and that was something I'd never known before. The moment I first laid eyes on you, I knew there could never be anyone else for me."

Kaitlin drew a quivering breath. "Why have you never told me that before? You don't know how badly I've wanted to hear you say that to me."

He shrugged helplessly. "I guess I'm not that great at expressing my feelings."

"But if you'd just come to me..." Kaitlin trailed off. The time for placing blame had long since past. Especially considering that they were both guilty of keeping their true feelings suppressed. "Sometimes I wonder if the difficulties in a Gallagher and O'Roarke union are just too great to overcome."

"Do you really believe that?"

"I never used to. But the animosity from our families, especially from mine, has put a terrible strain on our relationship. I've always thought that was the main reason you've thrown yourself into your work the way you have. You've tried so hard to live down your family's reputation, to prove to my father that you aren't just another O'Roarke—"

"You think I did that for him?" he asked with sudden anger. "I've never given a damn what your father or anyone else thinks about me. The only opinion I've ever cared about is yours.''

Kaitlin closed her eyes as a wave of emotion swept over her. She thought about what she'd told Fiona earlier. ''...*we were married for seven years. We still care about each other. We just don't love each other anymore.*''

How could she ever have believed that? How could she ever have considered for even a moment that her love for Dylan had somehow faded away?

Because at that moment, she'd never loved him more.

Dylan gazed at her so tenderly, a painful lump rose in Kaitlin's throat. She put a hand to his face and gently stroked the masculine roughness of his beard. He turned his head and kissed her palm. ''I've missed you so much,'' he whispered raggedly. ''I've missed being with you. Holding you...''

Kaitlin's breath quickened at the look in his eyes. In those blue depths, she could see the intimate secrets that they'd shared and the darker, more erotic mysteries that were still to come. She cupped her hand around his neck, drawing him to her, kissing him in a way that had him groaning against her mouth, that had both their hearts pounding when they finally broke apart.

She ran her fingers through his hair. ''We haven't kissed that way in years.''

''I'm not sure we've ever kissed that way.'' He seemed almost in awe of her as his gaze darkened.

And then they were kissing again. Long, deep, soul-shattering kisses that made Kaitlin's heart flail against her chest like a trapped bird. That made every nerve ending in her body dance with fiery anticipation.

She wanted Dylan as she'd never wanted him before.

She couldn't figure out what was so different about him...about her...but something had changed between them. For one thing, her inhibitions were gone. Even after seven years of marriage, Kaitlin had still been a bit reserved in bed. Had still waited for Dylan to take the lead. But no more.

In this apartment, away from their past, away from their family, away from all the hurt and disappointments and disillusionment, Kaitlin somehow felt free. Liberated. She quickly unfastened the buttons on Dylan's shirt and then shoved it down his arms. Shrugging out of the sleeves, he flung the garment aside, and then he was over her in a flash, bending to kiss her again. When she fumbled with the zipper of his pants, he put his hand over hers, helping her ease it open.

Slowly, she slid down in bed, kissing his chest, his stomach, ringing his belly button with her tongue before sliding even lower....

Dylan gasped. "Kaitlin..."

She kissed him again and again, touched him so intimately she knew he was about to lose control. She worked her way back up to his lips, and when they broke apart again, he stared down at her for the longest moment, trying to catch his breath. "What are you trying to do to me?"

Her laugh was a soft, throaty sound that seemed to arouse him even more.

He glanced toward the windows. "Maybe there's something to be said for all this anonymity after all."

"Do you suppose anyone can see us?" she whispered.

"The lights are out. I don't think so." He paused for a moment, his voice almost painfully hesitant. "Do you think we should stop?"

She didn't answer, but instead began to unbutton her pajama top. When he tried to help, she pushed him away. "No," she murmured. "Just watch."

And he did. He lay on his side, propped on his elbow as she rose to her knees and slid her top slowly down her shoulders. The bottoms came next and, because of her cast, less gracefully, but Dylan didn't seem to mind. His gaze on her was dark and hungry. "I've never seen you like this," he said reverently.

"Really? Because you haven't seen anything yet."
Slowly, Kaitlin looked up at the mirror.

Dylan glanced up, too, and even though it was dark in
the room, she could see his reflection. She knew that he was
watching her, watching them both, as she moved over him.
With his hands on her hips, he guided her exactly where
she needed to be, and then with her head thrown back, she
watched them, too.

Keeping her cast dry while they showered was a bit
tricky. Kaitlin wouldn't have been able to manage without
Dylan. He'd been helpful in so many ways, she thought with
a knowing smile as she watched him dress.

He glanced up as he finished buttoning his shirt. "Are
you sure you don't want me to spend the night?"

Kaitlin wanted him to stay more than anything, but she
didn't think it would be a good idea. It would be too easy
to pretend all their problems had just magically disappeared
after a night of great sex, but she knew from experience that
come morning, very little would have changed. It some
ways, sex only complicated the issues.

"We've got a long way to go before we're okay again,
Dylan. I think right now we could both use a little distance.
Some time to think. It would be too easy to fall back into
our old pattern, and I don't want that."

"I don't want it, either." But he frowned as he sat down
on the edge of the bed to put on his shoes. "I just don't
like the idea of leaving you here alone."

"I've been here by myself for almost a week," she
pointed out.

"I know, but you didn't have a broken foot until this
morning," Dylan said.

"I have my crutches. There's a pizza in the warming
drawer. A Hitchcock movie in the VCR. I'll be fine."

"Sounds nice and cozy," he said wistfully. "And here I
have to drive all the way home, catch a few hours' sleep
and then drive right back here first thing in the morn-

ing—'' He broke off at the look on her face. ''What's the matter? What'd I say?''

She was gazing out the window. ''Nothing. It's just...I guess I was thinking about how big our house is. How empty it seems sometimes.''

*''Do you know what it's like to feel as if the walls are closing in on you, Kaitlin?''*

She shivered as the stranger's words came back to her.

Dylan reached over and took her hand. ''Don't.''

Kaitlin glanced at him. ''Don't what?''

''Don't look that way. As if you already have regrets.''

She squeezed his hand. ''I don't.'' And she didn't. Not really. What she and Dylan had shared earlier had been...amazing. For a few moments at least, they'd never been closer, and Kaitlin suspected that was because, for the first time, they'd completely let down their guards. They'd been so open and trusting with one another that it was almost hard to imagine how far apart they'd drifted.

But one night wasn't going to bridge that gap, no matter how much they both might wish it to be otherwise.

Dylan finished putting on his shoes, then leaned over to kiss her. ''We'll do it your way, okay? Maybe you're right. Maybe some time apart is exactly what we need to put things in perspective. I know it's made me do a lot of soul-searching about my priorities.''

''Me, too.''

He smiled down at her. ''But I still hate leaving you alone. Will you call me if you need anything?''

''Will you stop worrying about me?'' she asked in exasperation.

''Yes.'' He bent to kiss her again. ''The very moment I draw my last breath.''

AFTER DYLAN had gone, Kaitlin found his cell phone on the dining room table, where he'd been working earlier, and she wondered if he'd left it there on purpose, to have a reason to come back. Such an obvious ploy didn't seem at all his style, but then, as she'd learned tonight, there were facets—intriguing facets—to her husband's personality that she'd yet to discover.

After making several trips to and from the kitchen, Kaitlin finally had everything in place and then, swallowing her medication, she settled back against the pillows to eat her pizza and watch her favorite Hitchcock film. But the opening credits had barely begun to roll when the phone rang. Freezing the frame, Kaitlin reached for the phone, wondering if Dylan had stopped somewhere on the road to call her. She knew he hadn't had time to make it all the way home.

"Hello?" There was silence at first and then that dark, silky voice whispered, "She has to die, Kaitlin."

Icy fear shot through Kaitlin's veins as the phone went dead in her ear.

*"She has to die, Kaitlin."*

Who? she thought frantically. Who had to die? The woman he'd left the message about earlier? What had he said about her?

*"...when I think about her with him, it kills me inside.... You have to stop me. I'm afraid of what I might do—"*

Okay, maybe he was just being overly dramatic, Kaitlin tried to reason. Or maybe she'd even misunderstood him. Maybe the painkiller she'd taken right before he called was already having an effect on her. The medication could be impairing her senses, making her hear things that hadn't really been said. Making her imagine things...

She did feel a bit strange, Kaitlin realized. Her stomach was queasy, too. But what if it wasn't her imagination? Or the drugs? What if that man really was planning to kill someone? Shivering uncontrollably, Kaitlin turned her head to stare out the window. Was he out there in the darkness? Was he watching her?

*"She has to die, Kaitlin."*

What should she do? Call the police?

And tell them what exactly? Kaitlin didn't even know who he was. The caller ID hadn't displayed his name or his number, which probably meant he was unlisted. Or he'd been calling from a cell phone. And she couldn't even be sure the apartment across the way belonged to him. Besides, he hadn't actually threatened anyone. Kaitlin was a cop's daughter. A cop's sister. She knew better than anyone the legal limitations in situations like this. There was nothing the police could do until he made an overt threat, and sometimes not even then. Sometimes they were powerless to act...until it was too late.

Her heart pounding, Kaitlin struggled to her feet and reached for her crutches. A wave of dizziness swept over her, and she waited for the room to stop spinning before she maneuvered over to the telescope. She bent to stare through the eyepiece, but the apartment across the street was pitch-black. She couldn't see anything.

She watched for several more minutes, and then lifted her gaze from the telescope to stare out into the night. So many lights...so many windows...so many invisible eyes watching from darkened apartments...

Her thoughts were drifting toward paranoia, she realized, and when the phone behind her started to ring, she whipped around but made no move to answer it. She let the machine pick up, hoping again that it might be Dylan.

"Kaitlin," that silky voice whispered. "I know you're there. I can see you."

The hair at the back of her neck lifted as she glanced around the room. The lights were off. There was no way he could see her. He was just trying to get under her skin. He was one of those sickos who got off calling strangers.

Fighting off a wave of vertigo, Kaitlin bent to the eyepiece and shifted the tube. His apartment was still dark, too. She couldn't see anything.

"Kaitlin." His voice was a singsong on the answering machine. "Pick up. I need to talk to you. We're kindred spirits, remember? Soul mates. No one understands me the way you do. No one ever will."

This had gone beyond creepy, Kaitlin thought with a shiver. This was downright scary. Terrifying...

"Pick up the phone, Kaitlin. Let me tell you how I'm going to do it."

A wave of nausea rose so strong in Kaitlin's throat that she barely made it to the bathroom before she became violently ill. She sank to the floor, hugging the sides of the toilet. But even after the nausea subsided, her heart continued to race, and the vertigo kept her on the floor. Leaning back against the tub, she pulled up her knees and buried her face in her arms.

She kept telling herself that the voice on the phone was just playing with her. A cat and mouse game designed to terrify her. There were people like that. The world was full of sickos. But what if he meant it? What if he really planned to kill someone? And why was he telling Kaitlin about it...unless he wanted her to somehow stop him?

*"You have to stop me. I'm afraid of what I might do—"*

Was that it? Were the phone calls a cry for help? First to Jane, and now to her?

Kaitlin had no idea how long she sat there before she was finally able to lift her head without the dizziness. She glanced at her watch. Dylan hadn't had time to make it home yet, and she couldn't call him in the car since he'd left his cell phone. All she could do was leave a message on the recorder at home.

Balancing herself with her crutches, she struggled up from the bathroom floor. And as she hobbled back into the bedroom, the phone started to ring. She hesitated, then picked it up, hoping that it was Dylan.

"She's coming over tomorrow night. I'm going to do it then."

Kaitlin gripped the phone. "Who are you?" she asked in desperation. "Why are you telling me this?"

"Because I want you to watch, Kaitlin."

She put a hand to her mouth as nausea rose inside her again. "Watch what?"

He laughed softly. "I thought it would be Jane, but since she's gone, it has to be you."

Kaitlin's heart was pounding so hard she could barely breathe. "What are you going to do?"

"I don't have to spell it out for you, do I?"

She closed her eyes. "Who is she?"

"It doesn't matter who she is. What matters is that she betrayed me…just like all the others."

The hatred in his voice sent another spasm of fear down Kaitlin's backbone. How had she ever thought his voice seductive?

She drew a deep breath, trying to rein in her terror. "If you want me to watch, you have to tell me who she is."

"Why? So you can warn her? So you can call the police? It won't do you any good. They won't believe you. It'll be just like in that movie. You know the one I mean. *Rear Window*. The police didn't believe Jimmy Stewart, either, remember?"

Kaitlin spun toward the VCR, where a little while ago she'd put in the very movie he was talking about. But he couldn't know that. There was no way he could know that….

Unless he was watching her…

When the phone had rung earlier, Kaitlin had frozen the frame rather than stopping the movie. It should have started playing again by now. But the TV screen was dark. Someone had turned it off. He'd been in the apartment while she'd been in the bathroom. He might still be inside, calling from a cell phone….

A scream rose in Kaitlin's throat, but she tried to swallow it back. She had to keep calm while she figured out what to do.

"Tell me something, Kaitlin. Have you taken your medicine tonight?"

The phone went dead, and Kaitlin dropped her gaze to the nightstand where she'd left her bottles of medication. She'd taken a painkiller and an antibiotic tablet earlier, right after Dylan left. And a little while later, she'd started to feel dizzy, then nauseous.

*Oh, my God....*

Had he tampered with her medicine?

Kaitlin grabbed up the painkillers, but her hands were shaking so badly, she couldn't work the childproof top. When the lid finally came off, the pills went flying. She watched as they scattered across the nightstand and some of them rolled onto the floor. Were they the same? She couldn't tell—

A noise outside the bedroom drew her gaze to the door. As quietly as she could, she picked up the cordless phone and carried it with her into the bathroom. She locked the door and, with shaking hands, dialed 911.

"NO SIGN OF A forced entry and nothing appears to be missing." Detective Doggett shrugged as he gazed around the bedroom. The two patrol officers who'd arrived on the scene first were still searching the rest of the apartment. "Not much to go on, I'm afraid."

"But I'm telling you he was in this apartment," Kaitlin said desperately. "He tampered with my medication. Put something in one of the bottles that made me sick."

Doggett walked over to examine the pills scattered across the nightstand. Then he read the label on the bottles. "Demerol," he muttered. "Some pretty strong stuff. Might make you imagine all sorts of things."

"I didn't imagine anything."

"So let me see if I understand you correctly then. You think he came into the apartment on two separate occasions tonight. He switched the pills while you were in the shower. Then he came back a second time while you were sick in the bathroom and turned off the TV."

"And probably switched the pills back. Look, I know how all this sounds." Kaitlin tried to suppress the quiver in her voice. "But I'm telling you the truth. You have to believe me. He plans to kill someone tomorrow tonight."

"And he wants you to watch." Doggett walked over to the telescope. "You watch him often, do you?"

She gasped. "I don't *watch* him. I only saw him once."

Doggett turned his laser-like gaze on her. "And then he started calling you. Telling you he plans to kill someone tomorrow night. A woman."

"Yes."

"But you don't know who this guy is or the name of his intended victim. You don't know what she looks like so you can't give us a description. You're not even sure the guy on the phone is the same guy you saw in the apartment across the street. Does that about sum it up?"

"You're not going to do anything about this, are you?"

"There's not a lot we can do, I'm afraid—"

"Kaitlin!" Dylan suddenly appeared in the doorway. "Are you okay? What happened? My God, when I saw the police cars outside—"

"What are you doing here?" Kaitlin asked in shock.

"I left my phone and decided I'd better come back for it." He glanced up at Doggett. "What's going on here?"

"Maybe you'd better tell me who you are first."

"Dylan O'Roarke. I'm Kaitlin's husband."

Doggett's brows lifted slightly. "The attorney? Your reputation precedes you." The two shook hands. "Could I have a word with you outside?"

Dylan turned back to Kaitlin. "I'll be right back, okay?"

When he came back a few minutes later, Kaitlin asked anxiously, "What did he say to you?"

"Come and sit down. You need to get off that foot." Dylan pulled her down to sit on the edge of the bed. "Kaitlin, why didn't you tell me about these phone calls? I asked you earlier if someone was harassing you. You denied it."

"He wasn't harassing me then. We were just talking—"

"You've been carrying on phone conversations with a complete stranger," he said incredulously. "And Doggett said you've been watching this guy through the telescope."

"For God's sake, don't look at me like that, Dylan. I'm not some weirdo."

"But you've been acting differently ever since you moved into this apartment," he accused.

"He said the police wouldn't believe me," she whispered. "But I never thought you'd turn on me."

"*Turn* on you? What are you talking about, Kaitlin? I'm just trying to figure out what the hell is going on here."

"You think I'm crazy. You think I imagined all this."

"Just calm down—"

But Kaitlin was becoming more worked up by the moment. More frantic. She knew she sounded crazy, but she couldn't seem to help herself. "A woman is going to be murdered tomorrow night, and no one believes me. No one is going to help me stop him."

Dylan sat back and stared at her for a moment. Stared at her as if she were a stranger to him. Then he saw the pills scattered across the nightstand, and reached over to pick one up. After a moment, he said, "How many of these did you take tonight, Kaitlin?"

"KAITLIN? Are you awake?"

She tried to open her eyes, but the effort was too great. She sank back into sleep.

"Kaitlin! Come on now. Rise and shine."

The voice was annoyingly persistent. When Kaitlin finally managed to open her eyes, the sunlight streaming in through the windows was so bright, she had to squint.

Someone was standing over her bed. "Honey, are you okay?"

As her visitor's red hair and vivid blue eyes slowly came into focus, Kaitlin stared up in confusion. "Fiona? What are you doing here?"

"Dylan had to be in court first thing this morning so he asked me to come by and check on you." v Kaitlin pushed herself up on her elbows. "How'd you get in?"

"Well, when you didn't answer my knock, I was all prepared to use my womanly wiles on the super. Or offer him a bribe. Whichever worked. But then I found this.'' Fiona held up a key. ''Not too smart of your friend to leave this over the door.''

Kaitlin stared at the key as realization hit her. That's how he'd gotten in last night. He'd known about Jane's spare key.

''Kaitlin, what's wrong? You look as if you've seen a ghost.''

She shook her head. ''Nothing. What time is it?''

''Just after nine. How about some coffee?''

''I want to get dressed first.'' Kaitlin swung her legs over the side of the bed and reached for her crutches.

''Aren't you supposed to keep that foot elevated?''

''If I don't get out of this room, I'll go stir-crazy,'' Kaitlin grumbled.

''Okay. I hear you,'' Fiona said. ''But if Dylan says anything, this was your idea. You know how he feels about me.''

''Same way you feel about him,'' Kaitlin muttered.

''Well, he is an—''

''O'Roarke,'' Kaitlin said with a sigh.

''I was going to say asshole in the courtroom, but yeah,'' Fiona agreed. She rummaged in the closet, then tossed Kaitlin a pair of black pants. ''I think these are stretchy enough to fit over your cast.''

Kaitlin grabbed a sweater, underwear and socks and headed for the bathroom. By the time she'd washed up, brushed her teeth and struggled into her clothes, she felt as if she'd put in a full day's work. Exhausted, she came back into the bedroom to find Fiona peering through the telescope.

''What did Dylan tell you when he called this morning?'' Kaitlin asked.

Fiona looked up from the eyepiece. ''Only that you'd had a rough night. I assumed he meant you were in pain. But

I'm getting the feeling now that something other than your foot was bothering you.''

Kaitlin glanced out the window. ''See that apartment directly across from this one?''

Fiona frowned. ''Yeah. What about it?''

''What if I told you that the man who lives there plans to kill someone tonight if I don't find a way to stop him?''

FIONA GLANCED uneasily over her shoulder. ''Tell me again why we thought this was a good idea.''

''Because we saw him leave the building carrying a briefcase,'' Kaitlin said. ''He got into a cab. He'll probably be gone for hours. This may be our only chance.'' Getting inside the building across the street had been almost too easy. A man had been coming out, and he hadn't thought twice about holding the door for a tall, good-looking redhead and a blonde on crutches.

Kaitlin counted the doors. ''This is it,'' she said with a shiver. ''This is his apartment.''

Fiona shivered, too. ''Okay. We'll knock on a few of his neighbors' doors and see if we can find out who this guy is. And while we're at it, maybe we can learn the name of the chick he plans to off tonight.''

Kaitlin shot her a look. ''I know you're just humoring me, but I appreciate your coming with me anyway.''

Fiona gave her a wry smile. ''Who better to track down a psychopath than me, right?''

But their plan didn't work out as they'd hoped. Only two people answered their doors, and neither of them was very helpful. One even threatened to call the police.

''Obviously, we need to regroup here.'' Fiona glanced at her watch. ''Unfortunately, I have a meeting…. Kaitlin, what the hell do you think you're doing?''

Kaitlin lifted one of her crutches and ran it across the top of the doorframe. When a key fell to the carpet, they both stood staring at it for a long, tense moment.

''We can be in and out in five minutes,'' Kaitlin said.

"He's bound to have an address book or a photo. Something that will tell us who this woman is."

"I can't go breaking into a man's apartment," Fiona said as she inserted the key into the lock. "I'm an officer of the court. Sworn to uphold the law." The door swung open. "Oh, dear. Look what happened."

She stepped into the entryway, then stopped so abruptly, Kaitlin bumped into her.

"What's wrong?"

"Nothing. It's just…creepy being inside his apartment. Especially if this guy is as big a whack job as you seem to think." Fiona glanced around. "Shall we start in here?"

Fiona was right, Kaitlin thought with a shudder. There was something creepy about the place. Something…evil.

The hair rose on the back of her neck as she thought about the stranger pacing back and forth, in this very room, contemplating murder. How had she ever thought him sensuous and sexy? How had she ever compared him to Dylan?

"Kaitlin." Fiona touched her arm. "Are you okay?"

"Yeah. I guess I'm just getting a little freaked out myself." She tried to shake off her uneasiness. "You search in here, and I'll take the bedroom."

"Okay, but make it quick. We have about three minutes by my watch."

Kaitlin headed down the narrow hallway. The layout was similar to Jane's apartment, so she assumed the door at the end of the hallway was the bedroom. She entered slowly and turned on a light.

It was some kind of study, all sleek and masculine with wood paneling and leather upholstery. Kaitlin started toward the desk, but the telescope at the window drew her gaze. She limped over and bent to the eyepiece.

The lens was focused on her bedroom window as she'd somehow known it would be. He'd probably been watching her for days.

"…*Jane told me so much about you that I feel as if I know you…. We're like kindred spirits, Kaitlin. Soul mates.*

*That's why I understand you so well.... I know you like to watch.''*

Abruptly, she pulled away from the telescope and turned back to the door. And that's when she heard it. A whimper. A soft, terrified cry.

It was coming from somewhere nearby, but Kaitlin couldn't quite pinpoint the sound. She maneuvered over to the door and called down the hallway to Fiona.

"Hold on a sec," Fiona called back. "I may have found something."

"Me, too," Kaitlin muttered as she listened for the sound again.

She was beginning to think it had been her imagination, her nerves playing tricks on her, when she heard it again. It was coming from inside the wall. She pressed her ear to the paneling and called softly, "Is anyone there?"

The whimper grew louder, more desperate. For a moment, Kaitlin thought it was a kitten that had somehow gotten trapped in the wall. And then she realized that a door had been so cunningly placed in the paneling as to be all but invisible. She ran her hands over the surface, searching for a latch or a catch—

There! She felt it!

She pressed the tiny button, and the door sprang back so abruptly she almost fell trying to get out of the way. Regaining her balance, she stepped up to the opening and glanced inside. She could see nothing but darkness at first. There were no windows, and when she felt along the wall, no light switch. Kaitlin knew she should wait for Fiona. But the whimpering was so loud now she couldn't ignore it. She limped inside, and as her eyes became accustomed to the darkness, she saw a woman lying on a narrow bed. She was bound and gagged, and as Kaitlin moved toward her, the woman's gaze rounded with terror. Her whimpers became even more frantic.

"So," a dark voice said behind Kaitlin. "You came to watch in person."

Kaitlin spun.

"Don't bother calling for your friend," he said. "She can't hear you."

*Fiona. Oh, God, Fiona...*

He grabbed Kaitlin then and dragged her back into the study. He shoved her roughly to the floor, and Kaitlin screamed in agony when she fell on her injured foot.

She gazed up at him in terror. "Why are you doing this?"

"Because it's so much more fun with an audience, Kaitlin. I learned that a long time ago."

As he started toward her, Kaitlin grabbed one of her crutches and swung it with all her might, striking him at his knees. He went down hard, howling in pain. She scrambled toward the door, but he grabbed her cast and dragged her back. Kaitlin screamed, in pain and terror, as he rolled her over, pinning her arms at her sides with his knees. She saw then that he had a knife. His eyes gleamed with madness as he lifted it over her chest.

The first bullet caught him dead center in the forehead. The second in the heart. He fell to the floor without a sound. Kaitlin turned and saw Dylan in the doorway. Slowly, he lowered the gun.

As THEY WALKED OUT of police headquarters and stepped into the sunshine, Kaitlin drew a long breath. Dylan was beside her, holding on to her arm to help her down the steps. She paused at the bottom and glanced up at him.

"Have you heard from the hospital?"

He nodded. "Fiona's going to be fine. She has a mild concussion, and your aunt Maggie said she'll probably be released within twenty-four hours."

"And the other woman?"

"Physically, she'll be okay, too, but emotionally—" he broke off. "Who knows?"

Kaitlin shuddered. Emotionally, it would take them all some time to get over this.

"Why do you think he targeted me, Dylan?"

He shrugged. "Who can really understand the motivations of a psychopath? I think he had probably been stalking Jane for months, and then when she left and you showed up, he simply improvised."

"He knew so much about me," she whispered.

"That's how they lure you in. It's a form of seduction. A game. Playing with the victim is half the pleasure. I have a feeling before this investigation is over, the police will find a string of dead women." Dylan closed his eyes briefly. "God, Kaitlin, when I think about what could have happened to you—"

"But it didn't happen," she said softly. "Because you believed me."

His blue eyes glittered with anguish. "I should have believed you from the first. I should have been with you instead of Fiona."

"You were there when it counted the most," she said. "You've always been there when it counted the most."

"If that were true, you never would have left me," he said grimly.

"We've both made mistakes, Dylan. We're both to blame for what happened to our marriage."

He gazed off into the distance for a moment. "Do you believe in second chances, Kaitlin?"

"After what I've just been through, I believe passionately in second chances." She lifted her hand to his face. "But it won't be easy, Dylan. Let's not kid ourselves."

"I know that. But if I've learned anything from your leaving, it's that all the success and partnerships and corner offices in the world don't mean a thing without you. I've loved you from the moment I first laid eyes on you."

"I love you, too, Dylan." Sometimes it left her breathless how much she loved him.

He bent and kissed her again, kissed her so deeply that Kaitlin almost lost her balance and he had to catch her. They both laughed, and then he kissed her again.

When he pulled away, Kaitlin said, "Can I ask you something, Dylan?"

"Anything."

"Where did you get the gun? Where did you learn to shoot like that?"

"I'm an O'Roarke, Kaitlin. Do you really want answers to those questions?"

She smiled ruefully. "No. Maybe not."

"What *do* you want, Kaitlin?" he asked softly.

"You," she whispered. "I want you."

Now, and for always, she thought.

# 24 HOURS
## Kay David

*Destin, Florida 4:30 p.m.*

IN 10 MINUTES, Sarah Greenberg's world was going to end.

If she didn't get to the bank, deposit her paycheck, and make it to the training field in the next 10 minutes, life, as she knew it, would be over. Her rent check would bounce. But worse than that, she'd be tardy, a major offense in the eyes of Lena McKinney, Sarah's boss and the commander of the Emerald Coast SWAT Team. As the information officer of the SWAT team, Sarah had been begging for a promotion. The exercise Lena had planned for today was Sarah's big chance to prove she was ready to move up.

Wheeling into the bank's crowded parking lot, Sarah slid her jeep into the last open spot and grabbed her purse. Working for the SWAT team was exciting, but Sarah longed for more action. A multicounty organization, the team handled all the dangerous situations the local police forces couldn't handle. With their extra fire power and special techniques, the SWAT team was a force of its own.

But Sarah's position on the team seemed mundane to her. Whenever there was a hostage situation, it was her responsibility to find who the captors were and how they could impact the situation. She garnered floor plans and telephone numbers, neighbors' names and relatives' jobs. If it was a domestic complaint or an assailant was holding a gun to someone's head, it was her job to discover who he was and why he was doing what he was doing. Her job was vital, but she could do more and she wanted to prove that fact to Lena.

Jumping from her vehicle, Sarah ran toward the door of the bank and slipped inside just as the security guard was reaching out to close it. She gave the gray-haired man a grateful look. She'd lived in Destin all her life and Tommy Tipton had been the guard ever since she had come here with her father. "Thanks, Tommy," she said breathlessly.

"No problem, Sarah." He grinned. "It's always a pleasure to see you, late or not."

She flashed him a smile, then hurried toward the front of the lobby. There were two tellers and a half-dozen waiting customers. Sarah almost groaned out loud. The wait would be forever! Before she could decide to leave or stay, a motion caught her peripheral vision. She focused without thinking, her cop's radar coming on, her gaze swinging to a man near the front of the line.

After a moment's study, she decided she was being paranoid. There was nothing that unusual about the stranger. Casually dressed and wearing sunglasses, he seemed anxious for the line to progress, stepping slightly out of the queue to look ahead. He was tapping his foot impatiently. She relaxed, but all at once, the feeling returned, even stronger than it was before.

Sarah looked again, her stare going down the line a little more closely this time. The man she'd first noticed had stepped back and she could now see the people ahead of him. Along with a couple of teenagers and a gray-haired retiree in shorts and dress shoes, there was a woman corralling two little boys, an impatient businessman batting papers against his leg, and a solitary figure dressed in black, standing completely still.

Sarah concentrated on the last person, her heart first stalling then accelerating. No one else had shoulders that wide or hair that dark. No one else could send her pulse into such panic. No one else could make her want to turn and run.

No one but Ray Maitland. The only man she'd ever loved and hated at the very same time....

*5:00 p.m.*

SARAH WHISPERED his name to herself. Ray Maitland. She'd known he was still in town, but they hadn't had any real contact or even spoken since they'd both been seniors in high school. She'd been young, and so had he, the last time they'd embraced, yet if she lived to be 100, she'd never forget the feeling of his body against hers.

As if sensing her stare upon him, Ray turned slowly and looked over his shoulder. His hair was longer—growing over his collar—his brown eyes even darker and more cynical than when he'd been 18. He searched the queue as she had, seeking the source of his discomfort.

A second later, he saw her. Before he could stop himself, everything that had once been between them flashed across his face. Love, hate, confusion, resentment. She could feel the searing heat as the emotions burned their way toward her. In a single heartbeat, she was eighteen again.

Back then, Sarah had thought nothing could separate them. She didn't care that his father wasn't around or that his brother was in a mental hospital. His mom did the best she could but a waitress's salary didn't put her in the same social set most of Sarah's friends and family enjoyed. Her parents had told her Ray wasn't good enough for her but she'd stood up for him. She'd loved him. Then he'd dumped her.

Sarah, her brother, and her mom and dad had gone on vacation. Almost as soon as their car had pulled into their driveway, Ray had called and told her to meet him. She'd grabbed her little brother for cover and stuck him in the backseat of the car, telling her parents he'd asked for ice cream. Five minutes later, she'd met Ray at the Dairy

Queen. He'd told her he had married Joan Wilson, a former girlfriend.

Naturally Sarah had been devastated. She and Joan hated each other, always had. The stepdaughter of the local sheriff, she'd been Ray's girlfriend before Sarah, and she'd never forgiven Sarah for "taking him away" as she always put it. Ray had married Joan.

Ray wouldn't explain, despite the barrage of questions Sarah had thrown at him. She'd cried and pleaded, making a fool of herself. Dignity fled. In the end, he'd said nothing but goodbye. The humiliation of being so wrong had hurt for a long time. After the pain had come the anger.

Unable to look away, Sarah met Ray's gaze, but she kept her thoughts to herself—or so she hoped. He stared back, his own expression under control once more. There were lines in the corners of his eyes and a hardness behind them. She'd heard the divorce had been a bad one, but he still had his business. Sometimes, she drove past it on her way to the beach. Maitland's Motors. He owned a high-powered mechanic's shop that specialized in expensive motorcycle repair and sales.

She broke their gaze by glancing down at her watch, then she cursed silently, her fingers tightening on the deposit slip and paycheck. She'd just leave. To hell with the rent. Her decision had nothing to do with Ray, she told herself. He meant nothing to her anymore. All that had passed between them was just that. In the past.

She turned to get out of the queue, but at the very last second, shock rooted her to the marble floor, her eyes disbelieving what she was seeing. The man behind Ray, the stranger who'd first caught her eye, had suddenly grabbed Ray. As Sarah watched, horror sweeping over her, he stuck a gun in Ray's neck.

"This is a holdup," he screamed. "Everyone down! Down on the floor, right now!"

*5:15 p.m.*

RAY COULD FEEL the gun pressed against his temple. He could smell the oil from the weapon's chambers, could feel the cold, hard metal. For just a second, though, he couldn't comprehend exactly what it meant. He could only concentrate on Sarah. Her shocked stare, as she saw what was happening, actually registered more powerfully with him than the .38 now jammed into his flesh.

Don't do anything stupid, he told himself. Not with Sarah here. God help him, he'd hurt her enough already. But his instinct for survival was stronger than his need for caution. He twisted abruptly and seized the man's arm. Squeezing tightly, Ray pulled at the weapon, but the guy seemed to possess an almost supernatural power. He held on and crammed the pistol even deeper into Ray's flesh. "Keep trying," he yelled, "and I'll shoot!"

Ray heard the note of insanity and recognized it; his own brother had screamed at him that way. He immediately went still.

"Everyone on the floor. Now!" The crazed man repeated his command then began to shout as one of the smaller children, not understanding, broke free of his stunned mother's grip and ran away.

The terrified customers watched helplessly, some shrieking, some frozen in shock. The robber pushed Ray to the floor, sending him spinning away from where they'd been. Ray stumbled and fell, but not before he realized there were more of them.

Three other robbers had now joined the first, each holding a gun. Ray's eyes returned to Sarah's. They were filled with a fear so palpable it made his stomach clench. He followed her gaze and saw the reason why. The man who'd first grabbed Ray now had the small child tucked under his arm.

Ray watched in horror as the mother cried out and ran for her baby. In a slow, almost graceful movement, the robber holding the toddler lifted his right hand and brought it down against the mother's head, the crack of his gun against her skull a gut-wrenching sound. Then he turned nonchalantly and handed the child to one of the other men.

The uniformed guard by the front door took two steps forward. Until that very moment, Ray hadn't even noted the old man's presence.

"D-drop that kid," he demanded. His weapon shook and so did his voice as he faced the other man. "Drop him and the guns right now, and no one will get hurt!"

Ray's heart faltered. The crook's expression held no understanding, no compassion. Nothing but blank determination.

"It's too late for that, old man." The robber raised the .38 and fired....

5:30 p.m.

THE SOUND of the gunshot echoed in the lobby of the bank, as pandemonium broke out. Sarah gasped as Tommy Tipton crumpled without a sound, a small dark hole opening up in the center of his forehead. She ran toward him, then stopped as the robber pointed his gun at her. "Forget him! Get away!"

Having no choice, Sarah stepped back and dropped to the marble tiles with the others, but her mind was spinning through the possibilities. She had to do something and do it fast. Then she cursed. She'd left her weapon locked in her trunk.

Lifting her head, Sarah watched the four men huddle together, hoping against hope she might figure out what to do. They split up and headed in different directions. At the front of the bank, one of the robbers stood in the middle and counted off the time, his eyes trained on a stopwatch. The one with the child stayed by the front door and the other one guarded the hostages. The fourth man, the one in charge, barked out instructions to the two tellers, sending one woman to join the others on the floor and ordering the remaining one to fill the bag he threw at her.

Sarah winced and held her breath as the older woman froze. Lucille Abbot had been with the bank forever and always greeted Sarah with the kindest of smiles. She'd lost her husband to a heart attack last summer, but she had two grandchildren and a third on the way.

"Move it!" he screamed. "Fill the damned bag."

"I—I can't...." Lucille clutched the bag to her chest and stuttered the words, the color draining from her face to leave two circles of blush.

He lifted his gun and pointed it at her, cocking the hammer with a smooth pull of his thumb. "Does this help?"

The clicking sound seemed to jar her. Without another word, she reached toward the nearest drawer and began to stuff money into the sack. Sarah let out the breath she hadn't known she'd been holding, and then suddenly she realized Ray was right beside her. As the confrontation had taken place, he'd used the opportunity to move to her side. No one had noticed, including her.

She held back a gasp, his dark eyes inches from hers, his head a heartbeat away. For just a second, she didn't know what was making her pulse race faster—the holdup or Ray's closeness. Her eyes went over his face, from the stubble of his beard to the fullness of his lips. They were as sensual and compelling as she remembered. He spoke urgently and she jerked her gaze to his, leaving her thoughts where they'd been.

"Have you got your gun?" he asked.

"It's in the car."

"What about your radio?"

"Same place." She glanced over her shoulder, and then looked back at him. "I've got to think of something, though. These guys mean business."

Together they looked at Tommy, then their eyes connected again. Ray's hand was on her shoulder, the heat of his fingers burning through her T-shirt, the strength of his grip digging into her flesh. A second later, Sarah heard Lucille gasp and she jerked her gaze to the woman's white face. The teller had finished filling the bag and had just seen Sarah. Lucille's eyes widened as the realization sunk in.

"Do something," the older woman screamed. "For God's sake, Sarah—do something! You're a cop!"

*5:45 p.m.*

SARAH WAS YANKED to her feet and found herself staring straight into the robber's eyes. Green and filled with anger, they were frantic in their intensity. Time was passing, and he knew it, the counting man a constant reminder.

"Is that so?" He shook her roughly, as if he were a dog and she a bone. "Are you a goddamned cop?"

"Yes, I am." She hoped she sounded calmer than she felt. Inside her chest, her heart felt as if it were about to explode. She'd been trained for situations like this, but actually going through one was something entirely different. She wasn't prepared for her fright. Knowing Ray was there didn't help, either. A rush of incompetence, sharp and edgy, sliced through her and her emotions pushed in, everything crowding her closer to panic.

Drawing a deep breath, she forced the terror back down, making herself speak with a clear, strong voice. "If you think you're going to get away with this, you're wrong. You made a bad decision when you picked this bank."

"Get over there and get those damned bags filled up!" he screamed over his shoulder at the man by the hostages, ignoring Sarah's warning. The other man nodded then ran past them and Green Eyes turned back to Sarah, his head tilting toward Ray. He'd obviously seen them talking.

"I picked the right bank," he said curtly. "You and your boyfriend aren't gonna stop us."

Sarah followed the track of his movement to where Ray was poised. A ripple of something went down her spine at the look in Ray's eyes. When they'd been together, every moment had seemed more intense, the light more blinding, the smells sharper. It had seemed as if he had the ability to turn up the volume on her senses. Looking at him now, across the lobby, she felt the same thing happen all over again, a sweep of emotions rushing over her. What was she going to do? How could she protect him and everyone else?

She pulled her gaze away and turned to the man who held her. "I don't think my boyfriend and I will stop you." She took a breath, then continued. "But you will be stopped. I'm sure of that."

"You're crazy—h" He swung his head around. "How many bags, Bobby Lee—"

"Five more! Maybe six—"

"The Emerald Coast SWAT Team is the best there is," Sarah spoke again. The longer she could stall him, the better the team's chances were of getting there. "Once they get involved, you're history."

"What the hell makes you think they'll find out?"

She shook her head and started to speak, then stopped herself. He didn't need to know about the silent alarm the tellers could trip with their feet. Surely Lucille had managed to get to it. Sarah opened her mouth to answer him flippantly, but she never got a chance. From outside the bank, the startling sound of a bullhorn could be heard.

"This is the Emerald Coast SWAT Team," a voice boomed. "We've got the building surrounded and you are now under our command. Put down your weapons and come to the front of the bank."

Sarah's heart leapt as she recognized Beck Winter's voice. A huge blond giant of a man, he was the chief negotiator of the team and she'd seen him in action many times. If anyone could resolve this without violence, it would be Beck. He was phenomenal, his tones liquid, his presence incredible. But her relief was short-lived. A second later, the robber's gun was at her head and his arm was around her neck. All she could think of was Ray.

*6:00 p.m.*

PANIC FILLED the elegant lobby once again and Ray jumped to his feet. Before he could get halfway up, the man with the gun at Sarah's head jerked the barrel and pressed it into her flesh, just as he had with Ray earlier. Ray felt his heart stumble then stop, the metal gleaming evilly in the bank's overhead lights. Sarah stood still within his grasp, her face white but her expression determined. She was going to do something, and Ray didn't wait to see what. He moved forward without even thinking.

The robber stared at Ray. His eyes were filled with a terrifying intensity. "Stop it! Right there." Turning to the others, he waved the gun. "Shut up," he screamed. "Shut up or I shoot the cop!"

The huddled group near the wall fell silent while outside the bullhorn continued.

"We know who you are and we have the bank surrounded. Put your weapons down and come to the front door now. Release your hostages."

The man holding Sarah tightened his fingers on his weapon. Ray could see his knuckles going white with the effort and that was all it took. Something seemed to explode behind Ray's eyes, a white-hot rage over the idea that anyone—anyone!—would dare to hurt her.

He started forward again, two long strides, but this time Sarah raised her hand to stop him. When the robber felt her movement, he yanked her back with an abrupt jerk. "Stay there, damn it!" he screamed at Ray. "I'm telling you, man! Stay there or she gets it!"

Ray had no choice; he froze, a giant hand constricting his

heart. Without another word, the man unexpectedly pivoted and pushed Sarah hard, his palm in the center of her back.

"Tie her up, damn it." Swinging the gun in Ray's direction, the robber pointed it at him. "And him, too! Then put them by the other wall." He looked over his shoulder. "Get out here, Bobby Lee, we got trouble!"

Sarah went flying across the room, stumbling into the arms of the robber who'd been counting off the minutes. He caught her roughly and tried to spin her around, but she reacted faster. With a vicious kick straight to his groin, she sent the man down. She turned instantly to the next one, but she still wasn't quick enough. The fourth robber was tall and muscular, a huge man with a beefy red face, the largest of the four men. He grabbed both her hands in one of his and despite her best efforts, subdued her quickly.

Seeing Sarah in the robber's grasp, a stab of something rippled down Ray's back. Something uncontrollable this time. He couldn't define the emotion but all caution fled as adrenaline surged through him. He barreled toward Sarah and the big man, a mist of anger filling his vision. Sarah cried out and shook her head, but Ray kept on.

A second later, he saw movement from the corner of his eye. His brain defined the motion and he understood what was happening—the man Sarah had kicked had recovered and he was coming at Ray—but Ray didn't really care. The only thing that mattered was getting to Sarah. The sharp report of the pistol filled the lobby, then unbelievable pain detonated behind Ray's temple, white stars on a field of black. He went down....

*6:30 p.m.*

SARAH SCREAMED. The bullet hit Ray and he collapsed to the floor. A line of blood welled up along the edge of his scalp, dark red against the tanned, smooth skin. Without thinking, she headed to where he'd fallen, but the big man jerked her back so hard, it felt as though her arm might pop from its socket. Pain ricocheted down her shoulder, all the way to her fingers, but she ignored the agony and struggled against the man. She had to get to Ray! Someone had to help him! Twisting and turning she fought until the robber subdued her again. The only reward she got for her effort was a quick glimpse of Ray's body.

What she saw made her ill. She actually went weak, her legs turning to rubber. The man she'd kicked was dragging Ray's limp form toward the wall opposite from where the other hostages were gathered, his head bumping along on the floor, a streak of red marking its path. She swallowed down a wave of nausea and pulled herself together. Was he alive? She couldn't tell. At least the SWAT team had arrived. Like a prayer, she repeated the words in her mind. The team was here. Everything was under control. The team was here. Lena, Beck, everyone else. They wouldn't let anything bad happen to them.

She repeated the mantra several times, as the beefy man at her back tied her hands then pushed her toward the wall. She crashed into the elegant paneling, then slid down into a pile, Ray right beside her. The second robber tied Ray's hands together then he sent Sarah a nasty look and kicked Ray once, hard and fast. Ray groaned and the man turned and ran to where the other three men waited. They converged, a frantic huddle as the bullhorn outside continued to sound.

Her eyes went back to Ray's face and as she watched, he moved slightly. She felt a wave of relief wash over her as he groaned again. At least he was alive! A second later, the robbers went back to their work, frantically filling the bags behind the counter. They acted as if they didn't care the team was outside. Didn't they understand what was going to happen? They'd never get out now!

Sarah hadn't exaggerated to the green-eyed robber. The Emerald Coast SWAT Team was the best there was. Every year they won competitions; every year they won awards. No one had a better record for arrests and safe recoveries. But they'd have to do their job, and Sarah knew better than most what that really meant. Her throat so tight, she could hardly breathe, she turned back to look at Ray. His wound was vicious—the bullet had cut a wide swath across his head and he was bleeding furiously. It needed immediate attention.

Her gaze then went to the mother still crumpled on the marble floor. A few steps from her was Tommy, obviously dead. She strained against her ropes but they were too tight. She'd never get out of them. Closing her eyes, she continued to struggle against them anyway. After a while, she gave up and did the only thing she could; she prayed.

Two hours passed.

Unable to move or do anything to help anyone, Sarah was growing desperate. The team continued to try to contact the people inside the bank, but so far the robbers had resisted all efforts. As long as they didn't talk, they seemed to think, they'd be safe. If they only knew, Sarah thought... There were plenty of ways to handle this situation and if things didn't start to move soon, something would break loose.

Lena didn't let incidents drag out. It wasn't her style; the team members wearied and then mistakes were made. By now, she'd have set up a perimeter and was probably getting information on the bank's layout. Guessing who was inside and praying for their safety. All the planning would be taking place in the War Wagon, a remodeled Winnebago that carried the team's equipment and Sarah's own workstation. She wished she were sitting there instead of here.

Once again, Beck Winter's voice filled the lobby from outside the bank. "If we don't hear from you soon, an entry will be made. Do you understand what I'm saying? An entry will be made!"

Sarah swallowed hard and inched her way toward Ray.

She'd been trying to rouse him for hours, but he'd fallen silent. She was getting more and more worried. He could have a concussion...or worse.

"Ray?" she spoke urgently. "Ray, can you hear me?"

He didn't answer, and all Sarah could do was think again about the men and women outside the bank. They were doing everything they could, she knew.

Another sweep of helplessness came over her. She should be doing something besides sitting here, thinking about what her team was planning. She looked across the lobby at the group on the other side. Lucille, the mother and two kids, the businessman...

With her hands tied and no weapon, there was little to be done, but the more Sarah thought about it, the faster the ideas came. Suddenly, she knew what she had to do. She gave Ray a final look, then she struggled to her feet.

"Hey!" she called out. "Hey, you..." She raised her bound hands and pointed them at the man in charge.

The startled robbers, in a group by the teller's counter, broke apart, their eyes turning her way. For a second, she didn't think they'd answer, then the man in charge broke away from the others. As he stepped toward her, a stutter of fear made its way down her spine. But it was too late now. She'd caught his attention.

"What?" he growled from across the way.

"Get over here," she said. "Right now. I've got a proposition for you."

*10:30 p.m.*

RAY'S FIRST impression was pain. His second was of Sarah. Sitting beside him on the floor, she touched him softly, her hands cool and gentle as they dabbed at his temple. Despite her care, he jerked as he became aware of his surroundings and tried to sit up.

"Stay still," she demanded. "You'll bleed if you move."

She was biting the end of her tongue, the tip of it sticking out as she concentrated on his wound. "I'm no nurse, but I found a first aid kit with bandages in it. I think I've got the bleeding stopped. You've been out almost two hours."

Ignoring her words, he eased up, and a swell of dizziness hit him. He closed his eyes for a second, then opened them and looked around, touching the gauze at his temple. They were in a small room lined with shelves filled with paper goods and file cabinets. "Where in the hell are we?"

"They locked us up in the supply room, in the back of the bank."

"What about everyone else?"

"They're gone," she said calmly. "I traded the other hostages for time. The SWAT team threatened an entry, but I got them to hold off. In return, the robbers let everyone go and sent out Tommy's body. I tried to get you out, too, but they wouldn't release you. I made them untie us, though. I think they're saving us to exchange for transportation."

"What do you think they'll want?"

"Who knows," she answered. "Some kind of car, maybe a plane. As much sense as they've apparently got, they might want safe passage to Timbuktu, who knows?" she repeated.

Ray nodded, then grimaced at the pain.

She put her hand out and touched his shoulder. "Don't move. It's a nasty wound. You're lucky to be alive."

Her touch etched itself into his skin, her fingers warm, the nails painted a pale shade of pink. It was the same color she'd always used, he realized with a start. How many times had he imagined her skin against his since they'd broken up? He answered himself quickly: too many to count. He reached out and covered her hand with his, raising his eyes to hers. Her blue gaze turned unsettled as he made the connection and spoke two words. "I'm sorry."

She hesitated for a long moment, and then said, "For what?"

"For not trying harder. There should have been some-thing I could have done—"

She shook her head quickly, her hair swinging back and forth, brushing whispers across her neck. "Don't worry about it. The team will come through—Beck's a great ne-gotiator and it'll work out. With the hostages out of the way, they have a lot more options." She paused. "You did the best you could."

"Did I?" His face shifted and grew hard. "That's what I tell myself all the time about us, too. That I did the best I could. But you know what?"

She licked her lips, her heart freezing in place as she waited for him to continue.

"I didn't do the best I could. I screwed up, big time. And I've regretted it every day of my life."

*11:30 p.m.*

THE SILENCE BETWEEN them thickened and grew until it was suffocating, the weight of their past too much to keep ig-noring. Sarah tried anyway, removing her hands from un-derneath Ray's, inching away from him as she did so. "It's in the past. We wouldn't have stayed together anyway."

"How do you know that?" he insisted. "We might have—"

Her gaze falling to her lap, she interrupted him. "Drop it, Ray. I don't want to go there. Now isn't the time to explain all that."

He waited for her to raise her face but she kept her eyes down. If she looked at him, he'd know she was lying, and she didn't want that to that happen. Not now.

"But I hurt you," he said bluntly. "And I shouldn't have. You didn't deserve it."

At his pronouncement, a flood of emotion overcame her, and she couldn't stop herself. The mask she'd constructed so carefully fell away. She jerked her head up and looked directly into his dark eyes. "You didn't just *hurt* me, Ray. I was devastated when you left me."

He pulled himself together with an obvious effort, a grimace of pain rippling over his face. "I know."

She blinked hard, the memory of that agonizing time suddenly as fresh as if it'd happened the day before. "You could have warned me."

"No," he said slowly. "I couldn't have."

"I don't understand. What do you mean you couldn't have? What kept you—"

"It was complicated. Too complicated—"

She interrupted him again. "Nothing's that complicated. Tell me what I did that was so horrible, tell me what I did that ran you off." She clasped her arms against her chest as if the gesture could protect her heart, the one he'd already broken so many years before.

"You didn't do anything," he answered wearily. "It had nothing to do with you. I told you that then and it's still the truth."

"You're lying."

Despite his pain, he leaned toward her. She didn't reach for him, but she didn't move, either. He clasped her shoulders with both his hands and looked straight into her eyes. They were blue, so blue it almost hurt him to stare at them.

"It's the truth, Sarah. I left you because I had to. You didn't do a thing. Something...happened. Something neither of us could control."

"What? Just tell me, Ray. "

In the past five years, Ray had played this scene a thousand times inside his head. He'd picked up the phone countless more times, wanting to call her only to put the receiver down abruptly. More than once or twice, he'd even driven past her apartment. She lived on a quiet side street, just off Highway 98, kept flowers on her porch and flew a bright blue windsock shaped like a cat. Sometimes she stayed up late and watched television. He'd seen the blue flickering light.

He took a deep breath. "We couldn't stay together, Sarah. I had to marry Joan. She was pregnant."

## 12:00 a.m.

SARAH'S HEART FLAMED, and then turned into ashes, leaving a gaping hole in her chest, where it had rested a moment before.

"Pregnant? You were sleeping with her *and* me? My God, all that time I—I thought you loved me and this is what was going on. I can't believe this bull—"

Ray tightened his hands on her shoulders, his dark eyes glittering, the heat in his touch reaching deep into the place she'd kept hidden all these years. "I did love you," he said sharply. "I loved you with everything I had inside me, Sarah. You were my world."

She tried to pull away but he wouldn't let her. "But how could you—"

"I said she was pregnant," he interrupted again. "I didn't say I was the father."

Sarah fell still, the words echoing inside her head, her brain incapable of unscrambling the situation. Through the years, she'd accused him of many different sins—in her mind—but this possibility had never entered the realm of thinking. Not this.

Ray dropped his hands from her shoulders but didn't move away. He was so close she could see his pulse jumping at the base of his neck, could smell the soap he'd used that morning. All her senses went on high alert and suddenly she was even more aware of him than she had been before. After a moment, she realized he hadn't answered her. With an almost Herculean effort, she pulled herself together and focused once more.

"Why did you marry Joan, then? Why would you do that

if you weren't the father of her baby? I don't understand...."

"She was raped," he said bluntly. "She went out on a blind date and the guy roughed her up then raped her. When she learned she was pregnant, she didn't know what to do. The guy was long gone and even if he'd been around, she would have had nothing to do with him.

"She came to me and asked for help." He raised his gaze. "I couldn't walk away from her, Sarah. She wouldn't have survived."

"Wouldn't have—" Sarah broke off her incredulous words. "She could have gone to the police! She could have told the counselor at school. She could have gone to her church. Damn it, Ray, there're a million places Joan could have gone for help besides you."

A sudden memory broke free. "Damn, Ray, her father! Joan's father was the sheriff! He could have found the guy. He could have—"

Ray shook his head, and then closed his eyes, his face going pale at the pain. It took him a second to look at Sarah again. When he did, she could tell the anguish he was feeling came from a deeper place than the wound he'd just received.

"She couldn't tell him, Sarah. He was a total son of a bitch and he would never have believed her. He'd been beating her for years and I believe he would have killed her if he'd known.

"I was the only one who could help her...."

*12:30 a.m.*

"OH, MY GOD..." Sarah said the words softly, each one holding the weight of her shock. "Sheriff Bentley? Ray, are you suggesting. . ."

He cut her off. "Believe me, Sarah I *knew* the man. He was brutal and angry and he had the size to back it up. Joan wouldn't have had a chance. He hated her...or at least he acted as if he did. Maybe it was something else and he couldn't allow that to happen...so he beat her instead.''

A sick roll of disgust washed over Sarah. "How horrible for her. I always thought..." She stopped herself and started over. "I never knew—"

He looked past her, to the window above. He had no idea what time it was, but behind the streetlights, there was total darkness. "No one knew. No one but me. Every night he'd come home and work her over...or her mother. I think Joan deliberately put herself in his way sometimes to spare her mom. Her life was hell, believe me."

Sarah thought back. Joan had been beautiful, a tiny girl with golden hair and dark green eyes. Sarah had always been so jealous of her, never knowing, never suspecting. Her heart clenched at what the other girl had gone through. She raised her face to Ray's, his expression torn with grief and sadness. "What about the baby?" she asked softly. "I didn't ever hear—"

"She lost the baby, which was a blessing, I guess." His face went tight and closed. "We tried to stick it out for a few years, then realized it was pointless. We didn't love each other and we never really had. Not like—"

Sarah knew what he'd been about to say.

She started to answer, although she had no idea what words to use, but all at once Ray shook his head then grabbed her. "Shh..." Pushing her behind him, both of them still sitting on the floor, he slid himself between her and the door as he whispered urgently over his shoulder, his hands on her legs. "Listen! I think I hear someone...."

She held her breath and concentrated, the heat of his touch burning through to her skin. The sensation was a familiar one; she'd dreamed about it for years. Frozen against the wall, she waited behind him, but her pulse was the only sound she heard. After a moment, he relaxed. She could see his shoulders slump and feel the tension ease from his muscles. He shifted to face her, but he didn't move back. Instead, he closed the gap between them and reached out for her....

*1:00 a.m.*

RAY PUT HIS ARMS around her, then pressed closer. He thought he could feel Sarah's heart beating, but he wasn't sure. Maybe he was imagining the sensation because he wanted to, because he needed to. It had been far too long since he'd held her this close. She raised her face to his, her skin glowing in the dimness of the office, her eyes bewildered. Was the shock of the situation finally reaching her or was it his embrace that had her confused? She touched her lips with the edge of her tongue, darted her eyes across the room, and then brought them back to his face.

"I thought they might be coming back," he explained.

She nodded. He made no effort to move away. And Sarah didn't, either.

Instead, he lifted his hand and cupped her cheek. Her skin was smooth, the satin softness just as sensual as when they were young and in love. Closing his eyes, he took a deep breath and pulled in the fragrance of her body. She'd never worn perfume, he remembered, but she hadn't needed it, either. A seductive essence—all her own—rose in the heat between them, and in a flash, he was eighteen and they were in the backseat of his old Camaro. He hardened with the memory.

"What are you doing?" she whispered. The words were whispered with a sexy hoarseness.

He didn't answer her. He couldn't. Instead, his throat closed down with a sudden, overwhelming desire, any words he might have spoken, trapped—just as he was—in the memories surrounding them. Then she touched him. It was a dove's feather across his brow, the brush of an angel's wing, but he felt it all the same. A thousand nights he'd woken from a dream, haunted by just such a sensation but knowing at the same time he'd never really feel it again—except in his dreams.

"I thought you hated me," she said softly. Her eyes were liquid; they pulled him into her heart. "I thought I did something terrible, something wrong, and you just stopped loving me."

His fingers tightened against her back and he brought her closer without even thinking. She fit against him as if she'd never left, her arms going around his waist, her hands smoothing his back.

"Stopped loving you?" His gaze connected with hers in the dark and something passed between them. He couldn't explain the feeling, couldn't even name it, but he recognized it all the same. Its unexpected appearance—and the strength of it—shocked him. He knew he couldn't lie and he couldn't hide behind anything less than the truth. Not now.

"I could never have stopped loving you, Sarah." The words hurt as they came out in a rusty whisper.

She gripped his back with her hands, her face expectant. Suddenly Ray understood, as he looked down at her, the reality of what he was really saying. He could never have stopped loving her. And he never had.

*1:30 a.m.*

WRAPPED IN Ray's warm embrace, Sarah felt her heart clutch. She'd gone through enough pain over their breakup. To have him say something like that and not really mean it would be beyond cruel. She had to make sure she was hearing what he was really saying.

"What are you telling me?" she asked quietly. "I have to know what you mean."

He didn't answer her with words. He brought his face to hers and covered her lips in a kiss that stole her ability to even think. Beyond the reality of what was happening, though, she understood. He loved her. He really loved her.

She kissed him back with abandon.

For what felt like a lifetime, they clung to each other and didn't let go, their bodies meshing in the old familiar way, their hands exploring the sweet paths of the past. He'd filled out, she thought, his shoulders wider, his hips more narrow.

She wondered if he could tell how her shape had changed, as well. Since joining the force, she'd slimmed down, toughened up. She felt a fleeting sense of anxiety; her soft teenage curves had been replaced by a leanness born of strenuous exercise. Would he still find her attractive?

She didn't have to ask. Ray murmured deep in his throat and dropped his hands. His fingers followed the lines of her hips then smoothed their way to her buttocks. He almost lifted her up as he brought her close and for a moment, she halfway expected him to do just that. She did nothing to stop him, either. She wanted to feel him against her, wanted even more. The need must have made itself known. He yanked her black T-shirt from the waist of her pants then slid his hands underneath it.

Like a heated torch, his touch imprinted itself against her skin, and Sarah gasped. It'd been years since they'd been together, years since they'd made love. In her memory, she'd imagined it, but all the images from the past had fallen short—as had every man who'd ever touch her since Ray. No one but him could make her feel like this. No one.

Her body took control and Sarah let it. With her hands, she pulled Ray closer and with her mouth she urged him on. Nothing meant anything but this, the moment taking on a life of its own. Later on, she wondered how it could have happened. How could she have lost control so easily? How could she have forgotten where they were, what was happening? It seemed impossible that a man could have that kind of power over her very sense of survival, but then again, maybe that's what the moment was about. Even in the face of danger, one had to survive, to feel…to live.

She had no real answer to her questions because nothing had made sense that day. She only knew she did what she did because she had no other option. In this moment, at this time, nothing was important but the feel of Ray's body, his skin against her own.

Their mouths still locked, they fell into each other's arms, their kiss deepening with a passion sending them straight into the past.

*2:30 a.m.*

THE DOOR OPENED without warning. Ray and Sarah rolled apart, Sarah gasping, Ray coming up with his hands fisted. He didn't know what was going on but he wanted to be prepared.

"Entertaining yourselves?"

The man with the green eyes stood in the doorway. Despite his mocking words, he wore an unmistakable aura of tension. His expression was tight and so were his hands, wrapped about his weapon. Ray shifted his gaze from the gun back to the man's face. The robber didn't let them answer, he simply turned and nodded to one of the men behind him. It was the big guy, Ray saw, as he pushed his way into the tiny supply room. Without a word, he walked up next to Ray and put a gun to his head.

Ray watched as Sarah started forward automatically, her hands fisted, her whole body ready to do battle. But Green Eyes swung toward her, grabbing her arm and pulling her toward him. "Not so fast," he said as he thrust a cell phone in her face. "Your buddies are back on the line. I want you to give them a message for me."

Ray struggled to contain himself. All he could think about was elbowing the creep with the gun, and then leaping across the room to smash the other man's face in. He could even see the action in his mind. Sarah had always been important to him, but the past few hours had confirmed what he'd reluctantly suspected. He loved her—and he wanted to save her.

His body must have telegraphed his intent. The man at his side reached out with a beefy hand and touched his arm. "Don't even think about it," he warned softly. "You'll regret it."

Despite the gun at his head, Ray shook off his touch and sent him a cold glance. Green Eyes spoke again, pinching Sarah's arm until the flesh went white.

"It's time to wrap this up. You're going to confirm what I've told your negotiator, then you're going to tell him they've got two hours to bring a helicopter to the parking lot. When it gets here, we're going to leave—with all our money and one of you. We'll tell the pilot where we're going once we're inside."

He held out the cell phone and Sarah took it, her hand steady. She brought it to her ear, then paused as the robber spoke again, his voice almost conversational.

"By the way, there's one more thing you might want to mention to your friends out there…."

She looked at the man with a neutral expression. Ray couldn't believe how cool she was, how unruffled. A few seconds before her heart had been pounding beneath his, her skin hot with desire. No one, including Ray, would have thought her anything but capable as she glared at the man beside her.

"What might that be?" she asked coolly.

He tilted his head in Ray's direction. "If our directions aren't followed and our hand is forced, we're going to start with your boyfriend. We'll shoot him one leg at a time and work our way up."

3:00

Sarah hadn't thought she could get more scared, yet when the robber made his pronouncement, she actually went weak, her stomach churning. She forced her eyes away from Ray's and stared at the robber from behind a mask of aloofness.

Her voice was chilly. "I understand."

Lifting his cell phone to her ear, she began to speak. On the other end, Beck Winters answered her. He was the SWAT team negotiator and there was no one better at his job. They kept the conversation short and blunt.

"They want a chopper," she said. "In the parking lot. You've got two hours to get it. When they leave, I'll be going with them."

From across the tiny room, Ray started to protest, but the man at his side silenced him with a rough backhanded slap. From beneath his makeshift bandage, a trickle of fresh blood appeared. Sarah held back a groan of her own. She didn't want him hurt but he wasn't getting on that helicopter. If anyone did that, it'd be her.

Beck quizzed her, as she'd known he would, but she couldn't answer his questions with anything but a grunt. Before she even managed two of those, the robber grabbed the phone from her hands and closed it with a flip of his wrist.

"Did he agree?"

"They'll do what they can," she said. "But they may need more time."

"Well, for your friend's sake, I hope they don't."

Green Eyes nodded to the big man at Ray's side. The robber tied Ray's hands again, as Green Eyes tied Sarah's. In unison, they pushed them into the hallway, Sarah following behind Ray with a gun in her back. She felt a rush of angry hopelessness. She ought to be doing more. But she couldn't.... And for the very first time, Sarah truly understood the meaning of teamwork. She *was* a cop, but she was also a SWAT member. By herself she could do nothing. She had to depend on the men and women outside to get her through this one. The things she normally did for the team were as essential as the officers who busted in with weapons drawn. Why had she never realized that until now?

For the same reason she hadn't realized she still loved Ray. The real truths of life had a way of getting away from you. When you were covered up in the details of living, you didn't have time for the larger picture. But she did now.

In the lobby, the robbers tied their hands again, then pushed them both to the floor—on opposite sides from one another. For more than two hours, they sat there, opposite each other, their eyes saying what their hearts couldn't. Sarah wasn't ready to give up, though. She used the time to work on the knots of the ropes binding her hands. After a while, she thought they were actually getting looser. After a little bit longer, just when she was sure they were, she watched as the big robber came over and spoke to Ray.

The guy's expression didn't change as he talked, but it was clear something was about to happen. A flash of shock and then surprise crossed Ray's face as the robber reached behind him and did something to his ropes. Sarah tensed, her mind spinning; if nothing else, she could create a diversion, do something, do *anything*…. But she didn't have time. A second later, Ray turned to her and mouthed three words. She was translating them in her brain—I love you—when the two men rushed the three remaining robbers and the bank doors exploded open.

*6:00 a.m.*

THE FLASH-BANG went off with a blast of noise and smoke, and the SWAT team poured through the door, a rush of black movement and noise. Sarah jumped to her feet and struggled to free herself in the confusion as Ray and the fourth robber attacked the three-gang members. As total chaos erupted, finally dropping her ropes, Sarah joined the fray.

Just as they were meant to, the SWAT team quickly

gained the upper hand. The men and women were trained, a superb team of lethal precision. Lena McKinney, the commander, along with four other officers, all garbed in black, instantly took control while the rest of the team checked the lobby and secured the area. No weapon was discharged.

Lena rushed to Sarah's side. "Are you okay?" Not normally a demonstrative person, the other woman wrapped her arms around Sarah, her gray eyes filled with tension and concern. "God, Sarah, I couldn't believe it when I realized you were in here—"

Sarah hugged her back then pulled away. "Lena, wh-what happened? How'd you know—"

Before Lena could answer, Ray and the big robber joined them. Sarah looked up at the huge man and blinked. "You helped us? I don't understand…."

Lena tilted her head toward the man who'd turned then back to Sarah. "Meet Jack Cutter, Sarah. He's under cover with the ATF."

The towering would-be robber held out his hand. "I'm sorry," he said softly. "I had no idea what was going on until he brought us in here and threw me a gun. I didn't have a clue."

Astonished, all Sarah could do was nod.

"Jack's been under cover for almost a year," Lena told Sarah. "But he sacrificed his investigation to end this."

Sarah followed Jack Cutter's gaze to where the three robbers stood, their hands already cuffed. The leader of the men was staring back, his eyes so full of hate, Sarah could feel it all the way across the lobby.

"I almost had him," Jack Cutter said. "He was planning a big drug buy from a pipeline out of the Caribbean, but he didn't have enough money." He turned back to Sarah and Lena, his expression filled with regret at what had almost happened. "That's why he was robbing the bank. He needed cash for the buy. If I'd had any notice, I would have told you guys."

Sarah nodded but she wasn't listening. All at once, she'd realized Ray was no longer by her side. Her eyes almost frantic, she jerked her gaze from one corner of the lobby to the other, searching, staring, disbelieving. She saw team members, bank officials, and EMS personnel, but no one that looked like Ray. Her heart spiraled down in a slow descent, the past rushing in with pain and disappointment. He was nowhere in sight.

He'd left her. Just like before.

## 11:00 a.m.

SARAH WAS A WRECK by the time she was debriefed and released to go home. Driving Sarah's Jeep, Lena chauffeured her there, another officer following in Lena's SUV. They hadn't wanted Sarah driving and that was fine with her.

They arrived and Lena parked against the curb, turning to Sarah as she killed the Jeep's engine. She spoke softly. "Are you sure you wouldn't rather come out to my place? We can have dinner, sit on the deck. You might not want to be alone tonight, you know...."

Sarah pushed a hand through her hair. It felt as tangled and confused as her emotions. "I'm okay, Lena. Really. It was...it was scary but I'll be okay. You don't need to baby-sit me."

"Now that sounds like something *I'd* say...."

Sarah smiled wanly. "I'll consider that a compliment."

"You should." Lena smiled broadly. "You did a great job in there, Sarah. You really kept your cool. I'm proud of you." She hesitated, and then asked, "Are you going to call the guy who was in the bank with you? Ray?"

Being on the team was more than just a job—they were a family and Lena knew Sarah's history. Nobody's private life was actually private.

"I don't know," Sarah answered. "I thought we might

get together again...then he was gone. I guess that pretty much tells me everything I need to know."

"Don't count on it," Lena cautioned. "You can't read someone else's mind, no matter how close you are."

"Maybe so," Sarah agreed reluctantly, "but we shared more than words back there at the bank, Lena. We connected. Ray explained everything that happened back when we were dating, and then we...well, we got to know each other again. I thought..." She let her words die slowly, her hopes going with them.

Lena reached across the seat and patted her arm. "Don't give up," she said. "You might be surprised by how things turn out."

"That might be true. I learned one thing from this experience, that's for sure, something valuable."

Lena's gray eyes turned curious. "What's that?"

Sarah took a deep breath. "I learned what teamwork means. Until today, I hadn't understood. We're all important, whether we break down the door or sit at a desk and get information."

"That's what I've been trying to tell you all along."

"I know that now," Sarah said.

"Well, it was a hard way to learn the lesson," Lena smiled, "but I'm glad you feel good about it now." She paused. "And don't worry about Ray, either. It'll all work out like it's supposed to. It always does."

Sarah went inside and shut her door behind her, sliding to the floor in a heap. All alone, she let the tears flow. Lena was an incredibly smart and unbelievably strong woman, but this time she didn't know what she was talking about. Things weren't going to work out right this time.

Not for Sarah and Ray.

*12:00 p.m.*

RAY STEPPED INSIDE his house and slammed the door behind him. He'd insisted on giving the cops his statement from the parking lot, and then he'd grabbed his motorcycle and taken off. If he'd stayed any longer he would have made an even bigger fool of himself than he already had. Walking to the rear of the house, he peeled off his T-shirt and jeans and stepped into his shower. He turned on the water full force but even the cold blast couldn't erase the image of Sarah from his mind.

Her soft brown hair, her startling blue eyes, her lips against his. Touching her had been a dream come true, the taste of her mouth against his even more sweet than he'd remembered. She'd become a woman since the last time he'd held her, and quite a woman at that. The memory of everything that had happened between them flashed inside his brain. He closed his eyes and leaned his head against the cold hard tile, the water streaming over him in freezing rivulets.

What on earth had he done?

He lifted his face and scrubbed it with his hands. She'd been living in his memory forever, and now, with a single rash choice, he'd renewed her license to stay there. The taste of her mouth alone would keep him awake for years. He stepped out of the shower and toweled off, shaking his head and slinging water drops to the mirror. It had to be ironic, he thought. He was no shrink, but it seemed like most people might come out of a failed bank robbery with some kind of traumatic anxiety. He didn't have that problem. The cold barrel of that gun against his head meant nothing compared to his emotions now.

All he wanted was Sarah. But he couldn't have her. He'd hurt her too much the last time and expecting her to come back to him—just because he'd explained—was ridiculous. She was a smart woman. She might kiss him, might even do more, but she wouldn't take a second chance on a loser like him. Not the kind of second chance he wanted—the kind that would last forever.

He padded into the kitchen with the towel wrapped around him, and headed for the refrigerator. Reaching inside, he pulled out a beer and drained it in two swallows. The cold bitter taste eased his throat but did nothing for his heart.

*3:30 p.m.*

SARAH WOKE UP late that afternoon, her head still fuzzy, and her heart still hurting. Stretched out on her bed, she thought back to the previous day. Barely 24 hours before, she'd been walking into the bank. It didn't seem possible, but in the course of a single day, her life had been flipped upside down and turned backward, as well. Her career. Her past. Her future. Nothing seemed the same.

She stared at the stripes of sunshine above her bed. They danced in the late afternoon heat, their shimmering lights reminding her of the dark gleams in Ray's eyes. He wasn't the young boy she'd known all those years ago. He'd grown up and become someone else. The cynical, jaded mask was still there, yes, but underneath it was a man with deep convictions. The sacrifice he'd made by marrying Joan was one few men would make.

Sarah felt a strange mixture of confusion as she thought about his actions. He'd done the right thing, but a part of her still hurt over his choice. On the other hand, had he made a different decision, she wouldn't have loved him as deeply as she did. He would have been someone else entirely. He would have been a man who didn't have the capacity to feel as he did. A man who wouldn't put others above himself. He'd done the right thing, she told herself, but in doing so, he'd hurt her in a way she hadn't really understood until today.

With a moan, she rolled to the edge of the bed and stood up, the sheets falling away into a pile. However she felt about Ray...however he felt about her...none of it really mattered, did it? He'd disappeared last night and she was sure this time, it was for good. Sarah would probably never see Ray Maitland again and if she had harbored any hopes that something else might come of their encounter, she was kidding herself. She walked into her kitchen, her sadness wrapped around her like a blanket with holes.

THE WIND RUSHED past his face in a stinging wave, but Ray gunned the motorcycle's engine to its outer edge and forced the big machine to go even faster. The passing scenery at his left—the blue-green water and pearl white sand—disappeared into a blur as the cycle responded. He wished he could make his thoughts blur as easily.

Unable to sleep, unable to work, he'd gone to his shop after cleaning up. The guys who worked for him had all heard about the bank robbery; some reporter yahoo with a camera had even caught his image as he'd rushed from the lobby afterward. He'd brushed off the mechanics' questions just as he had the reporters'. He didn't want to talk about the incident or his part in it. All he wanted to do was forget it had even happened.

But he couldn't.

Sarah's eyes haunted him with a vengeance. He couldn't get their blueness to leave his mind. His fingers still felt her skin, his lips still tasted hers. Reaching the limits of town, he slowed the cycle. There was nothing he could do. He was doomed. One way or another, Sarah would always be with him. In his heart. In his mind.

She'd seemed to accept what he'd told her about Joan, but her expression had given her true emotions away. Just as he'd known all along, he'd hurt her—hurt her so badly, she'd never forgive him. When you chose one woman over another, the reasons didn't really matter, did they?

Slowing to stop at a red light, Ray looked around him, his eyes burning with exhaustion and despair. The sad part was he'd told Sarah the truth yesterday. He loved her. Loved her with everything inside of him. He always had. He took off again, the cycle's motor screaming, the pavement streaming beneath him. Now that he'd said the words out loud—and to her—they'd taken on a life of their own. There was no way he'd go on pretending that wasn't the case anymore and suddenly he wondered why he'd even tried.

The question hit him hard, reality crashing all around him. He fought the cycle as he fought his thoughts, then finally he gave up. With a wild jerk on the cycle, he pulled the big machine over to the curb and braked, scrubbing his face with his hands. How could he have never wondered what this meant? How could he have ignored the truth for so long?

Through the years, he'd thought he wasn't good enough for Sarah. He'd made up all kinds of excuses and given himself dozens of reasons why he couldn't contact her. Every time he'd wanted to call her, he'd convinced himself she wouldn't talk to him. Why? Why had he done that? It made no sense at all.

Without any warning, the answer came to him swiftly, the power of his words to Sarah opening his eyes and laying out what had always been there. What he'd been too blind to see. A cold whisper of disappointment came over him, then anger, hard and fast. He'd wasted all these years, all this time, and he had no one to blame but himself. He slowly lifted his head and stared off to his right. The Gulf of Mexico stretched out before him, an endless vista of emerald waves and glistening light. He cursed softly, the wind snatching away his words and sprinkling them over the water. An hour passed then he started the cycle's engine and pulled away.

*5:30 p.m.*

SARAH WRAPPED her housecoat more tightly around herself and opened her front door, her house shoes shuffling against the concrete sidewalk. Without even thinking, she bent down to pick up the evening paper. The boy always left it directly on her doormat, but this evening it wasn't there. She straightened up and saw Ray.

He was sitting in the white patio chair she kept on her tiny front porch. The newspaper was spread around him as if he'd been there for a while. A foam cup of coffee rested on the concrete floor beside his feet along with a crumpled bag from Krispy Kreme Doughnuts. He raised one eyebrow and her heart melted.

"I didn't want to wake you," he said. "Hope you don't mind that I made myself at home."

She shut the door behind her and walked slowly to the empty chair beside him. She was making a mistake, she told herself. "Go back inside. Forget him." She ignored the warning as he offered her a doughnut. She took it and sat down.

"I have something to tell you," he said without preliminaries. "Something I should have said a long time ago."

The doughnut turned to dust but she continued to chew. He leaned closer to where she sat. He'd shaved and changed clothes. His dark hair gleamed in the evening's dying light and she felt a catch inside her chest as she remembered how soft it'd been when she'd run her fingers through the black strands.

"There are a lot of things I shouldn't have done in our relationship. I shouldn't have left you yesterday without a word. And I shouldn't have left you all those years ago and married Joan. I probably shouldn't have gotten into your life to begin with...."

He paused. "But the worst thing I did was ignore the truth, Sarah. And if it's the last thing I do, I had to come over here and tell you that."

Sarah swallowed hard. "I understand—"

"No. No, you don't." He interrupted her gently, his expression taking the bitterness from his words. "Because I didn't understand myself until just a little while ago."

He reached out and took her hands in his. "I was scared, Sarah. Scared to death. When we met and fell in love, I'd never cared for anyone like I cared for you. And I couldn't believe someone as wonderful as you could actually love anyone like me. I think I married Joan because it was the easy way out."

"The easy way out! You gave up your life to help her—"

"She made it safe, don't you see? That way I didn't have to be the person you thought I was."

"That's ridiculous!" Sarah gripped his hands. "You are the person I think you are. You're brave and smart and loving…you're everything any woman could possibly want."

"Any woman?" He waited a second and she felt as if her world were dropping away. "Does that mean you, too? Could you love me, Sarah? As much as I love you?"

It took her only a second.

"Yes." Her hands were holding his so tightly her knuckles went white. "It does mean me. You're the only man who's ever meant anything to me, Ray. Since I was 18 years old, I've loved you and as much as I wanted it to be different in the past, that's just not the case."

He pulled her out of her chair and into his, the warmth of his arms melting her heart as she pressed herself into his embrace. They needed no more words. The kiss they shared said everything.

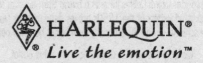

# DESPERATE JOURNEYS

### Four trips you *won't* want to take...

**DESERT DECEIT by Betty Webb**
The murder of a media magnate turns a dude-ranch cattle drive into a trail full of unforeseen danger. Vacationing private eye Lena Jones attempts to unmask a killer in Arizona's most rugged and remote area.

**THE FIRST PROOF by Terence Faherty**
Ex-seminarian Owen Keane accompanies his former lover to Maine to bury her estranged husband. But dark mysteries surrounding the dead man's family converge as a murderer strikes at the heart of a tragic past filled with buried secrets, blackmail and vengeance.

**DEATH ON THE SOUTHWEST CHIEF by Jonathan Harrington**
Danny O'Flaherty escorts his eccentric aunt on a cross-country train trip, only to discover his uncle's corpse in the next seat. When the body is stolen and replaced with that of a freshly strangled man, Danny has seventy-two hours to find a killer.

**STAR SEARCH by Nancy Baker Jacobs**
*Hollywood Star* reporter Quinn Collins inherits a house from a writer she never knew. Looking into blacklisted writers of the 1950s proves dangerous as Quinn exposes a killer's desperate scheme — and the stunning truth about her own parents.

Available May 2004 at your favorite retail outlet.

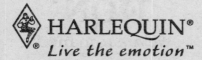

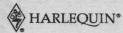

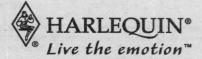